THE TOWERS STILL STAND

Best wishes,

[signature]

THE TOWERS STILL STAND

AFTER A FAILED 2001 PLOT TO DESTROY THE WTC, ONLY
ONE MAN CAN STOP TERRORISTS FROM STRIKING AGAIN

Daniel Rosenberg

ISBN-13: 9781530398829
ISBN-10: 1530398827
Library of Congress Control Number: 2016907257
CreateSpace Independent Publishing Platform
North Charleston, South Carolina

This book is dedicated to the thousands of victims of 9/11. A percentage of the profits will be donated to the 9/11 Tribute Center, which helps teach future generations about the impact of the attacks.

PART ONE: SEPT. 11, 2001

CHAPTER 1

KANDAHAR, AFGHANISTAN: 3 A.M. EDT

The call of the muezzin rang out from the towering, green-domed mosque at the center of town. The sun beat down, searing the low-roofed buildings of the Taliban's capital with 90-degree heat, about typical for lunchtime in mid-September in southern Afghanistan. The streets emptied as citizens entered the nearest buildings to worship. Failing to pray five times a day was a serious crime.

"Allahu Akbar," the muezzin's voice called, audible for miles through powerful speakers perched on buildings downtown.

In the main room of a flat-roofed, mud-walled home near the outskirts, a house like all the others on this unremarkable street, a black-bearded man – known by the rest of the world as Osama bin Laden but by his followers as simply "the Sheik" - was on his knees on a prayer mat with a small group of acolytes, bending over to kiss the ground as he prayed. Even on his knees, the Sheik towered over the group, and when they stood up at the end of prayers, his six-and-a-half foot height became fully apparent. The bright sun shone through the window – really just a hole carved in the mud building. The floor was bare concrete, with sandals lined up at the front entrance, where a blanket served as a door.

The house, like all the others in this community, was surrounded by a low mud wall with a darker brown door in the center, leading to the inner courtyard. The only thing that stood out about the place, other than the bearded Sheik himself, was the presence of two security guards in front of the gate – both armed with Kalashnikov machine guns and wearing military fatigues. They had also been on their knees praying, guns still strapped to their sides, but now they stood as a lone man wearing a dull brown robe approached along the empty street, carrying a clear plastic bag with a radio inside.

"The Sheik is expecting me," the visitor said upon reaching the gate. All of the men wore beards, and all wore wrappings around their heads to protect against the fierce heat. The guards eyed the radio in the bag suspiciously, and motioned for the visitor to hand it over. They turned it round and round in their hands, opening up the battery case, making sure it wasn't an explosive.

The visitor was a relatively young man, judging by the blackness of his beard and his spry step. From the dust on his robes, it was obvious he'd walked a long way. He waited patiently while the guards examined the radio, and then handed them a piece of folded paper. "Here is my identification."

The guards handed back the radio and looked over the paper. One of them nodded. "Yes, he is the Sheik's expected guest," he told the other. After briefly subjecting the visitor to a pat-down and finding no weapons, the guards escorted him through the barren courtyard to the home's blanketed front entrance. One of the guards briefly went in with the visitor's papers, and then quickly came back out. He motioned the visitor to enter. All of this was familiar procedure to the visitor, who had known the Sheik for several years.

Inside the hut, the Sheik watched as the visitor pushed through the blanket door into the relatively cool interior. The Sheik came slowly forward and embraced the man, who dropped his bag temporarily on the floor to hug the Sheik back.

"As-salamu alaykam," the Sheik said in his quiet, almost shy voice as the two embraced. His visitor repeated the words. They separated, stepped back to examine each other's faces, and both smiled. The Sheik's smile lit up his otherwise solemn visage for a moment, and the visitor looked him over, thinking to himself that the Sheik appeared thin and ill. His long, pale face looked even more pale thanks to the white wrap he wore around his head. His beard was more flecked with silver than it had been a few months ago, when the visitor was last here, and the Sheik - dressed in his usual flowing white robes which somehow never picked up dust like everyone else's - was obviously uncomfortable standing. Always thin, the Sheik now appeared skeletal. His frame could scarcely be carrying 160 pounds, the visitor thought. The three young acolytes who had just finished praying with the Sheik were back at their studies, sitting on the floor and trying to be unobtrusive.

"Ah, you brought it. Thank you," the Sheik said in Arabic, noticing the plastic bag for the first time. "It's battery powered, correct? We have no electricity."

"Yes, of course," the visitor replied. He pulled the radio out of the bag. "I brought extra batteries in case we need them. This radio is a special one. It can pick up broadcasts worldwide. We should be able to monitor things very easily. I'll show you." He held the device toward the Sheik, intent on explaining its capabilities further. But the Sheik waved him away.

"We can test it later," he said. "It's still several hours until we'll hear anything. Please put it over there." He motioned toward the bare floor by the wall, where the sandals lay. "Did you have the chance to say midday prayers? It's not too late."

The visitor, who had actually stopped in the road and prayed at the muezzin's call, let the Sheik know he already had done so. He put the radio down where the Sheik had motioned, still wondering why after years helping the Sheik with all sorts of complex technological implements, he had been asked to bring him a simple radio, and why it was so important that it be delivered immediately.

"Good," the Sheik replied. "Let's go inside and I'll get you a cup of tea. You've come a long way and you must be hot. We can catch up on your latest activities."

"Thank you so much," the visitor replied.

The Sheik limped as he escorted the visitor past the acolytes into another small room, and closed the curtain behind them. Outside, the street was quiet, baking in the sun. A mangy yellow dog walked slowly by, tongue hanging out as he searched for shade.

CHAPTER 2
NEW YORK CITY: 6:45 A.M.

The sun rose over New York on what looked like another beautiful late summer day. The sky was a deep, dark shade of blue. The towering profiles of the two World Trade towers punctuated the skyline, gleaming in the early sunlight. Despite the early hour, many office workers were already at their desks high up in the towers, getting ready for the opening of the U.S. financial markets or catching up on overnight market developments in Europe and Asia. Few bothered to look out of their windows at the dizzying views of city and harbor below. Only tourists wasted time admiring the scenery.

CHAPTER 3
BOSTON: 7:59 A.M.

An American Airlines 767 took off for Los Angeles from Logan Airport. Minutes later, a United Airlines 767 departed Logan for the same destination. Neither of them would make it.

CHAPTER 4

WHITE HOUSE INTERLUDE – 8:12 A.M.

Virgil Walker, the President's expert on terrorism, paced methodically back and forth across the ragged blue carpet of his office in the basement of the White House. His pacing was somewhat awkward due to the small confines of the room and because he walked with a limp, the reminder of a college football injury. He was alone in the room, most of which was occupied by a large wooden desk covered with papers and books in haphazard piles, some a foot high. A framed photo on the desk showed Virgil and President Clinton posing, Virgil looking intently into the camera and Clinton with that famous smile of his, arm around Virgil's shoulder. The photograph was signed by the former President, "Best wishes, Virgil. Remember to smile next time!" There were no family photos.

The curtains were closed, and the only illumination came from a small desk lamp that cast little light through its dust-covered shade. The walls held shelves of books, messy and disorganized, most of them concerning Islamic terrorism.

Virgil himself didn't look much better. He was wearing khakis and a wrinkled white Oxford shirt. He'd left his worn-out shoes under his desk and was pacing around in his black socks, one of which had a hole through which stuck his hairy big toe. His thick brown hair, with silver flecks here and there, especially along his unfashionable sideburns, needed cutting, and stuck out from the back of his head. He read a document as he walked, lips moving slightly. Not looking where he was going, he stumbled over a book, stubbing his bare toe.

"Dammit!" he yelled, and kicked the book into a corner. It flipped over, showing its title, "In the Shade of the Koran," by Sayyid Qutb.

Even as he read the day's briefing documents for the third time, he went over in his mind the last eight months since the new administration began. He couldn't remember a more frustrating stretch in his 25-year career in government.

The problem was, despite his high position, his constant warnings about a possible domestic threat from Osama Bin Laden didn't get listened to. His forehead, already lined with wrinkles, creased all the more as he considered his predicament. Part of it, he supposed, was his status as a holdover from the last administration, run by Democrats, not Republicans.

And maybe it was his height. He was a short man – no more than 5 feet 7 inches – and had always kept in shape. But now, at the age of 50, a slight belly protruded above his belt, reflecting too many late nights working and ordered-out, quickly-eaten meals. Many people literally looked down on him, and sometimes misjudged him as diminutive in importance as well. Those who knew him well were aware he'd been a star running back at his Division Two college despite being the shortest one on the team. He never missed a game, until the injury his senior year knocked him out of the sport for good and left him with the limp even now, 30 years later.

But in the new administration, no one knew that about him. He was just the little guy from the old administration, admired, certainly, for his knowledge, but also associated with what the new leaders saw as the prior administration's failings. He also couldn't glad-hand like the rest of them, especially the guy running things on the floor above.

Virgil pushed some papers from the corner of his desk and rubbed his nose. He reflected back on the President's Daily Brief report from intelligence agencies early last month warning that Bin Laden was determined to strike in the United States. Virgil had seen it as reinforcing the advice he'd been giving over the last months. But none of the others at the meeting gave it the attention it deserved. Instead, the President had asked a few questions and then moved on to the next subject. This despite Virgil's pleas to spend more time considering the situation.

"Something terrible is brewing; I'm sure of it," he had told the President and the rest of the national security team that day. But he sensed no urgency from anyone else, and he could almost hear them saying to themselves that once again, it was just Virgil, the old administration's hanger-on, Mr. Chicken Little.

CHAPTER 5
UNITED FLIGHT 93: 8:48 A.M.

United Flight 93 from Newark to San Francisco had taken off minutes ago and was climbing toward cruising altitude. In business class, where three Middle Easterners sat, a male flight attendant circulated through the aisle, handing out reading material. "Let's see," he was telling a business-suited, slightly pudgy middle-aged man in the third row. "We have the Economist, BusinessWeek and Fortune."

"I'll take a Fortune," the man responded briskly, reaching his hand out for the magazine without looking at the flight attendant. He was staring intently at his laptop, which was resting in his ample lap. He accepted the magazine without saying thanks, and the flight attendant kept the well-trained pleasant smile on his face as he walked to the next row.

Up front in seat 1B, Ziad Jarrah braced for action. There was no one in the seat next to him, so he had the row to himself. He was thin and olive-skinned, with piercing dark eyes. His face was well proportioned, with a somewhat prominent nose providing distinction. Until recently, he'd worn a thin beard with no mustache, but he had shaven it off. His clothes were "dress casual," khakis and dark green polo with a white t-shirt showing beneath it near his neck.

Jarrah glanced at his watch. Four minutes left until the planned time. Two brothers were in row five, and two more of the faithful were in coach. The decision of when to act was Jarrah's to make, and the others awaited his signal. He would pilot the plane into either the White House or Capitol.

In his right hand, Jarrah held his Nokia 7110, a black device with a small screen and an antenna at the top right. On this screen, he could monitor headlines, weather and email. And this phone, which all of the lead brothers carried, had been carefully modified by Jarrah, the group's chief technician, to allow connection to networks even while in flight. There was no other phone on the market with this sort of connectivity, and the brothers had found it quite reliable during their rehearsal flights across the country in recent weeks. Jarrah had been checking it nervously ever since the flight began. He knew that the brothers who had taken off from Logan airport in Boston should be reaching their targets shortly, and he was waiting to see the news flash across his screen. He looked at it again. Nothing.

This puzzled him. He checked his watch: 8:50. If the planes had taken off on time, they should have reached the target. It wouldn't take long, he knew, for the news to be reported. He held the phone up to eye level to check connectivity. Two bars. It was connected. Still no headlines crossed on CNN. The phone couldn't show him the actual CNN web site, only a list of headlines. But that's all he needed. His stomach tightened, and he shifted slightly in his seat. He turned around to look back at the brothers, but the flight attendant was in the way and he couldn't see them.

Jarrah's brow wrinkled, and he began methodically tapping his fingers on the armrest. The plan was for the four planes to hit their targets all around the same time, but the towers were to be hit first. What if something had happened to the other brothers and the plans went wrong? They'd never discussed this during their meetings, and he couldn't remember what the Sheik, if anything, about what should happen if plans failed. The Sheik and his second in command, a shadowy man known only as "the Director," mostly communicated with Atta, the lead hijacker on American Flight 11 from Logan, not with Jarrah. The Director's face appeared in his mind, with its burning eyes and snake-like smile. Jarrah shuddered.

He looked again at his watch: 8:53. Sweat began popping out on his face and under his arms. He checked the phone again. The bars were down to zero – no, wait – they popped up to a single bar. The CNN head-lines had updated again since he last looked. A single new headline now stood out at the top of the list:

"Two Planes Apparently Collide North Of New York City – Sources"

He stared, wide-eyed, at the screen. The time on the headline was 8:46 – seven minutes ago. The phone must have been out of range for a few minutes after all. He sat back, but no change of expression showed on his face. He still stared straight ahead, his dark eyes now betraying no emotion. There could be no coincidence, he knew. Something terrible had happened to at least one of the other planes. He had no idea how such a thing could have occurred, but there was no time to think of that now. He was on his own, and he had to decide the course. There was still a chance that one of the other planes would fulfill its mission, if it were still flying. He studied his phone, the fingers of his other hand tapping on the armrest, trying to will the headlines to update.

Another headline appeared and he leaned forward to read it.

"Update: New York Plane Collision: Authorities Say Planes Took Off From Boston's Logan Airport, Bound for Los Angeles"

Immediately after, a third:

"Update: New York Plane Collision: Authorities Say Flight Control Lost Communications with Airliner Prior to Collision"

It was 8:55.

Jarrah re-read the headlines with mounting confusion and frustration. Could *both* of the other planes be down? Was it possible, then, that the brothers on Flight 11 and Flight 175 had flown their planes into one another? How could that be? Had the mission to destroy the World Trade towers failed? And if so, what should he do?

There was a nudge at his arm, and he looked up. It was one of the "muscle" brothers who'd been sitting behind him in business class.

"Sit down," Jarrah said to him in English and pointed to the empty seat next to him.

The muscle brother's dark face was twitching anxiously. He combed his fingers through his black hair.

"What's wrong?" the brother asked in Arabic. "We're ready to go. You haven't given the signal."

Jarrah was the commander of this plane, and this brother and the others were there to serve simply as muscle – to help kill the flight crew and then subdue the infidels in back. These men hadn't been part of the planning, and some had only recently arrived in the United States, adding to their anxiety.

Jarrah didn't answer right away, and his cohort stared at him, wide-eyed, waiting for a reply. Thoughts rushed through Jarrah's mind. He realized he and the other brothers might never get as good an opportunity again as this one. Even if the brothers on Flight 11 and Flight 175 had failed to hit the towers, there was still a chance for him hit the White House or the Capitol, as they'd planned. And there was Flight 77, also up in the air now. It was supposed to target the Pentagon. Certainly Jarrah and Hani Hanjour, lead brother on that plane, could still accomplish their missions.

Then again, this wasn't about him. This was a much greater thing. The plan was to have all four planes hit the key targets – business and government. To finish the job begun in 1993 when the World Trade Center was bombed. To hit New York and Washington simultaneously – the two centers of American evil.

His phone vibrated and he jerked it up. A message, marked urgent. It was from the familiar email address – a generic-looking Yahoo account.

"I'm very sorry to inform you that today's meeting has been cancelled," the message read in Arabic. "We can discuss re-scheduling when you land in San Francisco."

Jarrah read the words with relief; the decision was out of his hands. The Director must have been monitoring things from Pakistan. He must have seen the same headlines and relayed his order across the Atlantic. The operation would be put off for another day.

"Let the other brothers know that today's meeting is cancelled," Jarrah told the brother next to him. "We'll try to re-schedule."

The brother nodded, didn't say anything and got up and went back to his seat, where he spoke quietly to the other brother. Then he rose again and walked into the coach section to tell the other two team members.

Jarrah's face stayed calm, displaying no outward change. Inside, he likewise remained calm. The fight against the infidels, he knew, would take hundreds of years. If his mission had to be delayed, it didn't make a difference. Justice would one day come for the Americans. At the same time, a feeling welled up from deep in his heart. A feeling of relief. He had thought he never would see Alev again. Now, maybe he would.

"OK, folks, this is your captain speaking," came a voice over the intercom, momentarily interrupting Jarrah's thoughts. "Glad to have you aboard today on our flight to San Francisco. I know we got out of the gate on time, but it looks like we'll be fighting a headwind all the way to the West Coast, so we might be getting in about half an hour later than we thought. We'll give you an update on our ETA just a little later on. But for now, please sit back, relax and enjoy the flight."

The overweight man with the laptop cursed under his breath. "Of all the lousy luck," he muttered.

CHAPTER 6

AMERICAN FLIGHT 77: 8:58 A.M.

A dark-haired, pony-tailed female passenger with sharp, pale features on the flight from Newark to Los Angeles glanced to the side when the clean-cut young man sitting beside her leaned back. The man, who looked Arabic, was dressed in business casual clothing. He had thick, prominent eyebrows. His lips moved a little, and she gave him a closer look. Was the young man praying? He'd been so quiet ever since he got on. She wondered where he was from and why he was headed to Los Angeles. For business? Which reminded her of the report she was working on. She was already behind and there would only be a few hours on the flight to get caught up. She bent back over her laptop.

The message Hani Hanjour had just received came as a shock. The other brothers had failed. The plan would be put off for another time. The towers still stood. He glanced at the American woman sitting beside him, tapping at her keyboard.

Her day would come, Hanjour thought. He had no doubts that one day, they would succeed, Allahu Akbar. It was a pillar in his mind – a simple, unquestionable fact of life. Dying for Islam was sanctioned by the Koran itself, and by the Prophet.

CHAPTER 7

THE WHITE HOUSE: 9 A.M.

Virgil Walker's forehead wrinkled as he glanced at the television set mounted from the wall opposite his desk. It was tuned to CNN, but muted. Something on the screen had caught his eye. He grabbed the remote control and turned up the volume.

Just minutes ago, CNN said, there'd been a strange mid-air collision about 50 miles north of Manhattan. First reports were that a United 767 and an American 767, both bound for Los Angeles, had collided about half an hour after taking off from Logan. There were also disturbing reports from the Federal Aviation Administration that at least one of the planes had been hijacked. Bodies and airline parts were raining from the sky over the town of Peekskill, and a neighborhood was on fire.

"It's too early to say for certain, but we're being told the chance of any survivors is very low," the CNN correspondent said. "Both planes were fully loaded with fuel for their cross-country flights, and witnesses say the explosion was extremely bright and loud. We're told there were 90 passengers and crew on the American plane and 64 on the United. If all have indeed perished, this would be the worst mid-air collision in terms of lives lost in U.S. history."

"Do you have any word yet on what may have caused the planes to collide?" the anchor asked the correspondent. "Could this have been some sort of pilot error?"

"Well, Frank, it's only been about 25 minutes since this happened, and the people we're talking to say they can't discuss possible causes yet," the correspondent replied. "But air traffic control has very sophisticated systems in place to prevent this sort of incident, and that's why it's so rare. It's been more than 15 years since we had a major airliner involved in a collision, and that was with a small plane near Los Angeles. To have two major jet planes colliding – well – we saw it happen five years ago in India, but I don't believe we've ever seen such an incident here in the U.S."

"Thanks, Phil," the anchor said. "We're now looking into reports that say at least one of the airplanes may have been hijacked before the collision. If that's the case, it would be the first plane to be hijacked on U.S. soil since the 1970s…"

Virgil was listening to the broadcast but gazing intently at his computer screen. The information he was getting over his secure channels was that the transponders on both planes had been turned off shortly after takeoff, and that both planes appeared to have turned south from their approved flight paths. There'd been a strange transmission to controllers from one of the aircraft, something along the lines of, "We have some planes."

His phone rang and he picked it up. "Yes," he said in a clipped voice. "I'm on my way." He put down the phone quickly, grabbed his briefcase and headed upstairs.

A few minutes later, an out-of-breath Virgil, wearing black socks with the toe still sticking out, stepped into Vice President Dick Cheney's office. Inside the expansive room, decorated with a blue carpet and gold curtains, Cheney, wearing his trademark large glasses, sat at his heavy wooden desk talking to National Security Adviser Condoleezza Rice. They both glanced at Virgil when he came in, and Cheney motioned with his hand for Virgil to sit next to Rice.

"What do you think?" Cheney asked him as he sat down.

Virgil looked back at the Vice President, folded his hands in his lap, and said, "Can I be blunt?"

"When are you not?" Cheney replied with a slight smile. Virgil had known Cheney casually for years, but this new administration was their first time working closely together. He didn't doubt why others referred to the man as "Darth Vader." When he stared at you with those gimlet eyes, you could almost feel lasers piercing your heart, and the small smile he offered now didn't help one bit.

"OK, you asked for it," Virgil said. "I think we need the military on high alert so we can be ready to take action if any other aircraft are hijacked. I'm convinced this is just the first wave."

"Wait a minute," Rice interjected. "Other planes being hijacked? Who said anything about that?"

"There was a strange transmission," Virgil replied. "The FAA said it sounded like someone saying, 'We have some planes.' I advise shutting down all air traffic right away and forcing all planes in the air to land. It's like I've been telling you – Al-Qaeda has threatened to attack us, and it looks like it's happening. We knew they might use hijacking as a tactic; that's been clear for years."

"OK now," Rice responded. "We have no evidence that this is Al-Qaeda, and we don't know of any other hijacked planes. You want us to force every plane to land? That's never been done in history. Have you stopped to think of how we'd look if forced thousands of planes to land and inconvenienced millions of people, and there wasn't any real danger? The implications would be enormous. I agree we need to keep planes on the ground just in case until we can be sure there's no more danger, Dick, but I think Virgil's idea is far too dramatic."

Virgil admired Rice for her expertise on foreign policy. At the same time, he didn't feel she took the threat of domestic terrorism seriously enough. She was a Russia expert, not a Middle East expert. The regular meetings to discuss Bin Laden had been cancelled. Virgil could no longer make his reports directly to the President – instead, he had to send them through a committee she had set up, which rarely met. At one meeting, she'd looked at him from across the table and asked him point blank how he could be so sure Bin Laden was targeting the U.S. homeland. "We know Bin Laden is a serious threat in the Middle East, but what solid evidence is there that he's targeting us here?" she'd said. A fair enough question, he supposed, but one that revealed a lack of understanding about the depth of Bin Laden's organization and its reach. He'd responded with a bromide citing various reports, but obviously didn't get through to her. Now, with the facts flying in her face, she didn't see "any real danger," and still worried about "inconveniencing" citizens.

At that moment the phone on Cheney's desk rang and the VP pushed the button on the conference line.

"Hi there, everyone," the President's Texas drawl came over the speaker. "I heard we had some very bad piloting up in New York State this morning. Tell me what's going on. Do we have a security situation, or is this just your typical airplane accident?"

"Mr. President," Cheney said. "We're convinced there's more to it than a simple airplane crash. We're pretty sure at least one of those planes was hijacked, and the word is that Middle Eastern men stormed the cockpit and took control of the plane before the collision."

"OK," Bush said. "Sounds like a very serious situation. Tell me more."

"Mr. President, this is Virgil Walker speaking," Virgil spoke up. "This looks to me like Al-Qaeda. We knew back in 1998 that Bin Laden might use hijacking as a strategy. I think there's more to come."

The President hesitated just a moment. "I knew you'd have some sunny forecasts for me today, Virgil old boy," he finally said. "Well, let me know what the worst-case scenario is. I always can count on you for that."

"Mr. President, it's my job to think of the worst case scenario," Virgil said, trying to hold his temper. "But since you asked, let me remind you of that memo you saw last month. It notified us that Al-Qaeda was determined to attack U.S. targets. And we know that hijacking is one of their game plans. Almost three years ago, President Clinton received a memo titled, 'Bin Laden preparing to Hijack U.S. Aircraft and Other Attacks.' I have it right here." He pulled open his old briefcase and started to comb through papers in a folder, getting increasingly tense as he tried to find the pertinent document. "Damn it, I know it's somewhere in here."

"Virgil, I'm aware of that memo," the President said in a clipped voice. "But we need more than a three-year-old warning to be sure Al-Qaeda is involved."

"We're not talking three years, Mr. President -- " Virgil started to reply, but Rice broke in.

"Mr. President, Virgil here says we need to shut down all the airports in the country and order all planes to land immediately. I appreciate his expertise, but I'm not convinced that's the right thing to do. I propose that warnings be sent to all planes in flight to keep cockpit doors locked and be on the lookout for possible cockpit incursions, and that all takeoffs be postponed until we can be sure we're on top of the situation. No need for everyone to land immediately. That would cause absolute chaos." Virgil thought he could see Rice and Cheney exchange a knowing glance as she finished.

It was quiet for a moment. Over the speakerphone, they actually could hear the muffled sound of the President's car accelerating as the motorcade pulled out of the parking lot at the elementary school in Florida where he'd been reading to youngsters when news of the collision broke. They heard the cheers of spectators, and Virgil visually imagined the President waving to the crowd as the motorcade left.

"All right," the President said, and then paused for a moment. "Look, I know some people say Virgil over-reacts sometimes, and I realize we have to think about the safety of everyone flying today. Virgil, I respect your advice, and I'm going to go along with your idea to cancel all takeoffs. I'm also going to agree with Condi's suggestion to warn all cockpits, but no forced landings. Can the FAA and the airlines carry out an order like that?"

"I'll coordinate the agencies, Mr. President," Rice said. "Can I get started on that now?"

"Yep – please go ahead," the President said. Rice got up and hurried out through the office door.

Before Cheney could say anything, Virgil spoke up. He stood by the VP's desk, and had been chewing nervously on a toothpick as the President talked. Now he took the toothpick out of his mouth and held it between his fingers. He faced the phone directly, as if the President could somehow be seen through it.

"Mr. President, with all due respect, sir, do you think it's OK to let those planes keep flying to their destinations in this situation?" Virgil asked. "Some may have just taken off, and could have destinations hours away. We're taking the chance that more hijackers could be out there. And we have to consider what exactly these hijackers had in mind. I think it's very concerning that both planes turned south, toward New York. We know Al-Qaeda has talked about using planes to target buildings. If there are other hijackers up there, other buildings might be targeted. Maybe even this one." He looked out the window nervously, as if he'd just realized the danger they might be in.

"What do you think, Cheney?" the President asked.

"If something were going to happen, we'd have heard about it by now," Cheney said, giving Virgil an annoyed glare as he spoke. "I talked to the NSA and to the FBI a few minutes ago and they're monitoring the situation closely. We also have the military on alert and planes ready to scramble if any airliners make unauthorized moves. I think we're pretty well covered."

THE TOWERS STILL STAND

"OK, Cheney," Bush responded. "Virgil – I want you to find out everything you can about this. If it turns out this is Al-Qaeda, that's a very serious situation. I didn't think they had the power to reach right into our country and manufacture something like this. If Bin Laden was involved, he's going to hear from me. So get me that info ASAP."

"Yes sir," Virgil said, still limping around the VP's office, chewing his toothpick.

"I also want us to consider right away who else might be behind this," Cheney said, leaning back in his chair. "We can't discount the possibility that Saddam Hussein might have sent operatives into our country to hijack planes. We have people on the ground in Kuwait and Saudi Arabia, and they have contacts in Iraq. I expect we'll have some evidence very soon and I'm recommending we pursue this angle very closely, Mr. President."

"Right; I agree," the President replied. "Over and out, everyone."

"Thanks, Mr. President." Cheney hung up the phone. Virgil still stood looking at the VP as Cheney sat straight in his chair and stared back.

"Do you need anything?" Cheney asked, reaching up to re-set his eyeglasses.

"Only your assurance that we're going to follow the President's instructions to pursue the possible Bin Laden connection to this and not just focus on Iraq," Virgil replied, looking straight at him. "I know you've had an eye on Iraq ever since you got here, but I'm not convinced Saddam had anything to do with this."

"Virgil, I don't think you take Saddam seriously enough," Cheney replied, staring Virgil back down. "We wouldn't be doing our jobs if we didn't investigate any connection Hussein might have, and I expect you to do just that. Is that understood?"

Virgil just kept looking Cheney in the eye.

Finally, Cheney sighed, and said, "Of course we'll pursue Bin Laden as well. It's what the President has ordered us to do. I just want to make sure we don't forget Saddam is out there. We know Bin Laden and Saddam despise each other, but remember, 'The enemy of my enemy is my friend.' "

"All right; I see the sense in that," Virgil replied, not sure if he really did. He turned and limped out of the office.

The Vice President stared at the door for a while after Virgil left, and then picked up his phone again.

CHAPTER 8

KANDAHAR, AFGHANISTAN: 8 P.M. LOCAL TIME

The sun had set over the dusty city an hour earlier, and the last remnants of twilight glowed purple and red on the horizon. Sunset prayers were over, and it would still be some time until the Isha prayers before bedtime. Though it was still warm, temperatures were down significantly since sunset, and stars had begun to twinkle brightly. There wasn't widespread electricity in this part of the world, and with the moon waning to a thin crescent, this was a night a stargazer would treasure.

In the nondescript hut, now lit inside by the pale glow of candles, Bin Laden, also known as the Sheik, sat on the floor, receiving more visitors. His son-in-law, Sulaiman Abu-Ghaith, head wrapped in white over his dark beard and mustache, sat with the Sheik and with the Sheik's technical adviser as the technician worked the radio dial and the antenna, trying to get a clear signal. The radio could pick up broadcasts from all over the world, and the technician was trying to get the feed from Al Jazeera, which broadcast in Arabic from Qatar. The Sheik was no fan of the Qatar government or of Al Jazeera, both of which he considered to be under the control of infidels, but even he had to admit it was the best possible source for the news they were waiting to hear.

The Sheik exchanged small talk with his son-in-law, but it was plain he was under stress, the technician thought. By this point, the mission should have been launched, and, if successful, would be the world's biggest news. But when he finally was able to get Al Jazeera tuned in, they heard only the ordinary news. The biggest story in the Muslim world now was the assassination over the weekend of Ahmad Shah Massoud, known as the "Lion of Panjshir" and the Sheik's sworn enemy as head of the Northern Alliance, which was fighting the Taliban in Afghanistan. The Sheik, of course, was aware of this news, which had first broken two days earlier, and he showed no emotion as broadcasters read the latest bulletins about the assassination. The technician was pretty sure the Sheik had known all about that assassination before it even had occurred. He wasn't privy to all of the Sheik's plans, but it would take a simple-minded man not to put two and two together this time.

Now, at the top of the hour, the newscast turned toward events outside of the Muslim world, and the Sheik leaned forward almost eagerly when the broadcaster began saying the words, "Today in the United States..."

"This could be it," his son-in-law said, tapping his fingers on the concrete floor where he was sitting. The Sheik turned toward him and motioned him with one hand to stay silent.

"There are reports that two commercial planes collided over a small town about 50 miles north of New York City today," the news anchor said. "The accident happened only in the last hour or so, and details are scarce, but it appears at least one of the planes had been hijacked. We're still waiting for the U.S. government to make comments about this tragedy, and for more details on the possible hijacking. It's believed more than 150 passengers and crew were aboard the two planes, an American Airlines and a United Airlines plane, both bound from Boston to Los Angeles. If all perished, this would be the worst mid-air collision in U.S. history..."

The broadcast feed, which had been somewhat weak, blurred out to static, and the technician started playing with the controls again, trying to get it back, but the Sheik motioned him to turn it off.

"We know what we need to know," the Sheik said. His face showed no particular emotion and seemed as calm as ever. But Sulaiman thought he could detect disappointment in his father-in-law's deep eyes, even in the soft glow of the candlelight. He himself wasn't sure how to feel. He'd known for several days about this operation, and had sent his wife and children to Kuwait to keep them safe in case of possible ramifications, but he hadn't been in on the planning. He knew this operation meant everything to his father-in-law, and to hear of this horrible failure was certainly shocking, if failure it was. The Sheik certainly seemed to think so.

"How can you be sure, sir, that the planes that collided are the ones flown by the brothers?" he asked.

"I cannot be sure, but I have a strong sense that they were. The coincidence would be too great," the Sheik said. "Didn't the Director tell us two of the planes would take off from Boston heading for Los Angeles?" He looked at the ground for a while and then looked up again.

"This is my failure," the Sheik pronounced. "I chose the crews personally, and they couldn't carry out the mission." He shook his head. "The fault can't lie with Atta. I had the utmost confidence in him. He was unshakeable. If I hadn't chosen him for this mission, he might have risen far in our organization. No, one of the other pilots must have failed."

"Weren't there more than two planes?" Sulaiman asked, trying to remember the scraps of information he knew about the operation. "What will happen to the two that didn't collide?"

The Sheik didn't seem surprised by this question.

"The Director and I planned for possible failures," he replied. "If the Director did his job, the brothers on the other planes have already received orders to stand down. We will keep them on the ground there if possible to plan for future actions."

The Sheik struggled slowly to his feet, and Sulaiman got up too to provide support should his father-in-law need it. He had noticed the Sheik limping earlier.

"I need to get communications quickly to the Director," the Sheik said. "We can't communicate electronically, but he will be sending me a message about the operation at some point in the next day. Sulaiman, I need you to get word to him that he is to come to me."

Sulaiman nodded. "I'll leave now for the Continental. I'm staying there and they have Internet access. I can contact him from there."

The Sheik signaled that this was OK. His son-in-law wasn't being tracked by any foreign agencies, they knew, and frequently served as a source of safe communications for the Sheik when he had to get word out of the country. Sulaiman prepared to leave. He embraced his father-in-law.

"May Allah look over you," the Sheik said, letting go of the younger man. Sulaiman pushed through the curtain and was gone. The Sheik stood in the center of the room, and no one disturbed him. He stood there for a long time.

CHAPTER 9

KARACHI, PAKISTAN: 11:30 P.M. LOCAL TIME

The Director was angry. He was fuming. His dark face had turned as red as a turnip. At times like this, no one wanted to come near him, not even his most trusted accomplices. But tonight, they had no choice.

The Director and his men had gathered in the back room of a popular Karachi night club to watch the proceedings on television. They were prepared to celebrate once the news hit, almost like a group of sports fans awaiting their team's victory. The room was theirs alone, curtained off from the rest of the place and guarded discreetly by a rather large, bearded man with no visible weapon, but a bulge in his right hip pocket. Life carried on as always at the rowdy club, with drink flowing and popular music blasting out of speakers, but that was a world apart for the small group of men sitting in the room behind the curtain with the Director.

By 9:30, the Director, his narrow face highlighted by a neatly-trimmed mustache and beard, had drummed his fingers on the table in anticipation, a twinkle in his usually sleepy eyes. The televisions in the room, some tuned to Al Jazeera and others to CNN, competed for attention in English and Arabic. The Director knew both languages well, and, although he'd grown up in Kuwait, was able to move around the huge city of Karachi like a native. It was he who, along with a few others, had designed this operation, had lobbied for it with the Sheik even against long odds, and had put all aspects of the plan into place.

For the Director, the motive may have started out as a religious one, but over time it had become more of an all-consuming obsession. He'd nearly come to blows several times with others in the group as he resisted their plans for other martyrdom operations. He feared those would distract them from their ultimate goal and perhaps unwittingly draw attention their way, interfering with the main plan. Although the Director was close in some ways to the Sheik, their relationship wasn't always a placid one. The Sheik's calm demeanor couldn't have contrasted more with the hot-headedness of the Director, and they often disagreed on tactics. The Director chafed at the Sheik's efforts to pick the hijackers, saying the Sheik relied too much on some inner sense rather than a complex, researched scrutiny. That was an argument he had lost, and the Sheik had chosen men for the operation, sometimes after just talking to them for a few minutes. They both agreed Atta was the best man to lead, but had clashed on the muscle men for the operation.

No one in the room, other than the Director, was certain when the TV reports would start broadcasting the news, because none other than him knew exactly when the operation would begin. But it was morning in the United States, and the Director had gathered them here, so it was apparent he expected something to happen. And soon.

When CNN began broadcasting reports of a plane collision in New York State, the Director jumped up from the table and began shaking his fist at the screen. Luckily, there were no waitstaff in the room, or they would have had a hard time figuring out why a tragic plane crash thousands of miles away could have caused someone to get so angry.

"No – it can't be!" the Director yelled. "No!"

"What happened?" asked one of his men, who had just come back from the bathroom and was now walking toward the Director.

"What do you mean, what happened, you bhen chot!" the Director fumed, spittle flying from his mouth, using an epithet that implied the man had engaged in illicit relations with his own sister. It was one of many Urdu swears he'd picked up from his years living in the country. He shoved the man, and the surprised victim of his rage fell backward, bumping his head on the floor. "Look at the damn television! That's what's happened!" the Director yelled. The man picked himself off the floor, rubbing a bump on his head, wondering at the strength of the 5'4 Director.

Ramzi, the Director's most trusted co-conspirator, got up slowly from his chair and walked across the carpeted floor toward the Director, who now was staring down at the ground in front of one of the televisions, where the news program had moved on from the plane collision to the latest word on the assassination of Mashood. Ramzi, a younger man who had worked closely on this holy operation with the Director for months and who had tried but failed to travel to the United States to serve as one of the hijackers, put one trembling hand on the Director's shoulder. The Director turned to him, his eyes blazing with anger at this interruption.

"Sir," Ramzi said quietly. "We must contact the others – now."

The Director grew visibly calmer and nodded. "Yes; as we planned."

Ramzi left the room with his phone. He hadn't addressed the Director by name, because he, like the others, wasn't sure what the Director's actual name was. The Director had about a dozen different aliases, and didn't reveal personal information to even his closest associates. But Ramzi knew the Director was the man who had planned the hijackings, with authority from the Sheik.

In the following hours, as the group watched the news disconsolately, it became clear that the Director had been correct. Both of the planes had been theirs, they knew. Although the Director, like the others, never touched alcohol, the effect of the news, as the night continued, was like that of heavy drinking. He stumbled around the room, sometimes banging his fist against the walls. He ordered the televisions turned off. He refused food.

"Everyone – out!" he finally fumed. "Out!"

The men gratefully rose to their feet and left before he could change his mind. Only Ramzi stayed. The diminutive man, who looked less like a terrorist and more like a young medical student, wearing Western clothes including a pink Oxford shirt with heavily starched collars and a carefully trimmed black mustache, continued sitting quietly in his seat. He was a thin man and didn't tend to eat much. There was an untouched plate of pita bread in front of him on the table.

Now the Director marched up and grabbed a slice. He smeared hummus on it and stuffed some quickly into his mouth. He chewed loudly and smacked his lips. Aside from his mustache and beard, he looked far from militant. He wore clothes that fit right into the modern Karachi scene, and no one would have picked him out in a crowd in the streets of Karachi. His looks belied his fierce militancy, and few would have guessed that not long ago he'd worn a long, bushy beard that made him look a little like the Maharishi Mahesh Yogi.

As the Director chewed, crumbs falling on the floor in front of him, Ramzi looked quietly down at the table.

"What is your diagnosis?" he finally said.

The food had calmed the Director down somewhat, as did the presence of his trusted lieutenant and the departure of the others. The televisions were off now, but they could still hear the crowds of infidels whooping it up in the front of the nightclub.

The Director shrugged and sat down, tired at last.

"It's too early to make a diagnosis," he replied. "But if I had to guess, it would be that some of the men weren't up to the task. Not Atta; he was well suited and trustworthy. I picked him myself to lead the operation. But I had my doubts about some of the others, and I expressed them many times to the Sheik, but he wouldn't listen."

He played with the half-eaten piece of bread in his hands, twisting it and causing small chunks to break off onto the table. He put the bread down and began pushing the chunks around in front of him into patterns only he could decipher.

"I had doubts too," Ramzi said quietly. "I was particularly concerned about Jarrah. I never felt his heart was really in it. He wasn't a true brother. Remember how he lived with that German girlfriend?"

"What are you talking about him for?" the Director asked petulantly, turning to look at Ramza from under his bushy eyebrows. "He didn't do anything wrong. He's on his plane now, probably going to land in California soon. If Atta is gone, Jarrah is the best one we have left. You confirmed he and Hanjour received our message, correct?"

"I did," Ramzi said. "They stood down. No one will know what they were planning, assuming they all keep their mouths shut."

"That reminds me," the Director said. "We have to take care of Moussaoui. He's a loose cannon. They arrested him three weeks ago and he's liable to wag his lips. Please make him your next job. We need to put that 'pagal bandar' out of commission."

Ramzi took out a little notebook and a pencil and wrote down the order. Then he tucked the notebook back in his pocket. They sat silently for a while.

"What next?" Ramzi asked, finally.

The Director, who had been in an almost trancelike state, opened his eyes. He didn't speak right away, but thought for a while.

"First thing is, I go visit the Sheik," he finally said. "Like it or not, we can't do anything without getting him on board, Allah bless him. He may have mucked up this operation, but we need his backing and his money if we're going to get this done."

"Get what done?" Ramzi asked.

The Director looked at him with contempt.

"Do you really think I'm going to let this stop us?" he asked. "Do you really think I'm going to let those incompetents prevent us from our ultimate goal? We're carrying on. We'll bring back the ones we don't need, but the leaders will stay. We will work with them to make this martyrdom operation happen. We're going to bite off the snake's head. I don't care if it takes us 10 more years to achieve our goals. The towers are mine!"

CHAPTER 10

LOS ANGELES INTERNATIONAL AIRPORT: NOON LOCAL TIME

American Flight 77 landed uneventfully at LAX. Hanjour and his accomplices walked dejectedly down the jet way to a destination that they hadn't planned on living to see. Those among them who had checked their luggage picked up their bags, and the five of them piled into a cab. "Where are we going?" one of them asked Hanjour.

"I know a place," Hanjour replied. The cab sped out of the airport.

CHAPTER 11

SAN FRANCISCO INTERNATIONAL AIRPORT: 12:30 P.M. LOCAL TIME

Jarrah and his helpers also arrived at an unplanned destination, and stood in the waiting area after disembarking, unsure where to go. Jarrah checked his phone for instructions and motioned the men over. He talked to them quietly. They nodded. After they dispersed, Jarrah sat down at the airport McDonald's, ordered a coffee, and looked again at his phone. He'd missed a call from Alev. He'd put her as far out of his mind as possible these last few weeks, but now he could see her again if he wanted to. He put his face in his hands.

CHAPTER 12

WHITE HOUSE: 4 P.M. ET

Virgil stepped forward, punching up the volume on the television.

"The two planes that collided above New York State today have been identified as American Airlines Flight 11 and United Airlines Flight 175," the CNN anchor said at the top of the hour. "A total of 150 passengers and crew were aboard the two planes, and so far, there are no reports of survivors. Let's go to Becky Martinez, our reporter who is on site not far from the wreckage of the planes. Becky, are you there?"

The camera had switched to a petite young woman with curly black hair and a smart blue blouse, standing on a New York street and talking rapidly into a hand-held microphone. Behind her was yellow tape labeled, "Police Line: Do not proceed beyond this point." Smoke still swirled in the distance, and the noise of helicopter blades echoed. Fire fighters rushed to and fro. Virgil could see ruins of at least one house in the background, flames still licking at the roof, and hear sirens as the reporter talked.

"Hi Bill," the CNN reporter yelled, trying to be heard above the noise and confusion. "I'm here about 200 yards from the site where one of the planes went down, and it's still very smoky. If you look behind me, you'll see that some of the wreckage is still burning, and we're being told the fires might not be totally extinguished for a while. Fire departments from six towns are here fighting the flames. We have no idea yet how many people on the ground may have been hurt or killed."

"Becky," the anchor broke in. "Did the planes hit the ground together or far apart, and how much total damage are we talking?"

"Bill, it appears the planes fell to the ground less than a mile apart. One fell in an open field, so we don't believe it damaged any residences. The wreckage of the other is behind me, and it's in an area of small homes about a mile from the center of the town. I've been talking to the fire chief here, and he believes about a dozen homes may have been destroyed. As I said, no word on the possible death toll on the ground, but we're worried it could be high."

"Thank you, Becky," the anchor said. "We'll be going back to Becky regularly for any updates. As we know, this wasn't just any plane accident. The National Transportation Safety Board has told us at least one of the two planes had been hijacked shortly before the collision. We don't know yet who hijacked it, or how. And we don't know the motives. But some experts we've talked to are surmising that the hijackers, who may have been Middle Eastern, might have tried purposely to cause the collision.

"So far, none of the known terrorist groups have claimed responsibility, and there are competing theories about what the hijackers' ultimate aim may have been. For thoughts on this, we're now going to talk to Harry Deaver, a former CIA and Defense Department official who is an expert on terrorist groups. Good afternoon, Mr. Deaver."

Back in Washington, Virgil's ears pricked up. He knew Harry, a former Defense Department man like himself, and a man who knew how to hold the television viewers' attention.

"Hey there, Bill, what a horrible day," said Deaver, a well-built, salt-and-pepper haired man now appearing on the split screen of the television. He was in his 60s, wearing an open neck plaid shirt and khakis, sporting a belt with a big buckle and sitting in a chair in front of a bookshelf in what appeared to be his home office. Confident but in a non-cocky, very approachable way. The way news stations liked their talking heads, people who viewers sensed were both knowledgeable and "one of them" as well.

"So Mr. Deaver, you spent many years studying terrorism, and you most recently worked on a report about the 1998 embassy bombings in Kenya and Tanzania. Who do you think today's hijackers may have been, how could they hijack a plane in this day and age with the security measures in place, and what were their motives?"

"Well, Bill," Harry said in a slow Southern drawl, an almost friendly nod to his head as he looked comfortably into the camera. "This is no surprise at all to me, and shouldn't be to anyone who's familiar with terror groups like Al-Qaeda. For many years, we've been aware that Al-Qaeda was interested in hijacking planes, and perhaps bombing them or trying to bring them down in other ways. I don't think we should consider this the same type of hijacking we saw back in the 1960s, when hijackers wanted pilots to land planes somewhere and hold passengers hostage until they achieved their goals. No, I believe this is something far more serious. I reckon these fellas today were planning on taking some lives. And maybe their own, as well."

"So Mr. Deaver, are you saying these were suicide hijackers, and they crashed into the other plane deliberately?"

"Well, Bill, we don't have any information on that as of now, but I think the FBI has to explore all possibilities. Maybe they were going to bomb the plane but messed up and flew it into the other one. Or maybe they planned to crash the plane somewhere. These are schemes we've been warned about, but it's always one thing to talk about it and another to actually see it happen."

"Mr. Deaver," another anchor broke in. "How could hijackers gain access to planes? Wouldn't the security measures we have prevent them from getting guns and knives aboard?"

"Well, we don't know exactly what tools these people used to hijack the planes. But whatever measures we have in place, they apparently didn't work too well this time," Harry said. "Look, I don't know of any system that's fool-proof. I'm sure the FBI and the White House are studying this very carefully right now, and although I'm not a betting man, but I'd wager a lot of new security measures will go into place very soon."

"And knowing that hijackers could board planes, are you comfortable with the decision this afternoon to allow planes to take off again?"

Harry's brows pulled together and his lips tightened.

"No, sir, I'm not comfortable with it. Now the FBI and the White House probably know what they're doing, and it's not for me to second guess, but with groups like Al-Qaeda, there's always a Plan B. I'm guessing the folks in control of the government have good reason to believe there's no danger at the moment, but I think we need to keep our guard up in the days ahead."

Virgil angrily snapped off the TV and threw his remote control to the other side of the room. He couldn't believe the flight ban was being lifted, against his advice. He'd been pacing up and down again, toothpick firmly in his mouth, as he watched the broadcast, getting angrier and angrier. He had done a lot of pacing around today. He was always like that. Even at home on the rare weekend he wasn't at work, Virgil's wife complained that he constantly puttered around the house, never comfortable sitting back and relaxing. The only time he ever really relaxed was on his long walk back up to his 19th-century, five-story townhouse in the wealthy D.C. neighborhood of Kalorama, about a mile and a half north of the White House, at the end of the day.

On his computer screen now was a letter to the President and Vice President. Virgil debated whether to send it right away or think it over between now and tomorrow morning. He was usually a man who liked to say what had to be said and say it now, but something held him back.

It had been a very long day, and he didn't know when he'd get home. He'd spent all afternoon shuttling between phone calls and meetings. There were calls with the heads of the CIA and FBI, another meeting with Cheney and Rice, and calls with his best sources on Bin Laden and Al-Qaeda, people who'd been monitoring the group for years. His people were convinced – all of them – that this collision had the hallmarks of an Al-Qaeda attack, and that more attacks might come. One of the people he'd spoken to, actually, was the fellow who'd just appeared on CNN, Harry Deaver. He and Harry went way back, all the way to the 1970s, when both of them had worked in the Defense Department under Donald Rumsfeld, the current Secretary of Defense. Harry suggested that Virgil ask Hofelder over at the CIA to do a check on the names of all Middle Eastern passengers on the two jets to see what links they could find, but Virgil had beaten him to it. That search was well in motion and Virgil expected to have the results soon.

Oh yeah, he'd also talked to Rumsfeld. It was no surprise, Virgil thought bitterly, to hear the Secretary of Defense take up the same view as the VP – that the hijackers may have something to do with Saddam Hussein. Rummy, like the others, was obsessed with the guy. Virgil himself felt the United States had done a pretty good job these last 10 years keeping Hussein from being a problem. The real danger, he believed, was Al-Qaeda, and Hussein was an enemy of Al-Qaeda – another reason it could be helpful to have him around.

The letter to Bush and Cheney on Virgil's screen reiterated Virgil's advice from the morning meeting. It warned that hijackings were part of Al-Qaeda's known arsenal, and that it was far from certain whether this was isolated or the first of many. He warned that Al-Qaeda had talked of plans to target buildings with planes flown by suicide bombers, and that the planes involved in the collision had turned away from their assigned flight paths and toward New York City before the attack. He argued that the United States needed to warn the Taliban to hand over Osama bin Laden and his men, or face a U.S. attack.

He also spelled out the reasons why it was unlikely that Saddam Hussein would have launched an attack like this, most notably because the man was addicted to power and an attack like this, if traced back to him, would mean the end of his reign. He spelled out his concerns about the hijacker's cryptic comment about having "some planes." He noted that other hijacking cells might exist even now, ready to attack again. His letter concluded, "Let's move on Al-Qaeda now. Quickly and immediately. Or our first warning of another attack here could be buildings burning in New York or Washington."

The phone rang in his quiet office. Outside, it was getting dark. Very little light now made its way through the small window high on the wall. Virgil headed to his desk and picked the phone up. It was Harry Deaver.

"Harry," Virgil said. "Just saw you on TV. You looked good."

"Thanks, Virge," Harry said in his slow, deep-voiced southern drawl. "I hope I talked some sense into a few people, assuming they were watching."

"I'm trying to do the same here, Harry," Virgil said. "I'm writing a memo to them now. I'll share it with you soon and see what you think."

"Sure, sure, fine," Harry said. "Look Virge, you know and I know those bastards are going to try to use this as an excuse to ramp up the pressure on Iraq. We both know what a mistake that would be. We have to keep up the drumbeat here against Bin Laden."

"You're preaching to the choir, Harry. I said the same thing to them myself over and over today. It's like talking to a statue. The bunch of them, they're all together on this."

"I don't mean to pitch a fit, but why the hell did you lift the flight ban?" Harry asked. "That was one mighty stupid thing to do."

"*Me?* Hell, I insisted they ban all flights. Look, Harry, I do what I can around here, but I'm an army of one. And I lose too many battles," Virgil said, pacing the room again.

"Well, it's time to stop carrying the load by yourself," Harry said. "If they don't take you seriously, you need to get this message out any way you can. I can go on CNN and talk all I want, but I'm not in the White House. I don't have the power of office that you do. If you don't get what you want from them, I'm encouraging you to go straight to the media."

Virgil pondered this for a minute. He could hear Harry breathing on the other end of the phone. The two tended to see eye-to-eye on foreign policy issues, maybe because they'd spent so long in the trenches together. Harry was a conservative Republican and Virgil was part of the endangered species known as liberal Republicans.

"Harry, I'll consider the media, but only as a last resort," Virgil finally said. "Taking that route would probably be the end of my job, and I might be able to do more here in the White House than I could out there being a talking head on CNN, no offense."

"None taken, sir," Harry replied with a bit of a chortle. Then he continued in a more serious tone. "But just think about it. This is too important to put your job ahead of it."

"Understood, old friend," Virgil replied. He poured himself a glass of bourbon as he held the phone between his ear and shoulder. "Come on by my place over the weekend, Harry. We can talk some more. I'm still on Bancroft Place."

"Yeah, I remember your place. One of the nicest. I'll let you know if I can make it over."

"OK, thanks for the support, Harry. So long."

"All the best, Virge. I reckon you'll do the right thing."

"I'll sure as hell try," Virgil replied. He hung up and tilted back his glass. He drank it all in one gulp and closed his eyes.

CHAPTER 13

WORLD TRADE CENTER: 6:30 P.M.

The sun was sinking low in the west, its red rays lighting up windows in the two towers of the World Trade Center. In the towers, workers rushed to get home, and the elevators were packed. Vacuum cleaners began to roar in the hallways, and janitors collected garbage from offices. Below the lobbies, crowds pushed and shoved their way onto subway trains, rushing by the restaurants and shops in the underground mall.

Up at the very top of the north tower, it was almost prime dinner hour at Windows on The World, whose windows faced north and east toward Midtown and Brooklyn. The lights of the Brooklyn Bridge twinkled far below as men in suit jackets and women in their best clothes waited for guidance to their tables by hosts and hostesses also dressed in crisp white shirts and jet black slacks. Those already at their tables looked over the menu, which offered well-to-do guests the chance to order a $3,000 bottle of wine.

Aside from the horrific plane crash north of the city, it had been a fairly normal day at the World Trade complex, a day that for most of its denizens would soon fade in their memories among the thousands of other work days in their lives, combining into a single blur as the years moved slowly by.

PART TWO: SEPT. 11 AFTERMATH

CHAPTER 1

THE WHITE HOUSE BASEMENT

Virgil was back in his White House basement office at 4 a.m. the morning of Sept. 12, wearing the same rumpled clothes. They looked even more rumpled now. There were dark circles under his eyes, and he needed a shave. Virgil was never the kind who could go long without shaving. He tended to develop five-o'clock shadow at around noon. Now, it was 16 hours past noon, and there was no shaving gear anywhere near.

But his own scratchy face wasn't on Virgil's mind at this graveyard hour. He was putting the finishing touches on the letter to Bush and Cheney and trying to decide if he should read it to Harry first. But emailing it to Harry was out of the question. This was very confidential, and the chances of someone hacking into the system and stealing it were too high. Within the White House, a secure email server protected internal messages, but it didn't protect documents once they left the building.

Virgil scratched his head and yawned. He'd been sitting in the same chair for several hours, and his legs cramped and his back ached. He got up and did a few toe touches, allowing his weight to stretch tired muscles and fatigued bones, then jogged in place for a minute. He made himself another cup of black coffee, twisting his neck gently from side to side as it brewed. Virgil was always a solitary man, and late nights weren't unusual, as he could think best with everyone gone. But this was late even for him. Earlier, a janitor had gone by in the hallway with a vacuum, and had looked in through Virgil's open door with a surprised glance to see someone still around.

Virgil finally decided against sharing the letter with Harry. Even calling him and reading it over the phone presented security issues. He knew Harry would agree with what he was saying. And if the President and Vice President didn't take it seriously, then he'd reconsider Harry's advice about leaking it. But leaking wasn't really in his nature. He was a team player, even if he didn't love his teammates.

Though he had no plans to leak any information yet, he believed the administration was going to try to hold back too much. Throughout what was now the previous day, at a number of meetings, the emphasis coming from above was to let information out slowly to the public, if at all. Virgil was warned especially against airing publicly any of his hunches about this being Al-Qaeda, at least until they had more information. Virgil agreed this would be prudent, knowing his teams needed more time to research the Al-Qaeda connections and flight manifests to see who these hijackers were. Best not to show your cards until you knew which ones you had, he thought.

But the President and Vice President wanted to only share the minimal information about the hijacking (or hijackings, he thought bitterly). The flight control transcripts and recordings were immediately labeled classified, and FAA and NTSB people familiar with them were told to keep their mouths shut. There'd be no public airing of the "we have some planes" transmission. There was even talk about classifying the two planes' black boxes, once they were found, with national security cited as the reason. That would be pretty much unprecedented. Virgil had worked in several administrations, but this one was the most secretive. He sensed that Cheney and Bush had decided the hijacking was something that could reflect poorly on their abilities to secure the country, so they wanted to let out as little information as possible. He smiled wryly to himself. The media wouldn't like that.

CHAPTER 2

THE WHITE HOUSE PRESS ROOM

The reporters shifted impatiently in their seats in the small White House press room, grumbling about the late start of the briefing. Nancy Hanson, the New York Times' White House correspondent, kept looking at her watch and sighing loudly enough for those around her to hear. "Typical," she said in a disgusted tone to the Wall Street Journal reporter on her right. "I've been doing this 10 years, three administrations. Nothing ever changes. They always treat us like this. Why tell us the briefing is going to be at 8:45 if they aren't going to be ready? I'm betting it starts right at 9." The Wall Street Journal reporter nodded his head knowingly, as if he'd heard this many times before. Finally Press Secretary Ari Fleischer walked in at the top of the hour, 15 minutes late but not looking particularly sheepish about it.

"Good morning, everyone," the Press Secretary said, standing at the podium. His bright eyes behind his glasses took in the audience quickly "Thanks for being here. My apologies for the late start."

"Apologies, my ass," Nancy grumbled under her breath.

"The President is still out of town and I have no announcements from him at this time," the Press Secretary said. "However, I want to update you on yesterday's tragic incident in New York State. The plane collision is still under investigation, but we have confirmed that the American Airlines flight was hijacked by several men who appeared to be Middle Eastern, we don't have all the information yet. These men apparently killed or disabled the flight crew and took over the controls. The United plane and the American plane collided about 15 minutes later. Both planes had deviated from their planned flight routes. We're investigating at this time whether the United plane was also hijacked.

"Obviously, two coordinated hijackings, if confirmed, would constitute a major terrorist attack, and any hijacking is definitely one hijacking too many. We're exploring how the terrorists got through security, what if any weapons they may have used, what their intentions were, who financed them and planned this action, and any links they may have had to terrorist groups like Al-Qaeda or terrorist leaders like Saddam Hussein. Right now, there's still a lot we don't know, but I can assure you the skies are safe. We decided out of prudence yesterday to prevent all takeoffs for several hours, and we spent that time working closely with the FBI and CIA to determine if any other attacks were imminent.

"After determining that there were none, we allowed planes to begin taking off again at 3 p.m. ET yesterday, more than six hours after the hijackings. As of now, flights are in the air, and all security systems have been raised to the highest possible level as a matter of precaution. But we see no current danger. In fact, my own wife is flying on a commercial jet as we speak. With that, I open the floor to questions. Nancy?"

Nancy, who had been first to wave her hand, now stood up and faced the Press Secretary, holding a notebook and pen and with a no-nonsense expression on her face, which was framed by medium-length, curly brown hair. Her face showed some middle-aged worry lines, and there were plenty of silver hairs mixed with the brown. Life as a Washington political reporter can take its toll.

"Thanks, Ari," Nancy replied. "I have a lot of questions, but the most urgent one is how do you know there's no further danger? How can you be so sure this isn't just the start of something bigger? And how can Americans feel safe in the air?" She stopped talking and stood there, bright green eyes staring down the Press Secretary, pen at the ready.

"Well, Nancy, that's actually about three questions, but that's no surprise coming from you," Fleischer said. There were titters from the other reporters. "I'll try to address them the best I can, but I'll first reiterate that there is no danger of further terrorist attacks at this time. Our national security team has been monitoring all of its channels into various terror groups, and it hasn't detected any plots. We believe this was an isolated event, but we'll be ready at first notice to ground flights again if we sense any further danger."

"Ari," Nancy said, continuing to scribble in her notebook even as she looked the press secretary squarely in the eye. "Weren't your people monitoring all their channels *before* yesterday and they still missed yesterday's plot? How can you have confidence they aren't missing something now? And what do you think these hijackers were trying to do?"

"Nancy, Nancy, Nancy," Fleischer responded with a smile. "There's three more. No one else has gotten to ask one." He smiled indulgently, then turned his full attention to the man at her side. "Let's see what the gentleman from the Wall Street Journal wants to ask." More titters rose at Fleischer's obvious dismissal of her, and Nancy reluctantly sat back down, her jaws clamped and her eyes glaring. "John – you have the floor."

"Thanks, Ari," said the Wall Street Journal reporter, who wore a tweed jacket and a somewhat unkempt beard. "My question is similar to Nancy's. Was there terrorist chatter before the attack and what do you think the aims of the hijackers were?"

"Well, John," Ari replied. "We're still working closely with the FBI and CIA, and with our national security team, to determine what if any sort of terrorist chatter they may have heard in the days and weeks prior to yesterday. It's too early for that investigation to have yielded any results, but I'm sure we'll learn more in the coming days. As to where the terrorists were taking the planes, or whether they meant to collide them – all that is under investigation, and I really don't have answers yet."

More reporters waved their hands frantically, and Fleischer answered a few more questions, as vaguely and evasively as he had earlier in the conference, Nancy thought. She wasn't able to get any more words in. Another 15 minutes and Fleischer thanked everyone for coming, walked briskly away from the podium, turned and disappeared behind one of the doors at the back of the room even as reporters kept shouting more questions at his retreating figure.

Reporters packed up to go. Camera operators fussed over their equipment in the back, and there was a low buzz of conversation as everyone rushed to put their stories out as soon as possible.

"So what do you think, John: are we being bullshitted here?" Nancy asked as she and the Wall Street Journal reporter prepared to file out of the briefing room behind a crowd of others.

"Well, you're the one with the patented bullshit detector," John replied. "What's it tell you?"

"The bullshit detector is at 10 out of 10," Nancy replied as they left the room and walked down a little hallway that led to their offices in the West Wing. "They're holding back from us, can't you tell? I think it's because they messed up and let this attack slip through. They know more than they're saying, but they don't want us to know because they want to protect their asses."

"Maybe you're over-thinking it a little, Nancy," John replied. They'd reached their offices and were standing outside in the hallway. "There is a lot of information they need to process, and it takes more than one day to figure out how something like this happened."

"Well," Nancy said. "I don't like being spoon-fed bullshit by them and then having to report it. Makes me feel like a mouthpiece for the administration." She shook her head, saw others in the hall scurrying to their desks and felt a tired sigh breaking through her anger. "I've been at this place way too long. Maybe it's time to look for something else."

"It would sure make my job easier if you left," John said with a smile. "Then you wouldn't be able to scoop me any more."

"Oh, I'd find a way, even if I retired," Nancy joked, and John laughed. They went into their respective offices and closed the doors.

Nancy sat at her computer and began typing a brief story about the press conference. There wasn't much new information to share, and she was disappointed not to be able to add much information beyond what she'd reported yesterday. In 15 minutes she was done, and she pressed the button to send her story to the bureau, where it would be edited. She wasn't worried about editors giving her any trouble. They pretty much left her alone. She guessed the story would be out on NYT.com within a few minutes, without any questions from any of the editors. It was like playing a sport, she felt. Once you established a reputation with the refs, they tended to call things your way.

But reporting from a press conference was the easiest part of her job. She could do it robotically. The challenge was finding a way to get information no one else had. She wanted to know where the planes had been headed, what the hijackers' motives had been and where they came from. And on this story, she knew whom she needed to talk to. The problem was, that person was Virgil Walker.

Nancy had been in D.C. long enough to know there were certain people who'd talk on background, meaning not for attribution, and certain people who wouldn't. She had a number of what she thought of as "deep" contacts in the administration who would give her insight on decision-making and behind-the-scenes debate as long as she never mentioned their name. Some would even call *her*. That's how she got a reputation for scooping other reporters. She had a knack for developing trust, which served her well. Just two weeks ago, one of her White House sources had given her a heads up about the President's decision regarding stem-cell research. Her article had wound up on the front page, and had been the talk of the town.

Nancy hadn't written much about terrorism recently – it hadn't been a big topic since last year when the U.S.S. Cole was bombed. So she didn't have a great network of Administration experts on the subject. However, word was that Virgil, a former Defense Department official, was the foremost expert in the White House on Al-Qaeda and other terrorist groups. So just on general principle over the last few months, she'd decided to develop him as a contact. Or had tried to, at least. She'd learned his office number through her web of contacts in the White House secretarial pool, but he'd refused to take her calls. And the one time she'd approached him in person, after the President held a press conference a few months ago to discuss terror threats, he had smiled shyly, shook his head and put a finger to his lips when he saw her press badge and walked quickly in the opposite direction. She hadn't pursued him then, but she would now.

CHAPTER 3

THE DIRECTOR AND THE SHEIK IN KANDAHAR

A group of three horses, each with a rider, headed down the dusty street outside Bin Laden's compound. On the middle horse sat the Director, looking unsteady and uncomfortable, sitting stiffly as he clutched the reins. The Director had spent the last years in Karachi, Pakistan's largest and most cosmopolitan city, and he wasn't used to four-legged transportation. When the horses stopped outside the Sheik's home, the Director tried his best to scramble off the horse gracefully, but wound up unable to bring one foot down off the animal while his other foot rested in the stirrup. One of the other riders, an older, bearded man wearing a turban and hoisting a machine gun over his shoulder, walked quickly over and helped the Director down.

"What a godforsaken place," the Director said out loud, looking around the empty street lined with mud walls. Not for the first time, he wondered if the Sheik gave up all of his wealth and luxuries because he truly wanted to sacrifice on behalf of the cause, or if to some extent he did it as a prop to make himself more palatable to the fighters he directed. Whatever the case, the Sheik did lead the life of an ascetic, so the Director supposed he deserved credit for it, no matter the underlying reason. As for himself, he couldn't imagine living in such a way. This horse riding, for instance, was at the Sheik's request. The Sheik believed cars were too easy for enemies to trace, and could be wired with a bomb. Since the Sheik had never heard of a suicide horse bomb, he insisted that his key people ride horses or walk when they came to visit. Sometimes the Director thought the Sheik was a little over the top when it came to security. Then again, he lived a pretty dangerous lifestyle.

"Stay out here with these confounded animals," he ordered the men who had come with him. "We can shoot them later." The men showed no sign of appreciating his humor, and stood stone-faced by the horses, toting their guns. The Director approached the security guards at the gate and they stood up to open it. There was no need for a security check this time. They knew the Director well.

Inside the mud walls, a hut stood across the dirt yard. The sun beat down on the courtyard as the Director walked toward the hut, dust floating with every step. The Director paused when he saw the Sheik stood at the door waiting for him; this was quite unusual, the Director thought. Typically, the Sheik would stay inside whatever cave or hut he was living in, and one would have to approach him as a supplicant would, asking for his approval. Even the Director, who'd come up with the 9/11 attack idea and handled its execution, still felt the Sheik looked down on him. This didn't matter to the Director, because he bowed to no man. But he knew others who were easily cowed by the Sheik's presence, and realized the Sheik relied on that reaction.

As always when they met, the two embraced. The Sheik's body seemed thinner and weaker than the Director had remembered from last time, several months ago. After they let go, they looked at each other for a moment, grim faced, and then the Sheik motioned him inside.

In the shade of the hut, the Director sat on a soft cushion while the Sheik made tea for him in the next room. The Sheik always insisted on making tea himself, saying no one else could make it the way he liked. He could hear the Sheik clinking dishes and pouring water in there. This was the Director's first time at this hideout, but he guessed that the other room was a kitchen. The windows were covered with curtains to keep the midday heat out, and the mud walls kept it cool as well. However, there were no window screens, and flies flew about, landing on the Director and then buzzing away when he slapped at them.

The Sheik emerged from the other room bearing two cups of tea. He walked to the Director in his stooped manner, handed him a cup and then sat down slowly and carefully onto another cushion nearby.

They sat looking at each other for a while. The Director, who'd asked the Sheik for this visit, decided the Sheik was waiting for him to speak and opened his mouth to begin talking. But the Sheik, seeing this, held up his hand and shook his head. He seemed to be waiting for something, and sure enough, within seconds, the midday prayer call came echoing through the windows. The two put down their teacups and knelt on cushions facing west toward Mecca to recite their prayers.

When the praying was over, the Sheik turned to the Director and asked in his melodic voice, "What next?" The Director, who had come here to discuss what went wrong and why, was thrown off for a moment. This wasn't how he'd expected things to go.

"With all due respect, Your Highness, I think we need to discuss what went wrong on the blessed day before we decide what to do next," the Director said. "There is no point moving forward if we don't learn from our mistakes."

The Sheik put his hand up again.

"The mistake was mine," the Sheik said, again surprising the Director. "I chose the brothers for our sacred mission, and I chose wrongly. They failed us."

The Director knew better than to react, although he most certainly agreed with that assessment. Instead, he broke in with, "Certainly not all of them failed. Atta appears to have done his job as we discussed. His plane was hit by the other. The brothers on that plane – Shehhi and the others – they were the ones to blame."

"Yes, yes," the Sheik said impatiently. "There is no sense dwelling on the past. The brothers are gone and we can discuss these matters with them when we reach the next life. I only have one observation to make. I think poor judgment was used in stopping the sacred operation after the first two planes crashed. We still had brothers in the air on the other planes, ready to strike. Please explain your decision."

"It was quite simple, your Highness," the Director replied. "The failure of the first planes was a sign to us from Allah, a sign that we were not meant to succeed that day. Rather than sacrificing the others and risking the ruin of everything we had planned, I decided it was best we should wait for another day, and preserve the assets we had. Also – the towers were the most important target. They are the symbol of U.S. Jewish power. A strike at the government buildings and not the towers would have left the snake free to bite again."

The Sheik nodded, but from the look on his face he didn't seem completely convinced. The Director knew the Sheik thought that he, the Director, was obsessed with the World Trade Center. And that was true enough. Ever since the semi-successful attack of 1993, which had killed six but failed to bring down the towers as planned, the Director had made it his life's work to complete the job. As he saw it, the towers represented the financial power of the United States and all the evil those finances brought to the world. Particularly the billions that the U.S. pumped into the Zionist entity – Israel.

"What's done is done, and now it's time to discuss our next actions," the Sheik finally said. "You're in touch with the remaining brothers in the United States, correct?"

"I am," the Director said. "We are sending the fighters back home but Hanjour and Jarrah will stay where they are for now, so we can easily use them for future plans. Hanjour, as you know, is a trained pilot and our best pilot there now that we've lost Atta. And Jarrah may be the most intelligent operator there with Atta gone. He can do brilliant things for us."

"He can, but not now," the Sheik said.

The Director looked at him questioningly.

"Do you mean later, then, we'll move ahead?" the Director asked. "Of course we need to lie low for a bit with the Americans on high alert, but they're not going to stay that way for very long. You and I have been to America; we know how they act. They are a weak people enslaved by the devil Jews, and they value sloth and fornication over faith. They love their 'freedom'," he spat out the word contemptuously, "too much to stop us."

"The Americans are a vulnerable people, that much we know," the Sheik said. "They will hear from us before long, God willing. But the failure of this sacred mission has made me think. I don't believe we have the power to succeed in such a complex undertaking so far from our holy lands. We need to look closer to home, particularly to the holy land itself, where the infidel soldiers still pollute the soil. We need to target the sham government that calls itself the protector of the holy sites. The failure in America was God's sign to us that we must re-focus. An attack on the oil fields in Saudi Arabia should be our next mission. We have the operatives to do it, and in that way we can punish both the Americans and the infidel house of Saud."

The Director had listened to this speech with less and less patience as it went on. He'd known the Sheik had never truly believed the September 11 plan would work, and that he might push back on any attempt to get it back in motion at this point. But he hadn't expected this bad of a reaction. After spending several years devoted to the fabulous plan he'd developed, and then seeing it all break down just minutes before the sacred battle was to be won, the Director wasn't about to let Bin Laden walk away from another attempt without putting up a good fight. The Director wasn't always good at holding back his anger, even from the Sheik, but this time, he thought fast and came up with a plan even as he spoke.

"I agree about the wicked house of Saud," the Director responded, as the Sheik nodded. "We will strike them with a vicious blow. But I leave the planning and direction to you, your highness. I am headed to the United States."

The Sheik's eyebrows rose, just as they had years ago when the Director had first proposed the hijackings and suicide missions into buildings, with the Director himself as one of the pilots, though not on one of the suicide planes. The Director's plane was to have landed, with the Director then emerging to declare victory over the infidels. The Sheik had rejected that plan with obvious distaste, and now he looked skeptical again. "What do you propose?" the Sheik asked.

A few minutes later, after the Director had told him the new plan, the Sheik's beard was wagging as he nodded his head.

CHAPTER 4

VIRGIL'S DECISION

It was 5 p.m. on September 14 when Virgil shut the door of his office and headed out through the underground hallways toward the east exit of the White House. He carried a small brown wrinkled briefcase that looked like it had been stuffed under airplane seats more than once, and nothing else. He was alone.

Leaving at 5 was a first for Virgil. In fact, the last three nights he'd been in his office until the early morning hours. He could easily do so today; there was plenty of work to do. But he was leaving. He'd had enough for now.

He walked by the guardhouse and out of the east gate of the complex onto the sidewalk, passing huge buses lined up to carry the last White House tourists of the day back to their hotels. It was another pleasant late summer day in D.C., with the temperature around 70 and a few puffy clouds overhead. The sun was beginning to sink in the west, where a large jet plane arched up into the sky from National Airport across the Potomac River. Like any true Washingtonian, Virgil didn't even notice the plane taking off. It was so much a part of the Washington scenery it wasn't even worth mentioning.

Virgil limped through the little park across from the White House, where the omnipresent protesters stood with their signs urging the United States to exit the United Nations, and then turned north onto Connecticut Avenue. He always tried to walk the mile and a half from work back home. It was uphill, so it gave him a bit of a workout. And walking always seemed to help his leg, although his limp never went completely away.

This was a pleasant change, he thought; walking the streets in actual daylight. No one noticed him. He looked like any other office dweller hurrying home at the end of the day. All around him the typical noise of the city flowed – taxis honking, planes taking off one after the other, tour groups chattering, hotel doormen blowing their whistles. He blended easily into the scene, and no one would have known he was a top adviser to the President. As he waited for the light to change at M Street, he glanced over at a Washington Post newspaper machine. The headline, which he'd already seen this morning, screamed out at him again: "America Mourns Terrorism Victims." Above the fold of the paper but below the headline were photographs of the passengers and crew of the two planes, arranged in rows like someone's high school yearbook. He knew the photos continued below the fold where they couldn't be seen through the newspaper box. Virgil looked quickly away and walked across the street when the light changed.

Cheney and Rice, along with Tenet from the CIA, had led various meetings he'd been to since the terrorist attack, and a consensus had been reached. The attack appeared to have links to Al-Qaeda, judging from the histories Virgil and his team had been able to research about the Middle Eastern men on the planes. Both planes had been hijacked, but it was unclear what their aim had been. The collision apparently was an accident, judging from the black box recording they'd listened to that revealed the struggle in the cockpit of Flight 175. But what the hijackers had planned to do with the planes if they hadn't collided remained unclear. Although Virgil had persisted in arguing that the hijackers had buildings and monuments in mind, others weren't so sure. One school of thought was that the hijackers meant to land the planes somewhere – perhaps at JFK or National airports – and start killing passengers one by one until certain demands were met, such as pulling U.S. troops out of Saudi Arabia or releasing Palestinian prisoners from Israel.

What absolutely no one could prove, but which kept getting bandied about, was the Iraq connection. Cheney, in particular, was instrumental in pursuing this line of thought, and already had evidence, or so he said, that Atta had been in Germany meeting with a representative of the Iraq government sometime last year. While Virgil believed in pursuing any evidence, he was skeptical about Cheney's claim, because it seemed unlikely that Saddam Hussein and Al-Qaeda – sworn enemies – would have any-thing to do with each other.

When he'd mentioned this to Cheney, the Vice President had glared at him with those penetrating eyes and replied, "The enemy of my enemy is my friend." Virgil still didn't buy it.

Tenet, the CIA Director, had pushed for a warning to the Taliban to give up Osama Bin Laden or face invasion. Bush and Cheney seemed hesitant to go that far, but had ultimately agreed that a major strike on Bin Laden was necessary. Bush, in particular, was impatient to take some action, noting that the U.S. hadn't done so after the U.S.S. Cole bombing last year and perhaps, by hesitating then, had unwittingly encouraged Bin Laden to think he could get away with more. "We need to stop swatting at flies and take the fight to Bin Laden," Bush had said firmly, striking the table with his fist for emphasis.

Today, Bush and Cheney had authorized a strike against Bin Laden and had asked the Joint Chiefs of Staff to recommend plans for doing so. But they didn't want to move too swiftly, for fear of making the same mistake as the Clinton administration in 1998, when it had bombed Bin Laden-linked sites in Sudan only to find out Bin Laden hadn't been in any of them. The Joint Chiefs of Staff, along with Tenet and with help from Virgil, were to formulate a plan that would identify the exact whereabouts of Bin Laden and get actual boots on the ground to track him down and kill him.

This was all well and good, Virgil thought as he crossed DuPont Circle heading north. What he couldn't tolerate was the secrecy the administra-tion was imposing on any information about the Sept. 11 incident, as it was coming to be known. He was convinced the nation was at immediate risk of another terror attack and that it was the government's responsibility to take appropriate action to prevent one – even if it meant shutting down every airport in the country. Everything he knew about Bin Laden and his outfit convinced him that Sept. 11 was just the beginning of a major blow from the group and that there might well be cells right now in the country preparing for a second strike.

Bush and Cheney were certainly taking the right steps by imposing new security measures on planes, but these measures – such as impenetrable cockpit doors – would take months to implement. Between now and then, who knows what might happen, Virgil thought. And the President and

Vice President, he believed, needed to allow more information out about the threat so the public could judge just what sort of danger it may be in.

"Why are you insisting we play down the implications here?" Virgil had asked Bush and Cheney earlier that day as they sat across from each other in the Oval Office. "Why are we pretending this isn't a huge threat to domestic security? It's one thing to make sure we don't have panic, but it's another thing to put people in danger. Remember what the hijackers said: 'We have some planes.' Some! That doesn't mean just two. It means more. We have to go through the flight manifests of every plane in the air at that time and do background checks on every passenger with Middle Eastern origins…" His voice had gotten louder and louder as he spoke, his face turning the color of a rare steak, his words coming faster and faster.

Bush opened his mouth to interrupt, but before he could speak, Cheney broke in.

"Virgil," he had said angrily, staring him down. "We're not putting people in danger. You know we're taking the appropriate measures. Heck, you were the one who argued to hit Bin Laden, and now we're doing it, aren't we? We've done the due diligence, and we haven't found any sign of an immediate threat to the country. What's the sense of crying wolf? I agree – let's check the flight manifests. You're doing that, right? It's worth knowing, but I can assure you that anyone who was on a flight Tuesday morning has landed by now. And no other planes were hijacked. Besides," he added, as if to himself, "hijacking two planes at the same time was one hell of an operation. Who'd think of trying to do more than that?"

There'd been a moment of silence while Bush and Cheney stared at him, waiting for a reaction.

"Have it your way," Virgil had finally said, resignedly. "I'm putting together a memo with my recommendations and you'll have it on your desks over the weekend. Once it's done, I'll shut up. Take it for what it is." He'd gotten up and left.

Now he had to decide whether to make the memo to Bush and Cheney public. Doing so went against everything he had stood for over the years – being a team player, keeping the confidence of others and staying behind the scenes. His mind was torn, and he realized he'd have to talk to Harry to work things out. The problem was, he knew what Harry would tell him.

As he thought through all this, he walked west down Bancroft Place, a one block, narrow street lined on both sides with four- and five-story brick 19th-century town homes. The street was narrow enough that it felt like walking along a hallway, with the town homes serving as walls. It was a comfortable feeling.

Halfway up the sloping street, Virgil turned right and up the short walkway to the town home he and his wife shared, a five-story affair where they'd raised the kids. Now it seemed rather large for just the two of them, but Linda still used the first floor as her law office, and didn't want to give that up. She was the one who'd lobbied him to buy the place back in the late 1970s for a veritable song when the kids were toddlers, and it had proved a great investment. Now, five flights of stairs and two entire floors that Virgil and Linda didn't really need seemed a bit much. But Virgil was happy they still had all five stories. The tiny outdoor porch at the front of the attic gave a wonderful view of the city, including the Washington Monument.

The interior door to Linda's office was open and the lights were off. He remembered now; she had a dinner meeting and wouldn't be home until later. The house was silent. Sometimes he missed the noise and chaos of having the kids around, even though it had driven him nuts back when they were little. He thought about the boys for a minute. Keith was in business school in Chicago and Kevin was a senior at Amherst. Neither had been home for the summer except for an odd week here and there.

He climbed up the back stairs used by servants in days gone by to what used to be a maid's bedroom. The small, oddly-shaped room was now Virgil's home office, and was crammed with bookshelves bursting with volumes. A small couch sat in one corner, and Virgil, seeing it, felt exhaustion wash over him. He hadn't had a normal night's sleep since the plane collision, and now, seeing the couch, he couldn't resist reclining on it. "Just for a few minutes," he thought, gathering the white Afghan blanket over himself and curling up among the throw pillows. In minutes, he was deeply asleep.

Fire. He saw fire. A huge explosion billowing out of a skyscraper. Black smoke rising toward the sky. Pieces of metal falling to the ground and flames leaping out of windows.

Virgil jerked himself awake, sweating. He looked at the digital clock on the table. Only an hour had passed. Even in his sleep he couldn't escape. He sat up, rubbing his eyes. Just a dream, but it had seemed so true. And the burning building had looked like one he knew. Which one? He thought back and tried to remember every detail of the dream. His memory wasn't perfect, but he was pretty certain the building he'd seen burning had been the Empire State Building.

He reached for the phone and dialed the familiar number. Twenty minutes later, the doorbell rang and he came downstairs to let Harry in.

"If you don't do it, you're hurting the country," Harry said firmly. The two men were sitting at the kitchen table over glasses of bourbon. The sunlight was fading outside. "Think about it. I can pitch a fit on CNN till I'm blue in the face, and it doesn't mean a thing. I'm just some talking head who used to be in the Defense Department. But you're an insider. You've got access to stuff you're not even telling me about – I know how that goes. Stop thinking so damn much – that's always been your problem. Stop thinking and do something!" He stopped and took a sip of bourbon.

Virgil got up and turned on the overhead light. He re-filled his glass. "You want some more?" he asked Harry, but Harry waved him off.

"Don't try to duck the issue, Virge," Harry said. "You need to make up your mind. You knew what I'd tell you when you called me over here. So why did you bother calling me in the first place? Did you think I'd changed my mind?"

"OK, OK," Virgil replied. "I did know what you'd say. You'd tell me I think too much."

"Damn right," Harry said animatedly.

"It's not as easy as you think, Harry. I hate leakers. I've seen them in every administration I've worked for. Instead of trying to resolve things, they throw up everything they know all over the Washington Post or the New York Times. Then they write books about how they were right and the President was wrong, and then they go out and make speeches for $25,000 a throw. And now I'm supposed to be one of those bastards? That's just not me."

"Get off your high horse, now, Virge," Harry said. "Stop making this about you being a team player. Because the team isn't those guys in the Oval Office. The team you're on is the United States team. If that analogy doesn't work, think about football. If you're on a team and the coach is calling the wrong play, and you lose, and then he calls it again, don't you have to speak up?"

Virgil put his chin on his hand and looked down at the wooden kitchen table. It seemed easy for Harry to talk about taking action, but he was out of the loop and didn't have to go back and face angry bosses the next day. Of course, he thought, if Harry were in his position, maybe he'd do just that. Harry was the type of person who did what he thought was right, and lived with the consequences.

"Harry, I don't even know what I think anymore," he said with a deep sigh. "Cheney's been around as long as I've been, and no one's more paranoid than that guy. If he's not sweating this, why am I? And he's right you know. If I released that memo, it would cause panic." But even as he said this, the images of his dream reappeared in his mind – the black smoke rising from the Empire State building.

"Maybe panic is what this country needs," Harry said, leaning over the table toward him. "I don't mean run out in the streets tearing your clothes off kind of panic. I mean people need to stop feeling so damn comfortable. I know the country's pretty worked up right now. We have 150 Americans just killed by terrorists. Like Oklahoma City in 1995. But the anger doesn't last. I mean, who talks about Timothy McVeigh these days, now that he's executed? Pretty soon the newspapers will be full of shark stories again, and articles about that damn congressman and his dead girlfriend. People have a short attention span around here, Virge, and I mean in the White House and Capitol, too, not just in the streets. We're living in a very, very dangerous time. If you think there's imminent danger and you don't say anything about it, you're being the opposite of a team player."

"There's no 'I' in team, right?" Virgil said, with a wry smile.

"Fuckin A, Virge."

CHAPTER 5

NANCY AT HOME

C NN blared in Nancy's small but neat apartment as she cooked dinner for herself and her 12-year-old daughter, Joanna. The kitchen was part of the living and dining room, and a small window over the sink provided a less-than-lovely view into the brick walls of the building next door.

"Today, Osama bin Laden released what he called a 'Message to the World' in which he explicitly threatened Saudi Arabia with an attack," the CNN anchor read. "Bin Laden didn't claim responsibility for the airline hijacking and collision in New York last week, but he did give credit to the hijackers, or 'holy warriors,' as he described them, for striking against the United States, which the terrorist leader called a 'despicable evil empire.' "

"In his message, Bin Laden blasted the government of Saudi Arabia and other Arab governments in the region, saying, quote, 'The removal of these governments is an obligation upon us...and a necessary step to make the Shariah the supreme law and regain Palestine.' He said Saudi Arabia is ruled by infidels who helped the United States humiliate Palestinians, and that the regime has committed crimes against Islam that, quote, 'nullify its validity before God...' "

Nancy shook her head and quit listening as she reached for a spatula. She had become used to cooking for just two. Her divorce had finalized six months earlier, and her ex-husband now lived in New Jersey. It was close enough that Joanna could spend some weekends with her dad, but this wasn't one of them, for which Nancy was thankful. After the terror

THE TOWERS STILL STAND

attack last week, she felt better having Joanna close to her. She clicked off the little TV on the kitchen counter, not wanting Joanna to hear more about this stuff than she already had.

As she juggled between chicken breasts browning on the stove and arguing with Joanna about whether she and her friends should be allowed to walk around on 18th Street the next day with no adult supervision, ("Come on, Mom, Amy's mom is letting her"), Nancy was thinking back on her frustrating week at work. She felt as if she were running in place, not really getting anywhere with the story-behind-the-story on the attacks. She'd been cooking and cleaning to try to drive all that from her mind, but the damn CNN broadcast reminded her. Why did I have that channel on in the first place, she wondered.

Not that her competitors on the White House beat were doing much better, she thought as she flipped over a chicken breast and turned down the heat to keep the oil from splattering further. The whole White House press corps was frustrated with the secrecy and lack of access they'd seen from the administration since Bush took office. She wondered again whether it was time to ask for a change in beats. With Joanna, it would be impossible to take an international beat, as she'd long wished to, but she could see them moving to New York if something good became available at the home office.

Joanna had said something and she hadn't heard.

"What, honey?" Nancy replied, trying not to sound annoyed but not succeeding. Joanna was getting under her skin with her constant begging about tomorrow.

"I said if you let me go, I promise I won't spend more than $20," Joanna said. She was still quite small for her age, with red hair and freckles that reminded Nancy of her ex-husband. "Just my allowance, and the money grandpa gave me. We just want to have lunch and look at some stores, not buy stuff."

"Joanna, for the last time, the answer is no!" Nancy said in a voice that was louder than she had meant. "Do you think if you keep asking I'll change my mind? It's not going to work!" She immediately felt dreadful, and Joanna started crying, ran to her room and slammed the door.

Nancy stood there in the kitchen, clothes spattered by oil, the comforting smell of garlic, olive oil and chicken hovering in the air, and not for the first time wondered if it was time to consider a career change. The damn job kept getting in the way of her relationship with her daughter, just as it had with her husband for so many years. She sighed, put down her oven gloves and walked slowly through the green-painted living room toward Joanna's room to comfort her and apologize for yelling. But dammit, she wasn't changing her mind about tomorrow, and that was final. Give an inch and they'll take a mile, as one of her friends always said about children.

Later on, with the dishes cleared and Nancy and Joanna sitting under a poster of a cat on their old couch watching a movie on TV (it was *Shawshank* again – Joanna had probably seen it a dozen times but never tired of it, and Nancy had made sure it was the TV version without the graphic scenes), Nancy leafed through her notebook of sources. She wasn't actively working; just trying to decide if there was someone she hadn't tried yet. Her eyes fixed on the name and number of Virgil Walker again. She looked at it for a minute, and then shrugged her shoulders. "What do I have to lose?" she asked herself aloud.

"What, Mom?" Joanna asked. She'd turned away from the screen, where Tim Robbins was hunched in the prison yard with Morgan Freeman.

"Nothing, honey, just work stuff," Nancy replied.

"You're always thinking about work, Mom," Joanna said, rolling her eyes. "Can't you just watch a movie and not be distracted?"

"You're right, sweetie. I'll put this stuff away," Nancy replied, putting down her notebook and relaxing her feet on the ottoman.

But later, after Joanna was in bed, Nancy sat at her Pottery Barn desk in the small combination living/dining room and dialed the number. It rang about seven times, and Nancy was about to give up (who would be at work at 11 p.m. on a Saturday, anyway, she thought), when a male voice answered.

"Virgil here," the voice said, sounding exhausted. "Is that you, Linda? I promise I'll come home in half an hour."

"I'm so sorry, Mr. Walker, this is Nancy Hanson from the New York Times. I just meant to leave you a message. I never thought you'd be there at this hour," Nancy exclaimed, feeling embarrassed. Her heart beat faster.

Virgil said nothing for a moment, mentally admonishing himself for not checking caller ID. The name of the woman on the phone was familiar, for some reason. He wondered if she had been the Times reporter who approached him after the president's press conference on terror issues last month. She'd looked nice enough, but the press was the press, and talking to the press never ended up working out, as he knew from past missteps. He tried to remember if he'd seen her byline in the paper, but he hadn't had much time to read lately.

The silence grew uncomfortable.

"Mr. Walker," Nancy said. "Are you still there?"

"Yes, yes, I'm here. But it's very late, Ms... Hanson, was it?"

"Yes. Nancy Hanson, from the New York Times. You can call me Nancy."

"And what did you plan to leave me a message about, Ms. Hanson?" Virgil asked. He crumpled up a piece of scrap paper and tossed it in the wastebasket under his desk.

"Well," Nancy spluttered. "I'm working on a story about the plane collision, and I'm trying to get some insight on what these terrorists may have had in mind. No one's really answering my questions – like at the press conference the other day – so I've been trying some people I know, and I happened to have your number."

"How did you get the direct line to my office?" Virgil asked. "You must be a hell of a reporter."

"Oh, we have our little secrets," Nancy said, feeling a bit less nervous.

"Look, Ms. Hanson, you sound really nice, but I'm afraid I can't help you. I have no clearance to talk to the media. And even if I wanted to talk to you, there's nothing I could really tell you to answer your questions."

"Do you ever do off-the-record interviews?" Nancy asked. "I'd promise never to identify you as a source if you talked to me on background. I'm just trying to get an angle on this thing. I feel like there's a lot that we aren't being told."

Virgil smiled.

"I've had some media training in a past life, Ms. Hanson, and I learned never, ever to go on background with a reporter. Frankly, I'm uncomfortable just having this little conversation. If my bosses found out I talked to you, I could lose my job."

"I'm sorry," Nancy said. "I'll leave you alone. Can I just leave you my number in case you change your mind?"

"I won't, but you can," he replied.

After she gave him her cell number and he got off the phone, Virgil stood up and limped over to the cabinet, where he poured himself another drink. The bourbon bottle was pretty light. He'd given it a workout this week, but, as usual, the alcohol didn't do much to relax him. He took a few sips, set the glass down on his desk, and sat back down. He wheeled his chair back and forth, looking again at his memo to Cheney and Bush, still on his screen and in about its 10th revision. Damn, he thought. What the hell am I doing here at 11 p.m. on Saturday? He was starting to get grief from Linda about his hours, which was rich, considering her 70-hour weeks in corporate law.

He looked at the number that he'd hastily scrawled on a napkin as he'd spoken to Nancy. And he thought about Harry's words. "Which team am I on?" he asked himself. Without giving it further thought, he picked up the phone and dialed the number on the napkin.

"Nancy Hanson, this is Virgil Walker," he said when she answered.

"Did you change your mind?" Nancy asked, sounding pleasantly surprised.

"I guess you could say that," Virgil said, leaning back in his chair. "Where do you live?"

"I'm on Ontario Road in Adams Morgan," she replied.

"Meet me on the corner of 18th and Kalorama tomorrow at 11," Virgil said. "You know the post office there? I'll be right in front. I'm about 5 feet 7 with grayish-black hair, and I'll be carrying an old brown brief case that looks pretty beat up. That time OK?"

"Sounds good," Nancy replied, trying not to sound too excited. "I'm about 5 feet 3 and I have kind of curly brown hair. I'll be wearing a tan jacket."

"Good. At least I'm taller than someone around here," he said with a laugh. "See you then."

"Thanks," Nancy said, and put down the phone. She sat on the couch in her dark living room, wondering what he would tell her. Her face broke into a grin as she felt the old excitement, and realized this is exactly why she'd gone into journalism in the first place.

CHAPTER 6
JARRAH TAKES CARE OF BUSINESS

Zacarias Moussaoui, who was arrested Aug. 16 on immigration charges after arousing suspicion when he attended a flight school to learn how to fly a 747, had been a pain in the ass ever since arriving in jail, his guards agreed. Moussaoui, a bald man with a distinct goatee, had a bunch of habits that didn't endear him to the corrections workers. He threw his food out into the hallway, banged on his metal bed with a spoon and yelled vulgar language when told to shut up. The other day, two FBI agents came to the jail to question him, but the agents hadn't really gotten anywhere in their interrogation. The agents left after a couple hours, telling the corrections staff that eventually he would be removed from this facility to one in which more sophisticated methods could be used.

Moussaoui, already an irritant to other prisoners, didn't make himself any more popular on Sept. 11. When the plane collision occurred, televisions throughout the facility were tuned to CNN and other news networks. Non-stop coverage ensued, and all the prisoners watched intently.

"Allahu akbar!" Moussaoui yelled over and over as the news of the hijacking unfolded. "Allah is the greatest! Hurray for the mujahideen! Allahu akbar!"

"Shut the hell up, you son of a bitch!" an African-American prisoner in a nearby cell yelled back. "I'll allahu akbar your fuckin' head!"

"Yeah, shut up, you fuckin' Arab bastard!" another inmate yelled. "Just go fuck yourself!"

Moussaoui just yelled louder, and started banging a spoon against his metal bunk. "Allahu akbar! Allahu akbar!"

The rest of the prisoners in the cell block tried to drown him out, yelling, "Shut the fuck up, shut the fuck up!" every time he called out "Allahu akbar!"

Between the yelling of the prisoners and the clanking of the spoon, the guard on duty in the cell block, Christopher Rivera, ran out of patience.

"That's enough out of all of you, goddamnit!" he barked, marching down the cell block, trying hard to project his voice loud enough to cover up the noise from the prisoners. "Shut the fuck up! We're turning off the fuckin' TVs. Every damn one of them!"

"Aw, come on, Rivera," a middle-aged, overweight white prisoner with a huge, jagged scar over his right eye called from one of the cells. "Don't let that raghead ruin things for everyone else."

"Too fuckin' bad," Rivera said. He went back toward his desk to get the remote control that turned off the TVs.

Moussaoui gave Rivera a dirty look as the guard walked by the French Muslim's cell. "You're next," Moussaoui said in his French-accented English. "We will win. America will be the loser."

"You're the only loser around this shitty place," Rivera replied in a gruff voice. "Shut the fuck up with that fuckin' 'Alluha Akbar' crap. You're driving everyone nuts, including me. You think I won't come in there and work you over? Just watch. You'll find out if you keep up that raghead shit." He knew his words were empty; "working over" prisoners didn't happen in Minnesota in 2001.

"America is the loser," Moussaoui repeated. "The loser." Rivera looked at him disparagingly and moved on.

On the morning of September 16, Moussaoui received his first visitor since arriving. The visitor, an intense-looking Middle Eastern man with a heavy beard wearing thick-framed glasses who had identified himself as Moussaoui's brother when applying the previous week to visit him, met Moussaoui in the visiting room and they shook hands and hugged as guards watched them closely. The conversation was in Arabic, and Moussaoui stayed uncharacteristically quiet, nodding a lot but letting the other man do the talking. None of the nearby guards spoke Arabic, so none of them understood what was said. But they did notice that Moussaoui was pale and silent when they escorted him back to his cell and his visitor walked casually out of the room and back into the free world. Rivera was the guard on duty. He carefully shut Moussaoui's door and moved along to the next cell. More prisoners needed escorting to the visitor's room, and there was no time to worry about Moussaoui's strangely quiet behavior. Rivera was just grateful for the peace.

That evening, the doors in Moussaoui's cell block opened automatically at the sound of a buzzer, and the prisoners filed out as usual to walk to the dining hall. All but one of them. Rivera noticed a gap in the line of men where Moussaoui normally would be. Rivera walked into Moussaoui's cell, the overhead light beaming down on the guard's shaven head.

"Wake up, Zachy," he called out in his rough voice, using the nickname for Moussaoui that usually so annoyed the prisoner. "Come on!"

He nudged the prone form of Moussaoui, who was sprawled on his bed. "Come on!" Rivera repeated, now speaking more loudly. "You're holding everyone up!"

"Everything OK in there?" asked the guard standing in the hallway watching the other prisoners.

"He ain't moving," Rivera yelled. "Call the medic!"

Rivera turned Moussaoui over and saw the man's face for the first time. The mouth was open, the tongue white and the eyes sunken in their sockets. Rivera held his hand in front of the mouth and nose and felt no sign of breath. "Oh, shit," Rivera said.

Later that day, Ziad Jarrah, the man who was to have been lead hijacker of Flight 93, sped down an empty Minnesota highway, his mission of the day complete. He'd followed the Director's orders and taken care of Moussaoui, the inconvenient bastard who'd gotten himself arrested through his idiocy. Oh, Moussaoui hadn't been all that happy to hear what Jarrah had to say, but to his credit, he understood why the action was necessary, and was ready to take his life for the cause. Jarrah had held the small packet of cyanide in his hand and slipped it into Moussaoui's as they shook hands upon greeting. He'd explained how just a few grains on the tongue would serve their needs, and a pale and unnaturally quiet Moussaoui grasped the packet in his trembling hand as they spoke together. He hadn't protested much. Jarrah had no doubt Moussaoui would go through with the deed, but he'd check later with contacts to make absolutely certain the operation was a success.

Upon leaving jail, Jarrah discreetly removed the fake beard and glasses and tossed both into a dumpster about 10 miles away. Then he pulled his rental car into the parking lot of an office complex a few miles further along and abandoned it. He'd walked from there to a local Hertz office, and was now driving a different rental car. His papers, including a driver's license with a false name and address and a State Farm insurance card, all checked out just fine with the car rental place, as he knew they would. After all, he'd created the documents.

Creating false papers was no big deal for Jarrah, who also could fly airplanes, doctor passports, pass lie detector tests, procure cyanide and conduct minor surgery in a pinch. He also was fluent in English, Arabic, French and German, and was a trained engineer. Additionally, he always seemed to know where to find the best beer and beaches in any locale, which made him a hit with those friends of his who weren't Islamic extremists. His many talents, he knew, made him an invaluable asset to Al-Qaeda, and that's why the Director put so much trust in him, even though his religious bona fides (and, to be perfectly honest, his religious convictions) weren't in the same league as many of the other terrorists in the group.

Moussaoui had high aspirations, Jarrah reflected as he drove south through the thinning urban sprawl and then the endless green corn and soybean fields south of Minneapolis, but his maturity was suspect, and he'd never been seriously considered for the Sept. 11 mission. Moussaoui's decision to train in a 747 simulator was his own, and by the time he was arrested, the Director had already decided to get him out of the way. The arrest had been very unfortunate, but luckily the American authorities were too stupid to put two and two together and connect Moussaoui with the other brothers who'd taken flight training in the United States. But they'd eventually make the connection, and now, even though the Sept. 11 mission had been only a partial success, Moussaoui was a loose lip that had to be zipped. Besides, he was a Frenchman with Moroccan ancestry, and didn't really fit in well with the other brothers, who were all born and raised in Arab lands.

The Director and the Sheik had their concerns about Jarrah, as well, he knew. Just weeks before Sept. 11, there'd been some question as to whether Jarrah would be part of the mission. The Director didn't think Jarrah's heart was truly in it, and there had been times when the Director had been correct about that. There was a last-minute scramble over the summer to find a replacement for Jarrah if he bowed out. Jarrah's family and Turkish born German girlfriend, with whom he remained close, passionately urged him to return to his homeland and get back on a more secular path. He had told them he needed to see this job through, but would consider their pleas afterwards. They hadn't known his job was being part of a suicide mission and there would be no afterwards for him.

Finally, in late July, Jarrah flew to Germany and met with an important associate of the Director's, who had convinced him to stay in on the plot by repeatedly showing him the news video of the little Palestinian boy crouching helplessly on the ground with his father before perishing in a hail of bullets.

Atta, whose bossiness rubbed Jarrah the wrong way, seemed greatly relieved when he picked Jarrah up at the airport upon his return. From that point on, Jarrah had been a full participant, ready to die on Sept. 11. He had cleansed his mind of his former life, especially of the time he'd spent in Germany years ago living with Alev.

When his hijacking was called off at the last minute, Jarrah felt a strange mixture of relief at having his life back and frustration with the rest of the plotters for messing things up. He knew he was a better pilot than Shehhi, and felt Atta had made a mistake by not making him the pilot of United 175. Instead of crashing his plane into the White House or Capitol (it would be his decision which one), he'd ridden the plane to San Francisco, gathered the other brothers at the terminal, explained to them that their services weren't needed for the moment and gave them money to buy tickets back to their home countries and await further instruction. This was all as the Director had wished.

That much made sense. The longer the "muscle" hijackers remained in the United States, the greater the possibility one of them would be arrested, like Moussaoui, and reveal details that were better left secret, like who had hired them. They wouldn't, however, have been able to give details of the plot itself. Though the muscle men were aware they were on a suicide mission, they hadn't been aware that it involved crashing planes into buildings. And luckily, from what Jarrah could tell by carefully watching post-Sept. 11 newscasts and reading newspapers, few in the U.S. had any inkling that buildings had been in danger. So in a sense, they still had the advantage of surprise, and could lie low for a while until the worst danger passed.

But part of him was angry at the Director for calling things off when they still could have accomplished at least part of the mission. The Director had always been obsessed with the Twin Towers, and probably hadn't seen the point in continuing once the World Trade Center could no longer be hit. He'd never cared much for hitting Washington, saying that the Jews who ran America did so from New York, not the capital city. Even the White House and Capitol were after-thoughts for him.

Jarrah pulled off the highway outside Owatonna for a late lunch at McDonald's and steered into the drive-through. He ordered a Big Mac, fries, a chocolate shake and a box of McDonald's cookies decorated with pictures of Ronald McDonald, paid the attendant, thanked her politely in his near-perfect American accent and drove back onto the highway, where he put cruise control at the legal limit of 65. It would never do to be pulled over for speeding so soon after the mission to take care of Moussaoui. He left the food in a bag on the passenger seat to eat later as he drove, and the smell of greasy meat and potatoes quickly filled the car. He let his mind wander a bit, reflecting again on the unbelievable fact that he was still alive. He never thought he'd live beyond September 11, and all the conversations with his family started coming back to him again. He'd promised them and his girlfriend that he'd get back in touch, but those words were empty when he said them. Now he wondered if he should follow through.

A couple hours went by as the car hummed along steadily. The big southern Minnesota sky was flecked with fluffy, late-summer clouds, but it didn't look like rain. The crops in the fields along both sides of the highway looked green and healthy. Jarrah was getting ready to pull his burger out of the bag when his cell phone rang. He grabbed the phone from the passenger seat and checked the number, which was unfamiliar. That didn't matter much. No one on the team kept cell phones or phone numbers for very long. It was too easy to trace.

When answering a call, he always mentally adopted his alter-ego as a Middle Eastern student here in America to study engineering. That was a pretty good guise, considering his former course of study in Hamburg,

Germany, was in aircraft engineering. His nearly perfect accent and his clean-shaven face, along with his stylish European clothes and designer sunglasses, completed the image quite well.

"Hello, this is Ziad Jarrah," he said politely and earnestly.

"Jarrah, where are you?" said the familiar, grating voice of the Director, speaking in Arabic. He never identified himself when he called, but Jarrah was used to this.

"Hello, sir," Jarrah said, changing to Arabic. The Director's English was pretty bad, and, being the Director, he didn't try too hard to get better. He left that stuff to the underlings. "Nice to hear from you. I'm in Minnesota, and I'm going to head east tomorrow, per your instructions. How's the weather there?" He thought the Director sounded closer than the last time they had talked.

"Did you take care of things at today's meeting, as we discussed?" the Director asked gruffly, not bothering to answer Jarrah's meteorological query.

"Oh yes, things went very well," Jarrah replied, his eyes on the road ahead but in his mind imagining the fat face of the Director and his uneasy eyes. "Our comrade understood everything perfectly, and I expect him to follow through with the plan."

"Good, good," the Director said. "Look, I expect to see you in a few days. I'll call you when I'm near and then we can talk in person."

Jarrah tried to hide his surprise. He hadn't planned on seeing the Director face to face anytime soon. And certainly not in America.

CHAPTER 7

VIRGIL TAKES CARE OF BUSINESS

At 11 a.m. on September 16, Virgil approached the Kalorama Station post office. It was a sunny, warm morning, and the sidewalk cafes were full of brunch-goers enjoying their coffee and pancakes. A little boy ran up the sidewalk toward Virgil, obviously not looking where he was going, and bumped into him.

"Ethan!" the boy's mother yelled from up the street. She ran quickly toward Virgil and grabbed the little boy, who looked about five and was wearing shorts and a Ninja Turtles t-shirt. "I'm so sorry, sir," she said to Virgil. "You know…kids…"

"Been there, done that," Virgil said with a smile. "Enjoy them while they're still young."

"What do you say, Ethan?" the mother cajoled her son.

"Sorry," the boy said, not looking too chagrined. He stuck out his tongue at Virgil.

"Ethan!" the mother yelled.

"No problem," Virgil said, smiling at the child.

The incident with the boy took some of the heaviness out of Virgil's step, and he stayed where he was for a moment and breathed deeply of the warm late-summer air, redolent of coffee from the outdoor cafes and flowers growing in the window pots of the turreted 19th-century town homes. The sun shone brightly, and he looked up at the sky as if he'd noticed it for the first time in a while. A smile touched his lips and quickly disappeared. Then he walked purposefully toward the post office.

As he expected, a brown-haired, short woman was standing at the entrance, wearing a stylish tan leather jacket and a hesitant smile, as if she wasn't sure he was the person she was waiting for. She looked somewhat familiar, but he couldn't immediately place whether he'd seen her before. He approached her. "Ms. Hanson?" he asked.

"Yes," she said. "Mr. Walker?"

"Yep. Nice to meet you," he said, offering his hand.

"You, too," she said, taking it.

They stood there awkwardly for a moment as pedestrians walked by, and then he withdrew his hand from hers.

"Let's say we start walking," Virgil said quickly. "I know a good Thai restaurant down the street that's nice and quiet. We can talk when we get there."

"OK," Nancy said. They began walking, not speaking as they went, and minutes later were inside the Thai place being escorted to a corner table in a secluded nook of the restaurant. "The tofu soup is really good here," Virgil told Nancy as they sat down. A young Asian waitress took their orders and left them alone. The small room was crowded with young families, local by the looks of them, eating their meals and talking happily.

Virgil lifted his battered leather briefcase onto the table and unbuckled it. Only one of the two buckles still worked. He fished out a couple pages of crumpled paper and laid them on the table in front of Nancy.

"Go ahead, read it," he said, hands out on the table. He leaned back and sat quietly while she picked up the pages.

She spent a couple of minutes reading carefully, then looked up at him expectantly.

"You can keep it," Virgil said. "Do what you want with it."

"Can I say you gave it to me?" she asked.

"Whatever," Virgil replied. "Either way, it's the end of my career in this administration once it's out. They'll know it was me, whether you say it right out or not. I'd almost rather have you write that I gave it to you. At least that way it doesn't look like I'm sneaking around."

She nodded. "You realize this is going to cause a big hubub, right?" she said.

"That's the point, isn't it?" he replied, smiling.

Their soup arrived, and the waitress placed a bowl in front of each of them. Tofu for Virgil and Tom Kha Kai for Nancy. The smell of coconut and cilantro drifted tantalizingly up from the table.

Virgil took a spoonful of the hot soup, bit into a piece of tofu, and chewed slowly. Nancy was looking at him, waiting for more.

"What made you decide to release it?" she asked, still waiting for her soup to cool.

Virgil thought for a bit. He was uncharacteristically reflective today, he thought. At work, he usually spoke quickly, and often didn't wait for others to finish what they were saying before jumping in. But today, he felt different. Maybe it was because he'd made his decision and was at peace with it. There were no longer any dragons to slay, at least not any he could see right in front of him.

"Are we on the record or off?" he asked, looking her in the eyes.

"Off," she said. "You can trust me on that."

"Good. I do. No hidden tape recorder, right?" She nodded.

He coughed – the soup was rather spicy. After wiping his mouth with a napkin, he said, "I've been thinking of doing this for a while. The hijackings last week put me over the edge."

"You feel people weren't listening to you?"

"Right. I've served this country for nearly three decades, Ms. Hanson. I love it dearly. And I'm sitting here…sitting here watching it be threatened by some really dangerous people. I've been telling my bosses that for months and months, and they don't take me seriously. Then we had the hijackings last week, and they're trying to blame Iraq, which had nothing to do with it. Nothing. And they're not being straight up with the country about the threat we face. If they won't be, I will. It's going to cost me my job, of course."

"What do you think is driving them?" she asked, leaning forward. "I've been covering this administration for eight months now and they don't tell us anything."

"Oh, all administrations are like that," he replied, a slight smile on his face.

"Well, to some extent, I guess. The Clinton people certainly buttoned up a lot after that impeachment thing, but usually with a new administration you start out with some decent rapport. Until the going gets tough, anyway."

He took another spoonful of soup.

"You've got to realize," he said quietly after he swallowed. "What's driving them is the same thing that's driving me. They're determined to keep the country safe. Now, they think they can do that best by keeping things secret. I think it's best if the public is educated. It's just a difference of philosophy."

"Aren't you afraid that going public with this would tell the terrorists something they didn't know we knew?"

"No, no," he replied, his voice rising a little and his face reddening slightly. "What I'm giving you isn't anything that shouldn't be known. I was careful not to put anything in there that would give the terrorists a leg up on us. I just think the public has a right to know that there might be terrorist cells still in this country planning further attacks. And it may actually help us if the terrorists know we knew about their ideas to smash planes into buildings. Maybe it would make them think before trying it again."

"You really think they had buildings in mind? I mean, crashing planes into buildings? That's pretty out there."

"I'm not 100 percent sure, but I've spent a lot of time focused on this organization, and it is something they've talked about in the abstract. I've never seen any fully-formed plans, but it just haunts me so much that both those planes turned south – toward New York. If they hadn't collided…I don't know what might have happened." He thought about his dream and shuddered.

"You aren't doing this for any partisan reason, are you?" she asked. When he responded with a bitter laugh, she added, "I mean, you did serve under Clinton."

"Look," he replied. "I'm a lifelong Republican. That's pretty funny – that I'd be doing this for partisan reasons. Even Bush and Cheney might get a laugh out of that one. Of course, after today, I won't have to worry what they think."

"I feel bad that you're going to lose your job over this," she said, biting her lip and leaning back a little in her seat. "Are you OK with that?"

He thought for a bit while she spooned soup into her mouth.

"It's like I can't quite believe it's happening," he finally said. "I've always played it by the book, always been a team player, and now I'm turning into Benedict Arnold. I don't quite know how I feel."

"I'm sure you feel relieved that you're doing the right thing." She had finally gotten around to tasting her soup. Ugh – too much cilantro, she thought.

"Tell you the truth, I thought for a long time that the right thing was to stay in my job and keep pushing people to take my advice," he replied. "Seems like that didn't work out too well. Ah, well. There's no going back now. You've got the note, and my goose is cooked." He smiled.

"I can still give it back," she said earnestly. She reached for the note.

"No, no. No turning back now. I'll never get the courage to do it again. Now or never, I guess. I had a lot of drinks last night when I made the decision. You know, the older I get, the more I'm convinced I make better decisions after a glass of bourbon. What about you?"

"Oh, I'm not a big drinker," Nancy said as the waitress returned with their entrees and laid them down.

"Now that I've gotten this monkey off my back, I feel pretty hungry," Virgil said, taking a bite of his pad thai. "Wow," he said. "No one makes it better than this place. You been here before?"

"Oh yeah, my daughter and I come here. She loves Thai food."

"Funny," Virgil said. "When we were kids, who'd ever heard of a Thai restaurant? I don't think I had Thai food till I was 25. How old's your kid?"

"She's 12," Nancy said. "She's been sassy lately." She smiled. It was easier to talk about her daughter than to deal with her brattiness.

"Oh, I know sassy," Virgil said with a laugh. "It all goes by so fast. Just wait. One day you'll look up and she'll be off to college."

They ate silently for a few minutes.

"Do you have kids?" Nancy asked, looking up from her bowl.

"Yes – two boys. Both grown up. Sometimes their entire childhood seems like it lasted all of one minute. Speaking of which..." He looked at his watch. "I suppose you have to go file your story soon, right?"

"Oh, I will," Nancy said. "But I didn't think it would be polite to inter-rupt our lunch."

"No, go ahead," he said, waving his hand casually. "I'll pick up the bill. Might as well while I'm still taking a salary."

"Will losing your job be a financial burden for you?" she asked, a look of concern crossing her face.

"No, no – don't worry about me, Ms. Hanson. I'll be fine. My wife makes too much money already, and the government doesn't pay much, you know. Go on – get out of here and write your story."

She got up.

"Thanks, Mr. Walker. For everything."

"Don't mention it," he said.

She started to walk away and he called out, "Ms. Hanson?"

She turned around and looked at him.

"Yes?"

"Please treat me gently in the article."

"I will," she said, and stepped quickly toward the door.

Virgil sat at the table for a while, no longer feeling very hungry. He picked at his noodles and took a sip of water.

The waitress came by. "Is everything OK?" she asked.

"Yes, yes, everything's fine. Please bring me the bill when you have a chance."

Virgil sat there, his stomach jumpy. As far as his career was concerned, he'd just signed his own death warrant.

Later that afternoon, Virgil puttered around the house. Linda had taken a cab to the airport for a business trip out of town, and the huge home felt more silent and empty than ever. Maybe I should get a cat, Virgil thought. At least it would be someone to talk to now and then. Back when the boys were little, they'd had dogs, but he felt no need to get another. Too much work.

He realized he was purposefully ignoring his computer, not wanting to check emails or the New York Times' web site, fearing what sort of demon he'd unleashed by handing over that memo to the reporter. It was an unusual feeling for him, like floating. He couldn't ignore the growing pit in his stomach.

The phone rang. It was Harry.

"You did it, Virge! Nice job," Harry said when Virgil picked up. "I can't believe it. I never thought you'd carry things through."

"All right, Harry," Virgil said, a cold feeling spreading up from his stomach into his chest. "What does the article say?"

"You haven't read it yet? Damn, Virge, get online and check it out. Call me back when you're done. I want to hear your reaction. Fuckin A – I can't believe it. Have you heard from anyone in the White House yet?"

"No, but now I'm dreading it," Virgil replied, walking with his phone toward his little office at the back of the third floor. "Look, I'll read it and then call you back and let you know if I hear anything from anybody."

"You did the right thing, Virge," Harry said. "I'm proud of you. But I have some advice. Turn off your cell phone and don't answer any emails. The media's going to be gunning for you, and I reckon they can figure out your number if they try hard enough."

As if to prove Harry right, Virgil heard his call-waiting signal.

"Thanks, Harry – I have to go. Bye."

He hung up.

He clicked onto the other line, and it was Cheney.

"Virgil," the familiar icy voice said. "We have to talk."

"Yes, sir," Virgil replied, the uncomfortable feeling growing. "What have I unleashed?" he thought.

"Be at my office at 5:30," Cheney said. "And don't talk to any more reporters." He hung up.

Virgil stood there holding the phone for a moment, heart beating in his ears. He knew this would get him fired, but nevertheless, he felt like a child caught in some disgraceful act by his parents. What an odd sensation. Virgil had gone through his career saying what he thought, not worried about others' sensitivities. And now he was shaking like a leaf. He poured himself a glass of bourbon and took a few sips. Thinking of Harry's advice, he turned off his cell phone. Then he sat down at his cheap and chipped old desk that Linda always nagged him to replace, opened up his laptop, and clicked onto NYTimes.com. Nancy's story was the headline, sprayed across the top of the home page. Virgil leaned forward and read.

From *The New York Times*, Sept. 17, 2001:

"Administration Official Says New York Skyscrapers May Have Been Target of Tuesday's Hijackers; Warns More Attacks are Possible"

By Nancy Hanson

WASHINGTON – A top White House terrorism official has warned President George W. Bush that Tuesday's hijackers may have been targeting buildings and monuments in New York City, and that underground "sleeper cells" of terrorists may remain in the United States planning further attacks.

Virgil Walker, the President's chief advisor on terrorism, said in a memo to the President obtained by The New York Times that Tuesday's attackers were likely on a suicide mission, bent on crashing the planes either into the ground or into buildings. Although all of the terrorists on the planes died in the collision, which killed 150, Mr. Walker believes the United States needs to launch an operation to find any partners of the hijackers who may still be in the country.

"Tuesday's collision of the planes, judging from the evidence we have, appeared to have been accidental," Mr. Walker warned in his memo to Mr. Bush. "Based on the intelligence we've gathered over the last five years, as well as both planes turning toward New York City, I believe the terrorists had major U.S. buildings and monuments in mind as targets. We can't be assured that all the terrorists in this operation died in the collision. There may be others connected with the plot who are still in this country, preparing other attacks."

Mr. Walker added that the administration needs to make finding these terrorists and capturing or killing Al-Qaeda leader Osama bin Laden its top priority. He said he had warned the administration of possible terrorist attacks against the United States prior to last Tuesday, and that Tuesday's attacks vindicated his fears.

"Let's move on Al-Qaeda now," Mr. Walker's memo concluded. "Quickly and immediately. If we fail to take adequate, aggressive and timely measures to wipe out Al-Qaeda as a terrorist operation, our first warning of another attack here could be buildings burning in New York or Washington."

The White House reacted quickly to Mr. Walker's memo, issuing a statement noting that the administration is already targeting foreign terror groups, but warning the public not to panic over Mr. Walker's prognostications.

"President Bush is committed to rooting out and bringing to justice the plotters of Tuesday's tragic hijackings," the White

House's statement said. "A concerted effort is already underway to locate and capture or kill terrorist leader Osama bin Laden, and to learn which countries may be sheltering him or aiding him in his attacks against us. Furthermore, we have taken measures here in the United States to protect citizens from future attacks. At this time, we have no intelligence warning of any further attacks, but we remain vigilant. We urge Americans to continue going about their lives as normal, but to remain on guard and report anything suspicious to the appropriate authorities. There is no reason to worry about flight safety, as the type of attacks we experienced last Tuesday are now impossible to replicate."

The statement added, "Mr. Walker's decision to reveal sensitive intelligence to the public was not constructive, and appropriate measures will be taken to ensure that important intelligence that could protect Americans is kept confidential in the future."

A phone call to the White House inquiring about Mr. Walker's future in the administration wasn't immediately returned Sunday afternoon.

Mr. Walker's memo didn't spell out details of intelligence that led him to predict possible future attacks. Nor did it explain why he believed the hijackers may have been targeting buildings and monuments. If that indeed was the hijackers' plan, it would mark a major new development among terrorist operatives, who previously have used individual suicide bombers to attack planes and buildings, but have never sent suicide bombers into planes with buildings as their targets. Mr. Walker didn't provide evidence of any specific New York targets the hijackers may have been aiming at, but said the collision of the two planes was clearly not part of the hijackers' plan. He didn't explain how the collision had happened, or why he was convinced it was accidental. The government has not released the planes' cockpit voice recorder transcripts, but it is believed the hijackers took the controls of both planes after killing the pilots.

Mr. Walker also made it clear that he believes Bin Laden was behind Tuesday's plot, though he didn't provide evidence pointing to the Al-Qaeda leader. Bin Laden, in a statement last week, denied any connection to the hijackings, but did call the hijackers, 'holy warriors,' for striking against the United States, which the terrorist leader called a "despicable evil empire."

President Bush has not yet explained how he plans to target Bin Laden. In 1998, President Clinton ordered missile strikes against several targets in Sudan and Afghanistan, with the goal of killing Bin Laden, but didn't succeed. Those strikes came after terrorist attacks targeting embassies in Africa that killed hundreds.

Last fall, a suicide mission killed 17 U.S. sailors and injured 39 others aboard the U.S.S. Cole, which at the time was harbored in the Yemeni port of Aden. Until Tuesday, that was the last significant terrorist attack against U.S. interests, and many experts believe Al-Qaeda was behind it, though the organization has never claimed responsibility. There have been no U.S. reprisals in response to the Cole attack, and according to Mr. Walker, the lack of U.S. response to that terrorist mission may have emboldened Al-Qaeda, helping to inspire Tuesday's attack.

"Lack of a strong response to the Cole attack by both the previous and current administrations has Al-Qaeda convinced it can strike the U.S. and our allies without retribution," Mr. Walker wrote. "We cannot afford to let Tuesday's hijackings go unanswered as well, or we open ourselves up to further attacks."

Walker, who has served in administrations of both political parties over the last three decades and is believed to be a Republican, also served as an adviser on terrorism to President Clinton, and remained in his current job after the new administration took over earlier this year. He is known as a "lone wolf," with few friends in Washington, according to one associate, who spoke on condition of anonymity.

"He's dedicated his career to destroying terror organizations, and he's very frustrated with the response to terror of both the current and previous administrations," the associate said Sunday, referring to Mr. Walker. "I think he released this memo to force the administration to take a more aggressive response against Al-Qaeda, and also to alert the American people that they're not out of danger."

Mr. Walker's associate added that Mr. Walker has spent years focused on Al-Qaeda and Bin Laden, and may be the foremost U.S. expert on the group and its intentions.

Mr. Walker, when contacted by The New York Times, declined to add any further comments beyond those he shared in his memo to the President.

Virgil read the article twice, wondering who had called him a "lone wolf." It had to have been Harry. Who else would have known his motivations so well? He'd never thought of himself as a lone wolf, but he supposed he'd become one over the last eight months, hiding out in his basement office so much, only surfacing to deliver dire warnings of Armageddon. He smiled to himself. In Washington, there were plenty of lone wolves. What was the old saying? If you want a friend in Washington, buy a dog. Right. He got up and prepared to head to the White House to get his head bitten off. He turned his cell phone on and it started ringing immediately. There were several messages in his voice mail. He flipped the phone closed and turned it off.

CHAPTER 8

COMING TO AMERICA

The next day, around the time Nancy was writing her article about Virgil's firing, an Air France 767 landed at JFK airport. The passengers, some of whom had been a little jittery traveling overseas to the United States less than a week after the deadly hijackings, filed off, happy to be done with their journey. Deep in the coach section, a slight man in his mid-30s, with a prominent high forehead, thinning hair and a short black beard and mustache took his carry-on bag down from the bin and put the strap over his shoulder. When his turn finally came to exit, he walked behind the other passengers to the front of the aircraft. "Merci and thank you," the young flight attendant said as passengers disembarked. The man didn't reward her with an answer, walking by without a word.

The Director exited the jet-way into customs and looked around. This was his first time in many years back in the United States, where he'd attended college in the 1980s, doing mediocre work and piling up a series of citations for reckless driving. His English was extremely rusty, but his Pakistani passport was a good fake put together by Jarrah some time ago. He lined up among the other foreign passengers and when he reached the front, told the attendant he had nothing to declare. The attendant, who'd been on duty for six hours and needed a break, looked over the Director's identification quickly, saw nothing out of line, stamped his passport and waved him through. The Director left the airport in a taxi and disappeared into the streets of New York City.

Part Two – The Plot Advances: 2006

"Who knows if he's hiding in some cave or not? We haven't heard from him in a long time. The idea of focusing on one person really indicates to me people don't understand the scope of the mission. Terror is bigger than one person. He's just a person who's been marginalized... I don't know where he is. I really just don't spend that much time on him, to be honest with you."
-PRESIDENT GEORGE W. BUSH, ON OSAMA BIN LADEN, 2002

CHAPTER 1

German Connection (Summer 2006)

It was the middle of the night when Alev Asani's cell phone rang. She hoped it was just a dream, but the sound kept piercing her sleep, and she slowly swam back to consciousness, lying alone in bed in her small apartment in downtown Munich.

By the time it had rung seven times she realized whoever it was wasn't going to give up. She looked at her bedside clock. It was 3:47. Outside her window the sky was pitch black. She picked up the phone.

"Hello?" she said sleepily in German.

"Alev?" the familiar voice said.

"Ziad?" Alev said, suddenly wide awake. "Is it you?"

"Yes, it's me." Jarrah said. His voice sounded far away over the international phone line, but it was still the one Alev remembered so well. The two of them had lived together for several months in the late 1990s, but then Jarrah had left for America and almost vanished from her life. In mid-2001, out of nowhere, seemingly, he re-appeared in Germany, and they'd spent a few days going back to their old haunts, sleeping in her apartment at night. He'd been mysterious about his activities in the U.S., and wouldn't answer her questions about what he was doing there.

But she and her parents had strongly believed he was involved in some sort of terrorist activities, and she'd urged him to stay with her. He'd seemed to be considering it, but then left to meet a friend one day and never came back. She'd called him a bunch of times after that, but got no response. This was all so unlike him, compared to the happy times they'd shared as students a year or two earlier. Back then, he'd seemed happy-go-lucky, and always was the one relaxing with a beer, staying out of arguments. He hadn't seemed to give politics much thought, and seldom went to mosque.

When news broke of the Sept. 11 terrorist hijacking and plane collision, she'd frantically scanned the papers and Internet to see if his name was mentioned among those of the hijackers, but he wasn't one of them. In the five years since, she'd given up on hearing from him again, and had several other boyfriends, none of them too serious. She supposed at age 28 it was time to find someone to settle down with, but she was pretty busy with her career in dentistry and just hadn't found the time to commit to another serious relationship.

"Where are you?" Alev said into the phone. She was speaking quietly, and then realized there was no reason to do so. She was alone in the apartment and there was no one to disturb.

"I'm still in America," Jarrah said. "I've been thinking about you a lot the last five years."

"Then why didn't you call me until now?" Alev asked, a tinge of irritation creeping into her tone. "And why did you call me in the middle of the night?"

"I knew you'd be home," Jarrah replied. "Sorry I woke you up. I'm just glad you have the same number. I thought it might be hard to find you."

"No, I have the same one," Alev said. "I never changed it in case you decided to call."

There was silence for a moment. Alev turned on the light, swung her long, light-brown hair behind her shoulders – the light reflected on her almond-colored skin.

"Are you still in Germany?" Jarrah finally asked.

"Yes, Ziad. I graduated from dental school and I'm working in a practice here in Munich. Can you come visit?"

"No, no," Jarrah said, sounding sad. "I'm stuck here. Can you come see me?"

She thought for a minute before replying, her sleepy mind still trying to reconcile so many factors at once.

"I don't know, Ziad. I'm booked up with patients. It's a long trip. And it's expensive. Why did you disappear and not call me for five years?"

"It's complicated," Jarrah said. "I can't talk about it on the phone. Come see me. I'm in Chicago. I'll pay for your ticket."

"Ziad, we have to talk before I get on a plane," Alev replied, propping herself up on her elbow. "I'm still angry at you. You just deserted me. And you were mixed up with something bad, I could tell."

"I can explain things if you come here," he said. "It's not something we can talk about now."

Alev sighed. He was still going to be mysterious; that much was obvious. Her bright blue eyes reflected in the glass, framed by dark eyebrows that furrowed at this sudden turn of events. She looked out the window, where the sky remained dark. Headlights of a lone car passed slowly by on the street below, casting their light into her room for a moment.

"Let me think about it," she said.

Jarrah clicked the phone off and wondered what had made him call her. He hadn't planned to, but for some reason, her face kept popping up in his head, and he'd found himself dialing the old number, almost to test if it still worked. His mind had been focused on planning, logistics, next steps, and his daily prayers. But sometimes it seemed as if he were going through the motions, and that's when he'd think of Alev.

CHAPTER 2

NANCY CONTEMPLATES A CHANGE

66 I still don't see how you can do this," Nancy Hanson's mother was saying, for the umpteenth time, it seemed. Nancy and her mother were sitting in the den of Nancy's parents' home in Tucson, one of about 50 one-story homes in a gated community, each with its own pool. The home was one of those modern, "open" plans, with marble floors and no distinct rooms. Kitchen, living room and dining area all blended into one, making Nancy feel a bit exposed. She preferred the small, distinct rooms of her little apartment back in D.C. She also didn't like how her parents had decorated the place with a Southwestern motif. The walls were covered with cheap-looking paintings of cacti and cowboys. Now that her mom and dad had retired to Arizona, they suddenly fancied Frederick Remington prints. It was mid-September, five years after the events of September 2001, and still kind of early in the fall to be out here. The temperatures hit 100 every day, though it was a dry heat, like being inside of a laundry dryer, Nancy thought.

"Mom, I sometimes wonder too, but you've got to look at it this way – it may be my one chance to really get to the top of my profession," Nancy replied, looking her mother right in the eyes. It was 10 p.m., and Joanna and Nancy's dad were out seeing a movie.

"But honey, you are at the top of your profession," said her mother, who, like Nancy, was a small, dark-haired woman. She'd been a high school English teacher until retiring a few years ago. Her hair was graying prominently, however, while Nancy's only had a few strands of silver even at age 45. Nancy hoped she'd take after her father, who still sported a nice dark head of hair even now as he approached 70, albeit with a growing bald spot in back.

"To some extent, you're right, mom," Nancy replied, trying to sound calm. "Being a White House reporter for the Times is a very prominent position. But I've been doing this for so long, now, and I think I've been typecast. In journalism, if you stay in the same place for too many years, you start to get looked over."

"Well, what's wrong with that?" her mother asked, voice rising and putting her hand out and laying it over Nancy's on the table. "What is wrong with being looked over if you're still writing for the best paper in the country and you get to interview the President? All our friends are so impressed when they see your name on the front page. And besides, it's a safe position and you get to be with your daughter." She gazed unhappily into Nancy's eyes.

It all came down to that, Nancy knew, biting her lip to keep from saying anything she might regret. Ever since this chance of getting assigned to the Middle East arose, it had eaten away at Nancy as well. Joanna was 17, a senior in high school, and Nancy and her daughter had enjoyed such a nice life together. They still lived in the small apartment in Washington, which was cozy with their possessions. Nancy's ex-husband was still in New Jersey, and Joanna relished her weekends with him, which also allowed her to go into New York City with her friends and cousins. Everything seemed about as good as it could be — certainly better than she had thought when the divorce happened.

But she felt like she was treading water in her career. At the Times, it was the rare star reporter who didn't take at least one assignment abroad, at least for a few years, and, at 45, this might be her last chance. The White House beat, which to outsiders seemed romantic and exciting, was actually something of a backwater for reporters at the paper. You basically followed the President around and wrote down what he said, without a great deal of opportunity to really dig into issues. A lot of the time, you felt as though you were just spewing out whatever the administration wanted you to write, like a mouthpiece. She tried hard to avoid falling into that trap, but it was a constant danger. She relished the notion of spending time in the Middle East covering terrorism and the chaotic governments of the region. A few years over there, and she'd likely be able to come home to a higher position at the paper, perhaps even as a columnist. That's how Nick Kristof and Thomas Friedman had gotten their columns, anyway.

It tore her heart out to have to leave Joanne with her father while she was away, and she knew that bothered her parents as well, neither of whom had ever warmed very much to her ex, even before the divorce. Nancy felt Jake was a perfectly capable dad, and could handle things in her absence. And Joanna was an independent girl who could take care of herself well. She and Joanna had spent many evenings this last month at home and out at dinner talking about the possibility, and Joanna seemed to feel pretty comfortable with the idea of living with her father.

What Joanna, and even more so, Nancy's mother, did worry about, was Nancy's safety. And they had good reason to, Nancy supposed. She'd lain awake nights, wrestling with this over and over, and she'd come to the conclusion it was now or never. As hard as it would be to separate from Joanna and only see her a few times a year, she had to do this for herself. She'd sacrificed so much the last 17 years for Joanna.

"Mom, I know exactly how you feel," Nancy said, looking her mother in the eyes. There were tears coming down her mom's cheeks, she was surprised and alarmed to see them. "Please, don't cry." She stood up, walked over to her mother and tried to hug her. Her mother gently pushed her away.

"Honey, it's OK. I'll get over it," her mother said. "I'll try not to worry too much about you over there. But it's going to be hard."

"I promise I'll email every day, Mom. Remember, I'm not a kid any-more. I'm 45. I can take care of myself. And the Times takes security very seriously. I've been learning a lot about it. Actually, it might be hard to do any serious reporting there; I'll be in such a bubble." This wasn't entirely true, Nancy knew, but she hoped it would soothe her Mom.

"How long will it be, again?" her mother asked, dabbing her cheeks with a Kleenex.

"I'd be leaving later this month and spending two years there," Nancy replied. "I'll still get to spend a few weeks here at home every year."

"Fine, fine," her mother said, standing up and beginning to clear the dessert dishes, which were still on the glass table in the dining area. Nancy walked over to help her.

"Just do me a favor," her mother added as she gathered plates still flecked with chocolate cake crumbs. "No visits there by Joanna, OK? That part of the world just isn't safe for kids."

Nancy put down her dish and walked over to her mom, who this time accepted Nancy's embrace.

"Don't worry, Mom," Nancy said, holding her mother closely. "Joanna will stay here with her Dad. I won't let her visit me in the Middle East. I'll be too busy to show her around, anyway."

CHAPTER 3

VIRGIL CATCHES UP

Virgil shut his laptop with a sigh and stared out the window at the parking lot under the gray November clouds. He hadn't been able to get steady work since being fired from the White House five years earlier, though he had contributed some opinion pieces on terrorism to The Wall Street Journal and The New York Times. He was separated from his wife, who'd grown fed up with his late hours and inattention, and instead of living in splendor in a Kalorama, D.C. town home, he was stuck out here in McLean, Virginia, in this crummy one-bedroom apartment in a complex of boxy 1970s buildings. He couldn't exactly blame his wife for leaving; she'd put up with his odd hours for years, and enough was enough. Besides, they'd grown apart since the kids left home. Luckily the separation had been amicable, and she still sent him a check every month covering basic expenses and kept him on her health plan. He'd never worked outside of the government, so his savings were rather meager. By being fired, he'd forfeited his government pension.

For about a year, he'd been taking night courses at the local community college, working to get his teaching degree. He figured if he kept it up, he'd make a decent high school history teacher some day. But at age 54, he wondered how likely it was that he'd be able to find a job once he got qualified. There wasn't much of a market for people his age, he knew. And history teachers weren't exactly a sparse commodity.

The other project he had going was his memoir, which he'd started soon after his dismissal. It was now more than 100,000 words long, but he kept revising and revising it, never satisfied. He knew it would be interesting to some publisher if he could ever finish. After all, he'd spent nearly 30 years in the government – from the time he graduated college right up until that fateful day in 2001 in Cheney's office, where he'd heard the vice president chew him out in the most painful way imaginable. The book spent a lot of time assessing why the government had missed possible terrorist signals prior to the hijackings of 2001, and criticized both the Clinton and Bush administration's responses to terrorist acts such as the African embassy bombings of 1998, the Cole attack of 2000 and the 2001 hijackings.

Even now, the words Cheney used came back into his head clearly. "Treasonous, irresponsible, Al-Qaeda's best friend, self-centered." He'd been given 20 minutes to clear anything personal out of his office – under the eagle eyes of two silent Secret Service men, who were there, he supposed, to make sure he didn't run off with any sensitive documents. His computer and laptop had been confiscated, and he'd been escorted to the White House gate by the same two Secret Service men, carrying a shopping bag full of his meager personal items – framed photos of his wife and kids, the photo of him and Clinton.

Ah, what's the point of ruminating about the past, he thought. That was then and now was now. The public fallout had dissipated pretty quickly after his firing, with editorial pages splitting about 50/50 on whether he'd made the right decision to reveal his memo to the public. His thesis that the terrorists were planning to crash into buildings, which he still believed in strongly, withered on lack of evidence. Nothing in Al-Qaeda's communications prior to the hijackings or in Bin Laden's messages to the public afterward ever referred to such a plan.

And when the administration had bombed several Al-Qaeda training camps and hideouts in Afghanistan several weeks after the plane collision, it had wiped out the group's primary network, even though it hadn't gotten Bin Laden, who was presumed to be hiding somewhere in Afghanistan or Pakistan. The Taliban government, which Bush had also targeted in his bombings after the collision, was weakened but held on to power, as the United States never committed the ground troops that would have been necessary to dislodge it. There was no public appetite in the U.S. for such an action, anyway, and Bush had shifted his focus quickly to Iraq. The public's interest in Bin Laden and Al-Qaeda waned, and it was widely considered that the group had been adequately punished for the hijacking deaths.

Aside from a threatening message every half a year or so from Bin Laden, Al-Qaeda had pretty much filtered out of the newspapers and news shows.

The most recent speeches from Bin Laden, like his first one after the hijackings, focused on Saudi Arabia, other Arab governments and Israel. He also railed against the United States, but the terrorist leader's focus seemed closer to his own home in the Middle East. There'd been a terrible bombing of civilians in Riyadh in 2002, which proved once and for all to the Saudi government that Al-Qaeda saw the House of Saud as a target, and since then, Saudi Arabia had joined the U.S. in calling for Bin Laden's death. But the Riyadh attack, which killed 25 civilians outside a government building, seemed like something of a pinprick, considering how much more damage Al-Qaeda might have done had it targeted oil facilities or the U.S. military bases in the country, so that attack, too, after a while, had faded in most peoples' memories.

What also had faded, and was more disturbing to Virgil, was any sense of mission in trying to uncover the people who had been behind the 2001 hijackings. From his conversations with people in the government who'd still talk to him – including Harry, who had re-joined the Department of Defense in 2003 and had rapidly risen in its ranks lately – it seemed there was a sense among the foreign policy elite that by breaking apart Al-Qaeda's operating systems, killing some key leaders, scattering the group and putting Bin Laden and his top deputies on the run, the problem had been solved. "Americans have a short memory, Virge," Harry had said a few months ago when Virgil brought up his concern in one of their rare conversations. "That thing in 2001 was a long time ago, and we've been at war for three years in Iraq. Lots more on folks' minds now."

But Virgil still obsessed about "that thing," as Virgil called the attacks, because to date, it was only the second foreign terrorist attack on U.S. soil, with the 1993 World Trade Center bombing the other. He couldn't be sanguine about the possibility that some Al-Qaeda mastermind might still be out there planning more attacks.

"The CIA is all over this stuff," Harry had assured him in that same conversation. "You just don't know about it because you're out of the government. They've been combing through all the evidence for years, and they're pretty sure they know who the fellas are that put that attack together."

Harry couldn't tell Virgil the name of the "mastermind," because Virgil had no security clearance. But Virgil's own thorough research, and his continued talks with sources in the Middle East still willing to risk speaking to him after his fall from dignity, zeroed in on a native of Kuwait named Khalid Sheikh Mohammed, known to his associates as "the Director," and referenced in the CIA documents as "KSM." Evidence uncovered from some of the materials found at bombed Al-Qaeda sites made references to this mysterious figure, and there were also messages back and forth between KSM and Atta before the attacks. The CIA had spent a good deal of energy searching Pakistan for KSM, as that was his last known country of residence. But it had come up with nothing.

Virgil hadn't let his lack of a security clearance stop him from attempting to figure out what happened, but he faced a number of challenges. For instance, he'd wanted to go through the manifests of every passenger plane on the tarmac or in the air at the time of the collision. He was haunted by the reference to "some planes," a reference that he purposely hadn't included in his memo to the President because of its national security sensitivity. And the public was unaware of it as well, since the black boxes had been under lock and key since the day they'd been found, with only selected bits and pieces released. Virgil wanted to know who else may have been on planes that day, and if they had connections to Al-Qaeda, but he didn't have access any longer to the databases he needed to dig that information out. He'd talked to Harry about his concerns, and Harry had reassured him that the FBI had done the footwork and had the information it needed. For some reason, that didn't make Virgil feel any better. He was frustrated being on the outside, but saw no hope of getting back in.

On this gray November day, after the Republicans had suffered a thrashing in the mid-term election earlier in the week, there was rumor that Defense Secretary Rumsfeld would be the administration's sacrificial lamb. Virgil didn't exactly feel bad about this, knowing the smug bastard all too well. He'd been disappointed in the mid-term results, but understood the implications – someone would have to take the fall. And with the Iraq war going from bad to worse, it was Rummy's turn.

Today Virgil planned to drive into D.C. for a doctor's appointment. His leg had become worse as he grew older, and his limp more pronounced.

The pain was getting to be a more personal thing, as well, talking to him like a close friend, day after day. He likely needed a hip replacement soon. "What fun, getting old," he said out loud. He put on his coat, limped carefully down the outdoor stairs of his apartment building, got into his old Chevy with a grunt of pain as his leg brushed across the seat, and drove to D.C. The bridge over the Potomac offered a dramatic view of the Lincoln and Jefferson Memorials and the Washington Monument, but Virgil didn't pay much attention. He'd never been a big one for scenery. And on this chilly day, the whole city seemed to lack color and vitality.

The doctor's office was in his old neighborhood, and after he parked and paid the exorbitant meter fee, he limped across DuPont Circle toward the building entrance. A light drizzle fell, and it was about 45 degrees. It was midday, but car headlights beamed through the rain drops. Lacking an umbrella, Virgil limped as fast as he could, eager to get inside.

As he walked, someone called out to him.

"Virgil –is that you?" a man's voice came through the mist. Virgil turned toward the sound and saw a tall, slim man wearing a tan trench coat walking his way. Virgil tried to place the face with the voice, which sounded so familiar. He'd always had trouble remembering faces, and this put him in the uncomfortable position of being recognized often but not being able to recognize who he was talking to. It could be quite awkward at times.

"Hi there," Virgil replied, trying to sound cheerful and enthusiastic at this chance encounter, which wasn't the way he actually felt. "It's been a long time." He still had no idea who he was talking to.

"It sure has," the man said. "I haven't seen you since probably, 1998. Remember that SOB we worked for, that Clarke guy? I'm glad he's gone."

That was the clue Virgil needed. Now he realized who he was talking to. It was Frank Edwards, who had worked with him in the Defense Department many years ago.

"Yeah, Frank, I remember that, too," Virgil said. "It wasn't all bad. We had some decent times."

"Well, if we did, I sure don't remember them," Frank said with a laugh. "I was the one in that guy's sights, mainly, not you, I suppose. What are you up to these days? Man, it's great to see you. You're still out of the government, right? That was a messy thing back a few years ago. Wouldn't have wanted to be you, no way. That took some guts, going to the New

York Times like that. Phew. Talk about laying it all on the line." They were standing in the middle of the park at the center of DuPont Circle, with people hurrying by in both directions.

"Yeah, I'm still out of the government, Frank," Virgil said, feeling slightly embarrassed at the reference to his firing. "You really think they'd ever hire me back after that affair? You cross the Bush people, you're marked for life."

Frank laughed and pulled out an umbrella, which he opened over both of them. "I know how that is. Say, want to grab a cup of coffee? We should catch up. Lots of juicy rumors going around."

Virgil looked at his watch. "I'm running a few minutes early for my appointment," he said, intrigued to hear any rumors Frank might know. "There's a Starbucks right across the street. We could go there for 15 or 20 minutes."

"Good, good," Frank replied. "I'm out for lunch, but I wasn't going anywhere special. I'll pick up a sandwich at Starbucks. Or maybe some yogurt. I'm trying to lose weight – don't laugh."

They started walking across the street, where the corner Starbucks beckoned. "Lose weight?" Virgil replied. He guessed the six-foot man at about a trim 175 pounds, hardly any different from eight years ago when they'd worked together. Virgil felt all the more decrepit as Frank strode out briskly toward the coffee shop. "You look like you could use to gain a pound or two."

"Yeah, that's what my wife says," Frank said as they opened the door and walked into the cozy store, punctuated by the rich, dark smell of strong coffee. "Believe it or not, I put on a few pounds after my birthday last month. Can't let middle age creep up on me. I'm training for a marathon."

Virgil, who'd long ago surrendered in his fight with middle age and now had the paunch to prove it, was secretly jealous. Running a marathon was one of those things he'd long imagined himself doing, but he hadn't been able to run the last 10 years or so since his leg got worse. Now, he supposed, he never would.

Over a grande caramel macchiato (for Virgil) and a tall black (for Frank), the two spent a bit of time reminiscing before Edwards leaned forward and spoke in a lower voice.

"Don't say anything now, but I have it on pretty good authority that your old buddy Harry is a finalist to take over for Rummy," Frank said, punctuating his comment with a raised eyebrow. "Inside dope. It's all the talk at the DOD, anyway."

Virgil pondered this for a moment, sipping his sweet drink as Frank leaned back to check his reaction. Virgil had mixed feelings about his old friend Harry. They hadn't talked much in the last few years - their most recent conversation was the one a few months ago in which Harry had reassured Virgil - and Virgil felt it wasn't just because Harry was so busy with the Iraq war. He caught himself feeling resentful of Harry now and then. After all, Harry had pushed him to publicize his memo to the president, and it had ended up getting Virgil fired. Perhaps Harry sensed Virgil's resentment. Or perhaps Harry wanted to distance himself from the contaminated Virgil Walker. Of course, Virgil could hardly blame Harry for this. Careers sometimes had to come before friendship.

"Well, that's interesting," he said, trying to sound neutral about it. "Maybe I'll check in with him and see if there's anything to it."

"You go ahead and do that, Virge, but don't let him know you heard it from me. You know how the rumor mill works around this town. I wouldn't want to ruin my stellar reputation."

"Oh, your reputation is secure with me," Virgil replied with a smile. "I won't tell anyone what a gossip you are."

Frank laughed. "Just for that, I'm paying for your coffee next time," he replied.

The two said goodbye and Virgil headed to his appointment, thinking of what Frank had said. How odd to think that Harry might become a cabinet member. If it happened, it would be the first time a true friend of Virgil's reached such a lofty position.

The news from the doctor wasn't good. The latest x-rays showed that the hip was in worse shape than ever, and it looked like a surgical case. Virgil was disappointed but somewhat stoic. The hip had been through a lot, starting with that college football injury, and then like a fool he'd become a runner in his 30s. He mentally began resigning himself to the operation, and hoped Linda's insurance would cover enough to keep the costs down.

Later that afternoon, the phone rang back at Virgil's apartment. It was Harry.

"Virge, ol' buddy, glad I caught ya," Harry said in his drawling voice. "Sorry it's been a few months."

"Good to hear from you," Virgil said. "You've been pretty busy – no hard feelings." He actually had some, but he was willing to let bygones be bygones.

"I don't know if you heard, but it looks like your old friend George W. is going to be making a new appointment for defense secretary, and it's very likely to be yours truly. If I get the appointment, I want you back in the department."

Virgil blinked. This was about the last thing he'd expected, and he sat silently in his chair, letting it sink in.

"Virge, you there ol' boy?" Harry asked.

"Yeah. I'm still here," Virgil said, recovering his voice. "I'm just surprised, I guess."

"Look, Virge, I've never felt quite right about the way things turned out in 2001 between us. I reckon I kind of pushed you on that memo, and then left you high and dry. I've been feeling guilty about that for a while now."

"Well, thanks, Harry. I appreciate it. Like I said, no hard feelings. But I don't want you to hire me just out of guilt." Virgil tried to keep the butterfly feeling of excitement building in his stomach from affecting the sound of his voice.

"Oh, it ain't just that, Virge," Harry replied. "I value your experience and knowledge. This country isn't getting any favors by having you sit at home when we still face terrorist threats out there. Last I heard, you had quite a network of experts on Al-Qaeda, and I'm still eating my heart out that Bin Laden is breathing and eating while all those folks on those planes are six feet under. I'm hoping you can help me bring him to justice."

"Well, that's quite an assignment, and I'd be honored to serve," Virgil said, deciding not to ask what specific position Harry had in mind for him. Probably a senior adviser role of some sort, not that it mattered. Just to get back into the game at all was hard to imagine. He took a breath, suddenly aware how improbable this sounded. "But how the heck can you ever bring me back? Bush and Cheney wouldn't go for that. My name is mud with both of them."

"Time heals, Virge, time heals," Harry replied. "I know those two pretty well and I'm fixing to make a case for you. Just stay near the phone the next few days. If I get this assignment – and I think I will – I'll work 'em over. We'll have 'em eatin' out of my hand in no time."

"Well, like I said, I'd be honored," Virgil said. "Just keep me posted, and best of luck to you." He ran his hand through his receding hair, as if to make sure he was really there and this was real.

"Thanks – I'll be needin' it if I get this job," Harry said. "They ran Rummy through the meat grinder over there. Hopefully I don't bring as much baggage."

"I don't think anyone could, Harry, truth to tell," Virgil replied.

"True, true," Harry laughed. "You take care now, Virge. We'll be talkin'."

Virgil hung up the phone, wondering exactly what he'd gotten himself into. As much as he'd felt depressed and disconnected being out of government, he wasn't sure he was ready to get back in, and once again face the big egos who ran things. Plus, there were still a lot of people in town who thought of him as a traitor for that memo, or as some sort of agitator at the least. Especially Cheney. He didn't relish having to encounter the Vice President again, even if Harry was able to butter him up.

Ah well, Virgil thought. If it all goes through, at least I'll have government health insurance again for my surgery.

CHAPTER 4

CHICAGO CONNECTION

The alarm went off for the third time and instead of pushing snooze again, Adam Fenton reached for it and turned off the alarm function before settling his head full of bushy, curly hair back onto the pillow. He closed his eyes, not wanting to look around the disheveled room, where his dirty clothes from the night before hung haphazardly over his desk chair. As he lay there, his gray cat Elmer leaped onto the bed with a loud "Meow!" and started kneading the blankets, purring and shoving his face against Adam's hand simultaneously.

"Breakfast time at the zoo, Elmer?" Adam asked groggily. The cat kept purring but didn't have anything else to say.

"Ah, another day," Adam said, stretching out his arms and pushing off the covers. In doing this, he mistakenly knocked the cat, which jumped lithely onto the floor and began licking his paws.

Adam rolled his 200 pounds out of bed and managed to stand up on the floor, wearing only his boxers. His hairy belly hung over the elastic band, and he felt his scratchy face with his hand. He hadn't bothered to shave yesterday, and now a light beard was developing. "Shit," he thought. "Can't get away without a shave today. Or maybe I can. Who gives a crap?"

He pulled out a can of cat food and gave Elmer his breakfast, then looked in the refrigerator (across from his bed) to see if anything was left. A nearly empty milk carton, a six-pack of Budweiser and a frozen dinner stared back at him. "Damn it – meant to put that in the freezer," Adam thought. He grabbed the dinner and took a look. Hungry Man fried chicken.

He tore open the box, peeled back the tray's top and felt the food. It was cool, but definitely no longer frozen. Probably OK. He put the whole thing in the countertop microwave and sat back on the bed while it cooked. The cat smacked his lips over his breakfast across the room. Adam lit a cigarette.

Time to think. What next? He tried to recall the last few days and it all seemed blurry. Being fired from PetSmart after coming in late for the fifth time in a month. Going to the bar and drinking, trying to forget what a mess his life seemed to be. Not being able to forget. Coming back home and undressing and sleeping for 12 hours. What next? He thought through his finances. He had a couple thousand in the bank, which would pay rent for a few months on this crappy apartment. He certainly didn't feel like going out and asking anyone else for a job – not now. First of all, he'd have to get a haircut, and he didn't want to bother. And he'd have to get his one suit dry-cleaned. It all seemed too complicated.

The floor was littered with yesterday's newspapers and dishes of half-finished meals. The little studio apartment smelled like cat litter because he'd neglected to clean Elmer's litter box for the last week. It also smelled like old cigarettes, but Adam didn't even notice.

"Let's face it, Elmer. I'm a mess." Elmer didn't reply. The dinger went off on the microwave and Adam grabbed the tray and a fork.

Adam plodded over to his desk, put down his fried chicken and turned on his computer. The one bright spot in his life now was the Internet and his website. He'd started blogging five years earlier (they'd called it "web-logging" back then, not blogging). Now he had a site devoted to his passion: airplane disasters. The site had hundreds of followers, and he continually updated it with the latest news about airline accidents around the world. There were sections where you could listen to actual recordings of flight control and pilots during the last minutes before crashes. The site had dozens of transcripts of "black boxes," and articles about specific crashes and the causes behind them. When he thought back, he admitted to himself that he'd let the blog get in the way of his job. He'd showed up late for work several times because he was so wrapped up in his blog. Of course, writing and researching about jet crashes was far more exciting than stocking 20-pound boxes of kitty litter.

He turned on the CD player and the disc he'd had in last night – "Remains Nonviewable," by a punk group called The Effigies, began to spin. The CD case lay next to the computer, showing a dim landscape of firefighters combing through an air crash site with red flags marking the location of human remains.

The Effigies, who had some success in the mid-1980s, were Adam's favorite group, though he sometimes thought he might never meet another person who'd heard of them. They'd broken up years ago. The sound of raw, hard guitar blasted through the apartment. Adam looked at his watch. He realized now why he was so tired. He'd accidentally set the alarm for 7. How the hell had that happened? "Must have been drunk. Why did I set it at all?"

His web page came up on the computer and he began updating his article about the collision of Flights 175 and 11 back in 2001. Now that was an interesting one. The National Transportation Safety Board's full report on the crash had lots of blank places in it where parts had been blacked out for "security purposes." Even the cockpit voice recorder transcripts of both planes, usually a fixture in NTSB reports, weren't complete. The transcripts went up to the moment before each plane was hijacked, but no further. The last words on the transcript from Ogonowski, pilot of Flight 11, were, "Wait a minute – you can't come in here!"

The government had never explained the collision of the two planes to Adam's satisfaction. The government ultimately had blamed it on Bin Laden and his associates, but who those associates were – other than the hijackers on the two planes themselves – had never been made clear. The government said the lead hijacker, Mohammed Atta, had met with an agent of the Iraqi government in 2000, and that was one of the reasons the President cited for this current war, but Adam thought that was bullshit. Bush had always been gunning for Saddam, and pulling Atta into the story was just too damn convenient. There were other, more shadowy figures associated with the hijackings, the media reports said, but they remained unidentified. Presumably they were still out there, which was sort of scary to contemplate.

The ultimate goal of the hijackers was still under debate. Some said they'd planned to land the planes and start shooting passengers. Others, including that guy whose name he'd forgotten who'd been fired from the administration shortly after the hijackings, said he thought the hijackers wanted to steer the planes into buildings in New York City. Now that was a genuinely frightening prospect, but there wasn't much evidence to back it up. Adam wondered absently what had happened to that guy.

Anyway, you couldn't argue with Bush's national security strategy, Adam thought. No terrorist attacks since that day in the fall of 2001. Attacks on civilians in Riyadh in 2002, Madrid in 2004 and in London in 2005 did cause some brief periods of concern, but mostly, Adam thought, people didn't go around worrying too much about terrorism any more. Nor, like Bush, did they spend much time thinking about Osama bin Laden.

Well, if there was one advantage to being jobless, he had a lot more time to write some meaningful stuff now, he thought. He sat there in his underwear, his cat again cleaning itself nearby, and began typing. He soon got involved in his writing and lost track of time and even where he was. The phone rang, interrupting him.

Where had he put the phone? With the music still blasting from the stereo, it was hard to pinpoint where the ringing came from. He realized it was on the bed, and he walked over, wondering who it might be. There weren't many people who'd be calling him this early.

He picked up the phone and frowned at a smear of mustard on the earpiece. The pungent odor reminded him of last night's take-out dinner, and he looked down and realized he had slept with a half-eaten hot dog on the bed.

"Hey Adam, it's Bob," said the voice on the other end.

"Yeah, Bob, what's up?" Adam replied.

Bob, like Adam, was an airplane blogger, though his blog was less concerned about plane crashes and more about planes in general. The man was obsessed with planes and airports. A fun day for him would be driving out to the cell phone lot at O'Hare, pulling out his camera and spending eight hours taking photos of different planes landing, taking off and taxiing. He had a network of other airplane-obsessed hobbyists who sent photos to his site from various airports around the world, and he posted them all. You could search his site by airline, type of airplane, year, airport and various other aspects. Adam, who was more focused on air disasters, sometimes visited Bob's site to find photos of so-called "accident craft" – or aircraft pictured before they crashed. He'd found a good one through Bob of Flight 175 waiting on the taxiway to take off from Logan before the 2001 collision, and he used it as the illustration for his blog post on that accident.

"I'm out at O'Hare, Adam, and I'm seeing the same shit again," Bob said in his distinctive nasal voice. "Come out here and I'll show you what I mean. It's really weird."

"You mean that shit you were talking about the other day?" Adam replied, wiping mustard off of his ear with his hand. The sharp smell drifted up to his nose.

"Right. Just some weird shit, dude."

Adam thought for a moment. He didn't have anything going on today, and an El ride to O'Hare was only a few bucks. The weather looked nice. What the hell?

"OK, I'll come out there. Give me about an hour. Hopefully I won't have to wait too long for the Blue Line."

"OK, man. I'm not going anywhere. I'm in the cell phone lot."

"Yeah, I figured as much," Adam said. "See you later." He hung up the phone, feeling a little better. At least his day now had a modicum of structure. And he had a reason to get dressed. He pulled yesterday's clothes off the chair where they were hanging and began putting them on, not bothering to change his underwear.

For the past week or so, Bob had been noticing some strange goings-on with one of the airline ground crews at O'Hare. Through his binoculars, Bob had watched as uniformed ground crew members had gathered, sometimes exchanging small packages. Bob was convinced it was some sort of drug trafficking deal. Probably no one else would have noticed anything at all, but Bob spent about 300 days a year observing operations at this particular airport, so he'd be more aware than anyone if something was off-kilter.

As Adam finished dressing, he wondered where Bob got the money to live like that, anyway. Maybe he had a night job. The guy certainly didn't look like he came from wealth. In fact, he was arguably more disheveled than Adam himself. As for Adam, he was skeptical that anything really fishy was happening with the ground crews, but he thought he'd humor Bob by coming out and seeing what he was talking about. He'd always wondered if ground crews posed a security threat. After all, didn't they get in to some pretty secure places just by touching a card to a sensor? There had to be a few rotten apples among them, Adam thought, and maybe Bob had spied some. Could be an interesting article for his blog, he supposed, if it turned out to be anything.

"So long, Elmer," he called as he left. "Don't work too hard while I'm gone." He pulled on his coat, closed the door and walked down the stairs, heading to the train station.

CHAPTER 5
THE DIRECTOR IN NEW YORK

few days later, as November drew to a close, a very short, dark-skinned balding man with a short black beard and a bit of a potbelly boarded the elevator to the World Trade Center observatory in Tower Two. He wore dark slacks and a checkered blue and white dress shirt, along with a cheap-looking navy jacket. His growing belly peeked out below his shirt, which had come un-tucked. His somehow unpleasant face contrasted sharply with the light-hearted look of the tourists, most of whom were bundled up against the November chill. The tourist crowds had thinned with the coming of cold weather, and the elevator wasn't too crowded. The man, known as the Director by his colleagues, stood patiently, watching the floor numbers quickly turn as the speedy elevator advanced 107 floors in just over a minute. The doors slid open and he stepped out with the tourists.

The Director didn't pause to look out the windows of the observatory. Instead, he walked quickly, as if he knew the way well, to the escalator on the north side of the observatory, which led up to the roof deck. At the top, he stepped off onto the wide observation platform, where the November wind blew fiercely from the north, making a high-pitched roaring sound that rose every time the wind sped up. He cursed under his breath at the cold in a language that wasn't English, and put his head down and advanced to the railing. He was practically alone up here – few others had any desire to face these winds. Looking north, the other tower dominated the view to his front left, its tall antenna piercing up another 100 feet into the sky. Below spread the streets and buildings of Manhattan, reaching north toward the Empire State and Chrysler Buildings 50 blocks away. The cars and trucks crawled up and down the highways along the Hudson and East Rivers, and thin November clouds sped quickly across the blue sky, blotting out the sun with their shadows every few minutes. A few boats lazily prowled the rivers, but not many. Pleasure boating season was pretty much over.

The Director shuddered a little with the cold, and looked at his watch. Still 10 minutes until he had to go back down. The little man was very familiar with this place. He'd been coming here every few months for several years, not often enough to attract attention from the security guards, but enough to know the layout pretty well and become familiar with the view from every direction of the sky deck.

At first he'd told himself these visits were for reconnaissance, but after a while, he had to admit that they were to feed his obsession. The towers had been haunting his dreams for years now, starting even before the air crash fiasco, and the visits had become something like pilgrimages. He licked his lips, and thought he was like a cat playing with a mouse. The mouse was still alive, its legs moving weakly, still trying to walk, but the cat kept batting at it with his paws, not enough to kill it, but enough to keep up the signs of life until it was finished. Then the cat would bite into the mouse and crush the life out of its body. He could see the blood oozing out of the little animal, coating its fur. He could sense the rusty taste of raw flesh and blood in his mouth. He smiled without realizing it.

As he savored his thoughts, his mind turned to the operations in Chicago, where Hanjour and Jarrah were based. The work at O'Hare was a test, and he'd chosen that airport because it was one of the busiest, a place where they could try his hypothesis without drawing much attention. The Director knew because he'd scoped it out himself. As he'd suspected, the Americans, after a couple years of much more advanced scrutiny following the plane collision, had relaxed their security measures. As always, he thought, the Jews who ran this country placed money over everything else, and had pushed back against the kind of security strategy that might slow business but would advance passenger safety. Full inspections of foreign cargo were still sporadic; background checks of airport workers were half-assed and security checks of passengers were rather lethargic, with bored, overworked TSA officers unable to keep up with the constant intensity needed to thwart future plots. Yes, the Director thought, putting his hands in his pockets against the cold, things were going just as he thought they would.

After the brothers failed to smash the towers on that sacred day of Sept. 11, the Director had presented his new plan to the Sheik. Bin Laden, who hadn't wanted to focus on the United States after the Sept. 11 operation went awry, agreed to center his plans on the infidels in Europe and the false Muslims in the Arab lands. Bin Laden had given the Director his blessing to come to the United States, and promised to continue funding him and the other two brothers, Jarrah and Hanjour, while they lay low, waiting for the right time to strike. Meanwhile, the attacks on targets abroad and Bin Laden's regular messages to the public castigating the evil House of Saud and the Zionist entity would keep America's eyes off the ball.

Indeed, the United States had helped their cause a great deal by attacking Iraq in 2003, which took the focus off of the remaining Mujhadeen in Afghanistan, where the Taliban government still offered protection. Sure, the U.S. attacks on Afghanistan back in 2001 had caused some ruptures, and a few key brothers had died, but the Sheik survived, and remained solidly in charge of the organization. And he, the Director, was safe here in America, living under his assumed identity, with all the necessary documents. Meanwhile, the chaos in Iraq had provided the group a new opportunity to directly target Americans, without the trouble of having to attack them in their homeland. At least not for now, the Director thought, smiling to himself again.

The cold grew more intense and the Director took the escalator back down to the warmth of the observatory. He was here to meet Hanjour. His team, he knew, thought he was insane to hold his meetings with them in this place, within feet of security guards in a building that had been specially protected against terrorist attacks since 1993, when he had planned the successful bombing that had killed six people. But he relished the irony of meeting here, plotting to finish the job that they couldn't carry out in 2001. He formed the mental picture of a calendar, with a date flashing: May 2008. He had good reasons to plan the attacks for that month. Just a year and a half to go.

The Director fished a phone out of his pocket. It was a cheap throwaway that he'd purchased at Walgreen's. He bought new ones every few days. No one ever knew his number except him. And no one ever called him. The Director called you, and you damn well had better be ready to listen.

He dialed. "Hanjour, where are you?" he asked quietly in English, standing near a group of tourists ogling at the view over New York Harbor.

"I'm near the elevators," Hanjour replied. "I see you. I'll be right there."

The Director put his phone back in his pocket and waited impatiently, shifting from one foot to the other. He looked up and saw Hanjour, who had been scheduled to be the pilot aiming at the Pentagon on September 11, 2001, heading his way. Hanjour still had his thick, prominent dark eyebrows, and remained beardless. Like Jarrah, Hanjour had a clean record. As far as the Director and the Sheik could tell, neither of the 9/11 terrorists had ever been tracked down by the FBI or appeared on any watch lists. Even so, Hanjour and Jarrah treaded carefully. They kept themselves clean-shaven, spoke English as much as possible, wore Western clothes and even took jobs. Jarrah drove a cab in Chicago, and Hanjour had worked on construction crews and as a cook at a Middle Eastern restaurant. And of course all this was done under assumed names and identities, expertly manufactured by Jarrah. The Director thought they'd done a good job fitting in.

Hanjour approached. "Director sir?" he said. The Director's colleagues were always careful to show the proper respect when addressing him. It wouldn't do to have their heads bitten off. Hanjour, like Jarrah, wasn't quite sure of the Director's actual name – he went by so many - so they just referred to him by his title.

"What's the latest update?" the Director asked. They were standing side by side, looking out over the harbor. No one paid them any attention. The Director spoke in English, which had improved slightly in the five years he'd lived here. It still was pretty poor compared to the English of Hanjour and Jarrah, but the Director never felt the need to put a lot of effort into his language skills. Even when he'd been at college in North Carolina in the 1980s, he'd gotten along fine without being fluent. But sometimes Arabic was a bad idea – it drew attention.

"I have some troubling news, sir," Hanjour said. "We think Oak Street Beach is getting crowded."

"Oak Street Beach" was the code word for the Chicago operation. "Getting crowded" meant someone – possibly a law officer – had caught on to what they were doing.

"What makes you think this?" the Director asked. He kept a veneer of calm on his face, but inside he could feel his blood beginning to boil. The damned incompetents! Always having his plans spoiled by incompetents!

"We have photos we can show you," Hanjour replied, speaking more quickly, still in code. "Our people went to the beach the other day and they were engaged in volleyball practice when they drew some spectators."

"How many?" the Director asked, trying to control his temper. Maybe he should have had this meeting in private, after all.

"Just two," Hanjour replied. "Like I said, we took some photos. I have them with me."

"Show me," the Director said.

Hanjour produced a pair of pictures from his pocket. They showed two Americans, dressed in casual clothes – jeans and light fall jackets – behind a fence at what must have been the cell phone lot at O'Hare airport. The two men each had cameras in their hands, and one had a pair of binoculars hanging around his neck.

The Director looked at the photos and guffawed.

"Ha! They look like ghabbys," he barked, reverting to Arabic for a moment to call the men stupid. "What are you worried about?"

"We know who they are, sir," Hanjour replied. "They each run blogs."

"What the hell is a… what did you say, blog?" the Director asked. This was unfamiliar English slang.

"Sir, a blog is a website. These two each run web sites where they post photos of airplanes. One of them has information on his site about the events of five years ago. Jarrah and I have some concerns about what they might do with any photos they take."

The Director put his arm around his underling's shoulders. Hanjour plainly felt uncomfortable with this but made no move to resist.

"My friend, my friend," the Director said. "Let's go back downstairs and discuss this a bit further. I feel we've seen enough sights for the day, don't you? What a beautiful view this is."

"Yes, yes," Hanjour said nervously. "It is tremendous."

The Director directed Hanjour away from the windows toward the exit, still with his arm around the man.

"Yes, I've always wanted to visit this place," the Director said in a conversational tone as they approached the line for the elevators back down. "The view is worth the trip."

"It is," Hanjour agreed. The Director dropped his arm from Hanjour's shoulders when the elevator door opened. The elevator whisked them back to the lobby in a minute, and, with their ears popping, they stepped out onto the street. It was mid-afternoon, and the sun was beginning to go down behind the North Tower. Above them, the tower they had exited stretched toward the sky, looming above them and casting a long shadow over the blocks just east as the sun sank toward the western horizon. The streets were full of people rushing and taxis honking. Another typical November afternoon in New York.

As they walked over toward West Street to get a cab, the Director stopped and barked out his trademark harsh laughter.

"What is it?" Hanjour asked

"Look at this sign," the Director said, motioning him over. Hanjour walked cautiously toward the Director, who was pointing at the sign mounted on the sidewalk. The sign read:

"Coming, January 2007: World Trade Center Condominiums. Your Chance to Live Sky High. See www.wtc.com for more details."

The Director was bent over with laughter.

"Sh, sh," Hanjour urged. "You'll attract attention."

"Right, right," the Director said in Arabic, composing himself a little. "But just think, just think – people will pay to live here? These buildings shouldn't even still be here. Oh, they've got a surprise coming to them." He gazed up at the towers soaring into the darkening sky, the buildings whose destruction would culminate his life's work. Then his gaze followed the bustling crowds of decadent and ignorant Americans on the sidewalk. A smile crossed his lips. "The sign is right," he muttered to Hanjour. "It will be their chance to live – and die – sky high."

CHAPTER 6

JARRAH IN CHICAGO

That same evening, Jarrah drove his yellow Ford cab through the streets of Chicago, picking up passengers at O'Hare and dropping them off at a hotel downtown. It was only 4:30, but the late-November sky was already getting dark, the end to a gray, cold day. The weather forecast called for snow to develop over the weekend.

The hotel's doorman signaled Jarrah, and Jarrah raised his hand to acknowledge. The doorman guided an elderly couple toward Jarrah's cab, and Jarrah got out to help with their luggage.

"Going to O'Hare?" he asked, in his perfect, almost unaccented English.

"Midway, actually," the elderly man replied.

"No problem," Jarrah said, wrestling the man's overstuffed suitcase into the trunk while the elderly couple boarded. He slammed the trunk door, climbed back into the driver's seat and turned the key in the ignition. He eased the car carefully into downtown traffic and turned on his headlamps.

"OK if I play the radio?" Jarrah asked his passengers in a polite tone.

"It's fine, just keep it down, please," the man replied. Jarrah pushed the power button and National Public Radio came on. Jarrah had that as his default station because he liked keeping up with the news, and it helped his English. By now, after six years in this country, he was even dreaming in English.

"And there's big news from Capitol Hill today, where President Bush announced the appointment of Harry Deaver to replace Donald Rumsfeld as Secretary of Defense," the NPR announcer said. "Deaver, who has a long history with both the Department of Defense and the CIA, is considered an expert on fighting terrorism. But his first assignment in the administration, assuming he's confirmed by the new Democratic-controlled Congress, will be to help improve the declining situation in Iraq, where continued sectarian strife has taken the lives of 250 Iraqi citizens and 28 U.S. soldiers over the last month. New York Times correspondent Nancy Hanson is in Baghdad, and she joins us now. Hi Nancy."

"Hello, Bob," came a woman's voice. Jarrah listened carefully as he drove onto the entrance ramp to Lake Shore Drive, headed south. "Good to be here."

Bob asked Nancy about some of the challenges the new defense secretary would face with the Iraq war in the coming year, and Jarrah's attention drifted a little. The war in Iraq was the Sheik's business, not Jarrah's. The battle there against the Shiites was proceeding as planned, with the Sheik providing funding for some of the bombings last month. Jarrah wasn't tasked with any Iraq strategy. Rather, he wanted to know more about Harry Deaver's U.S. strategy. He knew from coverage of the plane collision that Deaver was far more tuned in to domestic terror threats than his predecessor, and that could have implications for the operations Jarrah was planning.

Finally, the announcer asked Nancy about the U.S. situation.

"Nancy, the United States has been surprisingly free from foreign terrorist attacks and threats the last 13 years. But Mr. Deaver said in a recent interview that he considers the U.S. to be very vulnerable, and that there needs to be a greater focus on terrorism. You covered the White House for many years, and you're familiar with Deaver's thinking. What do you think he plans to do here in the U.S. to lessen the threat?"

"Well, Bob," Nancy replied. "I think first of all it's important to remember that we haven't been completely free from foreign terrorism in the U.S. since 1993. People tend to forget because it's been a while, but we had the two planes hijacked by terrorists in 2001, and at the time there was some concern that the terrorists might have been targeting U.S. buildings and monuments. Now that's never been proven, but Harry Deaver has always been of the opinion that those attacks were precursors to something else, and that perhaps terrorist cells still exist in the United States. I'd expect a greater focus on prevention of domestic terrorism if Deaver

THE TOWERS STILL STAND

gets confirmed, and I think one thing he might want to urge the president to do is upgrade airline safety. But remember, Deaver's focus is on the military, and domestic terrorism is really not on his list of responsibilities, so I'm not sure how much influence he can have on that issue."

"And Nancy, what are your thoughts on Deaver's chances for confirmation?"

"Oh, it's almost certain he'll be confirmed," Nancy replied. "He's popular on both sides of the aisle, and with his record and the respect he has around the country, I can't imagine this will be an appointment that's seriously challenged by Democrats."

"Thanks very much, Nancy," said Bob. "Good having you here."

"It's always a pleasure, Bob," Nancy said. "Good night."

"That was Nancy Hanson, the New York Times' correspondent in Baghdad, where she's been stationed this fall after spending 10 years covering the White House," the NPR announcer continued. "Now we move on to Turkey, which is preparing for the pope's coming visit..."

Jarrah mentally tuned out the radio. He was fighting traffic on the Stevenson expressway, headed for Midway Airport, and a few drops of rain began to fall. It was now fully dark, and he turned on the wipers. The passengers in back were quiet, and he stole a glance into the rear view mirror and noticed the wife had fallen asleep with her head on her husband's shoulder. At that sight, he felt emotion stir in him briefly, and fought to stamp it out. He focused once again on the road in front of him, where a brief opening allowed him to shift into the middle lane. He slammed down on the gas and roared past the semi that had been blocking him.

The report on the radio steered his mind back toward the Plan, which they still had 18 months to get into shape and carry out. He thought back to a conversation he'd had earlier this year during the Director's most recent visit to Chicago, when Jarrah had driven him aimlessly around Chicago in his cab. The cab was an excellent place to hold meetings, as they had absolute privacy.

"It is no longer possible to hijack an airplane in the United States," Jarrah had told the Director then. "The measures taken by the enemy after the failure of our holy operation would prevent that." They had been speaking Arabic, which they always did in private.

"No, no, my friend," the Director had replied from the back seat. "That's where you're absolutely wrong. The fact is, it's even easier to hijack a plane now and accomplish our mission, because we know more about our enemy now, and because they think they know more about us."

Jarrah, unlike some others in Al-Qaeda, wasn't shy about challenging the Director. He knew the Director's bark was worse than his bite, at least with those he respected, and Jarrah was confident he had the Director's respect. The Director had told him more than once that Jarrah should have been at the controls of Flight 175, not Shehhi, and of course, Jarrah agreed.

But Jarrah found it hard to agree with the Director about hijacking. After all, hadn't the failed September 11 attacks shown the U.S. authorities that Al-Qaeda was intent on hijacking U.S. airplanes on U.S. soil? And hadn't the government taken appropriate measures to better secure airlines afterward? Surely, hijacking planes and flying them into the towers – the Director's original plan – was no longer viable, and they'd have to find some other way to attack the buildings.

Not according to the Director, though.

"Listen, my friend," the Director had said from the back seat. "Think of this as being like a game of blackjack. In 2001, we showed our first card, and the enemy saw it. But our second card is still face down on the table. Think! The enemy knows we can hijack planes – yes, we showed that. But the enemy doesn't know what we intended to do with those planes, do they? Oh yes, one or two smart ones in the government thought about that, but they fired the one who spoke about that. They've gone to war in Iraq and forgotten about 2001. They think they're safe – that we wouldn't try the same tactic again. That all works to our advantage. Oh yes!" He cackled his mad laugh, which always annoyed Jarrah to no end. Jarrah said nothing in reply. At times like these, it was best to let the Director get everything out.

"Yes," the Director went on. "They have taken measures, but they haven't gone far enough. Have they made any real effort to check foreign cargo? No. Have they truly sealed the cockpits? No. Are the TSA crews able to tell with 99 percent accuracy who's an innocent civilian and who's a muhjadeen? No. They make little old ladies go through long security lines and check their hands for bomb residue, and at the same time you can go through without a second look, Jarrah. You told me that, right?"

Jarrah had taken some flights since 2001, testing out security measures. Indeed, there had been times when old ladies were subject to extra security, and he, carrying his assumed name and identification, had been waved through. But he had noticed the extra security aboard aircraft, and he'd read that the government now stationed security people on almost every plane. Besides, he thought, Americans were no longer blissfully ignorant about the possibility of hijacking. After the Sept. 11 collision, there'd been a campaign by the government to make people more aware of what do to in the event of a hijacking and how to recognize suspicious passengers. He also knew that pilots were far more prepared now to take measures against hijackers than they had been before 2001.

Jarrah told the Director as much, and the Director slammed his fist against the seat.

"Don't believe their lies, Jarrah," the Director had said, and looking through the rear-view mirror, Jarrah could see the Director's frenzied eyes, shining with zeal. "You say the passengers are educated? No, they're still ignorant. They still don't know what we planned to do with those planes. You can count on them to sit quietly and behave, like lambs to the slaughter. We did a good job of hiding our plans in 2001, and no one suspects anything. Don't try to talk me out of this. The plan is going forward."

And of course, Jarrah thought as he exited the expressway and headed south toward Midway with his two elderly passengers, the Director got his way. Backed by the Sheik, the plan took shape. It wouldn't be as complex as the 2001 attacks, of course. There'd be only two planes this time, and the planes would take off from Chicago for New York. But the towers were still the goal, and the date, May 14, 2008, to mark the 60th anniversary of the founding of the Zionist entity - was rapidly approaching. The tests they'd been conducting at O'Hare the last few weeks, designed to see how easy it would be to sneak weapons aboard passenger jets, had gone smoothly. They'd proven they were able to work with their ground crew contacts to put the test materials – in this case combination locks – aboard the planes without passing through a security check.

The problem rose when he had spied the two Americans watching their operation last week. Hanjour had traveled to New York to discuss the situation with the Director – you didn't call or email the Director about stuff like this. Now the Director had to make a decision. Killing or kidnapping the Americans would draw unwanted attention their way. But letting the Americans go to the police with their photos or put them on the Internet – Jarrah's fear – would also threaten their operation.

Jarrah's plan – which he knew Hanjour was sharing now with the Director – was a middle-of-the-road one that he thought would work. The airport workers they'd enlisted believed Hanjour and Jarrah were drug traffickers, and the workers were being paid off to sneak the locks onto the planes in hope of gaining even bigger payoffs once the actual drugs started flowing. Jarrah had no interest in directly confronting the two spying Americans, but Jarrah's airport worker contacts could be told about them and asked to run interference, paying off the spies to go away.

Certainly neither of the spies were wealthy. Jarrah had followed them back from the airport, learned their addresses and researched them online. A payment of $5,000 each and a request to shut up would probably suffice. If the Americans went to the police in spite of that, more dramatic measures would be needed, Jarrah thought. Either way, they had to act quickly. They'd first seen the spies four days ago, and Jarrah kept an eagle eye on both of their websites to see if they had posted anything. Nothing so far, and he doubted that even if they did so it would get much attention. But any leak was unwelcome, and he had to be on top of it. He could disable the websites if necessary, but he didn't think it would come to that, and he didn't want to yet, as it might attract more attention.

Midway Airport drew up on their right, bright red lights shining, signs pointing the way to long-term and short-term parking, and the Orange Line rapid transit station. Jarrah pulled into the circular terminal driveway and stopped the car. "We're here, honey," the man in back told his wife. "Already?" she asked sleepily.

"The fare is $40," Jarrah said and took the man's credit card. The man gave him a $10 tip, and Jarrah got out and helped with the luggage.

"Have a good trip," Jarrah said. The man thanked him quietly and slowly walked into the terminal carrying luggage, his wife at his side. Jarrah watched them for a minute and then got back into the cab, drove over to the pick-up area, and waited for his next fare.

As he waited, his phone rang. He checked the number. It was the familiar one.

"Hello, Alev," he said in his calm voice.

"Hello, Ziad," Alev said.

"Did you decide?" he asked. His heart beat a bit faster in anticipation.

"Yes. I'm flying in on December 5," Alev said. "You'll pick me up at the airport?"

"I'll be there. What flight?" He drummed his fingers eagerly on the steering wheel.

She told him. There was awkward silence again.

"Ziad?" she finally said.

"Yes?"

"Can you tell me why you want me all of a sudden?"

"I miss you," he said truthfully. "You're the only woman I've ever been close to. And I'm lonely."

"I'm lonely too," she replied. "I've never met anyone like you."

Jarrah smiled, knowing how right she was.

"I'll see you December 5," he said quietly.

CHAPTER 7
NANCY IN IRAQ

When Nancy finished the NPR interview, she rode the elevator back up to her hotel room. It was 2 a.m. in Baghdad, and she was exhausted, and wondering not for the first time why she'd ever come to the Middle East. A sudden wave of homesickness burst through her, leaving an empty feeling in her middle, and she pictured Joanna's face and felt once again the longing for her voice and touch. It was almost physical, this longing. She clenched her teeth as she stepped out of the slow elevator into the dimly-lit hallway and walked toward her room.

She collapsed on the lumpy bed without bothering to turn on the light. As she had promised, she took out her Blackberry and sent one more email to her mom and Joanna, telling them she had gotten through another day. Outside her window, the Baghdad horizon glowed orange from the city lights. Often she had lain here at night listening to explosions echo across the city. Sometimes they sounded very close. Even here in the protected zone of Baghdad where foreign journalists lived, she knew she wasn't completely safe. There'd been reporters killed not far from her hotel, and one hotel which had housed reporters had been bombed early in the war.

The irony was, she wasn't even supposed to be in this war-torn place. She'd come to the Middle East expecting to work out of the Cairo office, and had done so for several weeks. But then the paper had an unexpected need for another reporter in Baghdad as the pace of the war picked up, and Nancy's boss had asked her to come and fill in the gap until they could find someone permanent. The editors knew she had family reasons for wanting to stay out of a war zone, but then again, she was the one who took the Middle East job, and it wouldn't really do to say no, especially since this was a temporary assignment. She'd been here for three weeks, and a replacement was due in three days. Nancy was counting the hours till she could return to the comparative calm of Egypt.

The Baghdad assignment, of course, hadn't gone over very well with her mother and Joanna. Nancy tried to soothe her daughter, but it was hard to do from 5,000 miles away over the phone. They'd tried to Skype a few times, but the technology wasn't too good, so they'd given up.

Though Nancy felt incredibly guilty about taking on this assignment, and part of her wanted to quit and take the next flight home, the journalist in her was filled with excitement. Here was a chance to cover history as it happened, even though at the moment it seemed like a tragic one. Since arriving, she'd seen things she'd never imagined – mostly violent ones. The U.S. military kept reporters on a pretty short leash, but that hadn't prevented Nancy from doing some more aggressive reporting, getting out into the streets and interviewing the civilians who'd been impacted most by the situation. One of her articles, about a merchant in one of Baghdad's markets who'd lost his entire family in a sectarian bombing, had made the front page. Yes, she told herself, the stories here were nearly all tragic, but, as a journalist, this was how you made a name for yourself. The greatest journalists all covered wars, or at least went overseas. Every day, Nancy learned something new, and she'd actually become pretty good at Arabic, which she'd taken a crash course in starting back in the U.S. when she learned she'd get the Middle East assignment.

And even though part of her was counting down the days till she could get out of this awful place, another part of her regretted that her time here would be so short. Ever since that fateful day when she'd talked to Virgil Walker in the Thai restaurant in Washington, she'd been convinced that Virgil was right about Al-Qaeda being a threat to the United States. Here in Iraq, Al-Qaeda was ascendant, and many of the bombings were its doing. What better place than here to learn more about the terror organization, track down its leaders and write about their motivations? Not that it would be easy, of course. Al-Qaeda leaders didn't make it a habit to conduct interviews or let it be known where they hid, but she figured she had a better chance here than nearly anywhere else. She'd even asked her editors if after this temporary assignment in Iraq, she could travel to Pakistan, where she hoped to get a better handle on the terror group. So far, she hadn't heard back on that one.

It was 2:30 a.m. when Nancy finally fell asleep, knowing she had to be back at the bureau at 8 a.m. Outside, the sky over Baghdad glowed, and a dull roar thudded many miles away, the sound of artillery thumping outside of town. Despite the late hour and the distant explosions, cars still ran up and down the nearby highway, headlights on as late-night drivers headed to destinations known only to them.

Nancy was woken the next morning by the sound of the muezzin's cries echoing over the city. "Alluha Akbar," the voices echoed. She wondered vaguely if people here ever got used to these prayer calls enough to ignore them. Five times a day, the city rang with their somewhat mournful cries, and she still jumped each time. Maybe it's like moving to a farm, she thought. Eventually you get used to the roosters.

She showered, dressed, sent an email to Joanna and her mom ("Just three more days!") and then left the hotel for the bureau office a few blocks away. Both her hotel and her office were inside the so-called "Green Zone," where it was relatively safe for Westerners to move about. Outside, the day was pleasantly cool, around 70 degrees, and the palm trees blew in a light wind. What a shame that the city was so violent, she thought. It must have once been a nice place to live. Of course, this was fall. She'd heard the heat was brutal in the summer.

"Hi Nancy, how's it going?" the Baghdad bureau chief, Ron Kolarik, greeted her as she entered the office and walked toward her desk, where papers were piled in neat stacks next to her white coffee mug emblazoned with a photo of Joanna. "We've got some local treats this morning - Kleicha." He pointed to a plate on a table in the middle of the small room where there was a plate of Kleicha tamur, cookies filled with dates. The bureau consisted of one room about the size of a hotel room, with three desks crammed into the corners and a lone window looking out at palm trees and the calm brown waters of the Tigris River. A barge floated by lazily.

"Thanks, I'll take a pass," Nancy said, with a dramatic eye roll. Ron enjoyed teasing Nancy. Everyone in the bureau knew about her aversion to ethnic foods, and that she'd come to the Middle East with a huge supply of packaged American products. If she had to survive this assignment on PowerBars, then so be it.

"I figured you'd say that," Ron said with a smile. He was a sandy-haired, red-faced man in his mid-40's who'd spent 20 years stationed in several Middle Eastern countries. He spoke Arabic fluently, and often gave Nancy tips on how to improve hers. But she despaired of ever achieving his level of expertise. Ron moved through Baghdad as if he'd always lived there, and the Iraqi people seemed to accept him almost as one of their own. He'd spent part of his childhood in the Middle East, which helped him understand the culture in a way other reporters never could.

Still, Nancy wasn't intimidated. She knew she could cover any story, and Ron respected her talent. She had the same ability as he did to make sources feel comfortable, and to deliver big stories the competition couldn't get. She'd never be the seasoned Middle East expert that Ron was, but that wouldn't stop her from doing a good job. She approached every day just as she had in the White House, determined to push the U.S. military and government leaders for answers to her myriad of questions.

Today, Ron gave Nancy an assignment. In the past, she had set her own schedule and decided what to cover. But she'd given up a little of that freedom here in Baghdad as she learned about the country and the war, and this was one of those times. After Ron gave her the details, she returned to her desk and packed her green backpack to go out of the office for the day.

• • •

Three hours later, lying in the back of the hot SUV, mouth parched, the militants' excited voices in her ears, Nancy thought back upon what had happened. The day had started out normally enough, with Ron asking her to go along with U.S. troops to a neighborhood in Baghdad where the soldiers were helping dedicate a new elementary school. A U.S. general, accompanied by his Iraqi Army counterpart and about two dozen U.S. and Iraqi soldiers, performed a ceremonial ribbon cutting, and the little children – aged kindergarten through early teens – cheered. It had been a happy, feel-good event, and Ron wanted Nancy to write more stories about some of the positive attributes of the American campaign. "We've certainly written enough about the bad stuff," he'd said. "The paper is getting a lot of pressure from the military to provide 'balanced' coverage. I think the bad far outweighs the good, but when they do something right for once, I guess it's not a bad thing to highlight it."

After the U.S. General cut the ribbon and said a few words, his Iraqi counterpart had taken the podium, and that's when things got hazy for Nancy. There'd been a loud booming noise from out on the street, she remembered that much. Then there was the noise of children screaming, and she realized she was on the floor, covered with dust. All around her was chaos, with moans of pain, more screaming and excited voices in Arabic and English. That's when she'd noticed the pain in her left leg, and looked down and saw blood on her pants. She'd felt around the rest of her body and everything seemed to be in place, but she couldn't get up to move away from flames that were licking the wall nearby.

She had dragged herself in the direction she thought was the back of the room, hoping to get away from the fire, and had crawled right into a soldier lying on the floor. His face was covered with bloody pinpricks, and his legs were sprawled in an unnatural way. She couldn't tell which army he belonged to because his uniform was covered with dust, but his glassy, wide-open eyes told her he was dead. Nancy had seen enough dead bodies in her three weeks covering Baghdad to recognize that much.

Her leg ached with a dull, numb, prickly pain, but even as she lay there sweating profusely, clutching her leg, she realized what a great story this would be if she could get out alive. She cried out for help, but the air was filled with noise and dust. She couldn't see or hear anyone, and she supposed no one could see or hear her. She decided to stay where she was. Crawling was painful, and she was far enough away from the flames that they didn't seem like an immediate danger. Surely someone would come and save her if she waited.

A minute later, she saw a large man with a dark beard and a head wrapping emerge from the smoke in the direction of the front entrance. He looked down at her and the dead soldier and said something in Arabic that she didn't understand. He didn't appear to be an Iraqi soldier or a medical person, and Nancy's heart beat faster. Who was this guy? Could she expect help from him?

"Ma ismik?" he asked.

Ah, she knew what that meant.

"Nancy," she replied, trying not to moan from the pain in her leg.

"Oh, you're American," he said in accented English. "You're hurt."

"Yes, my leg." She pointed to the bloody spot. The pain wasn't too bad. She thought it might be broken, but it didn't feel like it had fallen off or anything. She'd heard of and seen too many unplanned amputations caused by bombs since she'd been here, and it was her greatest fear to come home missing a limb.

"I'll help you," he said, and bent down to pick her up. Carrying her in his arms like a baby, he stepped around rubble, pushed his way past a wall that was partially ruptured, stepped over a prone body and eventually brought her out to the street, where people were running around yelling amid smoke and dust.

When she looked from out of his burly arms at what was left of the school, she gasped. It was a miracle she was alive, she realized. Most of the building was gone, and flames shot from what was left of the wreckage. Ambulances zoomed up with sirens wailing, and U.S. and Iraqi soldiers ran around blocking off the street and pushing crowds away. Nancy wasn't the only victim coming out, she noticed. U.S. and Iraqi troops carried screaming children from the building, and the scene was absolutely pitiful. One child's legs were blown clear off, and she lay unconscious in the arms of a soldier. Blood poured out of her wounds despite a hasty tourniquet someone had wrapped around what was left of her legs. Nancy looked away.

Then Nancy realized she no longer had her bag. The bag had her computer and her notebooks. Luckily her Blackberry was still in her pocket. The man was hustling her to an SUV parked near the wrecked building. "Wait," she called out. "My bag!"

"What does it look like?" the man asked in accented English. "I'll go back for it after I get you into the truck."

"The truck?" she said. "Don't I need an ambulance?"

"The ambulances are all taken, so we're taking the less badly injured in whatever vehicles we can find," the man said. At this point, he'd carried her to a blue SUV and opened the back compartment. As he started to set her inside, she saw several Arab men already in the car, one of them holding a gun on her, and she started to scream. Instantly, the man's hand clamped over her mouth, and he stuffed her in the rear of the vehicle, slamming the hatchback shut before she could scream again. She pounded on a side window and started yelling for help, but a man in the back seat pushed her down with a warning glare. Amid all the chaos, it didn't appear any of the soldiers outside her window had seen what just happened.

Her "rescuer" now got into the passenger seat and yelled something to the driver. The SUV accelerated quickly from the scene and into a warren of streets Nancy didn't recognize from the floor of the back of the vehicle, and her leg started aching worse. She reached into her pocket for her Blackberry, but it wasn't there. The man must have taken it from her when he carried her to the truck.

"Where are you taking me?" she yelled. "I'm a journalist!"

"Don't worry, lady," said a man in the back seat, speaking Arabic, which Nancy was able to make out pretty well. "We're not going to hurt you."

"But my leg – it might be broken," she yelled, feeling adrenaline course through her. "You've got to get me to a hospital"

"We'll take care of you where we're going. It's not far," the man replied, again in Arabic, which Nancy struggled to understand, what with the pain and the bouncing of the vehicle on the potholed streets. Each bump made the pain worse. She tried to keep from screaming.

At this point, Nancy had stopped talking and considered her options: they were disappointing. She could try to break out of the car when it stopped, but with her injured leg she doubted she could crawl over to the door of the hatch back. And even if she could, she wasn't sure she could open it from the inside. If she did escape the car, the men would just stop it and come and get her. She couldn't get very far on her leg. Also, an escape attempt now might antagonize them and make her treatment worse. Begging to be set free wouldn't work with this crew, she thought. Best to stay quiet for now, as hard as that seemed, and see what would happen next. At least the men didn't appear to be homicidal. For now, at any rate.

At some point, Nancy had fallen asleep back there, overcome by the pain and fear. When she woke and looked out the window, she saw they were no longer in the city, but on a road somewhere beyond its outskirts.

She tried to recognize the place, but couldn't really tell. She hadn't been outside of Baghdad much since arriving, and from what she remembered, the scenery looked pretty similar whichever way you went. The road was only partially paved, and their vehicle was sending dust clouds into the air as it cruised along, going about 50 miles per hour, she guessed. There were groups of palm trees on the side of the road, and a telephone wire. The ground was covered with scrub grass, weeds and rocks.

"Where are we going?" she asked, surprised by the timid sound of her voice.

"We're almost there," one of the men in the back seat said. "Just five more minutes."

"We're taking you to headquarters, young lady," the man in the front passenger seat called out in English. "We have people who will take care of your injury. Don't worry."

"What headquarters?" Nancy asked. "Who are you people?"

"You ask too many questions," the man in the front said. "You'll find out everything in due time."

Nancy half-smiled to herself, thinking of the irony. All her life, wherever she went, whomever she was with, someone always told her she asked too many questions. Especially her school teachers. Now some Iraqi militant was telling her the same thing. Only this time, instead of it meaning a poor grade, it could mean her life.

Yet questions were her stock-in-trade. Finding answers, figuring things out, making sense of lies and inuendos, all tools she needed if she were to survive. She swallowed her fear and looked with new eyes at these men. They didn't look Iraqi at all. A few wore thick beards, which were unusual for men in Iraq. And although she was no expert at Arabic, the bearded men didn't seem all that comfortable with the language. And while Arabic was obviously the native tongue of the guy who'd lifted her out of the rubble, his accent in English wasn't like the ones she heard every day around Baghdad.

Fear rose inside her again. She realized then who had kidnapped her. These indeed weren't Iraqis. They must be from an outside group, perhaps one affiliated with Al-Qaeda that were spreading through the countryside, fomenting terror and sectarian attacks. These groups, which until mid-2006 had been led by a charismatic but bloodthirsty terrorist named

Abu Musab Al-Zarqawi, were still potent even now that Zarqawi had been killed by American bombs. From what Nancy knew, the groups were even more dangerous now than they had been during Zarqawi's lifetime, and were bent on revenge for his death. Kidnappings and terror bombings were their stock-in-trade, and apparently, Nancy had become victim of both in a single moment.

Just then, the man in the back reached over and put something over her head – some sort of hood – and she couldn't see.

"Don't worry," he said in Arabic. "This is just so you can't tell anyone where we are. We won't hurt you. The prophet tells us never to hurt women and children." Nancy said nothing, thinking of the scene back at the school, with the little girl's legs blown off. She decided this wouldn't be a good time to argue.

The smelly hood covered her face, but Nancy didn't make any move to tear it off. Her main concern wasn't so much what would happen to her next as the worry she'd be causing Joanna and her parents.

"Can I call my family and let them know I'm OK?" she asked. The truck was turning right off the main road and onto a bumpy, rocky track. Her leg cried out every time they hit another pothole, and she had to clench her teeth to keep from groaning from the painful bumps.

"We have your phone," the man in front called back to her. "We'll let them know. Don't worry."

That's a laugh, Nancy thought. Don't worry, indeed. Don't worry about being kidnapped. Don't worry that she had no idea where she was. Don't worry that she appeared to be in the company of some branch of Al-Qaeda militants. Her gut clenched at the likelihood of her deadly fate, but then she realized that in a sense, her wishes had come true. She'd wanted to track down Al-Qaeda and interview them, and now, through no planning of her own, she was among them. At least she thought she was. Her wish may have come true, along with her deepest fears.

At last, the truck slowed and then stopped. The driver turned off the engine and she heard the men getting out, talking to each other in a strange language. The hatchback opened, and someone pulled her out gently and carried her away. She could hear birds calling, but there were no other sounds. The air felt warmer and wetter than it had in the city earlier that day, and there was no way to tell the time. It was a vulnerable feeling, being blindfolded and carried by a stranger to somewhere she had never been. She had no reason to believe they had been telling the truth about not harming women.

At last, the man set her down on what felt like a soft couch. "Here, drink," he said, and a bottle was put to her lips under the hood. She hesitated. "It's just water," he said, soothingly. She opened her mouth and let in the liquid. It felt good, erasing that parched feeling. She wondered how much blood she'd lost. Her leg felt strange, as if it were somehow turned the wrong way, and she guessed it was broken. Maybe something had fallen on it when the bomb went off.

The man took the hood off her face.

She was in a room with mud walls and thin fabric curtains covering the windows. The room seemed to be part of a bigger house or building, because there were doors leading out of it in both directions. The couch she lay on was threadbare with yellow stuffing coming out of it from a number of holes, and across from her, on an equally shopworn piece of living room furniture, sat the man who had lifted her out of the rubble. He was now wearing white robes and an expensive-looking silver watch. He was middle-aged, with a full black beard, dark, bushy eyebrows and somehow soothing brown eyes. His skin looked weathered and rough – as if he spent a lot of time in the sun. He didn't hold a gun, but standing behind him were two other men in similar dress, and both carried automatic weapons.

"Please," she said. "Please call my family and let them know I'm OK."

The man smiled. His teeth were yellow and crooked.

"Don't worry," he said in accented but perfectly understandable English. "We'll make sure your family knows you're safe. I'll keep your phone and you may get it back at some point."

"Why did you bring me here?" she asked. "Do you know I'm an American reporter?"

She immediately regretted saying that, wondering to herself if that would set her up for some extra punishment. Well, nothing to do now but hope she hadn't set herself apart in a way that would come back to haunt her.

"Yes, yes, you told us you were a journalist," the man said. "You are Nancy Hanson, from The New York Times, correct?"

At first Nancy was befuddled, and then she realized how they knew. It was her phone. They must have checked her emails, calls, everything on it. She felt naked.

He smiled again, as if this were some pleasant afternoon they were spending at his invite. "We'll have plenty of time to get to know each other better, and then you'll learn more about us. Right now, your leg needs tending to. We also need to get you something to eat." He had a formal way of talking, and his accent made him sound somewhat cultured.

He made a strange sort of whistle, and two men came through one of the door openings.

"These two will take care of you," he said. "They both know how to splint a broken leg. And don't worry about the blood. It looks like you just had some minor cuts. You haven't lost much blood. But your leg is broken." He motioned the men to come over, and Nancy saw one of them carried a medical box with a red cross on it.

An hour later, with her leg splinted, some painkillers swallowed, and Nancy eating the bread and hummus the men had provided her, she felt a bit more like herself. The pain was now a dull ache, and she felt sure the injury wasn't life threatening. Her kidnapper ate the same meal, washing it down with tea, which he offered Nancy. She tried some, and it was a green tea, but stronger than the green tea she'd had in the past. And it had flavors of cinnamon and honey as well. Her kidnapper had dismissed the men with the guns, and it was just the two of them for now.

"Do you like it?" the man asked in English, taking a sip himself. "It's a specialty in the land of my friends here."

"Really?" she asked, feeling more comfortable. "This is Iraqi tea?" She'd never heard of such a thing, but there was a lot about this culture she didn't know.

"I didn't say our land was Iraq," he replied, smiling again. "Some of us are from Afghanistan, and that's where the tea originated. I personally am a Yemeni. But we are all Muslim, and that's what matters." He took another sip and Nancy once again pleaded for him to let her talk to her daughter.

"We have notified the public that you are with us and safe," the man said. "Your family will be aware of this, so there's no need for us to do more at this time."

Part of her was grateful to the man for the food and for making sure that her family knew she was safe, if that part was even true. But she resisted the urge to feel any gratitude; she wouldn't let herself become a victim of "Stockholm Syndrome," where the victim becomes sympathetic to her kidnappers. And just what had "the public" been told about her anyway? What game were they playing with her and the media? "How long are you going to keep me here?" Nancy asked.

"I don't have answers to all of your questions," the man said gently, putting down his cup and staring at her with his somehow friendly brown eyes framed by that thick black beard with no signs of gray. "I'm not the one who makes all the decisions. You will be here for some time, and we will make you as comfortable as possible."

"What's the point?" she asked, her voice rising a little. "Are you going to ask for a ransom? Are you going to threaten to kill me? What do you get out of this?"

"So many questions," he replied, waving his hand a little as if to brush away a fly. "I will tell you what I can. We are fighters of the Mujhadeen. Your country has done a great deal of damage here and to our people in other Muslim lands. Your country is our enemy, and you have no business being in our lands. How many of our people has your country killed? Too many to count." As he spoke, his voice grew louder and his formerly calm eyes flashed with anger. "Our children are sick and dying from war in Palestine and here in Iraq. Your country supports the dictators who deprive our peoples of their rights, and who falsely claim power over our holiest land. What is one kidnapping compared to all of that, I ask you?" He leaned forward on the couch, glaring at her, all pretext of civility gone.

"Yes," Nancy replied, squelching an inner shudder at the man's sudden change of character, but determined not to appear weak. "I'm very sympathetic to what people here are going through. I've seen many of them killed and injured, and I've seen bombings…" She stopped, struggling to think of something she could say to calm him down. But he broke in, this time, more angrily.

"Sympathetic!" he yelled, jumping up and standing over Nancy, who was lying on her couch with her splinted leg balanced on the end. Nancy shrank back against the cushions. "Sympathetic? If you're sympathetic, what are you doing here, writing about your country's war against the Iraqi people? Your newspaper is one of the evil ones that preached in favor of sending your troops here. If you write for them, you're part of the problem! Don't ever tell me you're sympathetic!" His eyes, seemingly so friendly before, now looked piercing under furled brows, and at his rage, the other men stepped through the doorway, checking to see what could have happened to make him so angry. He saw them and waved them away. His face had reddened behind his beard, and sweat dripped down from his forehead.

Nancy wasn't easily intimidated by noisy, angry men, having dealt with politicians in Washington for so many years. Of course, the politicians hadn't kidnapped her or held her at gunpoint, but she knew the best way to get respect in situations like this was to not show fear.

"I am sympathetic," she replied, looking right at him as he sat down again, the redness in his face retreating a little. "I am. But when I see things like I saw this morning, it's hard to feel that way. Your men bombed that school and killed those little children! I saw it! How can you justify that? If you care so much about people, why bomb them? And if you're from Yemen, what are you doing here?"

He looked at her, the sparks in his brown eyes subsiding, his tone soft once again.

"All of that may become more clear in time. For now, you don't need to know."

"Are you Al-Qaeda?" she asked, looking right back at him.

"That too, you may find out in time," he replied. "I see no need to tell you now. Enough questions. And enough arguing. I need to calm down a little." He whistled again, and the same two men came back through the door. He spoke to them in the same language she'd heard earlier, and the men came over to her and lifted her off the couch gently so as not to hurt her leg.

"What's going on?" she asked as they started carrying her toward the doorway.

"Oh, so many questions!" he said again, but this time with a smile. "I will answer you." He got up and walked behind the men as they stepped through the doorway into another room, this one with a cot and a small pot that she guessed was a toilet. There were no windows or other doorways in here.

"This will be your room for a while," he said. "We may have to move to another site if it becomes necessary. I'm going to ask that my men not chain you or make you feel uncomfortable. I'm certain you couldn't get very far on that leg even if you managed to escape, anyway."

The men laid her gently on the cot, which had a small blanket and an even smaller pillow. There was no other decoration or furniture in the room, and it was dark except for light coming through the doorway. She realized that when they left and closed the door she'd have no light at all.

"Can you at least give me a light and something to read?" she asked.

"I'll see what I can do," her kidnapper replied. "We're going to leave now. If you need anything, just call. Someone in the next room will hear you."

The first two men exited, and her "friend," as she was beginning to think of him, was about to walk out as well when Nancy called out, "What's your name?"

He turned to her and smiled.

"Just call me Ram," he replied. He went out, and she heard the click of a lock after the door closed. The room became dark.

A while later (she had no sense of time, because they'd taken her watch as well), the door opened again, this time letting in an artificial light. She assumed it was nighttime. It was Ram, and he had a small flashlight and three books. "Here you go," he said, handing them to her.

"Thank you," she said.

He left and she turned the flashlight on and examined the volumes he'd brought in. One was an English copy of the Koran. She knew the book well, having studied it before she came to the Middle East. The other books were cheap Iraqi novels, written in Arabic. Well, at any rate, she could spend a little time trying to decipher them, she thought, and brush up on her language skills. She picked one up and began reading, trying to ignore the dread feeling in her stomach. As she read, she wondered what her parents and daughter might be reading about her now, and shuddered at the thought. Her conversation with her mother back in September played in her mind. She'd assured everyone she'd stay safe. But she'd been unable to keep her promise. She gave up trying to read the book, and gave in to tears.

CHAPTER 8
FLIGHT TO CHICAGO

A lev sat in her coach seat on the Lufthansa jet, looking out the window somewhere over the Atlantic. Her face, which she had made up carefully, looked tan and healthy. Her smartly-ironed light blue shirt made her bright blue eyes look even bluer than ever under their dark brows, and she wore her dark hair smooth and long over her shoulders. The sun shone brightly into the cabin, and she could see tiny white waves far below in the endless ocean. She'd brought several books on the flight, including the newest Jane Smiley novel. She loved American literature and was fascinated with the country, which she'd only visited twice. But she couldn't concentrate on reading. Even now, her mind raced, and she wondered why she'd agreed to go in the first place. Part of her wanted to stay at the airport after landing and look up the next flight back. But she knew she wouldn't do that.

What future could there be with this man, who had left her without warning five years ago and disappeared into another country? A man she knew had contacts and friends who may have been involved in terrorist plots?

But something she couldn't fight drew her toward him at the same time. There was something so different about Jarrah. They'd had such good times together in Germany. He wasn't like other Muslim men from the Middle East whom she had met; he had a fun-loving side, and he enjoyed a good beer and a good meal. He never acted fanatical about religion, which was good because she felt no interest in the subject whatsoever, and he knew it. She had never been able to understand why he hung around with religious fanatics, or his habit of mysteriously disappearing for months at a time without warning. Her friends teased her about her infatuation with the "dark stranger," and she supposed they had a point. It just wasn't in her nature to fall in love with someone conventional.

Besides her very real attraction to him, she wondered if her decision to take the trip reflected cultural baggage she'd absorbed from growing up in her immigrant Turkish community. Although her own parents had been rather liberal, there was a lot of pressure in the community for women to assume old-fashioned gender roles and find men to take care of them. She was one of many educated Turkish women who moved comfortably in the modern world and took on a professional career. But it's hard to escape old traditions, and lately, her mom and dad had made it pretty clear that they were disappointed she was still single.

Her parents had liked Jarrah back in the old days, and had joined her that fateful afternoon in the Berlin coffeehouse when they'd begged him to stay in Germany and make a new life with her instead of going back to his friends in America. She could still remember the look on his face at that moment in August 2001. She'd read in novels about a "shadow crossing" a character's face, but until then, she hadn't known what it meant. Two days later, he had left again and never come back.

"Would you like something to drink?" the uniformed male flight attendant asked in German, interrupting her reverie. He looked at her with a polite but bored smile, hands on the drink cart.

"Just water please; thank you," Alev replied back in German, with a quick smile that revealed her rather small teeth. Alev often passed for German with her light brown hair and blue eyes, and she'd lived there so long her accent was almost native.

The plane flew on, and clouds built up beneath it as the jet approached the U.S. coast.

CHAPTER 9
CHICAGO INTERLUDE

"Earlier this week, I observed several ground crew members at O'Hare acting suspiciously. Are these men doing their jobs, or are they attempting to help criminals load drugs or other materials onto airliners? As I've written in the past, the airline security here in the U.S. is a joke. It's far too easy for a rogue grounds crew member to put dangerous materials onto planes, and we may be seeing just that in these photos."

Adam nodded to himself after re-reading his entry and clicked, "post," making his latest blog entry live on line. He slapped his laptop closed and lay back on his bed.

He was a facile writer, and loved the craft. You could look on Adam's site and find restaurant reviews, movie reviews, album reviews and the odd political rant, all delivered in the humorous tongue-in-cheek manner Adam specialized in. The blog attracted a loyal audience of readers around the country who enjoyed Adam's irreverent style and weighed in with comments below his posts.

The site now featured photos he'd taken at O'Hare with Bob last week of what appeared to be O'Hare ground crew workers putting packages into a waiting 737. It was hard to tell from the photos what exactly was in the packages, but the men certainly didn't look comfortable. It looked like they were trying to hide what they were doing. Bob was certain that he and Adam had come across some sort of drug deal, but Adam wasn't exactly sure what was going on.

However, it certainly reinforced in his mind the hypocrisy of current airline security regulations, which forced everyone to wait in ridiculous lines and go through sophisticated scanners to get on a plane, even while airport workers had access to the same planes without any checks at all after their initial security clearance. He'd written before about the utter foolishness of this system, and now he had photos to back up his views.

He'd titled the post, "Funny Business at O'Hare?"

The nice thing about a blog, he thought, as he lay on his bed listening to heavy metal blast away on the stereo, was that he didn't have to back any of this up with real evidence. If he suspected something was going on, he could build his case over time. He remembered working at his college newspaper, and realized he could never have published something like this back then without doing a lot more fact checking. He'd read somewhere that nowadays, with the Internet, everyone could be a journalist. So true, and so rewarding!

• • •

Across town later that same December night, Jarrah stopped his cab in a parking lot outside a Dunkin' Donuts and pulled out his laptop. Rain tapped steadily against the cab's windows. He clicked on Adam's website, "Aircrash.com" and looked at the latest photos. He frowned. There was no doubt. He'd have to disable the site and take care of this guy right away. He began typing quickly in the dark of the car, NPR still quietly playing on the radio.

"We have a further update tonight on the disappearance of New York Times journalist Nancy Hanson, who's been missing since going on assignment on Thursday in east Baghdad, where she was present at the school bombing that killed four Iraqis and two U.S. soldiers," the NPR announcer said, and Jarrah listened more carefully as he expertly worked to remove the offensive blog post from Adam's site. "According to a message we obtained, it appears Hanson survived the bombing and was kidnapped by a militant group. The group released a photo of Hanson holding today's newspaper and wearing a cast on her leg. The group said Hanson is safe and in good condition, but they will hold her captive until the United States agrees to release 200 militants from U.S.-controlled Iraqi prisons. We talked today to Ron Kolarik, the New York Times' bureau chief in Baghdad, and he said it's likely that Hanson was captured by a group that's affiliated with Al-Qaeda in Iraq, the terror organization that's claimed responsibility for the school bombing, which was apparently aimed at Shiites and American and Iraqi soldiers. Kolarik spoke with us earlier today, and here's what he said."

Kolarik's voice, which had a faint British accent from his many years living in that country, came on:

"We're glad to hear that Nancy survived the bombing, but we have it on good authority that the group holding her is affiliated with Al-Qaeda, which obviously has us very worried. Nancy is a valuable member of our reporting staff here, and we will work closely with the U.S. military to find out where she's being held and to get her released. We know this is very hard on her family, and it's also hard on our New York Times family. We urge Nancy's kidnappers to release her immediately."

The NPR announcer returned.

"The U.S. embassy in Iraq has also demanded that Ms. Hanson be handed back over, but said it won't meet the kidnappers' demands. An embassy spokesman told us, 'The United States doesn't pay ransom to terrorists.' Still, we believe that behind the scenes, the U.S. will work to get Hanson released, as it has in other recent kidnappings of U.S. citizens in Iraq..."

Jarrah stopped typing for a moment, wondering which militants had captured the American. It was quite possible that the Director was behind this. The Director had lots of side projects besides the one Jarrah worked on, and maintained close contact with the Sheik. But Jarrah knew he'd never hear the full story, as the Director played things very close to the vest. Jarrah's mind returned to the project at hand, and though again of how much work they still had to do between now and May 2008, just 17 months away. "Are you sure you want to delete this entry?" the server asked him. Without pause, he clicked the "OK" button and sat back and waited for confirmation.

CHAPTER 10

VIRGIL RETURNS TO GOVERNMENT

In his new closet-sized, windowless office at the Pentagon, Virgil had NPR on to the same report and listened intently until it ended. The desk in front of him was littered with papers thrown about haphazardly. The office featured no personal mementos, only the laptop and the scattered papers. Virgil's tattered raincoat hung on the hook of the closed door.

Congress had quickly approved Harry's nomination as Defense Secretary, and here Virgil was, back in the Department of Defense, with an office just down the hall from Harry. As promised, Harry had greased the screws with Bush and Cheney to allow Virgil back into the government. But he still had to keep sensitive documents far from Virgil, which might make Virgil's job difficult. Unbelievable, Virgil thought, that even back in government, he still couldn't get the information he wanted. The White House continued to be paranoid that he'd leak something important. Evidently, an office with a window was also out of reach. Well, he was grateful for the paycheck, anyway.

Ostensibly, he was Harry's adviser on Al-Qaeda, but that left a lot of room for interpretation regarding his job responsibilities. He had latitude to do whatever he thought might uncover threats from the group, using his contacts in the Middle East and the CIA. And although he didn't have access to some documents, he did have access to a database of research that the government had compiled on Al-Qaeda since he'd left in 2001, and he found it both fascinating and frustrating to comb through.

For example, one document detailed the government's attempts, shortly after the hijackings, to determine if other terrorists had been aboard planes in the United States at the same time that day, the very observation Virgil had given the president the morning of the plane collision. The searchers had compiled the passenger manifests of every airplane that was on the ground or in the sky at the time of the collision, and had honed in on some names of interest. It appeared there had been groups of men with Arab-sounding names on aircraft that took off from Dulles and Newark that morning, bound for Los Angeles and San Francisco. Both planes had normal flights and landed as planned. The researchers had interviewed the flight crews of both planes shortly after Sept. 11, and the crews had reported nothing abnormal about the flights. The only abnormal thing – if it could be considered all that abnormal – was the preponderance of Middle Easterners on board the planes.

The researchers had done background checks of those Middle Easterners, and their criminal records were clean. The odd thing, however, was that most of them had only recently arrived in the United States – some as recently as earlier that same summer – and none seemed to have jobs or other reasons to be here. Also, two of the men – Jarrah and Hanjour – had taken flying lessons during the previous year. It appeared most of the men had left the United States shortly after the plane collision, and the government had lost track of their whereabouts. All red flags.

Virgil, even in his new position, didn't have access to the government's final conclusions on the men, and bitterly he realized why. It was quite likely that Hanjour and Jarrah had connections to the hijackers on American Flight 11 and United Flight 175, and the information was top secret. It didn't take Sherlock Holmes to figure that out. He had no way of knowing if they remained in the United States. He hoped that someone in the FBI kept tabs on them. Perhaps they'd been arrested and were in some secret prison, maybe in Iraq. He wouldn't put that beyond the capabilities of a guy like Tenet and his team at the CIA, and it would renew his faith in Dick Cheney if it turned out the VP had indeed followed the mens' tracks and gotten them locked up. A Google search of their names turned up nothing consequential.

It occurred to him he should take the information to Harry to make sure he had it, and let Harry look into the matter to get a sense of whether the two men were under lock and key or still on the loose somewhere. The whole thing was so damned frustrating! Why bring him back if he couldn't access the information he needed to do his job? How odd to be back in the government, working for a man he respected, and still be dealing with the same type of roadblocks he'd had back at the White House.

"I understand how you feel," Harry had told him earlier in the week. Harry had been dressed in a new dark suit and sitting behind an antique wooden desk in his vast new office, but still managed to look casual and comfortable, leaning back in his brown leather chair with one cowboy-booted foot up on the desk. "We just have to be patient. I used up some of my good graces with them arguin' to get you back in the first place, so now we have to live with some limits, I guess. I reckon we'll have 'em eating out of our hands in a little while. You just do what you can now, and trust your instincts. Bring me anything you find and I'll try to polish the wheels so we can get it up the chain."

Another report he'd found in the database made some vague references to the shadowy figure who had worked with Bin Laden to direct the hijackings. This appeared to be the same Khalid Sheikh Mohammed, or KSM, whom Virgil's own contacts had spoken of. Further information on this character and his whereabouts were classified.

He was still searching through the database to see what else he could find when the NPR report came on about the New York Times reporter's kidnapping. It was the first he'd heard of it, and he immediately thought back to the conversation he'd had with Nancy back at the Thai restaurant five years ago. He hadn't talked to her since, but now her pleasant but somewhat intense face came to his mind. He had no idea Nancy had ended up in Baghdad, but the news report shifted his thoughts from the aircraft collision to his network of contacts in Iraq. One reason Harry had brought him in was to help get a better sense of who was behind the constant sectarian attacks in that country.

Al-Qaeda was obviously at the core of it, but the organization was a spider web of different affiliated groups, all working under its large tent but with their own leaders and sometimes their own intentions. Virgil, who had worked for the CIA and the Department of Defense during the 1980s and 1990s, when the U.S. funded militant groups to fight the Soviets in Afghanistan and had fought the Gulf War, had strong connections in the region, even with groups that were now fighting against the U.S. He sat back in his chair, ran his hand through his thinning hair and wondered who in Iraq he knew might be able to help rescue the reporter. He thought about notifying Harry before taking on this new project, but didn't want to bother the man, who was no doubt slammed with meetings as he adjusted to the new position. He didn't think Harry would mind much if he did a little digging on this.

His mind turned to an Iraqi friend of his, a man who had lived in both the U.S. and Iraq, and made a good living trading stocks on the Iraqi stock exchange. He hadn't talked to the guy in years, and now he fished out his huge old Filofax (he'd never gotten used to keeping track of contacts electronically) and flipped through the battered hand-written notecards, some of them stained by long-ago coffee spills. Ah, here it was. Aban Kanaan. He smiled when he saw the notecard, thinking about the fellow, an irascible jokester whose sense of humor got him through his country's hard times.

Kanaan had been a good source for him back in the days of the U.S. food for oil program in the 1990s, as Kanaan had contacts with Iraqi food companies that he invested in and could give Virgil a sense of whether U.S. food deliveries were getting to the right people. He knew Kanaan had a pretty wide network across various business groups in the country, but he'd also dabbled in some more interesting (and lucrative) products than food, including weapons and military gear.

The man certainly took some risks getting involved with that side of things, but Virgil figured that might make him a valuable source of information on weapons shipments and who in the country was aiding militant groups, as well as a possible source for ideas on who might have kidnapped the reporter. The question was, would Kanaan even remember him, and how would he get in touch? He looked at the cell phone number on the card and realized it was at least seven years old. People changed cell phones all the time.

Of course, helping rescue U.S. reporters kidnapped by Al-Qaeda wasn't exactly in Virgil's job description, but then again, he didn't really have a job description. Since Virgil was frustrated with his lack of access to documents related to Al-Qaeda in the United States, perhaps he could go through the back door and probe into the group through its presence in Iraq. Without pausing for further thought, he called the number on the card. He immediately regretted dialing the phone, realizing it would be about 3 a.m. in Iraq, but the loud beeps of a foreign phone ringing were already pulsing in his ear, so it was too late now.

"Ebn el metanaka!" a voice swore in Arabic. Virgil recoiled at the noise. From his rusty knowledge of Arabic, he knew what the words meant. "Son of a bitch!" He hung up the phone gently, hoping it was a wrong number. If it were Kanaan, he might not be too happy once he found out the caller was Virgil. But no, that wasn't how Kanaan would react. Kanaan was used to late-night phone calls. Probably a wrong number.

He Googled Kanaan and found what appeared to be the man's number at the company he ran. It was worth a try, anyway, but just in case, he'd wait until daytime in Iraq.

He got in touch with Kanaan the next morning.

"Virge!" the voice at the other end of the phone exclaimed. "A salamu a laykum! What's happening, man?" Virgil smiled, remembering how Kanaan, from the time he'd spent in the United States, had picked up some U.S. slang to mix into his accented English. The phrase, "What's happening, man?" coming from Kanaan sounded slightly amusing.

"Well, Aban, I got shipped off to the retirement home for a few years, but now I'm back," Virgil said, putting his shoeless feet up on the little desk in his office. "I'm wondering if you can put me in touch with anyone there who might have some sense of who kidnapped that New York Times journalist last week – Nancy Hanson. It's kind of a personal thing, not official you know. She's an old acquaintance of mine."

"Oh yes," Kanaan said. "I know all about that – it's all over the news here. But I don't deal with people like that – Al-Qaeda. You learn to keep away from those guys if you're here – they'll kill you quick. I got out of that weapons stuff a long time ago. They would have beheaded me, and I think my neck looks better with something on top of it." He laughed. "I still have a bodyguard, you know. I'm too well known."

"Why don't you leave the country?" Virgil asked. "I'm sure we could keep you safe here. You helped us a lot back in the day."

"Yeah, but that would be the easy way, bro!" Kanaan said with another laugh. "I don't do things the easy way, you know. I've got a business here. I couldn't just leave all my people behind. Besides, there's money to be made. Look, I'll see what I can do to help you with this reporter thing. I know some people who know some people. Maybe they can track her down. You guys going to pay their ransom? They want a couple hundred prisoners freed, right?"

"I don't know, I don't know," Virgil said, running his hands through his hair. Seemed like he could feel more of his bare scalp every day. "Just see what you can do. I appreciate it."

"No problem, man," Kanaan said. "If I hear anything, I'll let you know."

Virgil hung up, again trying to swallow his feeling of irrelevance. He told himself not to think about Nancy. She'd been the one to accept the assignment over there, and she'd known the risks. But it was one thing to read about terrorist kidnappings; it was another to know the victim. He wondered if he was somehow responsible for it, indirectly. Perhaps if she hadn't gotten so much acclaim from that scoop he'd given her, she wouldn't have been promoted to go over there in the first place.

"Dammit," he said, and brought his feet down from the desk.

CHAPTER 11

CHICAGO BREAK-IN

ang! A crashing sound woke him. Bang! There it was again. Someone pounding on Adam's door. It was easy to hear because his apartment only had one room, and he slept just feet from the front entrance. His cat Elmer ran under the bed to hide.

"Open up, buddy!" someone called from the hallway. "Wake up, little sleepyhead," came a sing-song voice.

Adam's heart pounded in his chest. He glanced at the bedside clock. It read 2:17 a.m. He wondered if he should just pretend not to be here. Maybe if he was quiet long enough, whoever it was would go away.

"All right, buddy. I know you're there," came the voice. "I'm waiting for you to come out, even if I have to wait till morning."

Adam reached for the phone to dial 911. Just then, the door came flying open and a heavyset black man, about 6 feet 4 and wearing a black ski mask that revealed just his eyes and mouth, stormed into the apartment and tore the phone out of Adam's hands before he could dial. A thick, hairy arm covered his mouth, stifling his scream, and he was dragged into the corner. The man used a booted foot to slam the front door even as he pinned Adam down against the floor and kept an arm over his mouth. Adam moved his head around trying to get away, but the man's grip simply tightened on him. The faint light from a streetlight outside the window glistened in the man's glaring eyes.

"Buddy, you listen to me and listen close," the man said, more quietly but firmly. "We know what you're up to. We've seen your website. We've seen you out at the airport. We have a pretty big deal going down, and you and your numb nuts buddy can't stop it. So do you know what we're going to do?"

Adam shook his head as well as he could with the man's arms wrapped around it.

"Well, we're going to make a little deal," the man said. "I'm going to give you a small amount of funding, and you're going to take it and agree to never tell anyone what you saw, and to never put anything on the Internet about it. You're also going to give me your user name and password for the blog. Break our little deal, and we'll break you, my man. We'll break you and your pal. Now does that make sense?"

"Yeth," Adam struggled to say, his mouth still buried in the skin of the man's arm.

"Good," said the man, still holding Adam tight. He thrust a pen and a notepad at Adam and watched carefully as Adam wrote down the blog information and handed it back. "Very good. This had better work, buddy."

"It will," Adam said, regretfully. He didn't have the courage to give fake information.

The man stuffed the pad into one of the pockets of his blue down jacket and turned to leave. Then he turned around to face Adam again.

"Oh yeah," the man said. "I have a small envelope for you that I'm going to leave on your bed before I go. Any phone calls to the police, and you're going to hear from me again. But trust me, fatso, you don't want that to happen."

"OK, OK – just let me go," Adam stammered, finally getting his mouth away from the arm and into some fresh air. The man smelled of cigarettes and BO.

The man loosened his grip and patted Adam gently on the head. "Very good, very good, my man," he said. "I'll be leaving now. And let's not see each other again, OK?"

"Yeah, yeah," Adam said, struggling to get his breath as he lay sprawled on the floor. The man got up, drew an envelope from the pocket of his dark jacket and tossed it on Adam's bed.

"Nice place you got here, buddy," he said, looking around at the dark, messy little room. "You sleep tight now. No hard feelings, OK?" Adam shook his head to show that yeah, everything was just hunky dory. He even managed a weak little smile. The man playfully wagged his fingers good-bye and stepped out the door, closing it quietly behind him.

When Adam finally stopped hyperventilating, he raised himself off the floor and stumbled over to his bed. He flipped on the bedside lamp and opened the envelope. Hundred-dollar bills tumbled out onto the blanket.

CHAPTER 12
A POTENTIAL OPENING

Virgil sat at his desk, still simmering with resentment about not getting access to the material he needed. Suddenly, he heard the distinctive thump outside of Harry's polished brown cowboy boots, and the door swung open. Harry wasn't much for knocking on doors. He just walked in as if he'd been invited. This bothered Virgil, but he was getting used to it. Harry held a file in one hand and waved it at Virgil, a smile lighting up his leathery face.

"Virge," Harry drawled, walking up to Virgil's desk and dropping the file on it. "I got this from a buddy over at the FAA the other day. I guess they don't have a lot goin' on over there, so they spend some time surfin' the web, and they came across something I thought you might find interesting. Or maybe you won't, but I'll let you decide." Virgil looked down at the file.

"Go ahead," Harry said, "open it up."

Virgil opened the file. There was just one page inside – a copy of an Internet page, it seemed. And not too professional either, from the look of it. Probably someone's homemade web site. He read the paper while Harry watched, a half smile on his red face.

"*Funny Business at O'Hare?*" was the title.

"*Earlier this week, I observed several grounds crew members at O'Hare acting suspiciously. Are these men doing their jobs, or are they attempting to help criminals load drugs or other materials onto airliners? As I've written in the past, the airline security here in the U.S. is a joke. It's far too easy for a rogue grounds crew member to put dangerous materials onto planes, and we may be seeing just that in these photos."*

There was a photo under the article, but it was hard to make anything out. It appeared to be of a grounds crew loading a package onto a plane. The photo itself didn't look too extraordinary to Virgil, but the implications were obvious.

Virgil looked up at Harry. "Does the FBI know about this?" he asked.

"Oh yeah, they're aware," Harry said. "I happen to know they're on it. But I wanted you to see it because..."

"Because of the terrorism implications," Virgil interrupted.

"Yeah, exactly," Harry replied.

"We've always known airport security is a weakness," Virgil said. "I've never felt the measures taken since 2001 did much to protect anyone. Far too many ways to get around them."

"Yeah, and it looks like these folks were tryin' to do just that," Harry said.

"Any sense if they were successful?"

"Well, not yet, anyway. The plane you see in the photo there took off and landed with no incidents. The FBI thinks these fellas might have been doing a test run, you see."

Virgil nodded, tapping his fingers on his desk at the same time. "Right," he said. "They probably made contacts with some disgruntled airport ground workers, paid them to load items onto some planes and checked to see if they could get away with it. Probably started with some non-lethal items, and maybe now they'll work their way up to something bigger."

"Now we're not sure it's lethal stuff these folks have in mind," Harry said, scratching behind one of his big ears. "This may be a drug thing. We've seen that before."

"True, true," Virgil said. "But my job is to look into any terrorism implications. Let's just say, for the sake of argument, that these guys are planning to hijack a plane. How do you do that nowadays, with the post-2001 measures we've taken? You can't get on a plane with a box cutter any more. And it's probably going to be tough for a whole group of terrorists to board a plane, with the better background checks we have now. So what do you do? You streamline your operation and raise your weapon profile. Maybe just one or two terrorists, but this time with guns instead of box cutters. You get the disgruntled airport workers to get the guns onboard for you, because they don't have to go through a metal detector. It's a huge hole in the security apparatus."

"Yeah, but how do they get into the sealed cockpit?" Harry asked.

"Oh, that's pretty simple, I suppose," Virgil said. "Put a gun to a flight attendant's head and force her to open the cockpit door. Or wait till she's delivering breakfast to the pilots and force their way in then."

Harry nodded. "Yep, that sounds right to me," he said.

"Now of course this is all just theory on my part," Virgil said. "I have no sense of whether there's a plot afoot. It's like I told you last week – I don't have access to a lot of the stuff I need to track down those guys who may have gotten away in '01. Have you gotten to my memo yet?"

"Yeah, yeah, I'm sorry, Virge. This job, it's a bitch. The Iraq thing – it just takes all my time. I promise I'll get to the memo as soon as I can and get you what you need."

"OK," Virgil said. "And I promise not to jump to conclusions based on this. By the way, has the FBI been able to track down the perpetrators?" He stood up and began pacing around the room.

"Not yet," Harry replied. "But I reckon they have a decent idea. Maybe they're closin' in."

"What about the guy who runs the blog?" Virgil asked. "Any info on him?"

"I'll leave that to you and the FBI, Virge," Harry said, cracking a smile. "I'm no good at snoopin' the way you and your friends are over there."

"Mr. Secretary?" a voice came in from the hallway. Harry turned. His assistant was standing in the door.

"Well, now, looks like I spent too long chatting with my buddy Virge and got running late," Harry said. "How late am I, Vic?"

"Not too bad sir," the assistant said, glancing at his wristwatch. "About five minutes."

"Ah, that's the nice thing about being on top," Harry said to Virgil with a smile. "They all have to wait for me. OK, I'm comin'. Let me know where you get with that, Virge."

"No problem," Virgil said. "I'll keep you posted."

"Say, Virge," Harry said. "Did I ever tell you about the memo Rummy sent to me and a few other guys a couple years ago?"

"I don't think so, Harry, why?"

"The subject line was, 'Issues with various countries,' and the memo went somethin' like, 'We need to solve the Pakistan problem, and Korea doesn't seem to be going well. Are you coming up with some proposals for me to send around?'"

Virgil's laughter followed Harry out of the room.

Once Harry left, just for the hell of it, Virgil typed in the URL of the airplane web site to see if there was anything further. But when he tried to get on, he got a message that the site was down. He tried refreshing it a couple of times, but no luck. "Dammit," he muttered to himself. He just had to learn to get better at this Internet stuff. Being 54 in 2006 was no picnic. His sons were both in tech-related jobs, and they could run circles around him on the computer. Maybe, Virgil thought, he should have one of them be an assistant. Of course he'd probably drive them nuts with his grumpiness. "Dad, you've always been a glass half-empty kind of guy, haven't you?" his younger son Keith had told him last weekend when they met for coffee and Virgil had complained about his lack of access to documents. He didn't like hearing that from his son, but he had to admit there was a lot of truth there. Kids these days seemed to be OK saying anything they wanted to their parents. He couldn't imagine telling his own dad something like that back when he was 24.

Harry sighed and Googled Adam's name, but didn't come up with much. It was pretty difficult to find out anything about anyone on the Internet, Virgil reflected. He guessed that the FBI was probably working to track the guy down and put it out of his mind for now.

Later that day, Virgil's phone rang. It was his buddy Kanaan in Baghdad.

"Hey, my man," Kanaan said. "How's the weather over there?"

"Pretty good," Virgil said. "A lot better here in the winter than the summer, the way I see it."

"Oh yeah, same here," Kanaan replied, laughing. "You know the scene over here – 120 degrees all summer. Sidewalks practically melting. Probably the sun drives everyone crazy. Maybe you move everyone in Baghdad to Washington, and no more wars. Ha ha."

"Yeah, right," Virgil said, impatient with the man's jokes. "So, did you find out anything?"

"Look, Virge, about your friend the reporter, you never heard nothing from me," Kanaan said. "I don't want to get my head cut off, you know. But I do have some buddies over here, and they think they know a bit about those guys that took her. Do you have a pen?"

"Yeah, I'm getting it now," Virgil said, fumbling for a pen in his can of writing utensils. The first one was broken and he threw it across the room. The second one worked.

"OK," Kanaan said. "They're almost certainly Al-Qaeda. No one's claimed credit for the bombing at the school, but it's just like all the others they've done. You know – killing the Shiites, suicide bomber, all that."

"Right," Virgil said, nodding.

"What my guys can't figure out is why this lady got kidnapped," Kanaan said. "Usually there's just one car and it blows up and that's it. But it sounds like this time there was another group of guys behind the first car, and they went in and tried to find someone to kidnap. Guess they thought it would be easier to do with all the smoke and stuff, you know, grab someone and take them away for ransom. Anyway, someone saw this truck leaving the scene with some foreign-looking guys in it. No way they're Iraqis, no way. The truck went off to the east, but no one knows exactly where, but they know the make and model and I got one of my best guys looking into it. He'll let me know if he finds out anything."

"Very good, Kanaan, very good," Virgil replied. "Good to have friends like you."

"Hey man, you help me, I help you," Kanaan said. "One hand washes the other, that's what they say, right?" Virgil smiled, once again amused by Kanaan's quest to learn American slang. They hung up and Virgil's mind returned to the Chicago thing, wondering what step to take next.

CHAPTER 13

ALEV AND JARRAH

I t was Alev's third morning in Jarrah's small but neat apartment, and the two were lying together in bed. They'd gone right back to intimacy as if five years hadn't passed, and Alev still felt comfortable and safe in Jarrah's arms. She'd had relationships with other Muslim men, but they hadn't treated her as kindly and thoughtfully as Jarrah, nor as gently.

They'd spent the last two days exploring the city, with Jarrah giving her a private tour in his cab. He took her to the top of the Sears Tower, to Pizzeria Uno for Chicago-style deep-dish pizza and to the Museum of Science and Industry, which they both loved — no surprise considering their respective engineering and medical backgrounds. At the museum, he'd grabbed her hand as they watched baby chickens pecking their way out of eggs in a huge glass-covered incubator, and said casually, "It would be fun to take our children here someday, wouldn't it?" They looked at each other and smiled, and her heart skipped a beat at the thought that he might finally be ready to settle down with her for the long term. But that was the only reference he'd made to any future plans. His actual life remained a mystery to her, and except for that one comment, he seemed reluctant to talk about anything beyond casual topics.

Now he lay back, silently, naked on top of the generic blue blanket that looked like a Wal-Mart special. She snuggled closer to him, but he pulled away and got up, starting to dress in the clothes he'd hung up on the chair next to the bed before retiring last night. The morning sunlight poked through the cheap white shade.

"Where are you going?" Alev asked, rubbing her eyes. "It's Saturday, you know."

"Saturday is a big day if you drive a cab," Jarrah said, tying his shoes. "I want to get an early start."

Alev yawned. She was naked too, but still under the covers.

"Why do you drive a cab?" she asked. "You studied engineering. Why can't you get a job doing that?"

"It's really complicated," he said. "Look, I'll be busy this morning, but do you want to meet for lunch? I know a good place. You'll like it."

"Do they have any vegetarian choices?"

"Oh yeah. Definitely. It's a Mediterranean place." He came up and kissed her cheek. "I'll pick you up at noon."

He left the apartment, giving her a house key so she could go out if she wanted. But she wasn't familiar with this strange American city, and didn't know where she'd go if she did go out.

Instead, she sat in Jarrah's small living room, which had a window overlooking the El tracks. Trains rattled by every 10 minutes or so, like clockwork, and the entire 1920s three-story brick building shook each time one passed by, as if the building were somehow tied to the elevated railroad. She noticed the trains didn't come as often on weekends as they had the last few days, but the noise still surprised her each time. She wondered if people living near the tracks ever grew used to it.

Jarrah's apartment resembled a blank book. No family photos or any souvenirs of his life. Bland-colored furniture that looked seldom used. The pantry held some bare essentials, including coffee, which she was sipping now. It was a weak American brew, she found to her dismay. His few and simple clothes hung neatly in the bedroom closet, and he made his bed every day as neatly if he were in the army. Not a wrinkle to be found.

The shelves held a small assortment of books, and she got up and looked through them again, as she had when she first arrived a few days earlier. There were multiple copies of the Koran, which she thought was strange considering she'd never known Jarrah to be very religious. And there were some other volumes related to Islam, including one by Sayyid Qutb that she hadn't noticed before. She vaguely remembered Qutb as the founder of the Muslim Brotherhood in Egypt, who'd been hanged by the Egyptian government back in the 1960s. She thumbed through it for a few minutes and a quote jumped out at her.

"History has recorded the wicked opposition of the Jews to Islam right from its first day in Medina. Their scheming against Islam has continued since then to the present moment, and they continue to be its leaders, nursing their wicked grudges and always resorting to treacherous schemes to undermine Islam."

She frowned. She hadn't remembered Jarrah ever talking about Qutb, but the book brought back her fears about what he might be up to. Had he fallen back in with his old friends? With an unconscious shake of her head, she placed the book back and looked at the rest of the shelf. There was nothing else too interesting. Just some Chicago guidebooks and maps, and a few detective novels.

Suddenly she felt guilty. Why was she spying on Ziad? Well, she justified to herself, he hadn't been very open with her about why he was living here, and tomorrow was her flight home. Studying his bookshelves seemed logical enough. She decided today's lunch would be her best chance to get an understanding of his plans. Did they have a future together? Would he consider moving back to Germany? And why was he driving a cab in Chicago? She knew one thing: her feelings for Ziad ran deep, and spending this time together with him reinforced her desire to be with him. Her skin tingled at his touch and she longed to truly know this man she loved. But what of his feelings for her?

Not long after noon that day, the two sat at a window table in the tiny, Persian-rugged storefront restaurant on North Broadway in Chicago's busy East Lakeview neighborhood. They sipped warm, savory carrot soup and Alev decided it was far and away the best thing she'd eaten since she'd arrived in Chicago. She could even forgive the place for its choice of music: The Gypsy Kings. After they ordered their entrees, Jarrah picked at a piece of pita bread and seemed preoccupied. Outside on the sidewalk, the weekend crowds bustled by wrapped in warm coats but undeterred by the chilly December weather.

"Ziad?" she asked, when things grew quiet for a moment.

"Yes?" He turned to her. He'd been looking out the window.

"What do you think of Jews?" Alev asked.

His forehead wrinkled.

"Why do you ask?" he said slowly, folding his arms. He was wearing a blue button-down oxford shirt.

"I saw you had a book by Qutb on your shelf, and he's an anti-Semite. I read a quote in there and it called the Jews wicked."

"The book says a lot of things, Alev," Jarrah said, looking at her intently. "It's not just about Jews."

"You don't like them though, do you?" she asked.

He stared at her for a minute. "It's complicated," he finally said.

"Why do you keep saying that?"

"What?"

" 'It's complicated, it's complicated,' " she parroted, and was glad to see his brow furrow, because she knew she was getting through enough to annoy him. "Ziad, life is complicated. But saying so doesn't give you an excuse not to talk to me about things." As always, he was being mysterious, and it frustrated her to no end.

"We've talked about a lot of things since you got here," he said, picking up a piece of pita and dipping it in his soup. "I'll talk to you about anything you want."

"OK," Alev said, taking a careful sip of the warm, comforting soup so as not to drip it on her black sweater. "What are you doing here?"

"You know that," he answered matter-of-factly. "I'm driving a cab."

"Don't talk to me like I'm stupid, Ziad. I know that. But why here, and why now?"

"I'm making good money," he said, looking away again. "It's not forever."

"What about us?" she asked quietly, reaching across the table for his hand. "You said something the other day about having kids. Did you mean it?"

"Sure, sure," he said, dropping her hand and turning red, as if embarrassed that he'd said such a thing. "But that's a long way off. Let's just live one day at a time."

"No," she answered firmly. "I lived one day at a time with you back in Germany and you never committed to me. Then you left, and didn't call me for five years. Five years! If you want to be with me, you have to make a commitment. You're very important to me and I care about you a lot, but I'm worried." Her blue eyes looked into his imploringly.

"Why are you worried?" he asked, reaching for her hand again. She dropped hers into her lap and continued to stare at him.

"Because you're hiding something from me," she replied. "You've gotten mixed up with those bad people again, haven't you?"

He looked down, not meeting her gaze.

"I'm going back tomorrow," she said firmly. "You can come with me. Even if there aren't any seats on my flight, you can book another ticket and be back in a few days if you want." He continued to look down and away from her. She took a breath and sat up straighter as she finished. "But if I go back and you don't agree to come too, we have no future together. I'm not just someone you can call out of the blue every few years and keep me around till you get tired of me. You're going to have to choose. It's me or them."

This time, she really meant it about cutting things off. This visit wasn't turning out the way she had hoped. She thought if they spent time together, he'd be his old self, but the person sitting across from her seemed like a stranger. Her heart ached to see, once again, that she'd lost the man she cared for so much.

He continued to gaze at the table, randomly pushing around bread crumbs with his fingers. There was silence as the server, a small, brown-skinned young man with a moustache, set down their food – vegetable kababs for him and vegetarian couscous for her. Neither of them picked up a fork.

Finally, he looked up again and spoke.

"Alev, I can't make a promise like that," he said. "I've made a commitment to people here, and they're counting on me. I've got to go through with it."

"Go through with what, Ziad? Driving a cab?" she asked, looking into his eyes.

"No, not the cab," he started, and then quickly added, "Nothing. Nothing. It doesn't concern you. But I've got to stay."

"Then why did you call me?" she asked, finally taking his hand. "What made you want to see me?"

"It's like I told you; I'm lonely," he replied. "But I can't go back with you. I just can't. I'd like to, but it wouldn't be right."

"It would be right to go back if you're mixed up with those bad people again. Don't you see? They want to hurt others. They hate non-Muslims.

They hate women. You're not like that, Ziad. You're just not." There were tears in her eyes as she looked at him. He looked away.

"Stop crying, Alev," he said quietly. "You know I don't like that."

"I don't care," she replied, but she wiped away the tears anyway. Then she took her fork and began eating, tears still forming in her eyes.

After a few more bites amid more silence, she put down her fork.

"Ziad," she said slowly.

"Yes, Alev?"

"You're not planning to hurt people, are you?"

He looked back out at the sidewalk.

"Ziad...?"

"Let's eat," he said.

He began hungrily attacking the food on his plate, but she just twirled her fork around her couscous aimlessly, not taking a bite. He didn't seem to notice. But she'd noticed some things about him. He'd ordered vegetarian food, and hadn't eaten meat the entire time she'd been with him. He also hadn't ordered a beer, though he used to have one with every meal back in Germany.

Ava smiled as she thought back on those days, especially the weekend trip they'd taken to Passau, an ancient town of red-roofed houses, winding streets and churches perched on a peninsula stretching like a finger into the Danube. He'd loved going into towers of the old public buildings and climbing to the roofs to look out at the scenery. She'd never been much for that, preferring to sit at a café nearby with her book and listen for him to call down to her once he reached the top. "Ava!" he'd call, waving frantically at her from the rampart of an ancient castle or the uppermost window of a medieval church. She'd put her book down, smile, and give a small wave back, feeling slightly embarrassed as others looked at her, wondering what she was waving at. But he'd never let her get away without acknowledging him.

"Aren't you hungry, Ava?" he asked, looking up from his nearly clean plate. She'd been staring out the window as she thought, fork in hand. He wiped his clean-shaven face with a cloth napkin and took a sip of water.

"I'm just thinking back," she said. "Remember how you used to love climbing towers and waving to me?"

He looked confused for a second, as if he didn't remember at all. Then a smile slowly came to his face.

"We were so young and innocent back then," Ziad said, reaching across the table for her hand. His eyes gazed into hers for a moment, then looked away again.

"We're still young," she said, smiling back.

"You're younger than me, remember," he replied. "Now go on, don't let yourself get hungry. I'll wait while you finish."

CHAPTER 14

HELD HOSTAGE

After two weeks in her little room, with only a short break here and there for a blindfolded walk outside to breathe fresh air, Nancy was more bored than terrified. Her captors had let her write a note to Joanna and her parents, so that was good, but as much as she begged, they wouldn't let her speak to them. "We can't take the chance of cell phone calls," Ram had told her. "That would probably give away our position."

She'd started thinking of Ram as a kind of Jekyll and Hyde. She'd never been too interested in fantasy novels; her tastes ran more to political non-fiction like Bob Woodward and Arthur Schlesinger, and when she did feel like light reading it was usually something trashy like *Us Magazine*. But her daughter was a huge *Lord of the Rings* fan, and Nancy had sat through the entire film trilogy, swallowing her boredom the best she could in an attempt to be a good sport.

Ram, she decided, reminded her of Gollum, the character in the Lord of the Rings with the split personality, one side fawning and friendly, the other vicious and enraged. Ram could be pleasant for long periods, explaining patiently to her why his religion permitted the sort of terrorism that Nancy had seen throughout the country and why Shiites and Muslim rulers of Arab countries could be legitimately marked for death. The topics weren't pleasant, but Ram approached them calmly with her, and never yet had he or anyone else caused her any physical harm. He emphasized again and again that he and his men considered it theologically forbidden to hurt a woman. She wasn't about to mention that this contradicted what she'd seen and heard about their culture. She was just grateful she'd been treated well so far. Her leg seemed to be healing nicely, and she could place her weight on it a little. They'd given her a crutch that she used to get exercise in the yard, blindfolded and guided along.

But Ram could go from pleasant to enraged in a split second, and Nancy never knew quite when to expect it. Just yesterday, in a discussion that had wandered from Muslims and their acceptance of other religions to the coming Iraqi elections, Ram exploded when she mentioned Israel.

"Why is your country so supportive of the Zionist entity?" he'd cried out, waving his arms and stalking around the room. "Do the lives of Palestinians mean less to your government than the lives of others? Ever since I was a child, Israel has been killing innocent Palestinians with no response from America, using American weapons!" He continued pacing, and suddenly, with one hand, swept a newspaper off of a little table onto the hard mud floor. "And if one Israeli is killed by a Palestinian, whose cause is just, that's an excuse for more Israeli violence! Death to Israel! As the Sheik has said, 'We will stand by the oppressed Palestinians and fight the Jews and their allies!' "

Although Nancy was momentarily shocked by Ram's invective, she had grown somewhat used to his rants, so she waited patiently until the red drained from his face and he'd sat down to drink a cup of tea, usually a sign that the yelling was over. He'd said one thing that was interesting, and she asked him about it once he'd calmed down.

"Who's the Sheik?" she had asked.

Ram replied. "You really don't know? Well, I'll let you figure that out, yourself. He is near and dear to me, and you may meet him in time. May peace be upon him."

Nancy had her own idea about whom the Sheik might be, but decided to keep her mouth shut for now regarding her suspicions that Ram worked for Bin Laden. She'd work on Ram the way she'd learned to work on sources over time as a journalist. It was tough for someone with her lack of patience, and she had to fight the urge to probe Ram for further information. No use sending him off the deep end again.

"OK," Nancy said. "I'll look forward to learning more. In the meantime, can you give me a sense of how long you're going to keep me here? Are you holding me for ransom? You know America never pays ransoms."

"No, we're not holding you for ransom," Ram said, sitting down and taking a sip of tea. "We aren't hungry for dirty American money. We only want back what America took from us – our people. We were fighting in this land and the Americans interfered where they had no business. We want American troops out and our fighters back. That's how you'll get released. Do you think you're the only one we hold? Oh no. We have many Western prisoners, and the same demands for all of them. Your country will eventually yield to our demands. The Americans have no backbone for a long fight with us, especially in our own lands. I trust you will eventually win your freedom, but I have no control over when that will be."

"But you do have control," Nancy argued, deciding to press a little. "You have me right here. You could let me go any time you wish, so I can go back to my daughter."

Nancy thought she saw the man wince a little when she said this. She'd appealed to him in the past using her daughter as bait, and it seemed to be a good way to get under his skin. She didn't know much about him, but she did know he was far from home and family. Perhaps he had a daughter or son he missed as well.

"Enough," he replied in a less friendly manner. "That's enough for now. Time to go back to your room." He whistled for his men, and they came to escort her.

"If you're going to make me go back in, at least give me something different to read, will you?" Nancy asked, turning her head over her shoulder to look back at Ram as the men led her away. "I've gotten through the entire Koran, and those Iraqi novels are pretty hard to read, even if I were good at Arabic."

Ram spoke to his men in their language, which she guessed was Pashto or Dari, and one of them nodded. A few minutes after she was locked up in the room, which smelled of urine from the bucket that served as her toilet, the man came back with a few more books – hardcover ones. Nancy shone her flashlight on them. None were in English or Arabic.

"I can't read these," she said, knowing the man wouldn't understand her. Some of Ram's men spoke decent English, but this wasn't one of them. She tried again in Arabic.

The man shrugged his shoulders, shook his head and walked out. She sighed and sat back on her cot as the door slammed closed and the key turned in the lock. She wondered when she'd be able to get a shower. She'd had a couple of baths with a bucket since she'd arrived, and the men had given her a couple of changes of clothes – pants and shirts made for men. But she still felt disgusting. And what would happen, she wondered, when she got her period? She knew it could come any day, and she wasn't looking forward to asking Ram and his men for a tampon.

She threw the books to the floor and lay back with her hands behind her head. The cot was hard, but she'd grown used to it. She started the mental exercises she'd developed to keep from dying of boredom in this little cell, including writing letters in her head to Joanna and her parents, playing tic tack toe against herself, counting the number of days between today and the day she or Joanna was born (Nancy was approaching 17,000, if her math was right) – just the little things that occupied time.

But today, the mental games weren't working. Her mind was scattered, and she couldn't mentally add figures or picture tic tack toe boards. She got off the cot and spent some time exercising her leg, pacing back and forth across the dark, undecorated room with its mud floor. She counted her steps, with a goal of reaching 1,000 for the day. She'd read somewhere that if you took 10,000 steps a day, it would keep you fit. With her wounded leg, she'd set the goal pretty low, and it was still difficult and painful, even with the crutches they'd given her. She hobbled around, wincing now and then at the pain, and eventually gave up. She'd only reached 200.

She continued to wrack her brain trying to imagine ways to escape, or at least to get the message out about where she was imprisoned. The problems were her leg, which kept conventional escape a fantasy; and her absolute ignorance about her location. She ran through some ideas again about writing a coded message, but none of them seemed like they'd work. And how would she code it, anyway, and to indicate what?

For that matter, she wondered if her letters even went through to her family, as Ram had assured her. After all, what did he have to gain by actually telling her family anything? He knew the U.S. government didn't pay ransoms, and any sort of message coming from him or his men might give away their position. Also, she'd covered Washington and the White House long enough to know that hostages in foreign countries, even high-profile hostages such as she would like to consider herself to be, seldom made the top of the to-do list for senior officials. The U.S. hostages in Lebanon back in the 1980s, for instance, remained imprisoned for years and years with little U.S. action to free them. She shuddered to think of being here that long; but she also shuddered to think that only thing protecting her from a worse fate might be Ram.

She decided the best thing to do was to keep on developing her relationship with Ram, who she at least could have conversations with when he wasn't raving. He obviously had a human side, and she would use her experience as a journalist to chip away at him. It was like developing a difficult source, she told herself. Sometimes the longer you talk, the more they open up. At least she knew how to do this, and it gave her a bit of hope – the only hope she had at this point.

Nancy sat heavily on the mud floor and picked up the books the man had left there. She turned on her flashlight and opened one up. The writing must have been Pashto or Dari, and it was beautiful to look at, filled with flowing symbols. It didn't look much like Arabic, but it did remind her somewhat of Hebrew, as it seemed like the dots above and below the letters might serve as vowels. She had Jewish friends and had attended Passover Seders, at which she'd learned a little about the language.

Still, there was no way she'd be able to read the books. She sighed again and scrolled slowly through the pages, boredom growing. As she scrolled, she thought she saw something unusual on one of the pages. She turned back to where she'd been, thumbing through page after page until she saw the one that had attracted her attention. Her eyes widened.

In the margin of the otherwise uninteresting page, someone had done some scribbling with a pencil. The marks looked rather old, but were still very clear. Nancy's heart raced as she stared at the bottom of the page, where the scribbling ended. Below the last scribbles, someone had drawn a very small picture with the same pencil. The picture looked like two tall buildings standing next to each other.

Somehow, seeing that image brought to mind her long ago conversation with Virgil Walker, and his memo. Why had the drawing reminded her of the memo? She mentally thought back, and saw herself sitting with Virgil in the Thai restaurant, hearing the words he'd said then.

"I just think the public has a right to know that there might be terrorist cells still in this country planning further attacks," Virgil had told her five years ago. "And it may actually help us if the terrorists know we knew about their ideas to smash planes into buildings. Maybe it would make them think before trying it again."

"You really think they had buildings in mind?" Nancy had asked. "I mean, crashing planes into buildings? That's pretty out there."

She couldn't remember where the conversation had gone after that, but she recalled that he'd been concerned in his memo about the planes turning south off their planned courses toward New York City. Two towers together. New York City. World Trade Center.

Had Virgil told her the terrorists might have been aiming for the World Trade Center? She didn't think he had, but it seemed logical enough if they were going to attack New York. After all, she mused, the World Trade Center had been attacked before, and a bunch of people had died. Were the terrorists on the planes trying to finish the job by flying airplanes into the buildings? And had she, somehow, been captured by the same group that had planned the attacks? She shuddered. She wondered if Ram had been part of it. Could this be his book, one he'd had back then and scribbled in absently one day during the planning, forgetting afterward that he'd done so? She felt fairly certain she wouldn't have been given the book had Ram known the drawing was in it.

One thing she felt sure of was the need to communicate this finding to Virgil, if she could ever get out of this miserable place. It was probably nothing. Maybe there were two towers together outside the window of whatever room the book's owner had been in when he did the drawing. She was probably jumping to conclusions. Who could blame her after two weeks in this place with mostly just herself for company? But her conversation just now with Ram in which he mentioned the Sheik seemed to back up her theory. She knew from her studies of Al-Qaeda that Bin Laden's acolytes often referred to him that way, and she promised herself to press Ram for more details.

Now that she'd discovered the drawing, it seemed more important than ever to get out of here as soon as she could. She looked once again at the page, closed the book, and turned off the flashlight.

CHAPTER 15
OPEN HOUSE, WTC

"Oh my God, Terry, look at this view," the woman called to her husband, who hustled over toward the window to look out from the 96th floor of the World Trade Center's north tower across New York Harbor. "Isn't that just gorgeous," the woman asked. "Incredible," the husband answered softly, eyes focused on the vista.

It was opening day at the World Trade Center condos, and select clients milled around a model apartment. The views from the narrow windows were as dramatic as ever on this sunny December morning, with Lady Liberty plain to see and the harbor dotted with islands. The coasts of Staten Island and New Jersey stretched out for miles under the bright winter sun, and far out on the horizon the light reflected on the waters of the Atlantic. Even from between these narrow windows, the condos' best asset was their view.

The clients were select because to be here, they had to prove their ability to pay for one of these apartments. A simple one bedroom started at $3 million, and prices skyrocketed from there. The so-called "penthouse" on the 105th floor, right below Windows on the World, listed at a cool $100 million. That included prime northeast views toward the Midtown skyline, six bedroom suites, a library, a room just for exercise and a wine cellar (as strange as the concept of a cellar might be 1,100 feet above the ground). Monthly maintenance fees would approach $100,000 for some of the units, which had their own entrance at ground level and a windowed "sky lobby" on the 95th floor.

The developer was Pete Gladstone, Donald Trump's archrival in Manhattan real estate and a relative newcomer to the scene at the tender age of 35. Trump had tried to make a deal with Larry Silverstein of Silverstein Properties, who'd signed a lease for the WTC complex back in the summer of 2001. The lease had been a good idea, as the value of the property had climbed substantially in the five years since then, especially now that the economy had recovered from the recession of 2000 and 2001. The Dow Jones Average had recently hit new highs, and the buildings delivered Silverstein substantial returns in terms of office and retail rentals.

But Trump's idea of developing some condos on the top floors appealed to Silverstein. He never had gotten along with Trump personally, so he allowed Gladstone, a competing residential real estate developer, to handle the project. Both Gladstone and Silverstein had enjoyed seeing Trump have a tantrum in the media about how they'd stolen his idea and given it to someone else to develop. Gladstone figured if he could just get five floors to work with, he'd be able to make a fabulous profit, but Silverstein had designated 10 floors, all in the North Tower, dividing them between still lucrative office space (the highest floors generally rented for the most money) and condos.

"It's a growing trend," the usually reclusive and quiet Gladstone had told *The New York Times* earlier this year in a rare interview when asked about the conversion of office space into condos on high floors of skyscrapers. "They just did it in Chicago last year, in one of those big 1970s office buildings off of Michigan Avenue, near Grant Park. But we haven't seen as much here in New York, and never at an iconic property like the WTC. Just think of the address: One WTC. To say you live at One WTC says a lot about your status."

The décor of this model condo reflected the anticipated status of the buyers as well. One female client, obviously with an appreciation of art, eyed the minimalist modern John McCracken sculptures and paintings placed strategically around the apartment. They were from Gladstone's own collection; his family owned an art gallery in Chelsea where works started at around $20,000 and went up into the seven figures. The polished, marble floors in the condo's front hallway would fit right in at a French manor, and wide, Doric columns framed the arched door entries between rooms.

Gladstone, a tall, thin, pale man with neatly combed blonde hair, who dressed in the finest dark suits and seldom smiled, professed to not worry about possible terrorism at the property, despite the 1993 bombing and the scare five years ago when some had warned that hijackers might have been aiming planes at New York City monuments.

"We have a very strong security system here, and anyone moving into a property like this is used to having a lot of security in their lives – many of our prospective buyers already have bodyguards," Gladstone had told the Times. "We're not talking about the average Joe moving here. These are sophisticated world business and entertainment leaders. They know what they're getting into."

Several major celebrities and business people, including two Oscar winners and four Fortune 500 CEOs, had already signed leases. In addition several Saudi sultans had expressed interest in purchasing the 10,000 square-foot penthouse. Opening day would be shortly after the new year, on January 9.

Gladstone, in his customary dark suit and red tie, watched the tenants step off the elevators into the model condominium. He chatted with people now and then but mostly stood alone with a half smile on his face, holding a glass of white wine but never sipping. This condo was his baby, and he'd already chosen it as his own apartment, which he'd move into once it was no longer needed as a model. He loved the idea of entertaining up here, with the tall windows looking out over the harbor and fireworks lighting up the sky on the Fourth of July. Maybe he'd raise a family here, if he ever got married. Right now, life was too exciting to waste time on domesticity.

CHAPTER 16

ADAM MAKES HIS MOVE

There could scarcely have been more contrast in apartments than between the one Gladstone stood in, with its marble floors and electronic blinds, and Adam's tiny studio walk-up with a window looking across an alley to the dirty brick walls of another building a stone's throw away. Adam was in his apartment now, lying on the bed with Elmer purring on top of him, still trying to decide what to do.

It had been two weeks since the man broke into his apartment in the middle of the night, and he'd said nothing yet, except to his friend Bob, who'd experienced a similar late-night visit. Bob was petrified, and determined to stay out of the matter altogether. He had told Adam he'd never get involved again in any photography of people at the airport. From now on, he'd stick to airplanes. His site was still up, and anyone who wanted to look at photos of 737s from the 1980s or DC-10s from the 1970s could find thousands of them on his pages. That was good enough for Bob.

Adam's site was also still up, minus the offending photo and blog post. Those parts were gone. Adam hadn't bothered to put them up again, as he had no wish for further nocturnal encounters with his ski-masked friend. He hadn't changed his user name or password, either. Actually, he now had little interest in the site. It seemed polluted, somehow.

The man had warned him against going to the police, and had left several thousand dollars in hundred-dollar bills, obviously bribing him to forget the whole thing. The guy must have been part of some sort of drug deal, Adam decided, and he and Bob had just been in the wrong place (or the right place, you could argue) at the wrong time. He'd heard the heroin trade had really taken off in the Midwest, so maybe these guys were trying to get product onto airplanes using grounds crew people to do the dirty work and avoid security. It made a lot of sense.

Part of him wanted to forget it all, spend the money to pay a couple more months of rent so he could put off a decision about what to do next with his life, and move on. But another part of him fought back, saying he should do the right thing and report what had happened. It seemed dangerous, but maybe the police could give him protection. They'd probably be able to trace the criminals through the serial numbers on the bills, which he'd kept protected in an envelope in one of his kitchen drawers. He supposed the criminals knew that was a possibility, but counted on him to stay quiet in the face of their threats.

The other thing nagging at him was the possibility that the criminals weren't just drug dealers, but some sort of terrorists. He'd done a lot of research on air crashes, including the hijackings and collision of 2001, and was fascinated that the terrorists successfully boarded the doomed planes and seized the controls. He hated the bastards, of course, but you had to admire their pluck. That had been a hell of a plan, but he supposed it could never work again now that the authorities knew how they'd done it. The government had made a big deal about how hijackings were no longer possible, but Adam was a skeptic, and he didn't quite buy it. Certainly the ground personnel represented a flaw in the works, and it would be pretty easy, he supposed, to pay them off or even get them to help the terrorists under some circumstances. He figured whoever had planned the attacks in 2001 could probably have found a way to bribe some ground crews if necessary. It hadn't been necessary then, but now it might be the only way to successfully carry out a hijacking, considering how difficult it had become for a passenger to bring a weapon aboard.

What finally swayed him to go to the police, besides, he supposed, his sense of responsibility to the community, were the images he'd collected of the victims of that collision in 2001. The photos he had weren't the ones you could find on newspaper front pages. They were the ones the police and first responders had taken once the smoke had cleared, and they'd seared their way into Adam's head ever since he'd found websites showing them. One showed a boy of around eight, still strapped into his airplane seat, which now sat upright in a field. The boy was wearing a mud-stained baseball jersey and cap, his face was reddened with burns and his blank, dead eyes still looked startled. Another photo showed a man's half-naked body, muddy and sprawled across the ground with an arm over his face, as if to keep himself from seeing whatever one saw when falling onto a corn field from 20,000 feet in the sky. Severed limbs. A doll here; a magazine there. Signs of lives destroyed in a single second. He supposed he'd never forget those images.

Adam hadn't ever lived up to his parents' high hopes, and at 35, he felt he'd pretty much wasted his best years being lazy and uncommitted. Now, for the first time, he'd started feeling like he was getting old, and wondering what he'd do with his life to make it more meaningful. He figured he was more than halfway through, considering how overweight he was, and death had started to be more than a faraway concept – something that happened to someone else. It loomed in his future, getting closer all the time. Even if he reported this to the police and got wiped out by that masked man, wouldn't that be better than going on as he had been? At least he'd die for something meaningful. He pulled out his phone and dialed.

"Hello, this is Officer Polanski. How can I help you?"

Adam had called the non-emergency line of the local precinct of the Chicago Police Department. He figured it was better than calling 911, considering the crime was two weeks ago.

"Yeah, officer," Adam said. "I want to report a..." He had to think. It wasn't really a robbery that he was reporting. The man had broken in, but hadn't taken anything.

"Report a what, mister? Look, I'm pretty busy over here. What do you want?"

"I want to report a break-in at my apartment," Adam said firmly.

"All right. It happen today?"

"Actually, no," Adam replied, feeling sheepish. "It was a couple weeks ago."

"Aw, give me a break, buddy," the cop replied. "Is this a joke? What the hell are you calling me for two weeks later? Why didn't you call then? How am I supposed to help you now? Huh?"

"Well, the guy basically threatened to kill me if I said anything," Adam said. "I thought about it for a while, but I decided to report it."

"Good for you, buddy, good for you. But look, because this happened so long ago, you're going to have to go to Area headquarters and explain it over there. We've got crimes goin' on today, not two weeks ago."

Adam got directions to the Area headquarters and thanked the cop. An hour later, he was sitting on a plastic chair in a police department waiting room that smelled strongly of body odor. Adam sat there trying to read the book he'd brought. It was a courtroom thriller by Scott Turow, his favorite author.

It was lucky Adam didn't have other obligations, because he ended up waiting three hours to see a cop. The policeman he finally spoke to sounded impatient at first, but took down Adam's information and his contact number and promised to call him if anything came up. He didn't seem too interested in Adam's description of the activities he'd seen at O'Hare, or in his description of the intruder, but he raised his eyebrows a bit when Adam said the man had left him $5,000 in hundred-dollar bills.

"You still have the money?" the cop asked in his gruff but friendly Chicago accent. He was graying and probably in his fifties, with sagging skin on his face and bright red cheeks that were rough from too much washing and drying. He looked tired and used up, but his green eyes still twinkled.

"Yeah, right here," Adam said. He dug the envelope out of the front pocket of his black and red Chicago Blackhawks jacket and placed it on the desk. The cop opened it up, thumbed through the bills and gave an admiring whistle.

"This is quite a stash, buddy," the cop said. "I'll tell ya' something, I admire you for bringing it here and doing the honest thing. Let me keep it for now, and we'll see what we can find out from the serial numbers. Oh yeah – we'll test it for drug residue, too. Hold on a second – I need to register this."

Adam waited while the cop picked up his phone, and daydreamed through the policeman's quick conversation. Another cop came in moments later with a metal box. The first officer handed him the envelope. "Thanks, Mitch," the first officer said. "No problem," the second cop said, placing the envelope in the box and walking out of the room.

"OK, buddy," the first officer said, turning again to Adam. "We'll have those bills checked out. Now you realize if this is stolen, you won't be getting it back, right?"

"Yeah, I understand," Adam replied. "Anything else I can tell you?"

"No, no, we're good," the cop said. "I'm going to pass this story around and see if anyone's investigating anything similar. I got your number if I find anything out. OK?" He offered his hand and Adam shook it.

"Thanks," Adam said. "I hope it's just some kind of drug thing. I'd hate to think it's more serious."

"What do you mean, more serious?" the cop asked, staring at Adam intently with his green eyes.

"I don't know," Adam said, feeling flustered. "It's just that, you know, with airports, you think of a lot of bad stuff that could happen." He felt a wave of guilt, as if the cop might suspect him of some sort of malicious act.

"Right, right," the cop said. "OK – I'll let you know what we find. Keep your phone with you the next few days."

"Thanks, officer," Adam replied, hoping the cop wasn't now suspicious he was involved in some sort of criminal activity himself.

He mentally replayed the conversation as he trudged slowly along the empty sidewalk to the bus stop in the chilly December air, his breath coming out in misty clouds, and figured he hadn't said anything that would point suspicion his way. He'd avoided mentioning Bob, since Bob wanted nothing to do with telling anyone about this. Which might have been a mistake since Bob could corroborate his story – or maybe he wouldn't, considering how afraid Bob was of the masked intruder he had met. And if Bob refused to corroborate, that would make Adam look like a liar. He shook his head and told himself not to be so paranoid. "You've read too many crime novels," he said aloud, feeling slightly amused.

The bus dropped him two blocks from his apartment and he zipped up his jacket and started walking. The wind whipped down the street right at his face, cutting into his exposed skin like an icy knife, and he cursed himself for not bringing his hat and gloves. He suddenly had a frightening sense he was being followed. He turned around, but no one was there. More paranoia, he guessed. Now that he'd told the cops, he was probably going to feel this way for a while. That fellow at his apartment had certainly seemed to mean business. Maybe he should have asked the police for protection. He hadn't thought about that in the warm, safe glow of the police station, but now, out here in the dark, he felt stupid for not saying something then.

It was now fully dark, and the streetlights cast an eerie glow over the pavement. There were few other pedestrians out, and Adam supposed most people were home eating dinner. The few huddled figures he did pass walked quickly, eager to reach their warm apartments. He was on a side street lined closely on both sides with 1920s two- and three-story gray stone apartment buildings, each with its own little stairway to the front door. Anyone could be hiding in the shadows of any of those buildings, or in a dark alley, he thought, and shivered.

He sped up, glancing behind him now and then, and eventually reached his own building, a four-story affair with a long first-floor hallway leading back to an elevator that was often broken. Adam normally took the stairway, but tonight that didn't seem like the safest idea. He decided to wait in the well-lit hallway for the elevator. He fumbled for his keys to the lobby door, and that's when someone grabbed him around the neck, wrapped a scarf over his mouth and dragged him into the alley that ran between his building and the next.

Whoever it was shoved him against a wall in the dark alley, and Adam's head hit the brick with teeth-rattling force. His arms were pinned against the wall by the person's large body, and he couldn't cry out with the scarf now wrapped tightly around his mouth a couple times. He swiveled his head frantically but saw no one on the sidewalk to alert.

The man holding him against the wall wore the same black ski mask as last time, but this time also wore a dark jacket with a hood over his head, and black gloves.

"That wasn't too smart, big guy," the man said quietly. "I thought we had a deal. You're some kind of welsher, aren't you? Do you know what happens to welshers?"

"Oomph," was all Adam could get out. The man reached inside his coat for something, and Adam was sure this was it for him.

The man pulled out a long, sharp knife and Adam screamed silently through the scarf. Just then, two men appeared out of the darkness, grabbed the perpetrator from behind and wrestled him to the ground of the dark alley. The knife fell out of the attacker's hands during the struggle and rattled on the pavement, falling a few feet away "Don't move!" one of the men yelled. "FBI!" He pulled out a gun and the perpetrator lay still on the ground, hands in the air.

Adam froze in place and watched the two officers hold the man down on the ground with their knees and handcuff him. One of the officers stayed on the ground with the attacker and radioed for assistance, and the other approached Adam and put his hand on Adam's shoulder. The officer used his other hand to unwrap the scarf from around Adam's face.

"You OK, Adam?" the FBI man asked, breathing hard.

"I... I think so," Adam stuttered, trying not to hyperventilate. "Man, you guys got here just in time. I think... I think he was going to kill me." He found himself shivering all over. The man wrapped his coat around Adam and patted him on the back.

"You just try to get yourself together," the FBI man said, patting Adam on the back again. "I'm sorry it had to come to this. We've been tracking you for a while and we wouldn't have let anything happen. We knew we'd never find this guy if he didn't try to get you first, so we had to let things take their course. We figured you'd go to the cops eventually and this guy would go gunning for you. But we didn't think it would happen this fast."

"You've been watching me?" Adam asked, dumbfounded. He was still trembling. How close to death had he just come?

"Yeah," the cop said. "We've been tracking you ever since that blog post you made about activities at O'Hare. That got the government's interest. We need to get to the bottom of this case. Sorry we had to use you as bait, but hopefully this guy we're arresting can tell us more about what kind of shenanigans he's been pulling at the airport."

Two police cars pulled into the alley, lights flashing but without any sirens, and several cops stepped out, grabbed the handcuffed man and pushed him into the back seat of one of the cruisers. A small crowd had gathered on the sidewalk to watch.

"You the guy he attacked?" another cop asked, approaching Adam and the FBI man.

"Yeah, I am," Adam said, feeling oddly like he'd stepped into an episode of *Law & Order*. This wasn't really happening to him, was it?

"OK, then," the cop said. "We'll need you to come to the Area head-quarters with us and make a statement. You can get in this car here." He pointed to the cruiser behind the one holding Adam's attacker. Adam looked questioningly at the FBI man.

"It's OK," the FBI agent told him, nodding. "Go on with them. We're working with the police on this. We don't think this guy is the leader of the little gang. We think he's been paid off to get you out of the way. We're hoping he leads us to whoever's in charge."

"Do you think they're doing some sort of drug deal?" Adam asked. The FBI guy and the cop were walking him toward the cruiser.

The FBI man shrugged his shoulders. "You know as much as I do right now," he said. "We're hoping your friend can tell us some more."

Adam climbed shakily into the cruiser with the cop, and the FBI man waved goodbye. The two police cars again put on their flashing lights, pulled out of the alley, and headed quickly toward the station through the dark streets. Adam leaned back in the seat, and his mind began racing. Was that really the FBI, or was this still part of some crazy scheme? He'd certainly become paranoid, he decided, but perhaps that's what comes of having your apartment invaded and then being accosted on a dark street. Ah, nothing to do except go to the police and make his statement, he supposed. He wondered if he'd have to testify in court. Maybe they'd give him a new identity or something. "How did I get mixed up in all of this?" he thought.

CHAPTER 17

GOING HOME

The day after her lunch with Jarrah, Alev sat in the window seat of a 747, gazing out the window as the big plane lurched itself heavily from the runway and climbed quickly into the deep blue sky. Minutes later she could see the dramatic Chicago skyline framed by Lake Michigan. How strange that a lake should be so big, Alev thought, as the plane cruised thousands of feet above the water. She couldn't see the other side at all. It looked like the ocean. But it was fresh water, Ziad had told her. Now, in early December, the water was still liquid, and brilliantly blue in the sunshine. But Ziad said it got icy by mid-winter.

In the end, she couldn't convince him to come home with her, and she couldn't convince herself to call the authorities and share her suspicions about what he might be up to. She wasn't quite sure what she could say. After all, she had no proof he was actually up to anything. She hoped Jarrah wouldn't get mixed up in any plan that might hurt others. And she couldn't turn the police onto someone so close. In the world they both came from, family and tribe came before everything. Somehow, she still felt connected to him, and couldn't do anything that might hurt him.

But she had given up on the idea of a long-term future with him. She'd meant what she said, and when he dropped her off at O'Hare, she'd told him it was the last time he'd see her. He'd embraced her awkwardly in the front seat of the cab, and then got out to help with her luggage.

"Please, Ziad, consider one more time," she said as he gently placed her luggage on the sidewalk. "Will you come back with me now? You can just double park your cab here and never come back."

He shook his head. "You know I can't do that, Alev," he replied, putting down the last piece of luggage and coming back to where she stood at the cab's passenger door. "But you will hear from me again. I'll call you."

"There's no point, Ziad," she said, shifting her purse to her other shoulder. "I meant what I said yesterday. If you can't commit to me, I'm not taking your calls." This time she successfully held back her tears. If he felt like crying, he didn't show it. His face remained a blank.

"OK, if that's how you feel," he said, in a curiously flat voice. He gave her a perfunctory peck on the cheek and then walked quickly around to the driver's door of the cab, not looking back. She picked up her luggage and walked quickly into the terminal, forcing herself to look straight ahead. She knew this chapter of her life was over.

As the plane cruised up above the clouds, Alev closed her eyes. Though she felt certain she was through with Ziad, she didn't feel quite right leaving without trying harder to understand what he was involved in. She wanted to relax and fall asleep, now that she had eight hours with nothing to do, but the itching sense that she hadn't fulfilled a responsibility, not to herself, but to others who might be in danger, kept her awake. She knew she had to do something.

CHAPTER 18

A CHANGE IN PLANS

"Majdoube!" the Director yelled from the back of the cab, punching the driver's seat in front of him and startling Jarrah, who almost steered into another car. There was a loud honk from the other vehicle, and Jarrah gave the driver his middle finger. The Director had just called Jarrah an idiot. That was never good news, and this time, Jarrah was pretty sure the Director was right. Jarrah had been calling himself similar words for several days now, ever since the FBI sting that nailed the enforcer as he tried to catch the spy. Why the enforcer hadn't nailed the spy on the man's way to the police station instead of on his way back was a head scratcher, and now it was biting them all in the butt. The man obviously hadn't realized where the spy was going until it was too late. The Director was not a happy man, and his anger, coming so soon on the heels of Alev's departure, had turned this into a very bad week for Jarrah.

With the Director and Hanjour in back, Jarrah drove aimlessly around the city, taking one expressway downtown and then getting on another one and heading out toward the airport where he'd picked the two up earlier that day. It was dark now; the sun set early in the Midwest in December, and snowflakes danced in the air. The highway was jammed with rush hour traffic headed home, and the headlights of semis flashed in Jarrah's eyes, momentarily blinding him as they passed on the other side of the median. His heart still felt frozen, as it had ever since he'd dropped Alev off at the airport the day before. Part of him had truly wanted to go back with her and give all this up. But something had repressed that desire all through

her visit, and he never let himself open up to her. Deep down, he supposed, the mission still took precedence.

Jarrah and Hanjour had brought the Director up to speed on where
things stood, and the Director's mood grew blacker and blacker. He didn't
say much, just let out an annoyed grunt now and then and sometimes
cursed in Arabic - a bad sign. Now he punched the seat again, spewing
several more curse words. Jarrah knew the Director didn't drink, but it
sounded almost as if he were drunk.

"So here's how it is," the Director said, in a sneering tone, still in Arabic.
"Make sure I understand. The FBI figured out what was going on at the
airport. That's mistake number one. And then you – Jarrah – weren't able
to take down the web site in time. Mistake number two. Third problem –
the spy went to the cops, and number four, they arrested the enforcer. Am
I right? Did I miss any of your fuck-ups?"

"That's the situation," Jarrah said quietly as he drove. He opened his
mouth to say more but the Director wouldn't let him speak.

"Who knows what that guy might tell the FBI now that they've got
their hands on him!" the Director barked. "He doesn't know all of our
plans, does he? Does he?"

"No, no," Jarrah replied quickly. "We'd never tell the fucking
Americans our plans. He thought it was a drug deal."

"I see you did something right," the Director said, sarcastically. "How
nice. But this man – you call him what – the enforcer? Ha. Some enforcer.
Anyway, this man, he's going to tell the FBI that a bunch of Arabs worked
with him to get materials onto planes. He could be telling them this right
now! Our plans could be destroyed! Such sloppiness! Unacceptable!"

The Director leaned back, glowering, his beady eyes half closed, and
Jarrah could almost feel the little man's anger coming in waves through
his body as he drove. Normally, he wasn't frightened of the Director, but
he hadn't often been the target of one of his tirades. He clenched the
wheel more tightly in his hands and pulled into the left lane to get around
a truck. This whole thing was spinning out of control. The fire that had
burned so hot in his gut back in 2000 and 2001 seemed to have died
down to little more than red embers. Why had he let Alev go back alone?
What was he doing here?

THE TOWERS STILL STAND

Finally, the Director spoke again. To Jarrah's surprise, the little man's voice was both calm and quiet.

"What is done is done," the Director said. "It's too late to change what happened already. The spy should have been killed, not just threatened. The enforcer should have been more careful and not gotten arrested. All of that is behind us now. What matters is what we do next."

"What do we do?" Hanjour asked. "Do we abandon the plan for now? Should we go back home?"

"Eskoot!" the Director yelled, eyes flashing again at Hanjour, who raised his hands as if to fend off a blow. "Let me think!"

After five years of working quietly and carefully, their cover was blown. The whole thing seemed a bit unworkable in the first place, Jarrah thought – trying to hijack two planes with just two pilots and several Muslim militants from the Detroit area who they would train as muscle men but wouldn't know the full extent of the plot. Neither Hanjour nor Jarrah had dared to take any flying lessons under their assumed names, so neither had been behind the wheel of a plane since 2001, unless one counted simulator time. They were bound to be rusty. The very idea of being able to hijack the planes depended on sneaking weapons aboard, and now that idea seemed to be out of the question.

The Director had been impatient for some time now, even before this disaster. He'd never wanted to wait so long before moving against the towers again, but Hanjour and Jarrah had done everything they could to convince him it was best to stay under cover for a while to let Americans get lax. The thing that finally had won the Director over was the idea of doing the deed on the 60th anniversary of the founding of Israel. If there was anything that could sway the Director, it was mention of the Jewish state. Just saying the word "Israel" could launch him into near hysterics.

"No more waiting," the Director said now, after a few minutes of uncomfortable silence. "We move fast. How soon can we launch the operation?"

"What? When the FBI has its eyes on us?" Jarrah responded, incredulous.

"My friend, I said we should have made our move some time ago, but you talked me out of it, and now look at the trouble we're in," the Director said. "Haven't you made enough poor decisions already? If I say we're moving now, we're moving now. You will listen to me, and do what I say."

Jarrah exited the highway at Armitage Avenue, and now he turned west and drove beneath the huge underpass, lined on both sides with the cardboard shacks and shopping carts of the homeless who lived like trolls underneath. Jarrah's cab emerged from the darkness and stopped at the traffic light.

As they sat waiting to move, Jarrah turned around and faced the Director, whose hair had retreated a great deal these last few years. It had been difficult for a man like the Director to lie low for so long, Jarrah reflected. The Director was a man of action. Waiting wasn't in his makeup.

"OK," Jarrah replied. "What next?"

"I have many thoughts, my friend," the Director responded. The car behind them honked as the light changed, and Jarrah quickly turned around in his seat and pressed on the accelerator. "Despite this series of events," the Director continued, "I believe you two will be able to carry things forward, but you will need my active help in every aspect of the operation. Here's what we will do. First, you need to take care of this, this...what do you call him – enforcer?"

"But it's too late – he probably already talked," Jarrah protested.

"Eskoot!" the Director yelled again. "How long have they had him? Two nights? The Americans don't torture their own people. They haven't gotten anything out of him yet, I assure you. Remember the Massaoui operation? I need that done again. Use one of your American friends."

"But won't that call even more attention to us?" Hanjour chipped in. "Maybe we should just let him talk. He'll only say it's a drug deal – that's all he knows."

"Hmmph, we can't take that chance," the Director replied. "Let's cut the tongue out before it starts to dance. Got it?"

"Yes," Hanjour said. "I'll take care of it."

"Good. Now, Jarrah, the next step is – ahh! Watch out!"

A car had turned in front of Jarrah and he slammed on the brakes to avoid it.

"Pull over!" the Director ordered. "How can I think when we're driving around? I could drive better than this."

Jarrah found a space on the side of the street and backed the car in. This was a relatively quiet part of town, and traffic flowed sporadically. No one would notice the cab parked here with the three men inside. Jarrah turned in the driver's seat to look directly at the Director.

"Next, we need to accelerate the date of our operation," the Director said, his voice sounding louder now that the engine was off. "Today is Dec. 6. We move against the Americans on Jan. 9. Another Tuesday, just like last time. It's a symbolic date – the date our Palestinian brothers launched an attack against the Jews and crusaders in 1948. It's also the date that Jewish developer wants to open his condos in the buildings. We're going to give him an opening to remember. Got it?"

"Wait a minute, now," Jarrah stammered, for the moment losing all pretense of trying to please the Director. "We can't move in just a month. We don't have all the men in place, and we haven't had flight training. And how are we to be sure we can make the operation work at O'Hare now that our cover is blown? What if we can't get materials on the flights?"

"No," the Director said firmly, raising his hand to silence Jarrah. "You don't understand. Not flights – flight."

"Huh?" Hanjour asked.

"One plane, one tower," the Director said quietly. "We move fast, and we streamline the operation. We do it in the next month. That's about how much time we need to get it together. No Detroit helpers. Just the three of us."

Jarrah couldn't contain his shock. "Three of us?" he sputtered. "You?" This added a whole new dimension, and Jarrah couldn't think it through with the Director smiling his icy grin at him.

"Yes, Ziad," the Director said, still grinning smugly. "You didn't think I had it in me to sacrifice my life, did you? Well, I'm more complex than you give me credit for. I'm taking over. We're going to do this right."

The Director explained his plan to the two men. The streamlined operation would only hit one of the towers ("The one with the condominiums," the Director said with a grin). With their cover blown, it was essential to make sure things went right, and hijacking two planes at once – always something of a challenge – was too onerous to contemplate any further. They'd hijack one plane, and the Director and Jarrah would serve as muscle men while Hanjour – the best pilot among them – handled the controls. There'd be no need to import "muscle men" from Detroit, as they had planned, and they'd switch operations to another airport closer to

New York – either Baltimore or Philadelphia, the Director decided. He had contacts in both towns who could make necessary weapons arrangements with ground crews where the heat wouldn't be so strong.

"I'm not worried about the FBI," the Director said, spitting contemptuously onto the cab's floor as he said the word "FBI." Jarrah flinched as the Director defiled his squeaky clean car, but held his tongue. "Those fuckers are even less competent than you two. If you're telling the truth that you only told the enforcer this was a drug deal, they won't suspect what we're doing. And even if they did, they wouldn't be able to coordinate among themselves and the airport authorities to get anything done quickly enough to stop us. I'm convinced our plan will work at the airports."

"What about the Sheik?" Jarrah finally asked. "He's expecting this on the day of Israel's independence."

"The Zionist entity, please," the Director corrected him in a condescending tone. "There is no state of Israel! The Zionists and crusaders stole the land from the Palestinians, and the evil Americans propped it up with their weapons." The Director's eyes had taken on a zealous glint, his voice rising with each statement. "Our attacks will tell the entire world that the Jews are illegitimate pigs, and responsible for any American deaths! That much, I assure you, we will accomplish!"

"Shh," Jarrah said. "Someone outside might hear you." He'd grown tired of hearing the Director lecture about the sins of the "Zionist entity."

"Ah, you're worried about being overheard. Isn't that amusing, coming from the majdoube who let the FBI in on our plans," the Director said, lips curling.

Jarrah's teeth clenched at the accusation. "That wasn't intentional," he said, looking the Director right in the eyes.

The Director stared at him, half-lidded eyes gleaming. "So you say," he said quietly. "So you say."

Jarrah felt a glimmer of fear inside, and he swallowed quickly.

"Can I really trust either of you?" the Director said, almost as if to himself. "Can I trust anyone?"

"Are you going to tell the Sheik about the change in plans?" Hanjour interrupted.

"Eskoot!" the Director barked again. "I can take care of the Sheik. That's not a problem. I have couriers who will bring him the message. I don't know where he is now, but they do. He approved our plan many years ago, and I have full approval from him to move as I see fit."

The two men nodded. Now that Jarrah thought through it a bit more, he could see the sense in streamlining the operation. Less logistical trouble and less chance of getting caught, even if the results wouldn't be quite as explosive. Jarrah believed that the three of them, with the right weapons, could easily subdue a plane full of passengers. And Hanjour was definitely the better pilot. Hanjour was the only Sept. 11 hijacker with a commercial pilot certificate, and he'd spent some time on computer simulators the last few months, enough to keep him familiar with what the controls looked like and how they functioned. He'd be rusty, but maybe he could do it.

Still, after dropping off Hanjour and the Director and heading home to his quiet apartment, which felt emptier than ever with Alev gone, Jarrah's doubts crept back in. What would this mean, having the Director go with them? Part of him wondered if the Director even meant what he said. He was a shifty fellow. But if he were serious, that had major implications for the entire operation. Now Jarrah's job also included babysitting the Director to make sure he didn't go off half-cocked and mess things up in the middle with his volatile temper. And if the Director was serious about this, what might his attitude be like in the weeks before the attack? He might get more zealous and controlling than ever. Just thinking about the Director being on the plane with them made Jarrah's stomach roll.

Now he regretted inviting Alev. It was weakness, and it was yielding to temptation. What had he been thinking? He must steel himself to avoid emotion and put her out of his mind once and for all. He must prove his worthiness, now that the Director doubted it. The thought flashed in his mind that he had only one month to live if all went as planned, but he pushed the fear away quickly. He lay on his bed awake late into the night, staring into the dark.

CHAPTER 19

VIRGIL AND HARRY AT THE CAPITOL

Virgil struggled to keep pace with Harry as they walked through the subterranean labyrinth of tunnels underneath the Capitol. Two young aides accompanied them, carrying bulky packages of briefing books, and even they had trouble keeping pace with the energetic Secretary of Defense. The only thing that slowed the group down now and then were various congressmen and senators who kept approaching to talk to Harry.

It was Monday, Dec. 11, and Congress would soon break for its holiday recess. But now, in the period between Thanksgiving and Christmas, the scene was chaotic, with last-minute deal-making as the lame-duck Republican-led Congress tried to get bills passed before leaving town and handing control over to the victorious Democrats the following month. Harry had just finished testifying at a hearing of the Senate Armed Services Committee and was on his way to the Russell Senate Office Building, where he had individual meetings scheduled with several senators. The Iraq war was going badly, and Harry faced some tough questions.

He'd asked Virgil to come with him, hoping they'd have time in between meetings to duck into an office where Virgil could brief him on the "Chicago affair," as they'd come to call the strange breach of security at O'Hare. But they were running late for a meeting with Sen. McCain, and Virgil wasn't sure when he'd have even a few minutes to update the secretary. They'd just boarded the subway, a special line that ran beneath the Capitol to connect various buildings where congressmen had their offices, when one of the aides' phones rang. It was a quick call, and when it was over the aide said something quietly to Harry, who towered over her at 6'5 and had to bend down to hear.

"Thanks, Susie," he boomed. Then he turned to Virgil as the subway car began moving.

"Well Virge, it's your lucky day," the secretary said, not out of breath at all after the 15-minute walk, though Virgil was sweating. "Looks like McCain is running behind and wants to have me come by 15 minutes later than we scheduled. So we have a few minutes here. Susie, can you find us a quiet place to talk? Thanks."

Susie studied her phone intently for a minute, and then dialed again. Meanwhile, Harry had started a conversation with a congressman who shared the subway car with them, and was slapping him on the back and laughing loudly when Susie approached him again.

"Looks like there's a room available on the first floor of Rayburn. I'll take you there."

"That's great, great," Harry said. He turned to the congressman and finished his salutations as the train arrived at the Rayburn station.

"I'm sure I'll be hearing from you again at appropriations time!" Harry said with a laugh as the congressman stepped out of the car.

"You know me too well, Harry," the congressman said with a laugh, and rushed off in another direction.

"Congressmen and senators," Harry said to Virgil reflectively as they followed their aides upstairs. "They say they're all for cutting pork, but don't believe it a minute. It's all about gettin' jobs for their district. If there's a chance to get $1 billion for a weapons factory in their district, all of a sudden it's tax and spend time. I don't care which party they are. Sometimes the Republicans are worse than the Democrats."

"No need to tell me," said Virgil, who was breathing hard from the quick climb up the stairs behind the secretary. His leg was really starting to bother him, and he was wondering if following Harry over to the Capitol today had been a good idea. He hadn't realized how much walking it would involve. "Never believe any politician who calls himself a fiscal conservative. Remember that old joke – 'What's the definition of a tax-and-spend liberal? A conservative congressman whose district has high unemployment.' "

Harry laughed his hearty laugh. "Don't I know it," he boomed.

"Here we are," Susie called from ahead of them. She pointed to an open wooden door and escorted them into a small room with blue curtains covering the windows. A table and a few chairs were scattered around. It looked as if there'd been a meeting there that had been interrupted, forcing everyone to leave quickly.

Harry dipped his long, broad frame into one of the small chairs, and motioned Virgil to sit across from him. "We'll just be a few minutes, Susie and Adam," he told the aides. "Just wait out in the hallway."

"Yes, sir," Adam said. He was young, like Susie, probably in his 20s. Harry believed in hiring young people and molding them. He said he liked new ideas and perspectives.

"So what's the latest, Virge?" Harry asked when the aides had left. Someone was vacuuming in the next office and the noise came through the walls, distracting Virgil slightly. Harry's cell phone rang and he looked at the number, shook his head, and clicked the off button. "Unless it's Cheney or Bush, I'm not getting it," he said.

"Harry, the FBI is finished interviewing the Chicago suspect, and he only knows there was some sort of drug deal going on," Virgil said. "He said they were loading combo locks on the planes, trying to see if they could get away with it before the drugs came through. If the lock plan worked, they'd know they could get the drugs on, eventually."

"No talk of weapons, then?" Harry asked.

"Well, the guy denied it, but are you going to believe him?" Virgil replied. "Why use combo locks, or anything metal, if drugs were the goal? I suspect if they could get the locks on, they could get weapons on, too. The ground crews don't have to go through metal detectors to get onto the planes. I assume someone could find a meeting place somewhere, slip a weapon to one of them, and they sneak it on and give it to a passenger. It's a huge hole in the system, Harry. A big flaw."

Harry nodded, and his forehead showed some worry wrinkles. "I don't see how we could still have this issue five years after they hijacked those planes," Harry said. "I guess the urgency just isn't there."

"There's more," Virgil said.

Harry leaned forward. "Yeah? What?"

"I had the FBI interrogators show this fellow some photos of the Middle Eastern men we'd found in the passenger manifests on the day of the collision," Virgil said. He reached into his worn leather briefcase and fished through some papers. "Crap, I thought I had them here. Give me a minute – sorry."

Harry tapped his fingers impatiently on the table as Virgil sorted through the briefcase.

"No worries, Virge," Harry said. "Look, just get to the point."

"Ah, here they are," Virgil said, pulling out two color photos printed on paper. They were a bit wrinkled, but the images were clear. Two Arab men, both clean cut and intelligent looking, wearing Western clothing.

"This one here is Ziad Jarrah, and this one is Hani Hanjour," Virgil said. "One was on a plane headed from Dulles to Los Angeles on the morning of the collision, and the other was on a plane from Newark to San Francisco. We've done some research on both of them, and their criminal records are clean, but we believe both had spent some time in the Middle East before 2001 and may have been involved with Al-Qaeda. There's evidence they attended training camps. They entered the United States early this decade and they've pretty much not made a peep."

"All right, then," Harry said impatiently. "Why should I care?"

"Because I shared these photos with the FBI in Chicago and the suspect told the FBI he recognized both the guys in the photos," Virgil said. "He said they're the ones who've been paying him to be the courier of combo locks onto planes."

Harry uttered a low whistle of surprise.

"Now that's really somethin," he said, slowly breaking into a smile. "Nice job, Virge. I reckon you really stumbled onto something. This doesn't sound like a drug deal to me. So you think these fellas wanted to get weapons onto planes, maybe recreate what happened that day?"

Virgil nodded. "That's my sense of things," he said. "The problem is, we don't know where either of these guys are. The Chicago operation got busted, so they could have gone anywhere in the country."

"What do we do?" Harry asked.

"Well, we've put their photos out over the FBI hotline, and the entire agency is looking for them," Virgil said. "But we'll have to assume they're living under assumed names, and they're probably pretty good at disguising themselves. We're definitely going to have a big job trying to find these guys."

"We need to warn the airports," Harry said.

"Done," Virgil said. "Already done. Every airport security team in the country will be on the lookout for anything suspicious, like what we saw in Chicago. And we sent the photos of these guys to the FAA. I think we're doing everything we can."

"Good, good," Harry said, nodding. "Nice work, Virge. I know this stuff isn't really in my bag of tricks, but I'm glad you're on it. Any sense of the timing?"

The door opened and Susie poked her head in. "Sir? I think you need to start walking over to Sen. McCain's office now," she said.

"Yep – I'm coming," Harry said, getting up cumbersomely from the low chair. "John McCain, John McCain," he said. "I'm sure going to get sick of that little son of a bitch. Come to think of it, I already am. Ah well, I knew he'd be a pain in the ass when I took this job. OK, Susie, here I come. Virge, you can go back now. Thanks for the update."

"No problem, Harry," Virgil said. "We'll keep you posted. Oh – one more thing. I think we have a lead on that New York Times reporter kidnapped in Iraq."

Harry turned around as he left the room. "Huh? Oh yeah – good luck with that. See ya later."

Back in his office later that afternoon, Virgil tried to connect with his Iraqi contact, but the phone just rang and rang – no answer from Kanaan. Virgil looked at his watch. It was pretty late over there, he reflected.

He thought back on the progress he'd made with Kanaan over the last week. Kanaan had quite a network, and his contacts had been like a bunch of little rabbits scurrying around the outskirts of Bagdhad, looking for evidence. Someone found someone else who had seen the getaway car as it left the scene of the school bombing, and they'd searched a large area for it. Someone else knew that Al-Qaeda had some hideouts northeast of town, and that helped focus the search on that area, a fertile part of the country dotted with groves of palm trees that now was one of the most dangerous parts of Iraq due to Al-Qaeda attacks. Any American venturing into that region wouldn't go without a fully-equipped group of military guards for protection, and even that might not help. But Kanaan's contacts had no such qualms. They were locals who lived close to the land, knew the area well and could get around without too much notice, though, like everyone, they had to be careful for roadside bombs.

Yesterday, one of Kanaan's scouts said he'd seen the getaway SUV on a road near Baqubah, about 30 miles northeast of Bagdhad and one of the most dangerous cities in the country, an area where the terrorist leader al-Zarqawi had been very active prior to his death. Al-Zarqawi's death hadn't changed things much in this part of the country. Sunni insurgents had recently captured the region from the Iraqi army, and the city of Baqubah was under siege. The scout had followed the SUV to a remote area where it turned off the road onto a dirt path. Kanaan had emailed Virgil asking what to do next, and Virgil had been trying all day to get him on the phone.

Meanwhile, Virgil had used his Department of Defense network to connect with U.S. military in the area, and the U.S. Army commander for the district now knew where the kidnappers might be hiding. Typically, the military didn't stage raids on militants to free hostages, but in this case, with all the publicity surrounding the fact that the victim was a New York Times reporter, Virgil figured there was a chance they would break precedent.

As Virgil ruminated, his phone rang.

"Virgil here," he said quickly into the phone. He was hoping it would be Kanaan. He wanted to tell the man to hold off on further action. No use giving the kidnappers any sense they were under surveillance. He wanted the U.S. military to make the next move.

"Virgil," said a familiar voice. Virgil recognized it as General Rod Davies, a man who had the irritating habit of never identifying himself when he called. Luckily, Virgil was pretty used to this by now. The two of them had worked together for many years. Davies was one of the few military guys who'd forgiven Virgil for his breach of conduct in 2001, giving him the benefit of the doubt. Like Harry, Davies believed Virgil had done what he'd done out of concern for his country, not for his own devious purposes. There were many others who disagreed with that perception.

"General," Virgil replied. "What's going on?" He suddenly felt nervous, as if the general were going to tell him something had gone wrong. The general was a man of few words, and pretty direct, so Virgil figured he'd find out soon enough.

"Virgil, we've got pretty good intelligence that the reporter is where your people say she is," the general said in his usual unemotional tone. "Our air patrols think they've identified the house where she's being kept. I just want you to know that we're going to send some troops in there tonight."

"Great!" Virgil replied, "Thanks for the heads up." Suddenly sweat broke out on his forehead as he realized all the things that could go wrong. "Take care," he told the general, as Nancy's face rose in his mind. "Keep her safe."

"That's affirmative," the general said and hung up.

Virgil balled up a piece of paper on his desk and tossed it toward the wastebasket. It missed. "Dammit," he said.

CHAPTER 20
NANCY IN IRAQ

Night fell around a compound on the outskirts of Baqubah, and several men in black clothes patrolled outside the mud huts nestled among the palm groves. The men carried small arms – no machine guns. The stars had begun to peep out on this cloudless, cool winter evening, and the smell of citrus wafted in from nearby fruit groves. Frogs croaked in the distance, and sometimes, from farther away, came the unmistakable sound of gunfire. Sunni militants were still fighting government forces for control of the area, and had made a great deal of progress recently. Soon, the nearby city would belong Al-Qaeda.

Inside a primitive mud building, candlelight flickered in the front room. Evening prayers had ended, and several militants had laid small mattresses on the floor. Ram squatted on his haunches amidst the men, holding a cup of his cinnamon tea and taking sips now and then. As always, he was wrapped in a white robe, and his beard grew wild and untrimmed. There were flecks of gray in it that hadn't been there until recently. As he drank his tea, he mumbled to himself, and his men looked at each other questioningly. Ram tended to be quiet at most times, but he'd been quieter than ever today. It was as if he smelled trouble in the air.

Nancy was locked in her empty room, where she'd lived the last three weeks. She'd spent about an hour pacing around, counting her steps, trying to feel newfound strength in her gimpy leg. But she'd grown tired and was discouraged that the leg hadn't healed more quickly. It still was tough to make it to 1,000 steps. She'd been allowed to write another letter to Joanna and her parents, but Ram had forced her to add stuff about the plight of the Palestinians, as well as the captured Iraqis in U.S. military prisons, calling for their release and for the immediate withdrawal of U.S. troops from all holy Muslim lands. Nancy felt like a tool writing a letter dictated by Ram, but what choice did she have? It was her only chance to communicate with her family and let them know she was OK. If indeed he was actually sending the letters, which she could only hope.

Over the last week, since discovering the drawings in the book, escape had seemed more and more important. It was urgent that she get back in touch with Virgil about what she'd seen. He might be the only one in the government who'd recognize the importance. She'd outlined some plans in her mind – noting when her captors seemed to sleep and which windows might be ones she could climb through if she got the chance. But there was little opportunity. When she did go outside, it was always with Ram and armed guards, and they typically tied her wrist to the wrist of one of the guards. And she was always kept blindfolded on those expeditions. Even if she could somehow get away, her leg would keep her from moving too far, and she wouldn't have any idea where she was. Were American troops nearby? Who knew? The sound of gunfire not far off made it clear she was near a war zone.

Upon reflection, she realized she was probably safest staying where she was, especially with the area nearby evidently at war. They'd treated her well, aside from Ram's outbursts, which were becoming less and less frequent. The man seemed to have withdrawn into himself of late, and Nancy couldn't tell why. Perhaps he was discouraged by the lack of response to the kidnapping – no one had met his demands. Or perhaps he was concerned about being found. Just yesterday, he'd mentioned to a guard that they should consider moving her to a different compound. Perhaps that would happen soon, and then there'd probably be even less chance for her to be found. Her growing complacency troubled her. She was a reporter, dammit! She should be able to figure a way out of this one. The phrase "Stockholm Syndrome" flashed through her mind again, and she balled up her fists, vowing not to let that happen.

She thought she heard voices in the other room. It wasn't unusual for Ram and his men to talk after dark, but the voices sounded excited. She put her head to the door and listened carefully through the crack, where a tiny, flickering light came through. "Put out the lights," she thought she heard someone say, though her Arabic was still flimsy. It had gotten better after three weeks here.

The crack between the door and the wall darkened. How she wished she had windows in her little room! She kept her ear pressed to the door, and now she thought she heard something else, but it must be a dream, because it sounded like the steady clop, clop, clop of helicopter propellers. There were shouts now from the front room, and from outside, she heard the sound of gunfire. Could this be a rescue attempt? Her heart began beating so loudly she could hear it in her ears. What should she do? Try to break out? But that could be more dangerous than staying put. If this were a rescue, she could be in huge danger, either from friendly fire or from her kidnappers. She'd heard many stories of hostages dying in just this type of situation. And what if she was wrong? What if this was a fight between two groups of insurgents? She could be caught in between. Part of her wanted to yell for help, and part of her wanted to crawl under her bed and put her hands over her ears until all this noise was over.

Before she could think further, she lost her power to decide. The door to her room burst open, and Ram rushed in – she could tell it was him even in the dark. He picked her up roughly – at twice her weight he easily snatched her up, clutching her tightly. He whispered, "Quiet. No noise out of you." But he didn't take time to blindfold her or put anything over her mouth. He moved quickly but stealthily through the front room, and now there could be no doubt – someone was trying to rescue her. She heard more calls outside, and another short burst of gunfire. She decided this must be a rescue attempt. Why else would Ram seem so harried? And who but the allied military would have helicopters? The "whap-whap-whap" of rotors punctuated the air, but Ram – breathing hard - carried her quickly out of the house and in the direction away from the noises, into a grove of palms behind the mud hut. "Shh," he whispered to her again.

To hell with that, Nancy thought. She made a snap choice to risk all on the possibility that someone was trying to save her life. "We're here – over here!" she yelled. Ram swore and clamped a hairy arm over her mouth. Nancy struggled in his arms, trying to pull his hand off her mouth to yell again. But his hand held tight, and she kicked her legs uselessly as he pulled her further into the dark. "Damn it, damn it, damn it!" she thought, realizing this really was it. She might well die right here. And if she died, she'd never get the message out to Virgil about the two towers being in danger. She realized it wasn't just her own life that hung in the balance, but possibly the lives of thousands.

American voices rang out in the distance. "What was that?" someone shouted. Now there was no doubt in her mind – this was a rescue attempt. She kicked Ram harder and at the same time scratched her nails – which she hadn't cut since her kidnapping – against his bare arm. She felt warm blood flow out of his wound, but he just swore and kept moving into the trees.

"She's over there – I heard her," someone else yelled. "Let's go!" Nancy heard the sounds of pursuing feet behind her.

"Put down the woman!" a voice from behind yelled in Arabic. "Let her go!"

Nancy struggled again to escape Ram's grip, but it was pointless. He squeezed her tightly, one arm around her neck.

"They may kill me," he whispered to her, moving his hand. "But they won't get you alive." Suddenly, a burst of unbearable pain penetrated her chest and screamed.

A shot rang, and Ram groaned, dropping Nancy into the wet dirt below the palm trees. She crumpled in searing pain. Warm fluid flowed from her chest, making her shirt wet and sticky. Her breath became a gurgling gasp. Ram's motionless body lay nearby.

Someone ran up and crouched next to her. "Stay still," said an American voice. "Everything's going to be OK. We have to get you to the helicopter – quickly." As if to emphasize his point, gunfire rang out from somewhere in the distance. The soldier took her wrist to measure her pulse.

"Hey, Doc, we need help over here!" the soldier called. Someone ran up, a man with a small box. He opened it and began taking equipment out.

"She's got a chest wound," the first voice said rapidly. "Wrap it up quick so we can get her on the copter. We're taking fire."

"Got it," the second voice replied, sounding closer now. "Is it a gunshot? Did we hit her?"

"No – looks like the guy had a knife. Here it is in the dirt."

But the voices, and even the world, seemed distant to Nancy. She couldn't get enough air into her lungs, and warm liquid filled the back of her throat, making it feel like she was gargling. She started to choke, and the doctor shoved something into her mouth.

"No, no..." she managed, twisting her head to keep him from inserting the tube into her mouth. Wait! Focus! She needed to tell them something important. What was it? Her chest burned from lack of oxygen, and lights flashed in her brain. Her thoughts swirled. But she had to try.

"I have to get you ventilated," the man said quickly as he fumbled with his equipment. "Just stay still. We're helping you."

Suddenly, the blackness and flashes in her mind went away, and a memory came. She was 12, and her father took her to New York on vacation. She remembered her first view of Manhattan, dominated at the far end by...

"Two..." she moaned through the pain. "Two towers. Tell Virgil."

"What?" the man said, putting his ear to her mouth.

"Virgil...Walker," Nancy croaked again. It was very difficult to talk. "Tell him. Two towers."

"Virgil Walker – two towers. Got it," the man said. "Did you hear that, Billy? She said tell Virgil Walker about the two towers. OK, lady, stay still. This might hurt a little." He stuck something in her mouth and then she felt a needle prick her arm. She slipped out of consciousness.

The doctor felt his patient go limp. "OK, she's sedated and ventilated, and I've wrapped up her chest. Let's move," he said to the other soldier. The two of them lifted her and walked quickly away, holding her carefully between them. More shots rang, closer than before.

"We'll be lucky if we don't get hit on the way up. Think she'll make it?"

"Doesn't look good," the doctor said, shaking his head as they approached a copter. They handed Nancy to the medical team inside, quickly stating the meds they'd given her and the type of wound they'd found. With a nod, the leader of the team in the helicopter took over her care, closed the copter door and the two rescuers headed quickly toward the other copter.

"What was that she said when you were on the ground with her?" the soldier asked as they ran. Another soldier was standing on the ground next to it, motioning to them impatiently with his gun. Behind them, the helicopter with Nancy aboard took off, rotors blowing dirt around the area.

"Virgil Walker," the doctor said as they all got in and the copter lifted off. "The two towers."

"Isn't that a movie?" the other soldier yelled out over the noise.

"Huh?"

"I said isn't that a movie, 'The Two Towers?' " They didn't seem to be drawing any further fire. Hopefully they'd taken care of all the bad guys down below.

"Oh, yeah – I remember; that movie was out a few years ago. Why the hell would she say that? Must have been delirious. And who the hell is Virgil Walker?"

"Hell if I know. But you'd better tell Captain Isaacs, just in case. Maybe it's some intelligence thing."

"Yeah – remind me later or I'll forget." The two copters rose quickly into the night. Below them, flames leaped out of the ruins of the hut where Nancy had been imprisoned.

CHAPTER 21

BACK IN WASHINGTON

Virgil stood on the hospital steps, his face more careworn and wrinkled than it had been a few weeks earlier, his formerly paunchy midsection now a bit thinner. His scalp showed through the remaining locks of gray hair on his head. Harry was with him. They'd just paid a visit to Nancy's family, who were maintaining their vigil outside of intensive care, where Nancy remained after her transfer from a hospital in Germany. She was still in critical condition from the stab wound, but it looked like she'd eventually recover. Even so, her family had been far from happy to see Harry, who they blamed for putting her in danger. And Nancy had been one of the lucky ones. Two other American hostages being held by the same militants had been killed in the raid that freed Nancy. This was Harry's third visit to a grieving family in the last two days.

Coverage in the papers hadn't been positive, with editorial writers – particularly the *Times'* own – demanding to know why the failed raid had been launched when it could put Nancy and the other hostages in danger, and why the soldiers dispatched to free the Americans hadn't been able to better protect them once the raid began. As for Virgil, he couldn't get the site of Nancy's pale face as she lay in the hospital, tubes projecting from her body, out of his head. She hadn't regained consciousness since the raid, and it looked like she'd be in a coma for some time to come. How long, no one could say.

The Times' lead editorial today, Dec. 20, was titled, "A Misguided Military Raid," and called into question the Army's decision-making abilities. "The tragic deaths of two hostages and the horrific injury suffered by

New York Times' reporter Nancy Hanson is yet another example of U.S. military incompetence in Iraq," the editorial concluded. "The Defense Department needs to provide a full explanation as to why the raid was ordered, why it failed to provide adequate protection for the American hostages, and how lessons from this botched operation will be applied to future hostage situations in a war where news from the front just keeps getting worse."

"You goin' back to the office, Virge?" Virgil heard Harry asked. It sounded like it came from far away, but he nodded. They were the only ones left on the stairs, except for Harry's ever-present aides, a few steps behind and higher up. The reporters and photographers who'd followed Harry to the hospital to report on his visit were packing to leave. They'd already been told that Harry wouldn't take any questions, and there were several security officers barring media access to the sidewalk and the stairs beyond it, where Harry and Virgil stood.

Harry was blinking in the chilly January air, and he now took out a monogrammed white handkerchief from the pocket of his dark suit and blew his nose softly. Two of Harry's aides approached, each with a briefcase.

"Sir, should we call the motorcade?" Susie asked.

"No, wait a while," Harry said. "Virge and I will just wait here a few more minutes."

"OK, just let us know when you want to go," Susie replied. She walked back up the steps and got on her phone.

"You can ride with me," Harry told Virgil.

"No. I think I need to take a long walk alone," Virgil replied. He wrapped his coat around him more tightly. The sun had gone behind clouds, intensifying the December chill.

"I wish I could do that," Harry said. "They don't let you walk around by yourself once you're in the cabinet, you know. A damn shame." He blew his nose again.

Virgil stared at the ground. He wished he could crawl into it.

"Look, Virge, I know you're blaming yourself for this, but that's counterproductive," Harry said. "First of all, you were tryin' to do the right thing, and second of all, the orders to proceed came from the General, not from you. The raid failed because a lot of things went wrong all at once, and we were dealing with some tough customers in a really bad neighborhood. It wasn't anything you did."

"I've told myself that, Harry, but it doesn't really wash," Virgil said, shaking his head. "If I hadn't gone beyond my job responsibilities and tried to track her down, no one would have made the raid in the first place. Those hostages are dead because of me."

"Virge, they might have died without you doing that, too," Harry said. "Those Al-Qaeda guys, they were playin' for keeps. They might have eventually killed the hostages anyway. Not to mention other unspeakable things. Stop readin' the damn papers so much. Those newspaper people always want to blame someone, but sometimes, no one's to blame."

"Thanks, Harry, that means a lot, it really does. But I think this is it for me in government. I'm really thinking it is. Everything I've done has gone wrong. I'm not helping anyone."

A gust of wind came up and blew Harry's handkerchief away. "Damn thing," the defense secretary said. Susie chased it down and brought it back to Harry, who stuffed it back in his suit jacket. Harry went coatless despite the 35-degree weather.

"Don't you go steppin' down on me, Virge," Harry said sternly. "I still need you. And that reminds me. General Davies gave me a message that I think you'll find interesting."

"Really?" Virgil said, turning his face toward Harry's. He couldn't begin to imagine what sort of message Davies might have for him.

Harry fished a piece of paper out of his pocket and unfolded it. He handed it to Virgil.

Virgil read it aloud.

"Nancy Hanson, recorded by Cpl. Martin Simmons, M.D. 'Tell Virgil Walker: The Two Towers.' "

He stared at the paper for a minute. Harry watched him and waited for him to say anything.

"Two towers," Virgil said, as if to himself. "How...? How could she know?"

"I can't say I understand it myself," Harry said. "Had you talked to her since the time you gave her that memo?"

"No," Virgil replied. "Not once in five years."

"Did you tell her then that you thought the World Trade Center could be a target?" Harry asked. "I'm guessin' that's' what she's talkin' about. Unless you and her were secret Tolkien fans together, which I doubt rather highly." There was a brief sparkle in Harry's eyes.

Virgil frowned, and slowly answered. "No. No. I don't think I ever mentioned those buildings to her, and I know I kept them out of my memo. We didn't have specific intelligence pointing to any particular buildings, but those towers definitely would be a plausible target," Virgil said, speaking more quickly now. "I mean, you read her article back then, right? I was quoted saying buildings may have been targeted, but I never said…" he paused for a moment, and then added, "I didn't want to cause panic."

"I think you did, anyways," Harry said, with a small smile. "But the point isn't what you told her then, it's what she's tellin' you now. Why would she say those words right then? Why would she have thought of you?"

Virgil shifted his weight to favor his good leg. He'd been standing a long time on the hard concrete stairs, and his bad leg was starting to talk to him rather loudly.

"Well, I have to think about it," Virgil said. "But if I were to make a quick guess, I'd say she saw or heard something in captivity that made her think the buildings are in danger, or were in danger at some point."

"Yeah," Harry said, nodding. "That's what I think, too. I'm goin' to need to bring this up with the military and with some of the higher ups. People need to know if those buildings are targets. Those fellas you're following around, any luck trackin' 'em down?"

"The FBI's on it, but nothing yet," Virgil said. "They can't find a trace of any of them. It's like they've vanished from the country."

"Oh, we'd know if they left the country," Harry said. "Virge – no leaving your job until you help locate those fellas. You may know more about them than a lot of people, with all that research you've done. Now you run along and git me a talking points memo for Bush and Cheney. I want to discuss the next steps with them."

"Will do, Harry; will do," Virgil said, trying to sound enthusiastic. He didn't feel that way. Writing a memo for Bush and Cheney wasn't something he relished doing, knowing how they tended to react to any of his advice.

"Susie, I'm ready to go back – tell the motorcade to come," Harry called out. "Virge," he said, putting his arm around Virgil. "Take a short walk if you want, but then I need you on this case. Get yourself together, now, you hear? We're goin' to get through this. OK?"

"I'll do my best, Harry."

Virgil watched Harry's short motorcade pull away down Connecticut Avenue toward downtown, and he climbed slowly down the stairway, figuring he'd walk until his leg got too painful and then grab a cab. He realized he wasn't far from the restaurant he and Nancy had eaten in that time five years ago, the day all this had started, really. He thought about walking by, but decided not to relive that memory any further.

As he walked, the sun appeared again from behind the cloud, lighting up the busy street and immediately warming the air about 10 degrees. With the sun out, Virgil felt a sudden burst of inspiration, a new desire to move forward and find the people who'd done this to Nancy. To find the people who even now threatened his country. Now he himself had a personal reason to finish the job, and seeing Nancy's family suffering intensified his need to get back on this case and start moving.

"Taxi!" he yelled.

CHAPTER 22

ALEV REACHES OUT

After the terrorist hijackings of 2001, the U.S. government had set up a terror alert number. Anyone with a tip on a possible plot could call in anonymously and talk to the authorities.

Alev, sitting in her comfortable apartment back in Munich, had researched this fact on the Internet. She stared a moment more at the phone before she dialed the number from the cheap cell phone she'd just bought at the drug store down the street and waited. She'd been back in Germany two weeks, and Ziad hadn't called her. Despite what she'd said at their parting, she found herself wishing he would. She knew she'd still take him back if he'd come to her.

But despite her loyalty to him, she knew she wouldn't be able to live with herself if an attack occurred and she hadn't said or done anything to stop it. No, she wouldn't tell the authorities his name, but she would tell them that an attack was imminent and that the perpetrators seemed to be operating out of Chicago.

"Hello, FBI," a woman's businesslike voice said on the other end.

Alev, who spoke English with a slight accent but not enough to hinder her, told the woman what she knew.

"You say this is some sort of terrorist plot and it might be in Chicago, right?" the woman repeated to Alev when she was done.

"Yes, yes," Alev replied quickly. "It's my boyfriend. I'm afraid he's mixed up with it."

"Ma'am, you have to tell me his name, or I'm afraid we can't do much to follow up," the woman said.

"I can't do that," Alev said. "But he's in Chicago, and I think he's been with some criminals. I just want you to be on the lookout."

"OK," the woman said, sighing audibly. "Have it your way. But there are seven million people in Chicago, and it's going to be hard to find out anything if we don't have a name and an address."

"I know," Alev said. "But I just can't do that."

"Can we have your name?" the woman asked.

Alev pushed the "end" button on the phone, and without thinking too much she placed it in her desk drawer. Then she stood up and looked out the window at the headlights of cars moving along the dark street, feeling ashamed that she couldn't do more.

CHAPTER 23

"SECURITY" GUARD

John "Jack" Hardaway became a security guard at Baltimore-Washington International Airport in the 1980s. He was a tall, thin man of around 50, his pink head completely bald, with eyes that seemed to probe into people when he looked at them.

Hardaway boasted an exemplary job record. His supervisors praised him for his professionalism and his devotion to duty. His background checks were absolutely clean. Hardaway never turned down an extra shift, and commanded a group of guards who worked hard to stay in his good graces.

But in his personal life, things weren't so hot. His supervisors didn't know that Hardaway was a compulsive gambler who hung around New Jersey casinos during his off hours. Which explained why Hardaway recently went through a very unpleasant divorce from his wife of 25 years, including a fight over child support for their teen-age children. He lost the case, and now had to pay a rather large sum to his ex-wife every month. Recently, he'd become more aggressive than ever at the blackjack tables, intent on winning enough to cover his excessive child support, but the cards didn't favor him. As he drove to the bar now to meet his contact, he owed his wife $22,241.07 and had just $933.23 in the bank. Those numbers kept playing in his mind. He envisioned them outlined in flame, branding into his skin, and gripped the wheel harder as he drove through the early evening darkness.

Hardaway had an unblemished reputation with his superiors, but his reputation around town was slightly less clean. He'd taken payments in the past to ensure that certain packages made it onto certain planes. Never anything lethal – Hardaway wouldn't let that happen – just packages that might be better off not going through security. With Hardaway's security pass, he could access just about any area of the terminals and tarmac, and he also knew most of the luggage handlers who worked at the gates. Some of the luggage handlers could be convinced to look the other way when Hardaway asked them to, especially when he gave them $50 or $100 to shut their mouths. It wasn't something he did often, but it was a small side business, and the longer he did it, the better he got. Like many criminals who succeed over and over, he had become a bit brazen, and confident that he'd never get caught.

His recent financial troubles put Hardaway in a very difficult position. He needed thousands of dollars right away, or he could serve time for failure to pay child support, his lawyer had told him. He'd put out the message among his network that he was open to doing a job, and a possible order had come through rather quickly. It looked like some big money might be involved, and he was eager to learn more.

On this night, Dec. 21, the longest night of the year, Hardaway pulled his gray Chevy Impala into the parking lot at the anonymous-sounding Joe's Bar and Grill on a suburban road about three miles from the airport. As he got out and shut the car door, a big jet flew just overhead on final approach. The noise filled the world, but Hardaway didn't even notice, he was so used to it. He threw his cigarette butt on the pavement and stomped it out with a brown work boot. What was the world coming to when they wouldn't even let you smoke in a bar, he thought to himself bitterly.

He trudged through the slushy parking lot and walked into the warmth and dim lights and wailing country music of the bar, looking around. The smell of beer hung in the air. He'd been told the name of the contact - some guy named Julio – but not what he looked like. Now he scanned the handful of customers at the bar and the dark wooden tables, trying to see if anyone looked Hispanic. He checked his watch to see if he was early. Nope – right on time.

"Table for how many?" asked the young hostess, approaching him with a menu. The bar was on his right, and toward the back were some tables.

"I'm looking for my friend," Hardaway said. "A guy named Julio."

"Julio? Yeah – he's right over here. Just follow me." The hostess pulled a menu off of a pile sitting on a table at the entrance and walked past the bar into the seating area. Sure enough, Hardaway saw a dark-haired man at one of the tables. He didn't look particularly Hispanic, but he was dark skinned like some of those Mexicans, Hardaway thought to himself. Doesn't matter what he looks like, he supposed. None of the other tables nearby were occupied. The place was pretty much empty except for some old men nursing beers at the bar and watching basketball on TV.

"Here you go," the young lady said, putting a menu on Julio's table. "Can I get you a drink?"

"A Miller Light. Thanks," Hardaway said. He sat down across from Julio and the waitress bounced back toward the bar. Hardaway admired her rounded rear end as she walked away. Then he looked across the table. The man stared at him intently.

"Julio?" Hardaway asked, suddenly feeling nervous for some reason. "You're Julio, right?"

"Yeah," the man said quietly, hand on his mug of beer, his eyes never wavering from Hardaway. He had a slight accent, but it didn't sound Hispanic to Hardaway, who worked with lots of Mexicans. Maybe this guy was from South America or something.

"You Jack?" the man asked.

"Yeah – I'm Jack. Look, let's not waste time. What's the job and what does it pay?"

The man looked over Hardaway carefully. It made Hardaway feel uncomfortable, like he was being sized up.

"I've heard you do some business at the airport now and then," Julio said quietly.

Hardaway nodded. "That's right. I do. If the job is right for me. Come on. What's this job?"

The man held his right hand up to slow Hardaway down.

"I'll get to the job soon enough," the man said, and Hardaway decided the guy must be South American. Those Colombians did lots of drug deals, right? Maybe this guy was part of some cartel down there.

"First, I want to know if we can trust you," Julio said.

Hardaway laughed nervously and pointed to himself. "Trust me? Look, boss, if the money is paid up front, I'm good as gold for you. I've been doing this for years. Ask anyone I've worked with – you can trust me."

The waitress came over with a bottle of Miller Light and set it in front of Hardaway. They stopped talking until she left again. They were still the only ones in this part of the establishment. The Wizards basketball game played on a TV mounted in the corner.

"I understand you have some money worries," Julio said quietly when the waitress was gone. "Sounds like you could end up in jail if you don't pay up."

"Look," Hardaway said, a cold feeling spreading inside. "I don't know how you know that, but I don't see why it matters. Yeah – I've got some problems. OK. That's why I'm here."

"This is an important job," Julio said, changing the subject. "Have you ever handled weapons?"

"You mean have I ever shot a gun?" Hardaway asked. "Sure I have – I just got back from some deer hunting in Virginia--"

"Keep your voice down," Julio said quietly but firmly. "You didn't understand what I said. I don't give a damn if you ever shot a gun. I want to know if you've ever handled them."

"Oh, I see what you mean," Hardaway said slowly, feeling a bit sheepish – not a common feeling for him. "Well sure, yeah – I've done that before."

That, of course, was a lie. He'd never placed a weapon on a plane. He'd always done his jobs on the condition that no one gets hurt. He was just out to make a little side money, not to get blood on his hands. But this time was different and he was pretty desperate. So these drug guys needed some guns transported somewhere. So what? As long as no one was getting shot on the plane, he couldn't care less. The less he knew about this job, the happier he'd be. He always tried to maintain a comfortable distance from his clients. He had enough problems of his own without getting emotionally involved with the scum he was helping out.

"I understand you and your people have special access," Julio said, and Hardaway nodded. "But I don't want anyone but you involved with this job. If you tell any of your friends, we don't pay you anything beyond the upfront cash, get it?"

"Yeah, sure," Hardaway replied. He could handle that – he'd done jobs on his own before. It just took a little extra care to make sure he could spend a little time on the bird before the luggage was finished loading. On some of his previous jobs the clients had specified where they wanted the materials left – a specific overhead bin or seat pocket. He supposed this would be the same. But if the guns were really big, space could be an issue.

"These items you're talking about, Julio, are they large or small?" Hardaway asked.

"I don't see why that's any concern of yours," Julio said. Again his eyes went up and down Hardaway's face, an uncomfortable feeling. Hardaway took a quick sip of his beer.

"Yeah, well, what I meant was, I need to know because that affects where I can store them, you know what I mean?"

"I'll get to that," Julio said. "First you need the flight number and date. It's Tuesday, Jan. 9. The 9:11 a.m. Southwest flight to Boston." He took out a piece of paper and wrote down the info, then passed it across the table to Hardaway. "The items are small – they'll fit in the overhead bin."

"I'm your man, boss," Hardaway said, pocketing the note. "What's the pay and where do I pick up the materials?"

"What do you usually charge?" Julio asked.

"Depends on the job," Hardaway replied, taking another sip of beer to brace himself for the negotiation. This job was on his back alone – that meant a higher fee. And it involved weapons – ditto. This might be just the job he needed and just in time. "For something like this, it takes $10,000 up front and another $12,000 upon delivery. I have to charge more for certain items, you know."

"Agreed," Julio said, reaching across the table to shake Hardaway's hand. Hardaway shook back, a bit surprised that the deal was wrapping up so quickly.

"I'm going to the men's room and will be right back," Julio said, withdrawing Hardaway's hand. Julio got up and walked to the back of the place, where he disappeared into the bathroom. Hardaway glanced up at the TV. Gilbert Arenas had just made another three-point shot.

Julio returned from the bathroom a moment later and shook Hardaway's hand again, slipping something into it as he did. Hardaway knew to pocket the money before looking. He'd count it in the car. If the pay wasn't right, he wouldn't do the job. That's how he operated.

"The package will be in a gray duffel bag," Julio said quietly as he sat back down. There was still no one nearby. "I'll drop it off at your home tomorrow night. I want the package placed in the overhead bin above seat 2A and 2B. First class. Understood?"

"Yeah, boss," Hardaway replied. "Sounds easy enough. You know my address?"

"I do," the man said, looking at him again with those piercing eyes. "I know a lot about you, Jack. And if anything slips up, you'll be hearing from me again.

"Hey, no slip-ups," Hardaway said, holding up his hands as if to show he was too competent to ever let such a thing happen. "Never have been. Just ask any of my customers."

"I have," Julio said. "That's why I came to you.'

"OK. Good night, I guess?" Hardaway said. He wanted to get away from this guy. Julio gave him the willies.

"Good night for now," the man said. "Your doorbell will ring at 9 p.m. tomorrow with the package. Be there."

"Yep, you can count on me," Hardaway said. "See you around." He hurried to the door, eager to light a cigarette. This was the first drug dealer ever to really intimidate him, and he couldn't understand why he had this feeling of dread. But the money was real; he counted it as soon as he got into his car. A smile slowly appeared on his lean face.

Jarrah sat back in the booth for a while after Hardaway left, declining the waitress's offer for another beer. Normally, Jarrah liked a good beer as much as anyone. He'd started drinking a few years ago, against Islamic practice, to better fit into his American mission and found he liked it. But he didn't feel much appetite for it or for anything lately. The operation was getting very close, and he didn't feel the same fire in the belly as last time. It felt like he was going through the motions. Having the Director in charge instead of Atta probably was part of it. Although Jarrah and Atta hadn't always gotten along, he'd admired Atta for his powerful leadership. The Director just got on his nerves.

He also ruminated about what the government might know. The whole Chicago thing left a bad taste in his mouth, and Hanjour – much to the Director's frustration – hadn't come up with a way to eliminate the enforcer. They simply couldn't penetrate the Cook County Jail – where the man was being held – without blowing their cover. Even the Director had ultimately accepted this, albeit with a nasty glance at Jarrah. The enforcer's continued presence, and the likelihood that he'd given descriptions of Jarrah and Hanjour to the police, forced them to make some changes to their plans. For instance, now they only went out at night, stayed in disguise and avoided public places. Even a hotel desk attendant could potentially give them away.

And now Jarrah had to deal with an unfamiliar airport, try to rush the job and put his trust in this Hardaway guy, whom he wasn't completely sure they could count on. There was no doubt the government would be more alert now, after the thing in Chicago. They'd been monitoring the news carefully and hadn't seen anything, but that didn't mean much. If the security apparatus was going to take additional measures to combat terror in the skies, it probably wouldn't advertise it to the world.

Jarrah knew this Hardaway guy hadn't believed the "Julio" alias. Jarrah was the least Middle Eastern looking of the three plotters, and the one most accustomed to working with Americans, which was why the Director had chosen him for this particular assignment. But he still didn't fit a Mexican profile. He sighed. Didn't really matter what the guy thought. He had their money and it wasn't a difficult job. The guns were small; they only needed handguns. There were three weapons, one for each plotter. The strategy would be similar to last time. Wait till the plane was up in the air, storm the cockpit and kill the pilots and have Hanjour fly while the other two plotters handled the passengers. Although there'd been some added security measures over the last five years to protect cockpits, they weren't too worried about gaining access. They could put a gun to a flight attendant's head and demand entry if it came to that.

Jarrah was pretty convinced that the passengers wouldn't fight back, especially if they were told the plane was being diverted to another airport. They would tell the passengers a bomb was on board, keep them calm and keep flying the plane on its same flight path from Baltimore to Boston. The passengers wouldn't suspect they planned to make the jet into a suicide bomb, because no one had ever done that before – not to anyone's knowledge. Jarrah wasn't sure the passengers would go exactly like lambs to the slaughter, the way the Director characterized it, but he wasn't worried about an onboard rebellion getting in the plotters' way.

They also could learn from some of last time's mistakes, Jarrah thought. They'd studied the type of airplane involved, a 737, very carefully on the Internet, and had booked simulator time as well. They knew the proper button to push to talk to passengers, so there'd be no repeat of Atta's screw up in broadcasting information over the radio to controllers. Oh yes, the Director knew that had happened. How he knew, Jarrah had no idea. It certainly hadn't appeared in any press coverage he'd seen at the time, but the Director just had a way of knowing things.

Jarrah wasn't worried about accessing the plane, either. The three of them had booked their flights in a couple of weeks ago under their assumed names, which had served them well for several years now. The names weren't linked to any criminal activities or to anyone associated with Al-Qaeda. They'd used the names many times on past flights they'd taken to get familiar with the interior of the 737 – the type of plane Southwest flew from BWI to Logan.

He was more concerned with Hanjour's piloting and the Director's ability to control his temper. Hanjour hadn't been behind the controls of a real jet plane in five years, and had only gone up about half a dozen times in small planes that he had rented. But flying a single-engine propeller plane couldn't compare to flying a fully-loaded 737, and all three of them knew it. Hanjour was the only "real" pilot among then, in that he'd been through an actual pilot training program, but that had been many years earlier. He'd spent a lot of time flying simulated 737 flights on the computer, but they'd decided against trying to get him flight lessons. A man with a Middle Eastern accent applying for flying lessons would have brought attention, even from the most oblivious Americans.

At least Hanjour had the even temper needed on an operation like this one, but that certainly wasn't true of the Director. The man had no ability to keep his head when things went wrong, and Jarrah was sure at least one or two things wouldn't go according to plan the day of the attack. He'd tried to discuss this with the Director, but the man had waved him off.

"I've dedicated the last decade to this operation," the Director had told Jarrah haughtily last week, when Jarrah mentioned his concerns. "I should be the least of your concerns. You concern yourself with getting things right and not fucking things up like you did in Chicago."

Still, the Director remained a concern. It's true he'd become a bit easier to work with in the last weeks since announcing he'd participate. He'd given Jarrah more autonomy than he'd expected, and he'd agreed without much fuss to Jarrah's logistical plans. It seemed that the Director had begun to absorb what all this meant, now that his own life was about to end, and, aside from lashing out at Jarrah when asked about his temper, had taken a calmer, more thoughtful approach.

But this new, subdued Director might not last. What if they reached the date of the operation, boarded the plane, and got sidetracked by the Director not handling himself appropriately? The man could fly off the handle at the slightest thing. Even a flight attendant telling him to make sure his seat back was straight might set him off. Jarrah's blood pressure went up just thinking about the possibilities.

But the worst thing was, Jarrah didn't know if he could go through with it. He just didn't.

After living for five years in the United States, Jarrah had – despite himself – grown fond of the country and its people. There was something innocent about the men and women here; most of them had never tasted fear and want. And the way they showed affection for each other in public, which had seemed so alien at first, now tugged at his heart, like the elderly couple he'd carried in his cab a few days before Alev's arrival.

Driving a cab, he had spent many hours in close proximity to all sorts of Americans from different racial and ethnic backgrounds, and he was more and more impressed, and also puzzled, by how they all seemed to get along. Even the ones who were obviously Jewish had treated him with respect. He'd never known a Jew could act remotely human. He'd grown up believing Jews were devils. And yet in his final week driving a cab in Chicago, an obviously Jewish man had asked him so politely about his life in the United States, and then left a generous tip. Could they all be that way? He thought again about Alev's question, 'What do you think of Jews?' " He hadn't answered then, and now he was more confused than before.

Never too religious to begin with, Jarrah had entered Al-Qaeda as a young man with a chip on his shoulder about the Israeli treatment of Palestinians and illusions of grandeur. That was more than half a decade ago, and even then, it had taken Atta and others in Al-Qaeda a great deal of effort to get him to come back from Germany and go through with the Sept. 11 plot. Alev and her family had tried to talk him into staying, but he'd found the willpower to overcome the comforts of home and family.

Jarrah hadn't mentioned any of this to the Director or Hanjour. But he sensed that the Director suspected his heart wasn't in it. The conversation in the taxi that night in Chicago was proof that the Director, always extremely capable of reading people,had his doubts about Jarrah. In a way, that conversation had redoubled Jarrah's efforts to engineer a successful outcome, because if there was anything he didn't want, it was for the Director to doubt his capabilities. Rejecting Alev's plea to come back to Germany was part of proving himself to be reliable, he realized.

Then came the failures with the spy. Though the Chicago malfunction wasn't completely Jarrah's fault, it was the first time the Director had expressed lack of respect for Jarrah and his many abilities. That ate into Jarrah at a very deep level, deeper, perhaps, than the part inside of him that had grown used to America and respectful of its people. In the end, the need to please the Director, something that had been building in him for so many years, was winning out. But the process wasn't linear. Some days he wanted to kill the man and get on with his life. On those days, visions of Alev kept creeping into his mind.

He'd thought about discussing all this with Hanjour, and had even begun a conversation with him earlier today as they sat in Jarrah's anonymous hotel room. But talking to Hanjour was like talking to the Koran. The man was always so quiet, and when he did speak, it tended to be in platitudes.

"All praise is due to Allah who has given us life after our death and to him is the resurrection," Hanjour had replied when Jarrah asked if Hanjour was truly ready to die.

"You have no doubt, then, that what we're doing is right?" Jarrah had asked.

"I've asked Allah for guidance, and I've put myself in his hands," Hanjour had replied. "This is the destiny he has guided me toward."

"I wish I could be that sure," Jarrah had said.

"Why? Do you doubt our mission is holy?" Hanjour asked. "Surely you still feel now as you have in the past?"

"Yes, yes," Jarrah had replied quickly, not wanting to get Hanjour worried enough that he might discuss the conversation with the Director. "I believe in the rightness of the mission to highlight the plight of our brothers in Palestine and Iraq, but I just don't know if I'm ready to die."

"Remember, Ziad, when you have questions like this, do what I do. Put yourself in Allah's hands. The prophet said, 'In the name of Allah, I trust in Allah, for there is no power or might but with Allah,' Come now, Ziad, you seldom pray. Join me in prayer."

Hanjour went to the closet, brought out two prayer mats and placed them on the floor in front of the television. The two men washed their hands and then knelt on the rugs and began the morning prayer. Jarrah tried to focus on it, but found his mind wandering, as it always did when he prayed. He glanced over at Hanjour, who seemed to be in another world, completely absorbed in what he was doing. Jarrah felt a pang of jealousy. How pleasant it must be to know yourself so well and to have so few doubts.

Now Jarrah finished his beer, taking care to only have one. He needed to keep his wits about him this final couple weeks. With Jan. 9 getting so close, he felt like a man on death row who knew his execution date. He'd even gone to the local mosque a few times recently, trying to reconnect with his boyhood religion that had once seemed so important. And he spent hours reading through Internet accounts of Palestinian and Iraqi suffering, trying to remind himself of why he was going through with this, of the message they would be sending to the world. The strike against the Trade Center, he told himself, using language he'd heard many times from the Director, wasn't a strike against ordinary Americans; it was a strike against the American financial system that drove financial and military payments and assistance to the criminal governments of Israel, Saudi Arabia, Iraq and Egypt. The Sheik would make that clear in a speech he'd already recorded, which would be released immediately after the attack.

Jarrah dropped a $10 bill on the table and got up to leave. No one paid attention to him. He was as alone as ever. He walked over to his rental car and drove off to the Best Western where he was staying. The others were at hotels nearby. The final stretch was here, and there was no turning back. He ignored the voice in his head that urged him to call Alev.

CHAPTER 24
FAA WARNING

FAA Memo posted to flight crews and other flight personnel by the U.S. government:

Dec. 27, 2006
From: FAA Security
To: All U.S. airlines, pilots, ground crews and other flight personnel

Please post this message where accessible to your employees, and email to all flight staff.

Recently, the FAA became aware of a security breach at O'Hare Airport. All airlines, flight crews and ground personnel must be on guard for any attempts by criminal elements to penetrate airplane security and load illegal materials of any sort onto aircraft.

We aren't aware of any other location in which similar criminal activities have occurred. However, any breach of security – no matter how minor – must be immediately reported to FAA security.

Thank you for your cooperation.

CHAPTER 25

Facing a Tough Decision

On New Year's Day, Virgil sat in the local Starbucks, sipping his Venti Caramel Macchiatto (he'd recently moved up from a Grande) and reading news coverage of the FAA memo that he'd reviewed for the Defense Department. The President and Vice President had agreed to issue the memo to airlines and release it to the public after Harry had briefed them on the possible connection between the breach at O'Hare and the faces of the men who'd been on airplanes five years earlier, the day of the collision. There was a national FBI manhunt underway for Jarrah and Hanjour, and every airport was getting extra security. Virgil, with some pride, felt that at last his work had paid off. Having Harry as a friend certainly helped him get stuff done.

Today was the first day any of this had appeared in the media, and Virgil shook his head as he read it. The same old stuff as back in 2001 – with the public being told only half the story so no one would "panic." The whole country, he thought, had spent too many years since 2001 growing more and more sanguine about airplane safety. It scared the shit out of Virgil to think how easy it would be for determined terrorists to sneak arms aboard a plane and hijack it, but there was this crazy idea that all the danger was behind, and that the measures taken since 2001 had solved the problem. So untrue. So untrue.

The administration had given the media a vague account of what had happened in Chicago, and the coverage reflected as much. The Washington Post editorial he was reading complained about the scant information shared by the government, saying people had the right to know exactly what had happened so they could assess the threat. But the government didn't want to share too much information, fearing it could inspire copycats. For now, the only information reporters had was word of an airport ground worker arrested in Chicago for attempting to sneak unauthorized material onto planes.

He supposed some enterprising reporter would soon file a Freedom of Information Act request to get the full story, but for now, it wasn't going to be available, and this time, he wasn't going to the media. He'd already thrown himself on his sword once, and look where it had gotten him. Now that he was back, he'd try to do what he could from within the government both to catch the bad guys and to make sure the right people had the information they needed. Throwing up all over the newspapers wasn't the most targeted way to get out a message, he'd learned. So he was working on a couple of fronts to protect the country if his bosses wouldn't.

Virgil still felt the government wasn't going far enough to warn of the true threat. The warning to airlines and pilots hadn't specifically mentioned possible hijackings or the possibility of hijackers flying planes into skyscrapers. Virgil was certain the cryptic "two towers" utterance from Nancy as she lost consciousness was a reference to the World Trade Center, and he'd made his point in meetings with the FBI. Nancy herself remained in a coma and couldn't be questioned. Partly through Harry and Virgil's efforts, additional bomb detection squads were assigned to the grounds of the WTC, and extra security personnel were posted in the lobby, but none of that would do much good, Virgil thought, if someone aimed a plane at the buildings. That possibility still seemed too far out for most of the people he talked to.

But he was determined to make sure the right people in government knew about the danger to the buildings, and luckily, he had Harry's ear, and Harry had the ears of many Generals and the Joint Chiefs of Staff. As of yesterday, the Air Force had received orders to keep a special eye on any planes in unauthorized air space around New York City. Extra patrols were on duty, and fighter planes would be ready to take to the sky at short notice if necessary. Virgil and his team had done some research, and discovered that back in 2001, when the collision had occurred, the Air Force had been in no position to do anything to quickly protect New

York buildings. If the terrorists had the WTC in mind then, they would have easily hit it, with no interference from the military. This time, it would be different.

But that didn't mean it would be easy, Harry had told Virgil. They'd been in Harry's large office last week, sitting in armchairs, sipping coffee, and talking about the measures underway. The President and Vice President had agreed to the extra patrols and special alert, but neither one, Harry said, felt much concern about the threat.

"They just don't see it happenin', and sometimes, I have trouble too," Harry said. "I mean, it does seem pretty far-fetched, Virge. Based on some criminals in Chicago that we can't track who were supposedly engaged in some shenanigans out there, and what your reporter friend said in Iraq, with nothin' to back it up, it's not much to go on. Believe me, gettin' Cheney to buy into this hasn't been easy. I have to say, I've used up some of my credits with him on this. And the worst thing is, we'll probably have no way of knowin' if the threat is real. I mean, even if these fellas stand down because of what we're doing, how will we ever know they did?"

"I appreciate that you've staked your reputation to go along with this," Virgil had said, putting his cup of coffee on the table, an antique wooden piece of furniture that went with the big wooden desk and wooden bookshelves in the rest of the office. "But just keep in mind that we've identified the people behind the Chicago plot as the same people who were on planes that day in 2001. And we've traced the names back to training camps in Afghanistan. I really think we've uncovered a sleeper terrorist cell, and it's very likely that the guys who captured Nancy also were in on it. How else can you explain the coincidence of her coming up with those last words. The two towers. Damn. I just can't keep it out of my mind. I've even dreamed of them the last few nights. If we did nothing, and then those bastards flew planes into them, how would we ever sleep again?"

"I know that, and you know that," Harry said. "I swore to protect this country and that's what I aim to do. Now have you uncovered any more information?" He checked his watch. "I've got five minutes till my next meeting, and tomorrow I'm flying out to Iraq, so make it quick."

Virgil explained to Harry what he and his staff had uncovered. The man who'd kidnapped Nancy was Ramzi bin al-Shibh, according to documents found on his body. There hadn't been many other pieces of identification in the hut, which the terrorists had burned when the military approached, perhaps to destroy evidence. Al-Shibh was a Yemeni citizen who'd lived in many Middle Eastern countries. He had links to Mohamed Atta – the lead hijacker on American Flight 11 – and to Khalid Sheikh Mohammed.

"This is very important evidence connecting Ramzi to the attackers of September 2001," Virgil explained to Harry, who nodded. "To me, this is the smoking gun, and proves that Nancy's reference to the two towers has relevance. The thing we're still trying to determine is whether the two who seem to be in America – Jarrah and Hanjour – also had relations to Atta. We know Atta was a chief lieutenant of Osama bin Laden's. If we find out that Jarrah and Hanjour knew Atta, then we have the missing piece of the puzzle. It would mean they were part of a plot in 2001 that was bigger than we realized – a plot to hijack two other jet liners that day."

"And why didn't they, if you don't mind me asking?" Harry asked.

Virgil shook his head. "I just don't know, Harry. Maybe they decided not to after they heard that the first two planes had collided. But it just makes me sick with worry to think those two are still out there, somewhere, here in this country, and they rang an alarm bell at O'Hare last month. It's just by the grace of God that we know anything at all about this. So the evidence you called "far-fetched" just continues to build, and none of it looks good."

"OK, Virge," Harry replied. "Whenever I talk to you, I leave feelin' worse than when I started, but I guess you're just doin' your job."

Virgil smiled grimly.

"All right," Harry said, getting up. "I appreciate your help and I'm glad you're still on the team, no matter what my bosses might say about you."

"Do I want to know?" Virgil said, smiling.

"Oh, they think I have a Virgil Walker fetish, I reckon. I'll tell you, I sure hope you're wrong about this, but it makes me feel better knowin' we've taken some measures. But just tell me one thing. Let's say we see a 737 flying straight at the towers one morning. Now pretend you're me. How would you feel about recommending to the President that the military shoot down a passenger jet full of American men, women and children?"

Virgil stared at him, mouth half open. Now that Harry had put it like that, it really came home to him. He'd never actually thought of it in that sense. His whole focus had been on uncovering the plot before it took flight. He found he couldn't answer Harry's question.

"So you'd feel the same way I do, I guess," Harry said after a silent moment, shaking his head. "I sure as hell hope it doesn't come to that, because I just don't know what I'd do."

"If it does come to that, I'll be right here with you," Virgil said, looking directly into Harry's eyes. Harry looked right back and nodded silently. They both sat there for a minute, considering what they might have to face, but comforted to have each other's support.

CHAPTER 26

ALEV IN GERMANY

On the same day, in Germany, Alev returned very early in the morning from the New Year's party she'd attended, carrying a bottle of extra Champagne someone had given her. There'd been bottles left over, so she'd agreed to take one home. She entered her empty apartment and sighed. Another New Year's Day in which she ended up alone. She also didn't know why she'd taken the Champagne bottle, since she never drank the stuff. Where should she put it? Not the fridge – it would just take up space. Her eyes glanced around the room and landed on her desk drawer. Sure, there'd be room in there. She crossed the room, opened the drawer and looked inside. Lying there was the cheap phone she'd used to call the FBI. She'd meant to throw it away, but it had slipped her mind. Of course the battery was depleted, but she had a charger.

She picked up the phone and looked at it, wondering why she suddenly felt like she should charge it up. Maybe she should try calling the FBI again? She didn't want to call from her own home phone, not wanting to give up her privacy. She still felt ashamed of her cowardice the last time, when she'd hung up without giving her name. No – not now. She'd charge the phone and then decide later. She was too tired to make a decision now. She put the phone in the charger and fell into bed to catch up on the sleep she'd lost by staying out so late. When she woke up, she'd forgotten about the phone, and it remained in its charger.

PART THREE – TERROR STRIKE

CHAPTER 1

BWI AIRPORT

Hardaway walked into his office at BWI smoking a cigarette and carrying a gray duffle bag instead of his usual blue backpack. He joshed with some of the guys, made a bet on the Wizards game, and laughed at a new Polish joke told by his friend Pete. He felt good, partly because he'd used the $10,000 payment from "Julio" to pay off nearly half of what he owed in child support, and had promised his ex-wife the rest later this week. The bag drop-off from Julio had gone well, and he had what he needed to do the job, including access to today's 9:11 flight to Boston.

He donned his uniform, put on a thick black jacket to ward off the January cold, ran his security card through the machine and pushed open the heavy metal door to the tarmac, his breath smoking in the chill. The high-pitched noise of jet engines warming up pierced the air, and the sky was still gray and dark, with sunrise some time away. The lights of the terminals blinked red and green, and already, despite the early hour, dozens of jets waited at the gates. A United Airlines 737 taxied toward the runway, where ground lights would guide it through the darkness.

There'd been some interesting developments in the last week that he guessed might be related to today's operation. First, some of the big bosses had gathered him and his crew for a meeting to go over security operations. This wasn't too uncommon, but this time there was a twist. Any personnel with fewer than five years on the job would undergo full background security checks, they were told, over the next few weeks. Veteran employees would also be subject to these checks in the longer term. Of course, they'd all been checked when hired, but this sounded like an even more thorough investigation.

Also, a memo from the FAA was posted all over their offices and around the tarmac warning workers to be on guard for "criminal elements" who might try to load illegal materials onto planes. This was highly unusual, and the first time Hardaway had seen such a thing in his 20 years on the job. Obviously, everyone who worked there was charged at all times with doing just that – keeping illegal materials off of planes – but to have it posted in a special notice like that was disconcerting.

"What the hell do you think is going on?" Pete had asked Hardaway when the signs had gone up the other day.

"Damned if I know," Hardaway had said, stubbing out his cigarette on the tarmac with his booted foot. "Seems like they're trying to tell us we ain't doing our jobs the right way. What the hell. The bosses sit around their offices drinking coffee and worrying about all sorts of crap. Guys like us do the real work. But you can bet if something goes wrong, it's us who'll hear about it."

"Damned straight," Pete had replied. "Always think they can do our fuckin' jobs better than we can."

Hardaway felt a bit cocky, knowing that he had the inside scoop on this unusual warning. But his gut tightened each time his eyes landed on one of those notices. Were the authorities on to this specific operation he'd become part of? And if so, did they have their eyes on him?

And more alarming was the thought that perhaps he'd gotten involved with something a lot more dangerous than a drug deal. He almost began to have some second thoughts, but he decided it was too late. He'd already accepted the cash and had paid Cindy's lawyer. He couldn't very well go back now, and if he did, who knew what Julio and his friends might do. The guy hadn't looked like someone to mess around with.

Now, a few days after the first notices were posted, the fear had faded. No one had approached him, and the other workers now passed the signs without a glance. Hardaway felt strongly that he could do the job without any regrets. He had the weapons in his bag, and he knew the plane to Boston would be at gate D-22 by around 7. It was a Southwest 737 flight, and it wasn't coming from somewhere else – this was the start of its day. Once it arrived at the gate, it would be easy enough for Hardaway to climb aboard and place the bag in the overheard compartment where Julio had asked him to stow it. There was no metal detector to go through on the plane, and one of his jobs was to inspect the cabin for security prior to takeoff, so no one would be surprised to see him. He figured he'd have at least a few minutes alone on the aircraft prior to the crew boarding, which would allow him time to stow the bag without being seen.

Hardaway lit another cigarette, pulled on a pair of ear-protectors and a glow-in-the-dark vest and began his security patrol.

CHAPTER 2
FINAL WORDS

In the Marriott at the BWI Airport, Jarrah, Hanjour and the Director ordered room service in the Director's suite. The Director, who'd gained a lot of weight since he arrived in the U.S., put away a cheese omelet, three cups of coffee and a cinnamon roll, eating noisily and belching when he finished. Jarrah managed to keep a look of disgust off his face.

"Ahh," the Director grunted, with a burst of ugly laughter. "That feels better." He was still dressed in an old pair of blue pajamas, while the other two were already wearing slacks and oxford shirts.

Hanjour and Jarrah ate little of their breakfasts. Neither had slept much the night before. They'd spent the night going through their purification processes, including a ritual shaving and several cycles of prayer. Hanjour had thrown himself into the process enthusiastically, but Jarrah was only going through the motions – religion just wasn't too important to him now. He'd come to terms with what he was doing, and was ready to die. The attacks would be appropriate revenge, he felt, for the horrible deeds the United States and Israel had done in the Middle East with finances that originated in the two towers, and he knew he'd be a hero to millions of suffering Muslims for his actions. He'd won the fight within himself, and he was going to do what he'd set out to do so many years ago. But even through his resolve in the quiet moments between rituals and prayers, a small part of him resisted. It seemed to talk to him in Alev's voice, a voice he forced himself to tune out.

With breakfast over, Jarrah called the lobby for a cab to take them to the airport, and he picked up the Director's bags.

"No!" the Director said, shaking his head vigorously.

"What do you mean?" Jarrah asked.

"Put down my bags," the fat man said. "I'm not going."

This time, even Hanjour was incredulous.

"Why not?" Hanjour gasped.

Jarrah was speechless. He felt almost as if his legs couldn't hold him up, and he had to consciously force himself to remain standing. So this is how it is, he thought. They'd been played for fools. He remembered the night the Director had announced his intentions to fly with them, and his own doubt when he'd heard that. It turned out his doubt was justified. But even as all these thoughts went through his mind, a feeling of relief that was nearly palpable spread through him. Handling the Director had been his main worry today, and now he wouldn't have to. Arms folded across his chest, he looked at the man and waited for him to explain.

The Director stood up, all 5'4 of him, placed himself in the middle of the hotel suite in his pajamas and began gesturing grandly as he spoke in Arabic.

"As both of you know, I've been in constant communication with the Sheik," he said, raising his chin at mention of the Sheik, his eyes ablaze. "He and I have planned numerous operations overseas while I've been stuck in this country. Remember the Bali operation four years ago? That was *my* plan. And the female American reporter in Iraq? I also supervised that. There were many others as well, and some still in the works." He waved his hands as if the extent of his projects was too numerous to fully relate.

"I'm a valuable man, my friends, and by living here, I've been right under the Americans' noses while they searched for me in Pakistan. Their search was useless, praise Allah, and the Sheik wants me to continue as operational planner in years to come. He can't afford to lose me. Besides," he added, with a shake of a finger, "I need to work on a plan to destroy the remaining tower after you take care of the first one."

"So we kill ourselves and you stay behind eating omelets?" Jarrah asked, not even trying to hide his contempt. A hot fury burned up from his near empty gut.

"No, my friend," the Director responded with a shark-like smile. "Remember, too, that you don't just kill yourselves. You're destroying the financial power of the United States and the country's ability to pay for its crimes against our people. You're warriors in the battle against the infidels here, and your names will live forever. And don't forget the 72 virgins when you die."

"Seventy-two virgins?" Jarrah said. "Do you really believe that?"

"Of course!" Hanjour burst in earnestly. "The Sheik himself has said so."

"Thank you, Hanjour," the Director said gently. "The Sheik knows many things. And I trust him when he says today's operation is the right thing to do for our people."

He turned his attention back to Jarrah, his voice quieter but more serious now. "I've had my doubts about you, Jarrah, but I expect you to prove me wrong today. You've been hard working and loyal, and I've been able to count on you for many years. The Sheik sent me this note, and asked me to give it to you before today's operation." He waddled over to his bag, reached in, and pulled out a piece of notebook paper folded many times over. He handed it to Jarrah.

Jarrah unfolded the paper under the Director's watchful eyes and started to read the hand-written words. Then he looked up quickly, doubt in his eyes.

"Is this really from him?" Jarrah asked.

"Certainly, my friend," the Director replied with that same shark-like smile. "It's as I said. Read his words, Ziad. The Sheik believes in you, and he believes you're the right man to head this mission."

Jarrah began reading again, trying to decide if he believed the Director. He'd only met the Sheik once, and it had been for only a few minutes back in 1999. He wasn't familiar with the man's hand writing or style of language, so he had no way of knowing for certain if the Director was telling the truth. His eyes drifted away from the letters, seeing them but not really reading them.

The voice seemed to come from far away, but it was inside Jarrah's own mind. Even as the Director and Hanjour watched him expectantly, he felt as if he were somewhere else, back in the Middle Eastern restaurant in Chicago. Alev's bright blue eyes were shining into his, tears dripping down her cheeks. He heard her say again, "Ziad, you're not planning to hurt people, are you?"

Jarrah shook his head quickly, as if trying to stave off her question. The Director and Hanjour looked at each other and looked his way again.

Jarrah's mind returned to the hotel suite, and to the note in his hand.

"*My brother Ziad Jarrah,*" the note read. "*I have personally chosen you to lead this holy and sacred mission. Our martyred brother Atta has been shown his seat in paradise, and you will follow him. The blood pouring out of Palestine must be equally revenged. The world must know that the Palestinians do not cry alone; their women are not widowed alone; their sons are not orphaned alone. Take revenge on those who finance the Israeli atrocities and the atrocities against our people in Iraq and Chechnya. Remember, Ziad, despite what you may think from having lived there for so long, the American people are not innocent of all the crimes committed by the Americans and Jews against us.*" The letter went on further, but Jarrah stopped reading.

He looked up. Hanjour and the Director were staring at him expectantly.

"Well," the Director finally said. "Now do you believe the letter is from the Sheik? Because it is."

Jarrah found that he did believe the letter. His deep anger at the Israelis rumbled within him as he read the words, blotting out the voice and image of Alev in his head. The words of encouragement from the Sheik renewed his confidence in their operation, and he felt a sense of righteousness that was almost like a jolt of electricity. He would avenge the victims in Palestine. He nodded to the Director.

"Good, good, my friend," the Director said. "Ziad, you are in charge of this mission. Hanjour. You will take orders today from Jarrah in my absence. Understood?"

Hanjour nodded.

"As-salamu alaykam," the Director said, looking at both of them in a fatherly way.

They stood there for a moment, feeling the drama of what was to come that day.

"You had both better be going," the Director said after some time, looking at his watch. "It's 6:50. You board in an hour and a half. You still have to go through security. I hope that pig head American got the materials on board as we directed."

"He better have, for the money we paid," Jarrah said. He turned to Hanjour. "Come on, let's move," he said. Hanjour nodded and picked up their bags.

"I will monitor from the ground and send you instructions as necessary, just like last time," the Director told them as they prepared to leave. "May Allah be with you. You will both be in my prayers."

Jarrah took a last look at the Director. The two embraced.

"I know we haven't always agreed," the Director said quietly into Jarrah's ear. "But you are today's Mohammed Atta. Please make him proud with your actions."

"That is my aim," Jarrah said.

They closed the door and left, and the Director stood alone in the hotel suite, the smell of omelets still hanging in the air.

CHAPTER 3

MORNING IN MANHATTAN

It was a clear winter morning in New York, and the sun had just edged above the eastern horizon, throwing the first rays of light on the skyscrapers of Manhattan. The two World Trade Towers stood as they had for 35 years, tall and proud, like sentinels watching the broad harbor before them. Over the years, other, smaller buildings had been constructed nearby, but the two towers remained the undisputed kings of downtown New York, and it was difficult to imagine the city before their construction, so embedded were they into its very fabric.

Up near the top of Tower One, a number of Gladstone's condos remained on the market on this opening day, but Gladstone himself sat in his own unit, enjoying breakfast by himself at a small table next to the windows in his kitchen. He'd already been down to the lobby that morning to welcome the other residents moving in, greeting each one as they arrived in custom limousines he'd ordered especially for this day. Now he was taking a short break to eat. He'd moved in over the weekend – being the developer of the place had its advantages.

The kitchen had all the modern touches – granite counters, stainless steel appliances, hand-crafted cherry cabinets and a special chamber for storing wine. In the other rooms, his collection of modern art hung on the walls, just as it had when the unit was a model. Gladstone – a bit of a health nut – had added some more personal items, including a $2,100 Blendtec blender for his juicing needs and an $8,000 Hammacher Double Espresso machine. Gladstone sipped a double espresso from that machine now and read The Wall Street Journal. The big news today was some sort of special announcement that was going to be made by Apple CEO Steve Jobs at the MacWorld convention. Gladstone read the article carefully. He'd been a Steve Jobs admirer for some time, and wondered what the man had up his sleeve this time.

Gladstone put the paper down, took a sip of his espresso and looked out at New York Harbor 96 floors below. Not for the first time, he wished the architects would have designed wider windows, but even so, he never got tired of the view. In the first light of day, the harbor's water was a dark shade of blue, and he could see the Staten Island Ferry chugging past the Statue of Liberty toward the Battery, carrying commuters to lower Manhattan. Far beyond that, he could see the long New Jersey coastline, extending south and then east toward the ocean. It all seemed so quiet from up here. Gladstone knew he had to stop by the other condos soon to make sure moving day proceeded smoothly, but he wanted to savor the view one last time. He sat back in his chair and took another sip of espresso, trying to make this moment last.

CHAPTER 4

SECURITY CHECK

Southwest Airlines Captain Richard Billings and First Officer Kevin O'Rourke went through security at BWI as they got ready for their first flight of the day – a 9:11 run to Boston. After that, it would be back to BWI, and then back to Boston, where they'd be done for the day. Billings had just returned from a three-day break, but O'Rourke had flown into BWI yesterday, deadheading on a flight from Chicago. O'Rourke was ready for a day off – this was his fifth day in a row on duty – so it was a Friday for him, even if the actual day of the week was Tuesday.

"Damned security check," Billings complained to O'Rourke as they went through the metal detector after placing their bags on the conveyer belt. "Let me ask you – how much sense does it make for the airports to make you and I go through security every day? I tell you, it makes no sense at all."

O'Rourke nodded as he retrieved his carry-on from the belt behind Billings. "You said it, Rich," he said amiably. "It's so damn useless. I mean, come on, we're the damn pilots!"

"Well, it satisfies the Feds, I suppose," Billings said. They walked down the hallway toward the gates, dressed in their Southwest Airlines uniforms and dragging their carry-ons behind them. "If you want anything to make sense, don't ask the government to do it, right?"

"Exactly," O'Rourke replied. They'd reached D-22, where they greeted several other members of the flight crew. Passengers occupied every seat in the waiting area, and some watched a TV mounted on the wall, where a CNBC reporter was previewing the day's Steve Jobs event.

"Good morning, everyone," Billings said to the flight attendants with a sunny smile. "You all ready for another fun day?"

"Yeah, right," said Wendy Harris, the chief flight attendant, sipping a Starbucks as she stood near the gate. "This is way too early to be working." Harris, like O'Rourke, had been on duty for several days and was ready for a day off with her fiancé, who worked here in Baltimore, where she was based. After spending tonight in Boston, she'd finish tomorrow in Baltimore and have two days off. Unfortunately, her fiancé would be working. But at least they'd see each other and get to go out to dinner, maybe.

"Wendy, do you mind watching my luggage for a minute while I go get some coffee?" Billings asked.

"No problem," Harris nodded.

"I'll get on board and check things out," O'Rourke said.

"OK," Billings replied over his shoulder as he walked toward the nearby Starbucks. "You want anything?"

"Sure – bring me a grande mocha."

"With whip?"

"Yeah – thanks. Sounds good."

O'Rourke nodded to the security officer at the entrance to the jet bridge and walked through it to the 737. As he stepped on board, a tall, bald-headed man in a BWI security uniform with a radio on his belt and a gray duffel bag in one hand ambled casually over from first class and approached him. His security badged gleamed in the morning sunlight that poured in through one of the windows.

"Hi there," the security officer said. "I hadn't expected you guys to be on so soon."

"Oh, I like to get an early start," O'Rourke said. "Everything look ship shape?"

"Yep," the security officer replied. "I'm just doing my final check. I was already in the cockpit. You can head in there now."

"Will do," O'Rourke said. "Looks like a nice day to fly."

"Whatever you say, boss," the security guard said. "I'd just as soon stay on the ground."

"Once you get the flying bug, it never goes away, my man," O'Rourke replied, turning into the cockpit. "Have a good one."

"You too," the security guard said, and O'Rourke sat down in the first officer's seat, put on his headphones and began checking the controls.

Hardaway stood for a minute at the junction between the jet bridge and the tiny kitchen, and then stepped into the front of the passenger section. He glanced toward the cockpit to make sure O'Rourke was occupied, and then, very quietly and carefully, he opened the overhead compartment above seat 2C and gently laid the gray bag in. He closed the door softly and peeked back toward the cockpit. O'Rourke was talking to someone on his radio, not paying any attention to him. Whistling casually, Hardaway walked toward the back of the plane. The back door was still open, with a stairway leading down to the tarmac.

Hardaway casually walked down the stairs and stepped down onto the ground. He let out a deep breath. That had been a close one. The damned pilot had walked in just when he was about to open the overhead bin, and that would have caused some questions. Well, all had gone well and it was over. The drug gang would get their guns and Hardaway would get the $12,000 he was owed. No going to jail. He'd have to get back to the casino with some of that money and see if he could double or triple it before just handing it over to that son-of-a-bitch lawyer, he decided. His luck had finally turned.

CHAPTER 5

FINAL PREPARATIONS

Jarrah and Hanjour sat in the waiting area at Gate D-22, each of them pretending to read a newspaper, dressed in their neatly dry-cleaned business casual outfits. Per plan, they were on opposite sides of the waiting area, and once onboard, would be seated apart. Both had the plan down pat, and Jarrah was very glad the Director wasn't with them, now that the time had come. Half of his worries had been how to handle the Director, and that would have been a major distraction. The Sheik knew the Director as well as anyone, so Jarrah wouldn't be surprised if the Sheik had factored all that into the decision to keep the Director on the ground.

Still, his mind started to race as he thought of all the things that could go wrong. Would the weapons be in the overhead container where they should be? Would they be able to quietly convince the flight attendant to open the cockpit door at the right time without causing interference? Jarrah hoped it wouldn't be necessary to shoot anyone other than the two pilots, but he was prepared to kill the attendant if he had to. Both he and Hanjour had been to the shooting range numerous times, and could handle the weapons just fine.

He also worried about Hanjour's flying abilities. Both Hanjour and Jarrah had spent plenty of time flying single engine planes and on 737 simulators, and he told himself it was just a matter of steering. But steering a real plane, he knew, was far different than steering a simulator. Once in the cockpit, their plan was to put guns to the heads of the pilots to get the cockpit security codes so they could lock the door, then eliminate the pilots and have the controls to themselves. There'd be no need to herd passengers to the back as they had prepared to do five years ago. Nope - this plan was streamlined, as the Director liked to say. The question was whether they could carry it out. He could feel the sweat gathering under his arms and hoped it wouldn't show through his shirt.

As Jarrah checked his Seiko watch for the fourth time in five minutes, the announcement came over the loudspeaker:

"Welcome Southwest passengers to flight 143 to Boston, departing at 9:11 a.m.," the female voice said. "We're expecting a full flight today, but standby passengers please stay here at the gate and we'll be calling your names shortly. Thanks, and we're glad you chose Southwest today."

Jarrah stood up with his small Samsonite carry-on, and no one paid much attention to him. He had a few gray hairs that hadn't been there back in 2001, but he was still clean shaven and sharply dressed, and could have passed for any number of ethnicities, including Italian, Hispanic, Jewish or Arab. The name on his U.S. driver's license was Julio Garcia, a generic Hispanic name that he'd been using for a few months now. The Director liked to have everyone change their names every so often, which was easy enough to do, with Jarrah's expert knowledge of how to create fake documents.

Jarrah put his newspaper down on the chair and looked across the room toward Hanjour, who was sitting by the window with his own news-paper. Their eyes met briefly and Jarrah nodded his head slightly. Then he went over toward the front of the line and prepared to board. Hanjour followed closely behind. They'd paid extra for prime positions in line so they could sit at the very front of the cabin.

CHAPTER 6
VIRGIL IN D.C.

Virgil paced around his office, just as he had back on Sept. 11, 2001, although that office had been in the White House basement, a place where he was no longer welcomed. He was frustrated, just as he'd been then, and was still wondering about his commitment to this job, even though he'd promised Harry he would stay.

He was frustrated because the FBI's search for Hanjour and Jarrah had turned up nothing but dead ends. The agency found the apartments where the men had lived, but both living spaces had been cleaned and left pristine. It appeared the men had left Chicago a couple of weeks back, though Virgil wasn't sure how the FBI knew that. But there were no hints of where they might be now. It was like trying to track down ghosts.

He thought again about the one trace the FBI did get: A phone call from an unidentified woman overseas warning of a possible attack. The woman who had called refused to give her name, and when the FBI had tried calling the number back, there was no answer. They couldn't trace it to any given person or specific location, and only knew the call had originated in Germany. Either the person ignored the FBI's calls or the phone had run out of charge. Virgil's contacts at the FBI shared the number with him, and he had it in a notebook on his desk. He'd tried it several times a couple weeks ago, but no one picked up. There wasn't even a voice mail. He wondered who could have called. Someone who knew Jarrah? Someone who knew about his plans? Or more likely it was totally unrelated, maybe even a crank. Still, something about it intrigued him. He hadn't called the number since before the new year, but maybe he'd try again today.

Every day, Virgil looked at the calendar trying to determine if there was some symbolism associated with the date that might make it more likely for an attack. From his knowledge of Al-Qaeda, he assumed if there were to be an attack, it would be associated with some event on the same day in history. Today's date, he had noticed with trepidation, was the 59th anniversary of the Jan. 9, 1948, attacks by Arabs against Jews in what had then been northern Palestine. Of all the issues Al-Qaeda said it cared about, Virgil knew the Israel-Palestinian conflict was at the top of the list.

"The creation and continuation of Israel is one of the greatest crimes, and you are the leaders of its criminals," Bin Laden had written in his 2002 letter to America explaining why Al-Qaeda fought the United States. "And of course there is no need to explain and prove the degree of American support for Israel. The creation of Israel is a crime which must be erased. Each and every person whose hands have become polluted in the contribution towards this crime must pay its price, and pay for it heavily."

Virgil considered going down the hall to check in with Harry, who was back from Iraq. He studied Harry's calendar on Outlook, but, to no surprise, found that the secretary was booked in back-to-back meetings all morning. OK – he'd go get some coffee. That might settle him down.

As he walked down the hall to the small canteen on the same floor, he thought of what his son had told him last weekend when they met for coffee.

"Dad, you work too hard," Keith had said, when Virgil had told him he needed to get back to the office. "You worry too much. You need to get a hobby or something."

Virgil knew it was true, but didn't think he'd be able to relax until he knew where Jarrah and Hanjour had gone. He looked at the other people going by him in the hall and lining up for coffee at the coffee stand. They talked casually to each other about the ball game last night and the forecast for more snow. None seemed particularly stressed about anything other than the typical workday blues. He wished he could be more like them.

As he stood waiting to order, his eyes fell momentarily on a *New York Times* lying on one of the tables. Virgil stared over the reader's shoulder because a picture jumped out at him. It was of the two towers. The headline read, "Celebrities Plan Move Into WTC Condos Today." Suddenly he felt dizzy, and had to grab the counter to steady himself. A woman waiting at the counter for her drink turned to him, looking alarmed. "Are you OK?" she asked.

"Yeah," he grunted. "Just had a dizzy spell. I'm OK."

But he wasn't. Today was the day. Somehow, he just knew it. He steadied himself, grabbed his phone and started dialing Harry.

CHAPTER 7

TAKING OFF

Billings and O'Rourke received tower approval to begin their takeoff run. Billings, the pilot in control on this first leg of the day, turned the plane off the taxiway and onto runway 33L, which would put them on a northwest path at takeoff. They were cleared to climb to 10,000 feet and then turn right, where they would proceed to their 37,000-foot cruising altitude. Estimated flight time was one hour and 20 minutes. It would be one of those rides where they started descending almost as soon as they reached their peak altitude.

Billings pushed the lever to full power and the plane zoomed down the long runway.

"Vee one," Billings said as the plane hit safe takeoff speed.

"Vee two," he said a moment later, pulling back on the control stick. The front tire left the runway as the nose pointed up sharply into the clear blue sky. Soon, the big jet soared over the suburbs of Baltimore, where patches of snow from last week's storm still coated the ground in places.

"Still some snow down there," Billings said conversationally as they reached the assigned altitude.

"Yeah, it melts fast over here," O'Rourke said. "Seems like we have less every winter, doesn't it? Global warming, I suppose."

"You buy that story?" Billings asked. A controller on the radio interrupted him, telling them to climb to 37,000 feet. "Roger, Southwest 143, climb to flight level 370," he replied, and began pulling the wheel back. The engines gave a roar as he again applied full power and the plane started climbing.

"You mean global warming?" O'Rourke said, picking up the thread of their conversation. "Sure. It's what all the scientists say."

"You know those scientists just want funding for their projects," Billings said. "If they scare enough people with that global warming talk, it gets 'em in the papers. Raises their profile, you know. Helps with the funding."

"Sounds like you know more about it than I do," O'Rourke said. "You might want to watch your angle there – looks like we're climbing a little fast."

"Thanks," Billings said, pushing the wheel in slightly. "I got excited there thinking about that global warming stuff."

"No problem. Glad to help."

They were silent for a few moments, with communications on the radio from other flights the only noise in the cockpit. They leveled off at cruising altitude.

"Guess I'd better talk to our guests," O'Rourke said.

"Sure. Go ahead," Billings said. He examined the flight map.

"Good morning, everyone," O'Rourke said over the cabin intercom. "This is your first officer, Kevin O'Rourke, and I'd like to welcome you aboard. We're at our cruising altitude of 37,000 feet, and cabin service will begin shortly. Our flight route today will take us over Asbury Park, New Jersey, a bit out over the ocean, and then across Martha's Vineyard and on into Logan. You folks on the left-hand side of the craft should get a nice view of New York City coming up in about half an hour. Anyway, we anticipate arriving a few minutes early today, and hope to have you to the gate at Logan around 10:30. We'll give an update on connecting gates a little later. We expect a smooth flight today, so just relax and enjoy. And thanks for flying Southwest."

O'Rourke clicked off the intercom.

"There's Philadelphia over on my left," Billings said, pointing out his side window.

"Yep," O'Rourke said.

"Man, I shouldn't have had that Starbucks before we took off," Billings said. "Think you can handle things for a minute while I go make room?"

"Nothing to it, Rich," O'Rourke replied.

According to Federal rules, the two pilots were supposed to be together in the cabin at all times, but it was a rule commonly broken. Five years after the 2001 hijackings, most pilots took such rules with a grain of salt. After all, when you've got to go, you've got to go. And who could safely fly an airplane with an aching bladder? Besides, they'd already set the controls to auto-pilot, so the co-pilot had little to do but keep an eye on the settings.

Billings unclicked his belt and climbed out of the pilot's seat while O'Rourke watched the controls. The plane was headed northeast. Billings glanced one more time out the window. He could see the ocean for the first time, off in the distance. The New Jersey countryside, with more snow on the ground then there'd been in Baltimore, rolled slowly by under the wings. It looked like a smooth flight ahead.

CHAPTER 8

ATTACK

illings punched the security code that unlocked the heavy, fortified cockpit door and swung it open. He stepped out of the cockpit and turned to his right to open the door to the bathroom. As he pushed open the door, there was a strange flash in the corner of his eye. A shape flew toward him. He uttered a quick "whaa..." before the dark shape hit him. A fist went into his eye, and he collapsed on the floor in front of the kitchen, wetting his pants as he went down. A muffled sound penetrated his mind an instant before his consciousness plunged into silent darkness.

Jarrah had fired a shot into Billings' head with his silencer-equipped handgun. Hanjour – now standing right behind Jarrah – blocked the passengers from seeing exactly what had happened. "Everyone keep quiet," he said calmly to the passengers up front. "Keep quiet and all will be well. We have a bomb, so just sit still." A woman shrieked and he pointed the gun at her, which shut her up quickly. He turned around and walked to the cockpit door.

In the cockpit, O'Rourke glanced around over his shoulder to see what was going on. Hanjour walked quietly into the cabin through the open door and pointed a gun straight into his face.

O'Rourke put up his left hand reflexively. "No!" he called.

"Give me the security code," said Jarrah, walking in behind his partner and shutting the door, pressing his body against it to keep anyone in the cabin from opening it. Hanjour continued pointing the gun at O'Rourke.

"Come on!" Jarrah yelled, his face heating up, and Hanjour jammed the gun against O'Rourke's head.

"It's 34... 34405," the trembling co-pilot stuttered.

Jarrah lowered his gun and punched in the numbers on the keypad. Nothing happened. He tried again, unsuccessfully, and then turned quickly to look at O'Rourke.

"This isn't the right code, you liar!" Jarrah screamed at the co-pilot.

A sharp pain exploded in O'Rourke's leg. Hanjour had shot him. O'Rourke cried out and clutched his leg where the bullet had hit. Blood sprayed from a tiny hole in his flight uniform pants.

"The real number this time or the next shot goes in your head!" Jarrah yelled.

O'Rourke, moaning with pain, told him the code. Jarrah punched the code in, and he and Hanjour both turned to verify the light at the door's side, indicating the door was locked. When Hanjour turned back to look at the co-pilot, O'Rourke's right hand pressed a button on the control panel. Jarrah pulled the trigger and a bullet pierced the back of O'Rourke's head, ensuring that pressing the button was the last thing O'Rourke ever did. An astonishing burst of blood and brain matter spurted all over the control panel and splashed ugly red and white stains on the windows. O'Rourke's body, still strapped into his seat, didn't fall, but remained upright, quivering for a few seconds. Most of his head above his nose was gone, and blood, hair and gore stuck to the back of his chair. A nauseating smell filled the small space.

Jarrah stuffed the gun back in his duffel bag, shaking his head. Even with the silencer, the firearm's shot reverberated in the cockpit. He looked at what remained of the co-pilot with disgust for the mess it made, not with any empathy. His previous doubts and weakness no longer plagued him.

Jarrah and Hanjour now were completely sealed off, safe from any intrusion. There was nothing the passengers or flight attendants could do, as the system meant to keep the passengers safe by sealing the cockpit against hijackers had worked against them. As Jarrah had expected, O'Rourke and Billings had put the plane on auto-pilot as soon as they'd reached cruising altitude, so the jet continued to fly normally.

Jarrah stood in the cockpit for a moment, reflecting on the last few minutes. After all the years of planning, it seemed unreal to actually be here, in the middle of it. Things had gone as well as he could have hoped. Better, actually, because he hadn't anticipated that the pilot would leave the cockpit. He'd moved quickly from his second-row seat as soon as the cockpit door opened and knocked the pilot out with his fist, then quickly pulled the gun out of his duffel bag to deliver the finishing shot. This was the best scenario he could have imagined. He'd worried he'd have to put a gun to a flight attendant's head to get the crew to open the cockpit, which would have taken time, too much time. Luckily, it hadn't come to that. Hanjour had reacted just as quickly, backing him up instantly, addressing the startled nearby passengers and securing their entry to the cockpit in a matter of seconds. Jarrah saw the Director's face in his head, that shark-like grin penetrating the darkness. He shuddered. Things were far from over, he thought. Still lots to do.

A pounding noise startled him. He turned toward it and realized it was the flight attendant banging on the cockpit door from the other side.

"Kevin?" a panicked voice called. "It's me, Wendy. Are you OK? I think they killed Captain Billings."

"Try CPR!" they heard someone else call from behind the door.

Jarrah smiled. CPR wouldn't help the pilot at this point. The gun had worked well. The knocking continued. "Kevin, can you hear me?" the flight attendant asked. "Kevin!"

Hanjour was hunched in the pilot's seat, carefully examining the controls. He disengaged the autopilot but held the plane steady and on the same flight path as before.

"Hey, it's just like the simulator," Hanjour told Jarrah as he continued holding the wheel and staring at the dials in front of him on the panel. "It's pretty easy."

"Good," Jarrah replied, thinking quickly of the next steps. "Let me get this guy out of his seat and I'll help you out. Remember to turn off the transponder. We don't want them to track us."

He and the Director had planned for a possible military response, though neither thought it likely that the Air Force would scramble planes to shoot them down. After all, how would the military know they planned to turn the plane into a missile against skyscrapers? No one had ever done that before. Hijackers always landed planes and made demands, and that's what the military would expect. Still, it didn't hurt to have the transponders off, and if the military did figure out what they were up to, it would make the Air Force's work a little harder.

"OK," Hanjour said, flicking the transponder switch to its "off" position. "Praise Allah, everything is going according to plan."

Jarrah unstrapped O'Rourke and struggled to lift the big man out of his seat. It was a gory job, and soon Jarrah had O'Rourke's blood all over his clothes. Oh well – that wouldn't matter in 20 minutes or so, he supposed. A brief chill etched his spine when he thought of that.

He finally pulled O'Rourke's body around to the small jump seat behind the captain's chair and draped O'Rourke over it, head pointing toward the floor of the cockpit. Blood kept pouring out of the man like a fountain, and the rusty smell of it filled the little room at the front of the plane.

Jarrah stepped over O'Rourke's body back to the co-pilot's seat. It was covered with blood. He took off his button-down shirt and draped it over the seat to cover the mess, and then sat down with an audible "squish." He grimaced and looked out the front windows to get his bearings.

"You see New York yet?" Jarrah asked. He felt oddly naked wearing just an undershirt.

"Not yet," Hanjour replied, surveying the horizon out of the sun-brightened windows. "Probably in a few minutes."

"OK. You'd better start descending. We're way too high."

"I will. But take it easy. Allah will guide us," Hanjour said. He began uttering a prayer.

Jarrah gazed out the window, straining to see any signs of the city and ignoring the increasing noise of chaos behind the locked cockpit door. Someone was banging on it, but he paid no attention. Nothing below but farms, forests and little towns. But the blue line of the ocean was now evident in the distance. Hanjour began pushing the wheel in gently. Unlike five years ago, there'd be no need for any sharp moves off the flight path. That's why they'd chosen this route. No sense in having problems that had crippled the mission last time when Shehhi lost control of his plane.

There wasn't much for Jarrah to do now except speak to the passengers. They might be calling the ground with their cell phones, and it would be best if they heard that the plane would land safely. He was sure the information would be passed along to authorities, keeping them unsuspecting. He pressed the intercom button.

"Hello, this is the co-pilot," he said in his best American accent. "The plane has been hijacked, but I'm OK and I'm still flying it. The hijackers have instructed me to land at Kennedy Airport and assured me that passengers won't be harmed. We're getting near the airport, so you'll notice we're starting to descend. Please keep calm and don't panic. Everyone will be OK if we just listen to what the hijackers want."

There, that should do it. He turned off the intercom.

The hard stuff was over. And it hadn't been that hard at all. In fact, it had been easy. A twitch under Jarrah's eye echoed a twitch in his brain as something bothered him. He wished he could pray, like Hanjour, but prayer wouldn't help the anxiety he felt now. What bothered him was that it had been too easy. Nothing had gone wrong.

• • •

Potomac TRACON handles air traffic going into and out of all the airports around Washington D.C., Baltimore and Richmond. The heart of the facility is a round, windowless room, where computer terminals are arranged in several circular patterns, each wider than the rest, like a little solar system. At 9:48, a red light blinked on one of the terminals. Co-pilot O'Rourke's last move had set off the light, and now an alarm sounded as well, letting controllers know a hijacking was in process. The controller at the panel, who'd been monitoring Flight 143, had never seen such an alarm before, and now, as she tried to assess what was going on, she lost the signal from the plane – the transponders must have been turned off. Had only the transponders gone off, certain procedures would come into play – but along with that alarm? Shivers ran up the controller's spine as the impact of that red light hit home.

She collected her wits and remembered that procedure called for her to immediately notify her supervisor in this situation, which she did. The supervisor would then notify FAA headquarters in Washington. The FAA had a hijack coordinator, who was Director of the FAA Office of Civil Aviation Security.

After getting this process started, the controller tried to contact the plane on the emergency frequency, but there was no response.

"What's going on there?" the controller next to her asked.

"Damned if I know," she replied, hoping against hope it was only some technical fluke.

• • •

The Director of the FAA Office of Civil Aviation Security hadn't been on the job the last time planes had been hijacked five years earlier, but when he saw the notification from Potomac TRACON – a hijack alarm, no ability to contact or track the plane – he knew right away what he was dealing with. He picked up the phone and called the Pentagon's National Military Command Center to ask for a military aircraft to follow the flight. NMCC would then seek approval from the Office of the Secretary of Defense to provide military assistance. The Defense Secretary's office would coordinate with the North American Aerospace Defense Command to track the plane.

Everything started moving very quickly. At the Pentagon, Harry sat in his private conference room meeting with generals in Iraq (via a video screen). He had missed an earlier urgent phone message from Virgil. Everyone in the conference room swung their heads toward the door when it opened with no warning and an aide ran in and whispered in Harry's ear. This was very unusual, as Harry never allowed interruptions in a meeting unless there was an emergency. The generals in Iraq and in the conference room looked at each other nervously.

"I'll be back as soon as I can," Harry said, getting up quickly and rushing out of the room.

Harry stepped into his private office and closed the door. His first call was to the NMCC. They told him that two F-15 alert aircraft stationed at McGuire Air Force Base in New Jersey were taking off now to follow the hijacked plane. Because the transponders were off, it wouldn't be possible to track the aircraft's identity or altitude, only the plane's primary radar returns.

"The planes are carrying live missiles and ready to fire, correct?" Harry asked the fellow at NMCC.

"These planes are just for surveillance, sir," the NMCC official replied.

"I asked you if they're ready to fire!" Harry yelled.

"Well, yes, they are, but it's a hijacking, right? We're just supposed to track it."

"Let me speak with the commander there," Harry said. "Now!"

In the short time Harry waited on the phone for the commander, he sent a message to Virgil asking him to come in, ASAP. As the commander answered, Virgil burst through the door to Harry's office holding his phone and a notebook, and Harry held up his hand to silence him.

"Crowe, this is Harry," the Defense Secretary said into the phone as Virgil stood next to his desk, nervously shifting his weight from one foot to the other. "We have a hijack in process, a Southwest 737 that took off from BWI and is headed to Boston. There's no transponder signal and the pilots aren't responding to radio. You have two F-15s trailing this plane. I want to be kept apprised minute by minute on this. I have reason to believe the hijackers are heading the plane toward New York. Let the fighter pilots know we may ask them to take extraordinary measures. Got it? Good."

He set the phone down and held out his palms toward Virgil as if to say, "What next?"

"Do we know how far the plane is from New York City?" Virgil asked quietly, standing alert at Harry's desk. Beads of sweat formed on his face.

"Nope, but couldn't be much more than 20 minutes away," Harry replied. "It took off from Baltimore heading north at 9:11."

"We'll have to make a quick decision on this," Virgil said, a line of sweat now trickling down from his forehead. "Those planes might need to fire. Today's the day the WTC condos opened. Plus the anniversary of attacks by Arabs against Jews in what was northern Palestine. I don't think there's any coincidence."

"You know that and I know that, but any decision on this one has to be approved by the President of the United States," Harry said. He picked up another phone and began to dial.

• • •

Lead flight attendant Wendy Harris grabbed the phone with shaky hands to call the flight control center, yet forced her face to avoid showing the panic that tightened her lungs. The passengers around her near the front of the plane stared at her, looking expectant, frozen in their seats. A mother softly cried, rocking her baby, and an old man in a business suit prayed, as did a young couple behind him. They'd witnessed the struggle up front, and they'd seen the two men burst into the cockpit with a gun and shove the door closed. The passengers averted their eyes from Captain Billings' body, bleeding in the front of the cabin. Their eyes spoke of fear, but a calm fear, as if the worst was over; after all, even the hijacked plane would eventually land, like the one in Beirut back in the 1980s. They knew the 2001 hijackings had ended in a collision, but that had been an accident. And the co-pilot's announcement a few minutes ago reassured them that the craft was still in good hands.

Harris felt less confident. "Hi, this is Wendy Harris on Southwest Flight 143," she told Potomac TRACON. "We've been hijacked by two men with guns. They killed Captain Billings and they're locked in the cockpit with the first officer." She turned her back on the passengers as she continued. "I heard a voice over the intercom but I don't think it was the co-pilot. I think it was one of the hijackers."

"Please repeat yourself, did you say you're on a hijacked plane?"

Harris tried to control her temper. She spoke louder.

"I said, this is Wendy Harris. I'm the head flight attendant on Southwest 143. We've been hijacked."

"Thanks, Ms. Harris – yes – we're aware your plane has been hijacked. Has anyone been hurt?"

"I told you – they killed Captain Billings. They're in the cockpit now with the first officer – Kevin O'Rourke. I don't know who's flying the plane."

"OK, OK – Ms. Harris – let me get my supervisor."

Harris waited breathlessly. She was standing in the tiny kitchen right behind the cockpit. As she stood there with the phone, she looked out at front of the cabin again, where the passengers sat pale and silent, their anxious faces looking to her for direction. "I'm on the phone with flight control," she told the ones in front. "They're going to tell us what to do. Just stay calm." She knew her words were empty, and so did the passengers, yet the mother nodded, holding her baby close. The plane continued to fly steadily, with a reassuring hum from the engines, but it was descending.

"Wendy Harris, this is Bob Tucker," a voice said over the phone. "I'm in charge at Potomac TRACON. We're aware of the hijacking, and I want you to help us out. Whoever hijacked you turned off the transponder, so we need to track you down. Can you look out the window and tell us what you see?"

"Hold on a second," she said, putting the phone down. She walked a few steps into the cabin and stepped into the right side of the first row. "Excuse me," she said to the two passengers there – a business-suited young man clutching the arm rests and an older lady who looked like she was praying like the others. Outside, she could see a coastline – they must be headed out over the Atlantic. Just then, the craft's left wing tipped down (there was a collective gasp from the passengers) and the plane turned left. They were heading up the New Jersey coast.

She got back to the phone and told the controllers what she saw.

"How high up would you estimate you are?" Tucker asked her.

"Well, we were at 37,000 feet around the time this happened, but we've been descending," Harris replied. "I'd say we're maybe at 20,000 feet now."

"Thanks, Ms. Harris – I know this is hard, but you're helping us a great deal. Can you tell us the seats the two gentlemen were in?"

"Seats 2C and 3A," Harris said. "Please, can you tell me what to do?"

"Ms. Harris – can I call you Wendy?"

"Yes, OK," she replied.

"Wendy, we're trying to communicate with the cockpit. We're waiting to find out what these guys are demanding. Once we know, we'll escort them to a safe airport where they'll land, and we'll negotiate to let everyone off the plane. So you might see military planes out the windows. Let the passengers know they're only for escort. Believe me, we've planned for crimes just like this, and we have a playbook. The hijackers probably have a gun pointed at O'Rourke and will make him fly the plane where they want. Just make sure all the passengers relax and let them know they're going to be safe. Can you do that?"

"Yes," Harris said. "I'll try. Please – please don't go."

"I'll be right here, Wendy," Tucker replied. "I'm with you all the way."

• • •

In the cockpit, behind the heavy, sealed door, things continued to go smoothly for Jarrah and Hanjour. They had the plane under control, and had turned north to follow the New Jersey coast. The coast was like an arrow pointing right to New York City, and all they had to do was keep the plane in a straight line and ignore the steady calls over the radio asking them to state their position. Hanjour had his hand on the wheel and kept the plane in a steady descent, now down to around 15,000 feet.

"Level it out," Jarrah said. "We've still got a while to go."

"We're getting close," Hanjour said. He was peering out the front window, trying to get a glimpse of the city ahead, but so far, it wasn't visible. "I'll take it down to 9,000 and then it will be easy to go down to 900 when it's time. Al-hamdu lillah."

Jarrah nodded, even though he didn't completely agree. Hanjour was the pilot; he would leave him to do his job. Every now and then Jarrah turned around, as if to make sure the door hadn't somehow magically opened. He still felt jittery, waiting for something to go wrong. But his doubts about the mission were long forgotten. Now he was determined to see it through. "Watch out for other planes," he told Hanjour, thinking back to 2001. Luckily, there were no other hijackers with inexperienced pilots to worry about, but they had descended quite a bit from the position they were supposed to be in, and Jarrah feared some Cessna pilot might take off from a nearby small airport and run into them.

• • •

"We've got Flight 143 in sight," the head F-15 pilot, Captain Reggie Jones, told controllers, speaking on a military feed that the FAA, the NMCC and the Defense Department could listen in on. Two F-15 Eagles, each loaded with air-to-air missiles, had locked in on Flight 143 and trailed it closely, but below and behind it, out of sight from the cockpit. "He's at flight level 150 and descending, approaching Asbury Park headed straight north up the coast. We're right behind him. Awaiting further instructions."

"Roger," came the response from the controller at McGuire. "Stand by for further instructions."

"Roger."

Flight 143 was less than 70 miles – about 13 minutes flight time – from New York City.

In a matter of moments, air traffic controllers cleared the airspace between Asbury Park and New York of all other aircraft. Flight 143 had the skies ahead to itself.

The headset of Capt. Jones, the head pilot of the F-15s, crackled back to life with a call from NMCC. "We suggest you fly along alongside the cockpit of the passenger jet and see if you can get a glimpse of the pilots."

"Roger that," Jones said over the roar of his engines.

Jones maneuvered his craft alongside the jet, rising level to it for just a moment, and managed a brief look into the cockpit from just a few hundred feet before pulling away.

"It appears the hijackers have control of the plane," Jones radioed back to controllers. "I see no sign of the crew."

Inside the cockpit of Flight 143, Hanjour grabbed Jarrah's elbow in panic and gestured forward and to the left. A silver military craft with a long nose and two tails was flying past them at very close range.

"OK – just relax," Jarrah said, a bit surprised at how quickly they'd been intercepted by the Air Force, but wanting to calm Hanjour. "They know about us – no surprise. They're not going to do anything."

"Flight 143, please respond," a voice over the radio said. "We request you land at Kennedy Airport and release all passengers safely. The U.S. Air Force has you under surveillance. We can discuss your demands after we have a guarantee that no passenger will be harmed. Please reply."

"What do we say?" Hanjour asked, hands gripping the control wheel more tightly.

"Nothing," Jarrah said. "Let me do the thinking. You just fly this bird."

Jarrah felt surprisingly calm. The message over the radio actually contributed to his sense of control. It was obvious the military had no idea what they planned to do with the plane. They were treating this as a simple hijack situation. And their concern about passenger safety meant they wouldn't take any chances that might hurt the people on board. He was less worried than ever about their mission being thwarted. Even once they got near the towers, the military wouldn't realize until too late what they planned to do. He wouldn't reply to the radio calls. He was certain the passengers had already told authorities that the hijackers planned to land the plane. No use engaging in extraneous conversation.

Hanjour pointed ahead to the horizon excitedly. "Look – I see them! I see them! The towers! We're on target. We're going to destroy the infidels' monument!"

Sure enough, Jarrah could now see the tops of the two towers peeking over the horizon. They were still a good 30 miles away, but visibility was clear and they'd be there in minutes.

"You'd better descend some more," Jarrah said. Hanjour nodded, neither of them saying another word. Hanjour maneuvered the plane lower and the Air Force plane veered off to the left and out of view. The sour air seemed to palpate with their combined heartbeats, the adrenaline in them both coursing through their veins as they closed on their target.

• • •

In Harry's office, Virgil listened as the Defense Secretary spoke with the President. He could only hear Harry's side of the conversation, but he was too upset to sit still. He paced back and forth in front of Harry's desk. The transmissions from the Air Force pilot, which he and Harry had listened in on a few moments earlier, concerned him. It didn't sound like the military fully grasped the situation. They were going to let the plane keep flying, and it was headed right for the towers. To make matters worse, it didn't sound like the President understood, either.

"Yes, sir," Harry was saying. "I realize the import of such a decision. But I'm asking you to give me the permission to carry out the order if necessary."

Harry listened for a while, looking at Virgil as he spoke.

"Yes, Mr. President," he finally said. "I know it's unprecedented. But I feel very strongly about this. We could have thousands of civilians in danger... how do I know the plane is targeting the towers? Sir, there's no time to go into it all. You just have to trust me on this one."

Those words struck a dagger into Virgil's heart. His entire mid-section felt ice cold, and he could barely stand on his wobbly legs. He knew Harry's evidence was based on Virgil's own research and advice. If the President gave Harry permission to shoot the aircraft down, and Harry acted on it, the entire operation would rest almost solely on Virgil's hunch. And however good his hunch was, there wasn't necessarily any way it could be proven. After all, if the plane were shot down before hitting the towers, what proof would there ever be that the hijackers planned to hit them? Virgil's word – and Harry's belief in Virgil's word – was all they had to stand on. And there could be a price to pay, with more than 100 civilians on the aircraft dead and no proof the passengers had been in danger of being killed.

Harry nodded. "Yes sir. Yes sir. I will. Thank you sir. Bye."

He put the phone down and looked at Virgil.

"We have permission to shoot the plane down if it comes within five miles of the towers," Harry said with an air of finality. "I think it's our call, now."

The radio crackled again. It was the Air Force pilot.

"They're descending rapidly," Capt. Jones said. "We're awaiting instructions."

Harry had a direct line to the lead F-15 pilot, and he used it now.

"This is Harry Deaver, Secretary of Defense," Harry said. "Prepare to fire on my command."

Jones hesitated only half a second. He'd never heard of a scenario like this, with the Secretary of Defense giving an Air Force pilot a direct order. This was like something out of a movie. "Yes sir," he said. "Prepare to fire on your command."

Jones lined his plane up behind Flight 143 with the other F-15. The commercial jet was descending steeply – far more steeply than it should be. It looked like it was down to around 5,000 feet and still dropping. Jones knew the hijackers had told passengers they planned to land the plane at Kennedy, so he couldn't understand why he'd received orders to shoot the plane down. He had said he was ready to fire, but every fiber in his body twisted at that idea. He knew that a direct hit on the jet from his AIM-7F/M missile would tear that plane apart, causing fiery death for what had to be at least 150 passengers and crew. Businesspeople heading to work; families off to visit relatives; grandparents on vacation. All just innocently taking a trip. All in the direct sights of his weapon. His military mind was trained to simply follow orders, but the civilian inside him wondered what in the world the Defense Secretary could be thinking. "Holy shit," he whispered to himself as he locked in on the target and prepared to fire if ordered. He hoped he wouldn't have to. His hands shook and every muscle in his body pulled tight.

• • •

Back in Harry's office, Harry listened to the radio transmissions as Virgil fumbled with his phone, dialing frantically.

"Pilots, state your positions," came the order from NMCC.

"We're about 15 miles out from the city, 3,000 feet up," the F-15 pilot radioed. "We're heading right for Manhattan."

• • •

Just after 5 p.m., German time, the cell phone Alev had forgotten about began to ring. She wasn't in her apartment – she was coming up the stairs on her way back from work – she had the 7 to 4 shift. She unlocked her door and heard the unfamiliar sound, trying to place it. Then she remembered and froze. Should she get it? It must be the American government – no one else had this number.

She stood in the doorway, trying to decide what to do. The phone kept ringing, and robotically she paced across the room and picked it up.

"Hello?" she whispered, heart pounding.

The voice on the other end sounded surprised and breathless.

"Thank God you answered!" the male voice said. "This is Virgil Walker, with the U.S. government. We have a hijack situation here! You called us several weeks ago warning of a possible attack. Do you know Hani Hanjour or Ziad Jarrah?"

Alev fell to her knees in the middle of her room. "Hello? Hello? Talk to me!" the voice on the phone sputtered as she knelt there, her unseeing eyes on the blank wall in front of her.

Guilt and shame flooded her body. Ziad had indeed gotten wrapped up in something dangerous, and she hadn't tried to stop him. She fought the urge to press the end button and throw the phone across the room. She summoned her reserves of courage and spoke into the phone.

"My name is Alev. I'm Ziad's girlfriend," she said quietly.

"Look – there's no time for any formalities," Virgil's voice said. "We believe your boyfriend is one of the hijackers. Can you get in touch with him? Could you do anything to stop him?"

Alev closed her eyes. This all seemed like a dream.

"I can try," she said.

"Stay on – don't go anywhere!" came the voice on the other end. She heard conversation as the caller talked to someone else in the room. She couldn't catch anything but a few words. Then the caller came back.

"Do you have Ziad's cell phone number?" the voice said.

"Yes," Alev replied. She had it memorized.

"OK – here's the situation," Virgil said. He spoke for a moment and then fell silent. "Well?" he asked after a few more seconds.

"I'll try," she replied.

• • •

In the cockpit of Flight 143, things continued to go smoothly. Jarrah and Hanjour no longer could see the fighter planes, but assumed they were being followed. Even so, they weren't worried too much. No one knew their intentions, so no one would stop them.

The altimeter showed 2,500 feet, and the plane was about 10 miles across the harbor from the towers. Hanjour aimed straight for the north tower, with its antenna. That was the one the Jews had made condominiums out of, which so amused the Director. "Allahu Akbar, Allah is the greatest," Hanjour chanted methodically, and for once, Jarrah felt the call of his religion. Maybe it was death approaching just moments away, but Jarrah took up the chant as well, and found it very soothing. "Allahu Akbar, Allah is the greatest," they both chanted, as Hanjour continued edging the plane lower. Two thousand feet, 1,500 feet...

Jarrah's cell phone rang. Distracted by the sound, Jarrah stopped praying, grabbed the phone and glanced at the number displayed on the screen. It was a familiar one.

"What's going on?" Hanjour asked, turning toward him. "What are you doing? Is it the Director?" Out the window, the towers loomed, several miles ahead.

Jarrah glanced back at Hanjour. "No...not the Director," he said. "It's Alev."

"You can't talk to her – don't answer!" Hanjour tried to grab the phone from Jarrah. The plane dipped as Hanjour's hands momentarily left the wheel. From behind them in the cabin came muffled screams through the cockpit door. Someone pounded on the door again. More than one person, from the sound of it. "Let us in!" came a yell.

The phone kept ringing and Jarrah clutched it tightly. Hanjour kept trying to paw it away, and instinctively, Jarrah pushed Hanjour back and Hanjour fell half off his seat, wedged between the seat and the wall panel, cursing, the plane swerving. As he'd pushed Hanjour with his left hand, Jarrah's fingers on his right hand brushed against the answer button.

"Ziad? This is Alev. Can you hear me?" Jarrah and Hanjour heard the disembodied voice in speaker mode coming from the phone even as Hanjour struggled to get back into his seat. The plane – with no one in control, continued to dip and weave. The pounding on the door and screams from the cabin grew louder, more persistent.

"Ziad," Alev's voice said. "Please don't hurt anyone. Land the plane safely."

"No!" Hanjour cried, fumbling to re-settle into his seat and reaching for the controls.

"Ziad, can you hear me?" Alev asked in her sweetest voice. "Ziad, remember, I told you you're not like those other ones, the ones who hate everybody. You're just not. Please don't hurt anyone." Jarrah froze in his seat. The voice took him back to the restaurant meal in Chicago, his bedroom. For a moment, he was there, not in the cockpit of a plane descending toward its target. Toward death.

"Put the phone down!" Hanjour screamed. "We must kill them all! It's Allah's will!" He used one hand to control the plane and with the other began reaching toward Jarrah, once again trying to grab the phone.

Hanjour managed to pull the plane up out of its dive even as he struggled for the phone. They were about 1,000 feet above New York Harbor, rapidly approaching the towers just a few miles away. In less than a minute, their mission would be accomplished.

In the cockpit, Alev's voice continued to plead. The plane arched through the sky, directly on course to hit the tower.

The struggle in the cockpit continued. Images flashed through Jarrah's mind as he fought with Hanjour, whose free hand stayed on the wheel, keeping the plane flying nearly straight. He saw the Director's stern face, frowning, disapproving, and he flinched subconsciously at the memory. Then he saw his bedroom, the morning Alev had left. He could almost smell her perfume. He was back in his cab, watching through the mirror as the elderly couple held hands. Alev's voice brought all this back to him, and suddenly he felt a desire not only to live, but a revulsion at the horror he was perpetrating and at those who'd led him to this point. What was he doing here? Why was he hurting people? Who was he, really? The smell of the dead co-pilot's blood penetrated his senses, and he grunted a moan of disgust at his own actions, even as he pulled the phone out of Hanjour's hands. "Please, Ziad," Alev's voice pleaded. "You're a good person; I know it."

Jarrah lifted the phone and brought it down forcefully on Hanjour's head. Alev's voice abruptly got cut off. A glut of blood shot from Hanjour's skull and he went limp. His hand fell off the wheel. Jarrah grabbed it and started to steer the plane away from the tower.

• • •

From his perch high up in the North Tower, Pete Gladstone stood admiring the expansive view from his luxury apartment. He'd earlier done a quick walk-through of the condos, glad-handing the new celebrity residents and inviting them to join him later for a "move-in luncheon" in the tower's 106th-floor conference center. Already, caterers scurried around preparing for what would be a glittery affair, adding to the numbers of people already clogging the hallways. The new residents were busy directing entire crews of workers to this place here and that one there in their luxury suites.

Everything was perfect.

He sipped a second hot espresso from a delicate porcelain cup, his eyes sweeping along the waterfront and then up to the sky. At first he wasn't sure what he saw. He'd seen the high silhouettes of numerous aircraft passing overhead in the past, but this couldn't be an aircraft, it was too low. Then he realized he was staring straight at the nose and wings of a jet airliner dead ahead!

His mouth dropped wide open and his espresso trembled in his hand, spilling hot drops onto his fingers, as he watched the 737 approach, heading straight for his apartment. He tried to scream but nothing came out.

• • •

"They're less than two miles away from downtown," the lead pilot reported to Harry. "They're over the harbor. Heading right for the towers."

"Where is it headed? Direct line of site," Harry barked.

"Sir... the pilot's voice held a quiver as he reported, "they're heading straight for the World Trade Center's North Tower."

Harry turned to Virgil and shook his head. "Nothing more we can do, Virgil," he said. "Sorry it didn't work out."

"Fire on the plane," Harry ordered.

"Understood. Firing on the plane," the F-15 pilot replied.

Virgil slumped into a chair, a hand over his wide-open mouth. This isn't happening, he thought.

• • •

As Jarrah struggled to turn the plane away from the towers, he saw a flash of light – the brightest light he'd ever seen - and heard the loudest noise he'd ever imagined. The noise and light seemed to explode in his head. Then he was in the air, alone, flying, a rush of wind in his face. Something hit his head, he blacked out, and never woke up.

There were no survivors as the 737 exploded 1,000 feet above New York Harbor in a massive ball of fire. It took weeks to recover all the bodies. But the towers and the 20,000 people inside them were safe.

Epilogue

When recovery crews fished the plane's black boxes from the shallow harbor bottom, they listened to the cockpit voice recordings, which made clear that the terrorists had targeted the World Trade Center. Etched in history would forever be the words, "I see them! The towers! We're on target! We're going to destroy the infidels' monument!" Five years after the original Al-Qaeda operation to destroy the two buildings had failed, the world finally realized what the terrorists had been up to. It was a new era, with iconic U.S. buildings under threat. Measures that should have been taken five years earlier – such as installing air marshals on jet planes, forcing ground crews to go through metal detectors and treating hijackings as potential suicide bombing attempts – all went into effect.

Hardaway, the rogue BWI security officer who placed the weapons on the plane, ran from law enforcement but eventually got tracked down and arrested at a New Jersey casino, where he was trying to convert the few leftover dollars he had from the terrorists into enough money for a flight to South America. He received 20 years in prison for aiding and abetting terrorism, but escaped the prosecution's murder charges.

Hanjour's and Jarrah's shredded remains received Muslim burials in unmarked graves in New York City's potters field. No one knew, or would have cared, if they'd learned of Jarrah's last minute change of heart and his decision to steer the plane away from the towers. It would always remain a mystery to Jarrah's family and friends how the talented, fun-loving man had ended up in a terror operation.

President Bush and Defense Secretary Harry Deaver received high praise for their calm, intelligent approach to dealing with the hijacking, and the F-15 pilots, in particular, received commendation for their actions. But it was bittersweet, because the nation knew that its leaders, in order to prevent thousands of deaths, had caused hundreds. The victims of Flight 143 received heroes' funerals, and flags flew at half-mast for weeks.

Alev's and Nancy's roles in trying to prevent the terror act never became publicly known.

March, 2007, Washington, D.C.

It was a gorgeous, sunny spring day, and the cherry blossoms had started to bloom near the Potomac. Virgil Walker, recovering from his hip surgery, was walking with crutches along the hiking path that meandered between the Jefferson and Lincoln Memorials, being passed again and again by young joggers and bikers, as well as swarming crowds of tourists carrying brochures and wearing baseball caps. A light breeze blew from the river, tickling Virgil's neck as he walked. He was thinking about Nancy, who had recovered from her wound and been welcomed back to her old job at *The New York Times.* Her family had never forgiven him and Harry for the raid, and Virgil couldn't blame them or the other victims' families for their anger. None of them would probably ever understand how the raid may have actually saved far more lives than it took, thanks in part to Nancy's shrewd observations as a hostage.

After the thwarted terrorist attack of Jan. 9, Virgil decided to get his surgery over with while he still could do it on the government's dime. No one except Harry knew his role in combatting the events of that horrible day, but that didn't bother Virgil too much. He'd never been one to seek glory. And anyway, he didn't consider his job over – yet. The shadowy figure who had planned the hijacking was still out there somewhere. Khaleed Sheikh Mohammed. They'd scoured Pakistan and Afghanistan for the man, and were now searching Iraq, figuring he must be holed up in one of those countries. They'd found traces of his presence in Karachi, but the evidence was rather old and dusty. He seemed to have left Pakistan some time ago, but they couldn't determine where he had gone. Virgil didn't intend to rest until he found the son of a bitch. This operation on his hip was just a minor hitch in the plan. He'd be back in the office, working seven days a week, as soon as he was able. He thought again about his son's advice to get a hobby, and realized he had one. His hobby was tracking terrorists. Not a bad one to have, and certainly not a waste of time. At least Harry appreciated him.

Now, as he walked along the path, his cell phone rang. He stopped and looked at the familiar number as joggers scampered past him. He paused for a moment, thinking, and then pressed the answer key.

"Mr. Walker, it's Alev," the voice on the other end said.

"Yes, Alev, I know," Virgil replied. He walked to a nearby park bench and sat down. "I'm glad we finally got back in touch."

"I know," said Alev. She paused for a moment. "I'm...I'm sorry it took me so long to get back to you. I'm so sorry about what happened that day."

"You did your best, Alev," Virgil replied. "From what we could tell, the plane started turning away from the buildings at the last moment, but by then it was too late."

Alev looked out the window from her apartment at the evening traffic rolling by. But her head was in another place, thinking back to that phone call on Jan. 9. She'd heard someone's voice yelling at Jarrah to end the call, along with the noise of engines and screams in the background. Screams that haunted her every night and would for the rest of her life.

"Do you really think Jarrah tried to turn the plane away because of me?" she finally asked.

"Well, we can't be absolutely sure," Virgil replied. "But that's my belief. Please, try to rest easy. I know you feel this was all your fault, but it wasn't. There really wasn't much more you could have done." Deep inside, he felt a bit differently, of course. If Alev had followed through on her initial call several weeks before the hijacking, perhaps he and Harry could have tracked down the terrorists and prevented it. But it was no use rehashing what he was sure Alev already knew.

"It helps to know that," Alev said, and now tears flowed down her face as she talked. "You must believe me – Ziad was a good man. He was good. Down deep. Those men – they polluted him with their ideas. He wanted very much to please them. More than he wanted to please me."

"Until the very end, and then he changed his mind," Virgil replied. "Rest easy, Alev. I'm here if you ever want to talk."

Alev put down the phone and sat on her couch, head in hands, weeping.

Spring 2007 – New York City

The bodies had all been pulled from the wreckage at the bottom of the harbor; the aircraft parts lifted out by cranes. New Yorkers now knew just how close they'd come – not once, but twice – to epoch disaster. Once this year and once in 2001. Never again would living in New York feel quite the same. Everyone felt watchful. Real estate prices plunged, particularly in the most prominent skyscrapers. Gladstone's $100 million WTC penthouse wouldn't sell, and eventually the price was cut in half. Finally, it was snapped up by a Chinese billionaire, but he never moved in. The purchase was only for show. Gladstone kept his own condo, but he never could look out the windows again without remembering the helpless, shocked feeling he'd had that morning when the plane headed for his tower exploded into flames and plunged into the harbor in pieces.

Though the people of the city had changed, the skyline remained the same as ever. The two World Trade Towers remained in their prominent place near the tip of the island, still sentinels over the harbor, unbreakable despite three terrorist attempts to take them down. Perhaps they would continue to loom over the city for many decades and perhaps even centuries to come – who knows what eventually happens to 110-story skyscrapers? Could such an edifice ever be torn down? Maybe. Or perhaps global warming would eventually raise the waters of New York Harbor, flooding downtown Manhattan and leaving its buildings empty, with the tallest just peaking above the waves in some future century. If that were to happen, the two towers could be the last buildings to disappear before joining their brothers in a watery grave.

A yellow cab slammed on the brakes at the the corner of 63rd Street and Second Avenue in Manhattan, and a passenger climbed in. "Lincoln Center," she ordered the driver. "Through the park." She then got back to her cell phone conversation, not looking closely at the short, pudgy man driving the cab.

The Director shoved his foot down on the accelerator, throwing the passenger uncomfortably against the back seat, and pulled out into traffic. Another cab, which he had cut off, honked angrily, but he paid no attention. His mind, always active, wasn't on his driving. It never was. He had plans to make, operations to oversee. He owed the Sheik a letter. He bit into his bagel and cream cheese and sped down Second Avenue toward his next date with destiny.

THE END

A professional journalist, Dan Rosenberg's career includes stints writing for the *Wall Street Journal* and *Barron's*. He currently writes about financial markets for a major trading website.

Rosenberg is married, has two sons, and lives in Highland Park, Illinois.

Made in the USA
Lexington, KY
14 February 2017